RIGHT ON THE EDGE

SID DE BEER

Dedicated to my late parents, Sam and Joan De Beer, my two unborn siblings, and our unborn child.

Wish I had the opportunity to know our unborn child, watch him or her grow up like our other three daughters, and to have grown older with my unborn siblings.

I have always wondered what it would have been like to have had siblings, and whether we would have been close, rather than argue like so many other families. Well, I will never know!

Thank you to all those that have encouraged me to write a sequel.

To my besties, my seven grandchildren, Blake, Kegan, Shayna, Logan, Hunter, Ryder, and Sienna, who I love more than they will ever know.

'The world is your oyster, believe in yourself and make things happen.'

Also by Sid De Beer

Available at www.whitefright.com

Acknowledgments

Thank you to my youngest daughter Kim for her encouragement.

A special thank you to Dani Streay of Graphic, Motion, & Narrative Design from analteredaspect.com for his input and the design of the cover.

'Follow your dreams, they know the way'

-Kobe Yamada

Contents

Chapter 1

The White House

Washington DC

'*We are right on the edge,*' said the President as he turned to face his aides seated around the table in the situation room.

He placed the palms of his hands together, looked at the ceiling, and said a silent prayer.

'Dear Lord, please do not let this happen, as it will lead to the end of all life on earth,' whispered President Trent.

His face white with fright!

Still, in his pajamas and gown, his hair uncombed, as he had not had the opportunity to shave or change into a business suit since the crisis began earlier in the day.

President Trent turned to face Barnaby Heathcott the director of the CIA seated alongside him, and asked, 'what's happening Barnaby?' 'Has Ivan activated any launch code sequences yet?'

'No Mr. President, not yet sir.'

Continuing, Barnaby said, 'all our satellites are focused on the Russian nuclear launch sites, and whilst there is a lot of activity around these sites, as of right now they have not activated any launch code sequences, sir.'

The General concurred and added, 'we will know the instant they activate their launch codes Mr. President.' 'Our satellites are ready to destroy their satellites in space, and disrupt their communications as well as any incoming nukes they may launch,'

'We are primed, loaded, locked and ready to launch a counter-strike on Russia as soon as you give the order sir,' added the General.

'Well gentlemen, we had better hope like hell that all our systems work properly if it comes to that, and that the late President Reagan's Star Wars program, namely the SDI or Strategic Defence Initiative can destroy all ballistic and intercontinental nukes in flight with X-Ray lasers.' 'Pray that it will be effective gentlemen, and that we can destroy any nukes long before they reach our shores, or that of our allies and make contact with the earth,' said the President.

'From what I have been told, we have doubted that SDI would be effective in a full-scale nuclear attack, so what's your take on it General?' questioned the President.

'Well Mr. President, I am aware of the comments made all those years ago, however, we have tested our ability to successfully destroy any inbound nukes, and I can confirm that all the tests that we have conducted over the past ten years, including the most recent test done a year ago, concluded that we will be successful if it ever came to that.'

'So General, are you confident that we can destroy any nukes launched from their road-mobile launchers scattered all around the countryside in the Soviet Union as well?' questioned the President.

'Yes, Mr. President.' 'We know exactly where all of them are situated, and to be precise, there are exactly sixty-two of them sir.' 'We have a fix on all of them right now.'

The President nodded, leaned over to Barnaby, and whispered, 'is your boy wonder at his station in Paris?'

'Yes sir, he is there right now Mr. President.'

Weeks previously a CIA agent by the name of Rafael Dujon, using the alias given to him by Barnaby Heathcott, had hacked into the Russian and Chinese military systems. His real name of Yonti Barr was known only to Barnaby Heathcott the director of the CIA, the late Stan Noble, and Lieutenant Commander Claire Johnston, based at the USA Embassy in Paris, France. He was known as Rafael Dujon within the firm, and all documents relating to his real identity had been securely locked away in a safe in the Director of the CIA's office at Langley, Virginia USA from the day he started at the CIA.

They had gone to great lengths to hide his real identity, and he had used various undercover names on numerous missions. It was thought impossible to hack into the Russian and Chinese military systems, however, Rafael had used his expertise in computer science engineering and had managed to hack into their systems. He set up a foolproof system that could not be traced, and had hacked into the Central Processing Unit of the Russian and Chinese military installation systems, planted encrypted instructions into each of their systems, with full access to their launch code sequences. He had spent untold hours setting up algorithms, and hundreds of dummy Internet accounts around the world ensuring that the source was untraceable.

Rafael informed Director Heathcott of what he had done, and that he was confident that his instructions would work when they activated their launch code sequences. It would be impossible to trace the source of the hack as the instruction in both systems were encrypted and untraceable. He had also manipulated the architecture, as well as the arithmetic logic units in both systems that perform arithmetic and logical operations altering the instructions in their computer systems.

This altered the memory used to hold instructions and data.

He altered all four functions and strategic stages of the nuclear launch code sequences in the Central Processing Units of both countries, and had set up sleepers in their respective systems. The sleepers would only become active, if they ever activated their launch code sequences, and any attempt at tracing the source would be impossible as data would travel through thousands of Internet-listed accounts leading to a dead end. He was confident that it would be impossible to trace what he had done.

Whilst it was thought that it was impossible to alter a launch sequence, Rafael had managed to secretly access their systems, and installed the destruct instruction into the Russian and Chinese systems which meant that at the time of a launch, ensuring that a missile would self-destruct on the launch pad.

He had used two trusted operatives within the CIA fluent in Russian and Chinese to help him interpret the languages, and decipher any codes he encountered in their systems.

'I hope that what boy wonder has done actually works, because if Ivan does launch nukes, and what he has done, does not work, the whole world will go up in smoke,' whispered the President looking directly at Barnaby.

'Well Mr. President, I hope that we never find out whether it will work or not,' replied Barnaby in a hushed tone.

The President merely nodded as the General shot an inquiring look at Barnaby, wondering what he knew.

A secret service agent placed the Nuclear Football alongside the President. The Nuclear Football travels with the President whenever he or she is away from the White House, however it was placed alongside him as a backup. The briefcase is fondly known as the Nuclear Football, the contents of which are used by the President of the United States to authorize a nuclear attack while away from fixed command centres.

The President turned to the secret service agent and asked, 'is Vice President Tippence securely located in the Cheyenne Mountain complex?'

The complex is a short distance from NORAD and USNORTCOM headquarters at Petersen Airforce Base in Colorado Springs, Colorado.

'Yes Mr. President, I can confirm that Vice President Tippence is secure within the complex sir.' The second Nuclear Football travels with the Vice President as a backup.

'What's the status regarding our troops participating in the war games in the South China Sea General?' asked the President.

'We have mobilized the largest contingent of NATO troops ever in a peacetime exercise, consisting of eight hundred and seventy thousand ground troops.' 'Three hundred and fifty aircraft including three squadrons of B-2 stealth bombers, fighter jets, an armada of one hundred naval vessels that includes four carrier strike groups, each consisting of two destroyers, two frigates, a replenishment vessel, and two submarines sir.'

'Russia is a vast country, so our forces are split into eight main strike groups within numerous countries with large forces concentrated in Estonia where the British have increased their ground forces from one thousand two hundred to one hundred thousand men,' continued the General.

'We also have a further one hundred thousand troops deployed in Ukraine Lithuania, Georgia, Poland, Romania, Bulgaria, and Latvia, and backup forces of a further thirty thousand troops in South Korea, Belarus, and Latvia collectively.' 'There are a further twenty thousand backup forces in Germany, Japan, and the Philippines, all ready to deploy on your order, sir.'

'Our troops are mainly scattered to the west of Russia, so if we have to retaliate, then the forces based in South Korea would need to be brought into the fray and airlifted into Russia or invade through North Korea.' 'As I understand it from intelligence reports, the North Koreans may stand aside and not get involved in a war at all, allowing NATO troops access into Russia' stated the General.

'As you are aware Mr. President, North Korea has undergone some huge changes after the death of Kim Jong-un and his sisters.' 'General Du-Ho Cha, the Supreme Leader has demonstrated his willingness to accept your offer, and participate in the free world economy.' 'He has made an effort to improve relationships with the West, and has encouraged investment in their country.'

'I believe that for the first time in their history, General Du-Ho has seen a way out of poverty for the people of North Korea, and from what we have all seen, he is embracing the opportunity to participate in the world's economy,' continued the General.

'All the allied troops in the various countries are well equipped with arms, primed and ready to invade Russia on multiple fronts, Mr. President.' 'We have set up a command center in the Philippines which is away from the front for security and logistical reasons.'

He added, 'supporting the ground troops, are some five thousand vehicles, and we have shored up the tank battalions with an extra five hundred tanks.' 'So we now have around a thousand tanks in various countries, all ready for an invasion Mr. President.'

'We will hit them from multiple sides if the Reds make a wrong move Mr. President, and as mentioned, we have significant backup assets in place in various countries.'

'In total, we have thirty NATO nuclear submarines scattered around the South China Sea, the Pacific, the Arctic Ocean, Barents Sea, Bearing Sea, as well as in the Sea of Okhotsk, so we have surrounded them, Mr. President,' 'We have a fix on all the soviet submarines, and will blow them out of the water as soon as you give the signal to attack.'

'Well if that does not send the Russian President a clear message, nothing will,' said the President leaning back in his chair and nodding to himself.

'Are you keeping an eye on the Chinks?' Asked the President.

'Yes sir, we have six nuclear submarines strategically located in the South and East China Seas, ready in case the Chinese decide to enter the conflict, Mr. President,' said the General.

Wonder whether these assets will be able to destroy Russia if Ivan launches nukes, and we retaliate, thought the President as he glanced around the table.

'If Russia and China decide to declare war on the West collectively, we will be up shit creek without a paddle, because the Chinese can afford to throw a million men into the fray,' said the President in a somber tone.

'I have a video conference planned with the heads of government of all the NATO nations scheduled for later today as well as a press conference.' 'I will address the world and notify them that we are doing everything in our power to deescalate the crisis at hand,' said the President.

There was mass panic worldwide as people scurried to get out of major cities, and head for the hills in the foolish belief that a nuclear attack would not affect them. Supermarkets had been stripped bare of commodities as panic buying engulfed the nation, and highways were gridlocked with fleeing people, noted the President as he watched the major news channels.

'As I understand it, there is an emergency special session of the United Nations General Assembly planned for later today, and I have instructed our ambassador to reiterate our wish to have a face-to-face meeting with President Pushkin to de-escalate the tension,' said the President.

Continuing the President stated, 'to be honest, the meeting at the UN may well come too late.'

'Secretary of State, Pompello and I have repeatedly tried to contact Pushkin and his Foreign Minister, Lacrov, however, both have refused to take our calls, so that leaves us with no other alternative other than to use the United Nations to try and get Pushkin to attend an urgent face to face meeting,' stated the President.

The President glanced at Barnaby who was bent over speaking quietly into his mobile phone, and wondered what that call could be about.

He looked at his aides and said, 'our intelligence has been confirmed by research written by Hans M. Kristensen, director of the Nuclear Information Project with the Federation of American Scientists, and Matt Korda, a research associate with the project that was published in the Bulletin of the Atomic Scientists in The Nuclear Notebook column.' 'It confirmed that Russia's nuclear arsenal includes a stockpile of nearly 4,500 nuclear warheads.'

Continuing he added, 'of these, some 1,600 strategic warheads are deployed on ballistic missiles at heavy bomber bases, while an additional 985 strategic warheads, along with 1,912 nonstrategic warheads, are held in reserve.' 'The Russian arsenal continues broad modernization intended to replace most Soviet-era weapons.'

Pressing on he said, 'Russia is in the middle of a decades-long modernization of its strategic and nonstrategic nuclear forces to replace

Soviet-era weapons with newer systems.' 'President Pushkin reported that modern weapons and equipment now make up eighty-six percent of Russia's nuclear triad namely the Russian Federation, compared to the previous year's eighty-two percent.'

'He added that they expected that number to rise to eighty-eight point three percent by the end of twenty, twenty-one.'

'The USA is capable of destroying Russia on our own with our five thousand five hundred nuclear warheads, and with the NATO forces strategically placed, I hope that Pushkin has sobered up enough, thought long and hard about the outcome, if he does launch nukes at us or any of our allies,' stated the President emphatically.

'We have some one thousand eight hundred nukes currently deployed, and two thousand in reserve which have now been re-deployed.' 'There are four hundred land-based intercontinental ballistic missiles, multiple nukes in submarines, and three hundred in bomber bases scattered around the globe.'

'A further three hundred in various European countries, and many more that we have in strategic locations around the globe.' 'Some hidden in defiance of the nuclear disarmament treaty we signed with the Reds,' stated the President.

'I do not doubt that the Soviets have also hidden some nukes which they too have not declared.' 'France and the United Kingdom have a further five hundred and five nukes between them, or so we have been led to believe, thus collectively we can more than match Ivan's inventory.'

'Do the maths gentlemen, it's a very, very scary situation.' 'So gentlemen, do you think that the assets we have placed around Russia are sufficient to deter Pushkin from launching his arsenal against us and the western world?'

The aides sat in silence, pondering what he had said, staring at the President with nobody offering a comment.

'So to quote what Pushkin said when he tried to sail the container ship laden with high explosives into the port of Baltimore, the world will go, "Kaboom," for sure,' he said waving his arms in the air.

'To be honest, we had all better pray, and I mean pray real hard for divine intervention, because a retaliation from us will destroy all living matter on earth,' stated the President.

'It gives a whole new meaning to the phrase, "the shit is about to hit the fan," and as the Germans say, "Alles ist kaput", everything is broken,' added the President.

'What's the latest?' asked the President as he turned to face the General.

'Quite at the moment Mr. President,' 'Our satellites are picking up images of massive activity at all the Russian military bases.'

The President looked at Barnaby who was still hunched over and still speaking quietly into his mobile phone, and once again wondered who he could be speaking with.

Secretary of State Pompello returned to the situation room and notified the President that he had finally spoken to his Russian counterpart, Foreign Minister Damir Lacrov, and convinced him to speak with President Pushkin to deescalate the situation, and to get around a negotiating table with the four of them as a matter of urgency. The President merely nodded and stared at the array of monitors on the wall, then looked at the screens beaming images of people trying to flee the major cities with reporters from CNN, Fox News, and Aljazeera reporting on the chaos taking place. As usual, there was looting on an unprecedented scale.

Please, Dear Lord, don't let some idiot in Russia accidentally push the button, because the consequences would be catastrophic, thought the President.

He glanced at Barnaby again and was intrigued at how calm he appeared in this crisis. What on earth does he know, and is not telling me, thought the President?

Barnaby put his elbows onto the conference table, interlocked his fingers, and placed his two thumbs under his chin. He looked around at the aides seated at the table and focused on General Mitchfield. If only he knew, he thought to himself.

Barnaby seemed to be deep in thought, and the President wondered what he had up his sleeve. What on earth has he not disclosed, and what could he be up to?

Once again he turned his attention to CNN and Fox News being relayed on the television sets on the side of the room as the major networks beamed images of the mass panic as millions of people were trying to leave major cities throughout the world. Gas stations had run dry and supermarkets had been overwhelmed with hordes of people trying to buy the last remaining food supplies, civil disorder seemed to be everywhere, highways and roads leading out of the cities remained gridlocked. The National Guard struggled to maintain law and order. Those that chose to stay at home were heavily armed, protecting their assets as reports filtered through that many looters had been shot in various neighborhoods.

President Trent stood, 'anybody for coffee because this may be the last time I can offer you anything at all,' he said as he made his way to the sideboard and poured the coffees.

The President's catering steward entered the situation room with a trolley of mixed sandwiches prepared by the executive chef, and placed it on the sideboard table.

'Thank you, Jules,' said the President realizing that nobody had eaten for several hours, and invited his aides to help themselves to a plate of sandwiches.

Satellite images were beamed onto numerous monitors on the wall, and the President watched as Soviet military personnel scurried around their nuclear silo sites. Surely they would not have people running around these sites if they were about to launch he pondered. It had been a few hours since the satellites had honed in on the various Soviet nuclear sites, and the frenzied activity continued around these sites which were being monitored by both the CIA and the US military.

'Mr. President, there are reports on social media of UFO's flying over their missile silos sir,' said the National Security Advisor Michael O'Rourke in amazement.

Turning to face him, the President said, 'are you sure Mike, and if so where the hell did they come from?'

'Yes Mr. President,' said Michael, passing his mobile phone across the table.

The President watched as the Facebook social media platform lit up with multiple people in Russia interacting with the rest of the world. He once again glanced at Barnaby who had pushed his chair away from the conference table, leaned backward, and was calmly staring at the footage on his mobile phone depicting an air of self-confidence that troubled him. I wonder how the Director of the CIA can be so composed in the current climate. This bugger knows something that nobody else knows for sure, thought the President as he studied Barnaby more closely.

Chapter 2

James S. Brady Briefing Room
The White House

The world's media were crammed into the James S. Brady Briefing Room as the President entered with all standing as a sign of respect. The President had taken time to have a quick shave and shower, then got dressed into a business suit after his video conference with the NATO heads of government, as he wanted to portray an image of a man totally in control of the dangerous situation confronting the world.

A secret service agent positioned himself against the wall behind the President and put the Nuclear Football between his legs.

'Good afternoon ladies and gentlemen, please be seated,' offered the President taking a few moments to look over the room, and focused on the reporter from Aljazeera.

'As you all know, the world at large is on the cusp of a war with Russia.'

'Our forces, as well as those of NATO, have been deployed in several countries in war games exercises, aimed primarily at persuading Mr. Pushkin, the Russian President to alter course, and to stop the threats to America as well as the world at large,' said the President.

'As you are all aware the CIA uncovered a plot by President Pushkin to fly a commercial airliner towards Washington several weeks ago, and release a deadly poison that two of his scientists had developed over our city.' 'This poison would have resulted in the death of all living matter, human, animal and plant life within a radius of seventy-miles, if it was ever released.' 'It would have rendered our administration leaderless, positioning Russia to take advantage of the chaos, and dictate terms to the world at large,' stated the President.

'We have proof that the Russians tested this deadly poison over a remote village in Syria.' 'Within a two-hour timeframe all human, animal, and plant life ceased to exist in the village and to date, nobody has returned to the village,' said the President focusing on the reporter from Aljazeera.

'We also have irrefutable evidence that the commercial jetliner had a payload of a deadly poison on board, and as mentioned the Pilots were instructed to fly the plane to Washington by President Pushkin, then declare an emergency.' 'They were then ordered to overshoot the runway, circle around the city numerous times making it seem like they were dumping fuel, however, instead of dumping fuel, they would be dumping the deadly poison.' 'The pilots would then set a course back towards north Africa.'

'Our fighter Pilots intercepted the flight over the north Atlantic ocean.' 'Despite numerous attempts by our Pilots to get the Russian Pilot to divert to a North African country and land safely, he ignored these warnings, continuing on the flight path towards Washington which gave me no alternative, but to issue an executive order to shoot the airliner down,' said the President pausing for effect.

'The Nineteen twenty-five Geneva Protocol prohibits the use of chemical and biological weapons of war, and after twelve years of negotiations the CWC, the Chemical Weapons Convention was adopted in Geneva on the third of September nineteen ninety-three.'

'All parties were signatories to the agreement signed in Paris on the thirteenth of January nineteen ninety-four of which Russia was one, so they have contravened the agreement that they had signed.' 'Our ambassador will table chapter seven articles thirty-nine to fifty-one, concerning Threats of Peace and Acts of Aggression at the United Nations later today/' 'That is of course if we make it to this sitting,' said the President in a somber tone of voice.

'The CWC is the first disarmament agreement negotiated within a multilateral framework that provides for the elimination of an entire category of weapons of mass destruction under universally applied international control, that the Russians have simply ignored.'

'A Preparatory Commission of the Organisation for the Prohibition of Chemical Weapons known as OPCW, was established with the responsibility to prepare detailed operation procedures, and to put into place the necessary infrastructure for the permanent implementing agency provided for in the Convention,' stated the President.

'The headquarters of this organization was established in The Hague, in the Netherlands, and the CWC entered into force on the twenty-ninth of April nineteen ninety-seven, which was one hundred and eighty days after the deposit of the sixty-fifth instrument of ratification.'

'So ladies and gentlemen, as you now understand, we are dealing with a President in Russia that wants to dominate the world at large.' 'He has lost control of his country which is bordering on anarchy, and is desperately trying to retain his grip on power over the Russian people.' 'We have all witnessed the escalation of violence in Russia on television recently.'

'Not only did President Pushkin plan to release this deadly poison, but the CIA also uncovered another plot orchestrated by him to sail a container vessel laden with high explosives into the Port of Baltimore, and remotely trigger an explosion that would have been like a nuclear explosion being detonated.' 'The ramification of that blast would have destroyed everything within a radius of seventy miles.'

'The tsunami that would have ensued as a result of an explosion of that magnitude, would have caused a tidal wave estimated to be around one and a half thousand feet high, the likes of which the world has never seen.' 'One can only imagine the devastation that a wave of that magnitude would have caused, not only in America but also worldwide bringing death to hundreds of millions of people.'

'And yes, if either the deadly poison was deposited over Washington or the ramifications of the explosion at the Port of Baltimore were successful, it would have left the United States without an administration and rudderless allowing Pushkin to eventually control the world,' stated the President.

'Despite the ongoing rhetoric from President Pushkin and the Russian media, we have irrefutable evidence that the only people on board the jetliner were the Pilot, Co-Pilot, and Navigator, and as I have stated previously, I regret having been forced to issue the order to shoot the plane down, which has resulted in all three losing their lives.'

The President paused, then reiterated, 'as I said, this deadly poison would have killed all human, animal, and plant life within a seventy-mile radius of Washington within a two-hour timeframe.'

Two gentlemen entered the briefing room wearing dark-shaded sunglasses and peaked caps, flanked by secret service agents that positioned themselves on either side of both of them. They positioned themselves against a wall behind the President.

The President turned towards them and said, 'I would like to introduce both scientists that developed this deadly poison to you.'

'The names of these two gentlemen will be withheld for security reasons.' 'They were under direct orders from President Pushkin to develop this deadly poison, and if ever any knowledge of this poison got out, their lives, as well as the lives of their entire families, would have been terminated immediately.'

Another man, also wearing dark-shaded sunglasses and a peaked cap flanked by two secret service agents entered the room moments later. Turning to face the man standing to his right-hand side behind him, the President added, 'I would also like to introduce President Pushkin' former head of security, whose identity is also protected.'

'The head of Pushkin's security has irrefutable evidence of what Pushkin wants to achieve and has relayed vital information to the CIA.'

'So, as you can see, we have the proof that President Pushkin had planned these acts of aggression, and thanks to the CIA, these threats were thwarted.' 'The CIA extracted both scientists, and their families, as well as Pushkin's head of security, who are now all residing in secret locations somewhere in the USA.'

'I have tried to contact President Pushkin numerous times recently, however, he has refused to take my calls.' 'Secretary of State Pompello has also tried in vain to speak with his counterpart Mr. Lacrov in Moscow and he too has not taken any calls.'

'I wish to assure my fellow Americans, as well as all the people around the globe, that the USA and NATO are not seeking confrontation, however, we are loaded, locked and ready should Pushkin decide to launch any missiles against us, or any other country in the world.'

'The consequences of a war with Russia would ultimately result in a nuclear confrontation, and we all know that would be the end of the world as we know it.' 'I again wish to notify my fellow Americans as well as everybody in the world, that I am doing everything possible to avoid a war with Russia, and urge President Pushkin to meet me for talks as a matter of urgency.'

'I would like to speak directly to President Pushkin,' he said pausing, and staring directly at the array of cameras.

'Stop this madness, as it will lead to the end of all living matter on earth.' 'Get your military to stand down, and meet with me within the next day or two, and let's resolve this matter.'

'I appeal to our people to stop the looting and remain calm.' 'I can assure everyone, that if ever there is a nuclear war, no place will be safe other than a nuclear bunker somewhere deep in a mountainside.' 'Even if one was lucky enough to take refuge in a bunker, in time to come, you would need to come out of it, then the radiation, lack of food and water would kill you,' stated the President.

'Please remain calm people, and thank you, ladies and gentlemen.' 'I am afraid that I cannot take any questions at this time, as I need to return to the situation room as a matter of urgency, and will convene a further news conference as soon as I have more to say,' said the President, as he turned to make his way out of the room.

Chaos broke out in the briefing room as reporters jostled to try and get as close to the President as possible, all shouting questions at the President as he prepared to depart.

The reporter from Fox News shouted out, 'Mr. President, there are reports of UFO's flying over the Russian nuclear sites, do you have any comment, sir?'

The President paused at the door, turned to face the journalist, and said, 'nobody knows where these UFO's have come from, so maybe you can throw some light on it.' 'From what we have seen, these UFO's have appeared out of nowhere, and have flown over various Russian nuclear facilities,' continued the President.

'Can you confirm that these UFO's were not developed by the USA, and being used as a deterrent in Russia?' 'Are they a secret USA weapon developed by the US, Mr. President?' Questioned the reporter from Aljazeera.

'From what I have seen, these UFO's seem to travel at the speed of light with the ability to change direction, or stop at the blink of an eye.' 'I can assure you that the human species has not advanced that far to enable travel at hypersonic speed.' 'Maybe someday, but not today, and not in our lifetime.'

The President had no idea that the CIA had dismantled an alien craft that had crashed decades previously, reassembled it, and learned the inner workings of its propulsion systems. They eventually succeeded in flying the craft, and that this secret was closely contained to the directors of the CIA only. No President, or anybody in the military had any knowledge of this closely held secret, so the President's remarks were in line with what he knew.

The President again bid the journalist farewell, turned, and made his way out of the room.

Chapter 3

Reno

Nevada

A week prior to the crisis in Russia and the President addressing the nation as well as the world at large on all the major television networks informing them that the world was on the brink of a war with Russia, Barnaby left his office at Langley, and was driven twenty-eight miles to the Dignity Hospice and Palliative Care Centre at Chantilly in Virginia.

The black bulletproof General Motors SUV with tinted windows pulled up at the entrance to the complex, and Barnaby's security detail quickly exited the vehicle, checked the surrounding area before opening the rear door allowing him to exit. He made his way into the complex, and was shown to a room that catered for people with terminal illnesses.

'Hello Kit, I hope you still remember me,' said Barnaby, as he entered and made his way towards the side of the bed.

Staring back at him was a frail old man, now seventy-six years of age. The years had not been kind to him, as cancer had spread throughout his body taking its toll. He most likely only had a short time to live. Frail and thin, his eyes sunken into his eye sockets with dark shadows below the lower eyelashes confirming his age and illness.

'Yes I remember you, Barnaby,' 'Let's see, it must be some twenty-odd years since I last saw you,' replied Kit softly as he moved his head sideways to focus on the visitor's face.

'Still sharp as a tack,' said Barnaby smiling broadly offering his hand in a greeting.

'I see we have one hell of a problem with Ivan,' said Kit as he gently took Barnaby's hand.

Wow, how alert is the old codger, even in his condition, thought Barnaby as he closed the door, and pulled a chair closer to the side of the bed.

'Well one good thing is that it won't make any difference to me if Ivan launches, as I most likely will be very lucky to live much more than a day or two,' said Kit softly.

Kit Banasiewicz, whose parents were born in Warsaw and fled with their young son, when the Nazis took over the village of Przemyśl in southeast Poland, on the fifteenth of September nineteen thirty-nine. Having finished his schooling, he went on to study astrophysics at the UNLV, the University of Nevada Las Vegas located on the southern tip of Nevada, graduating with a master's degree in physics, astronomy, and science.

He was recruited by the CIA in nineteen seventy-five as part of Operation Conceal, and sent to Area 51 in Nevada as part of a three-man team tasked with dismantling the wreckage of an alien spacecraft that had crashed in Hart Canyon on the twenty-fifth of March nineteen forty-eight, about nine miles from Aztec in New Mexico.

The craft was one hundred feet in diameter, had landed completely intact, and had been securely housed in a heavily guarded hangar at Area 51 in the middle of a barren desert in Nevada for decades. The two deceased alien occupants were placed into two refrigerated cabinets in a morgue for future study.

The CIA had to be sure, that whoever dismantled the craft and reassembled it, had exceptional knowledge and skill to ascertain the inner workings of the craft, with the ability to replicate its propulsion system. The three scientists were tasked with disassembling and reassembling the craft, getting to understand the dynamics of its control propulsion systems, and eventually being able to fly the craft safely.

Kit and two other scientists namely, Orson Occhialini and Sven Usoro were sworn to secrecy, and expressly told that they were unable to ever mention, or discuss the work that they were doing at Area 51 with anybody including family, friends, or secret lovers. They could only discuss the project amongst themselves, and all three were fully aware of the consequences that they, their family, and friends would suffer if ever any word of what they were doing got out, and having taken an oath, all three complied. Kit was the last remaining scientist alive, and had kept that oath for all those years.

Unbeknown to the three scientists at the time, when they started dismantling the alien craft's propulsion system, it was radioactive which caused cancer in all of them. Over time, cancer took its toll on Orson and Usoro resulting in a lot of pain, suffering, and finally death. Kit too had suffered deadly cancer however, for some unknown reason he outlived the other two.

Barnaby gently closed the door to the room, and made his way back to the chair alongside the bed.

'So Kit, I am asking you for some honest answers,' said Barnaby.

'You tested Palmito over the Jackass Flats site, which of course has now been decommissioned at the Nuclear Rocket Development Station in nineteen eighty-five in Nevada and the US nuclear facilities at NTS, the Nevada Test Site sixty-five miles north of Las Vegas and Colorado in the mid-eighties,' continued Barnaby.

The CIA had named the alien craft, Palmito after the final battle of the civil war at Palmito Ranch that took place on the twelfth and thirteenth of May eighteen sixty-five on the banks of the Rio Grande east of Brownsville Texas. They believed that someday, the technology gained from this craft would help save America, and the world ending hostilities with Russia, just as the last battle at Palmito ended the civil war.

Continuing Barnaby said, 'I have read all the classified reports on the tests of Palmito, and as has been stated in these reports, the outcome was that the alien craft had been successful at neutralizing our missile sites, shutting them down as it flew over these facilities, so can you add anything else to that?'

'You are correct Barnaby, not only were the sites neutralized, but they were out of commission for a further ninety-six hours, and thank the good Lord, the Russians never found out,' said Kit in a hushed tone.

'It took the military the full ninety-six hours to fully restore the power to the missile sites, because the blackout caused a catastrophic electrical failure due to the surge of current in the systems resulting in overheating, and the loss of expensive equipment like protectors and circuit breakers.'

Continuing he added, 'President Ford would have blown a fuse had he known that it was the CIA that caused these sites to be out of commission putting us in a very vulnerable position.'

'As you are aware from the classified report, there were multiple UFO crashes from nineteen forty-five to nineteen forty-eight at various locations, and the CIA collected the debris from all these sites and stored them in two hangers at area 51.' 'Our team had full access to all the bits and pieces,' said Kit pausing to regain his breath.

'It was difficult to ascertain exactly what happened and why that craft had crashed, however, we tried as best we could to lay out the pieces of the various craft, and to get a full understanding of how they worked.'

'The classified report confirmed that the CIA withheld this critical information from President Ford and his administration at the time, as the Director deemed it classified and for the CIA's knowledge only.' 'It needed it to remain in-house for possible use in the future,' said Kit.

'As you know when the pulse of high-frequency electromagnetic waves detects an object, the signal then returns to the radar's antenna for processing,' 'The classified report states that we were able to learn and understand the dynamics of the crafts propulsion system, which is true.' 'We eventually learned enough to repair and reassemble the craft, take it for a test flight, then land it successfully,' said Kit smiling broadly as he recalled that memorable day, all those years ago.

'It was a proud moment, to be honest,' said Kit lifting his head off the pillow, as if to confirm that he and his two fellow scientists had made a huge contribution to America.

'So, we went about trying to fully understand the electromagnetic propulsion system of reverse engineering and gravity control, and to say the least, it was a massive learning curve.' 'It was much more than we ever expected.' 'We learned how E.T. built the craft, studied their advanced propulsion system, and eventually got to understand how the craft was propelled by anti-matter reactors,' said Kit in a shallow breath, as a faint smile creased his lips.

'The reactor defied the laws of science, as we knew them, without producing any detectible heat, exhaust pollution, or sound with astronomical power levels not seen by mankind.' 'We measured the speed at an ultra-hypersonic speed of Mach-thirty which as you know is a little over twenty-three thousand miles per hour with no sonic boom.' 'Gone in a flash, and clearly, there was a fuel source in the craft, so we tinkered around until we managed to get the reactor to operate, however, we were unable to fully understand how it worked at the time,' whispered Kit pausing to regain his breath.

'The test flights we conducted around Groom Lake near Area 51, resulted in many reports of sightings from people living in the surrounding area, and the authorities conjured up some creative stories at the time, trying as best they could to divert attention away from what was happening.'

Barnaby glanced at the section in the classified report detailing that one of the naval F/A18 Super Hornet Fighter Jets with a maximum speed of one thousand two hundred miles per hour, had followed an alien craft in twenty seventeen, only to see it veer off course and vanish moments later. The report confirmed that the craft was one of those that the CIA had developed from the technology they had gained, and was on a test run that had been kept secret.

He moved his chair closer to the edge of the bed, as Kit's voice faded and he gasped for air.

'Scientists named the fuel source "Element 51" or more commonly moscovium which is a super heavy element that has one hundred and fifteen protons in its nucleus.' 'It can be man-made and is an enigma really,' continued Kit slowly.

'Moreover, the seemingly insurmountable problem is that anti-matter is hard to produce in large quantities, and can only be "created" at facilities like the Large Hadron Particle Collider at CERN in Switzerland.' 'It would cost trillions of dollars to produce enough anti-matter for one small reactor, but what we, the people around the world can do, is demand that our scientific communities concentrate on solving this problem, and not on building bigger and more powerful weapons.'

'A first-hand account came from Professor Leonard Wiltshire, professor of physics at the University of Cincinnati in nineteen sixty-nine, and throughout his career, he had researched gravitation, quantum gravity, and general relativity.' 'Albert Einstein put forward a theory, that proposed that gravity is essentially a warp or curve in the geometry of space-time caused by mass,' said Kit.

Barnaby was aware of a round table discussion titled "Recollections of the Relativistic Astrophysics Revolution" held at the twenty-seventh Texas Symposium on Relativistic Astrophysics in twenty thirteen. Professor Witshire recounted his work on what he somewhat puzzlingly referred to as, "the discovery of anti-gravity." His research is classified as Barnaby knew, and he was fully up to date on all matters in that regard.

'So, we implemented all of what we had learned which was invaluable to the team I worked with, allowing us to get a clear understanding of how anti-gravity works, and the research that the Professor had done, getting to know how the alien craft flew,' continued Kit, now visibly tiring.

'We learned about the vortex-based technology, the antigravity fast-rotating machine, and one of my colleagues namely, Sven Usoro developed the antigravity magnetic system which we installed in one of the "Tic Tac" shaped UFO's that we had developed.' 'We named it The Guardian.'

'We successfully tested The Guardian on several occasions, and as you are aware from the numerous media reports at the time, hundreds of people witnessed sightings over several weeks as we continued testing the craft,' 'The other three crafts were named, The Saviour, The Shepherd, and The Protector,' continued Kit smiling broadly.

'When I left the program, the four craft that we had developed, were hidden in hangers at Area 51, and would only be used if ever we faced a possible nuclear holocaust as we are facing right now,' stated Kit struggling to breathe.

'Yes, thank you, Kit, you have been more than helpful, and you truly have a wealth of knowledge which I greatly appreciate my friend,' said Barnaby.

'I salute you sir, and thank you for your service to our country, and the world at large.'

'I am sure you are right up to date with all the classified information Barnaby, as well as the fact that these crafts are securely located in hangers at Area Fifty One,' reiterated Kit as he breathed his last.

Barnaby hit the emergency button. A moment later a doctor and nursing staff rushed into the room, and went to work, trying as best they could to save Kit, however it soon became evident that their effort was in vain.

Barnaby stood motionless in the corner of the room staring at Kit, then saluted him, turned, and made his way towards the exit. All three scientists had made a massive contribution and personal sacrifices to humankind, and all had paid the ultimate price, he thought as he exited the complex, nodding gently to himself.

Chapter 4

Saratov

Russia

The President returned to the situation room, officially known as the John F. Kennedy Conference Room, a 5,525-square-foot conference room and intelligence management center in the basement of the west wing of the White House. Moments later General Mitchfield, the Joint Chief of Staff shouted out that the Russians had activated a launch sequence code at the missile base at Saratov some five hundred and twenty-eight miles from Moscow.

'Mr. President, they are about to launch,' shouted the General.

'We need to act immediately and launch now sir,' he said in an agitated voice.

Repeating what he had just said, he demanded that the President approve the launch of their nuclear missiles at Russia.

'Mr. President, this is an act of war, and we should strike immediately,' he demanded in an agitated tone of voice.

The President held up his right hand as a gesture for him to stop, the fist of his left hand clenched under his chin, as he focused on the images being beamed from the satellites.

Barnaby interrupted the General and said, 'Mr. President our satellites have just captured images of a massive explosion at the nuclear missile site at Saratov, and I can confirm that this is the base where the launch code sequence has been activated.'

Images of the huge mushroom cloud were beamed onto the monitor on the wall from one of the CIA's satellites. The President asked whether there was any evidence of any nukes having been successfully launched and Barnaby was the first to respond.

'No Mr. President, we have no evidence of any ICBM's or Ballistic Missiles being launched at all sir.'

'I concur, Mr President,' stated the General sheepishly.

The President glanced at Barnaby who was once again speaking on his mobile phone, and seemed extremely calm and confident for some unknown reason that troubled him greatly. Moments earlier, the President was about to issue an executive order to launch, however, he hesitated for an instant as he suddenly recalled the conversion with Barnaby, about pausing momentarily before issuing the instruction to launch due to his agent having infiltrated the Russian and Chinese launch code sequences, and successfully having installed a self-destruct encrypted instruction.

He recalled Barnaby's words, which was that the encrypted message in the Russian and Chinese systems would affect the architecture and arithmetic logic units, and would activate when the Russians or Chinese activated their launch code sequence resulting in self-destruction on the launch pad. He wondered whether the self-destruct instruction that Barnaby's agent had installed, was the cause of the explosion.

I bloody well told you so Mr. President, and you doubted me as well as my agent, thought Barnaby as he made eye contact with the President.

'We are beaming more images of Saratov right now Mr. President,' said Barnaby as various monitors focused on the city in Russia.

Barnaby glanced at the ceiling and said a silent prayer of thanks to his maker. Thank you Rafael he thought to himself. The President leaned back in his chair, and focused on the monitors beaming satellite images of what remained of Saratov back to Washington depicting utter devastation of the entire city.

'Well gentlemen, anything else that we should be worried about?' asked the President calmly.

'No sir, as you can see there is mass devastation around the city of Saratov in southwestern Russia, and all is quiet at all their other sites,' said the General.

'As soon as the mushroom cloud clears, we will get a better understanding of the devastation to the area,' continued the General.

Barnaby quickly Googled the city of Saratov, turned to the President, and said, 'Saratov has an estimated population of around a million people, which makes it the seventeenth largest City in Russia, and it is around two hundred and forty miles from Volgograd.' 'Saratov is five hundred and twenty-eight miles from Moscow, Mr. President.'

They quickly repositioned the satellite images to capture a larger area around the blast site, and as the mushroom cloud slowly cleared, it was evident that Saratov had disappeared off the face of the earth. Volgograd and Samara had been severely impacted by the blast, suffering mass devastation and horrific loss of life.

President Trent asked for a situation report on all the other nuclear facilities in the USSR, and the General confirmed that no further missile sites had activated launch code sequences, albeit that there was huge activity around all of the sites. The President wondered what President Harry S. Truman must have felt like in the summer of nineteen forty-five, when he authorized the use of the world's first atomic bomb. He considered the horrible death that hundreds of thousands of people had suffered as a result of these nuclear blasts, and his mind wandered back to how those that had survived the devastation of Hiroshima and Nagasaki must have felt.

Barnaby sent an SMS message to Rafael on a secure line, well young man, you have just saved the world from total annihilation. Speak later.

Let's hope that these horrific images will make Pushkin realize the impact of using nuclear weapons, thought the President.

Russian President Pushkin was seated in the Main Building of the Ministry of Defence at Znamenka 19, in Moscow, and was enraged at what he had just seen. Turning to the Supreme Commander-in-Chief, Army General Oleg Sokolov, he demanded to know which General was in charge of the base at Saratov.

'General Morozov is the commander at the base Mr. President,' replied General Sokolov.

'Is the idiot still alive General Sokolov?' shouted an enraged President Pushkin.

Banging his fist on the table he shouted, 'I did not give the order to launch, so please explain to me what the hell has just happened?'

'Those bastard Americans have sabotaged the base,' he screamed in a blinding rage.

'I want General Alexei Morozov brought here immediately, and make sure that you order all the other nuclear bases to stand down until I issue an order to do otherwise,' continued Pushkin.

'I doubt that he has survived the blast,' replied General Sokolov turning to one of his aides, and ordering him to try and reach General Morozov.

Pushkin paced up and down, demanding an answer from his Commander-in-Chief. The General's aide tried to reach General Morozov, however, the base had been destroyed, and all communications severed.

Moments later, General Sokolov turned to face the President and said, 'We have tried to reach him, but I don't believe that he has survived the blast, Mr. President.'

Images of what was left of Saratov were beamed onto the wall depicting utter devastation, and the ruins of the once proud city, similar to the images of Hiroshima and Nagasaki in Japan after the Americans had unleashed nuclear bombs on those cities, that lead to the end of the war with Japan on the second of September nineteen forty-five.

An enraged President Pushkin turned to face General Sokolov again, and demanded to know how an explosion in one of their nuclear missile silos could possibly have happened.

'Explain to me, how this could have happened General?' He demanded banging his fist on the table.

'I have no idea My President,' replied General Sokolov.

'Well, you had better get off your backside and find out.' 'And I mean real soon,' demanded Pushkin.

'I want to know exactly why the nuclear missile exploded in its silo, and if there was any sabotage.' 'If there was sabotage, I want to know, who is responsible,' shouted Pushkin.

'Bring whoever is responsible to me, and I will show you how to deal with incompetence,' he demanded.

General Sokolov stared at Pushkin, full well knowing that what he demanded would be impossible to fulfill, as the city had been reduced to ruins, and there were unlikely to be any survivors. He was horrified by the satellite images being displayed on the screen, as the reality of what had just occurred sunk in.

We all know what the effects of a nuclear war would be like, however, to see the devastation with your own eyes in your own country was unbearable, thought the General.

'There are a couple of possible conclusions that readily come to mind My President, however, until we can gain access to the base and do a full investigation, we will not be able to ascertain who is responsible, why this has happened, or how this tragedy has occurred.'

Putin merely glared at the General without responding. Images of UFO's overflying the Russian nuclear sites were being displayed on monitors across the room.

'Where the hell did they come from?' demanded Pushkin.

'I have no idea Mr. President,' responded the General.

Continuing he said, 'they have appeared over all our bases in the last few hours, however, there are no images of them over the base at Saratov.' 'Each time one of these has flown over our missile silos, it has resulted in an electrical failure, meaning that we are unable to launch,' said the General.

'Effectively, we are unable to respond, if the Americans launch an attack right now my President.' 'We are scrambling to get our nuclear ordinance back online,' continued General Sokolov.

'If these supposed UFO's or something that the American imperialists have developed has anything to do with the blast, then I want to know, so get off your backside General and find out.' 'How come we have not shot any of these so-called UFO's down General,' shouted Pushkin.

The General knew that it was impossible to fly over the site at Saratov and do an evaluation, due to the radioactive fallout that could take up to seven hours to clear after a nuclear explosion, when residual radioactivity will have decreased to about ten percent of its original amount.

'Mr. President, I will get over the site in the next ten hours, and get a team on the ground to evaluate exactly what has happened.'

Saratov is due south of Moscow, so the trade winds blow from east to west, thus they would blow towards the west Siberian Plains diminishing the impact of radiation over populated areas.

President Pushkin, turned to face General Sokolov again and said, 'do you think these so-called UFO's are American-made, and if so, how did they enter our airspace without our radar detecting them?'

Having calmed down a little, Pushkin leaned back in his chair, and wondered whether the imperialists had copied and perfected their version of UFO's. From old intelligence reports he had read of this type of craft, it affected nuclear sites as they flew over them, which they had experienced in America years ago.

Reports continued to flood into the command center in Moscow, confirming that UFO's had overflown their missile sites, and every missile site had experienced a power outage resulting in a meltdown of all electrical equipment. This shut down their ability to launch any missiles right after the UFO's had overflown their sites. The President wondered what had happed at Saratov, and whether these alien craft had somehow managed to trigger a blast at Saratov, albeit that there was no evidence of them flying over the base.

'Get all the commanders of our missile bases on a video conference.' 'I want to speak directly with all of them right now,' instructed Pushkin.

Thirty minutes later all the commanders had linked into the Zoom conference and the Pushkin addressed them.

'So, can anyone of you tell me what has just happened at Saratov?' he demanded in an agitated tone of voice.

No commander offered any plausible explanation other than, Yegor Fedorov, a three-star General based at The Main Centre for Missile Attack near Solnechnogorsk outside Moscow.

He stated that there had been an electrical failure in all of their missile silos, all of which had experienced enormous surges of electrical current in their systems resulting in electrical meltdowns, as well as the destruction of equipment and circuit breakers. Somehow the UFO's flying over their bases had caused the malfunction at all of the nuclear silos.

'So general, are you saying that we cannot launch any missiles right now?' questioned Pushkin.

'Yes Mr. President, we are sitting ducks if the imperialist launch as we are unable to respond right now,' replied the general.

'I want to know how this could be possible, and I want an answer soon,' demanded Pushkin as he stared at the devastation on the monitors.

General Sokolov excused himself and made his way towards the exit, and headed to the Kubinka military air base which is close to Moscow, in preparation for a helicopter flight headed for Saratov later in the day.

Pushkin paced up and down in the room agitated as he pondered what exactly had happened. He turned to his aides and demanded to know how many lives had been lost at Saratov. A young Lieutenant notified Pushkin that the population of Saratov was around one million people, and it was unlikely that anyone had survived the blast. An aide notified Pushkin that the American President was trying to reach him, and had offered any assistance we may require.

'You must be fucking kidding,' he shouted.

'These imperialist bastards are responsible for this tragedy, and now dare to offer assistance.' 'Fuck them, we don't need their help.'

Chapter 5

Nuclear Armageddon

Russia

Hours later, Barnaby turned to the President and said, 'Mr. President, we have confirmation that all of Ivan's nuclear sites have suffered a severe electrical failure.' 'From what we have seen on the monitors, it appears that the UFO's that overflew these nuclear sites have somehow managed to cause an electrical melt-down, restricting them from launching any missiles.'

'Our intelligence, satellites and long-range radar systems, have not picked up any further launch code sequences having been activated, or any missiles having been launched.' 'So in my humble opinion, we may have averted the destruction of the earth thanks to our alien friends,' said Barnaby candidly.

Continuing he said, 'I wonder what caused the explosion at Saratov, and as we know, they did activate the launch code sequence at Saratov, and somehow, something has gone wrong.'

Barnaby had confidentially told President Trent, that his agent had infiltrated the Russian and Chinese Central Processing Units of their military installation systems, and planted an encrypted instruction that would result in a nuke exploding in its silo if they activated a launch code sequence.

Unbeknown to President Trent and all previous Presidents, the outcome was similar to the time that the CIA's UFO, aptly named Palmito, had successfully neutralized the US missile sites, shutting them down as it flew over them many years ago, he thought as a slight smile creased his lips.

He reminded himself that it took the US military a full ninety-six hours to fully restore the power to those missile sites. Neither the US military nor President Ford, the sitting President at the time, had any idea that the CIA was responsible, and that they had caused the meltdown. He simply nodded gently to himself, confirming that the UFO's that the CIA had hidden for decades, did not fail, and had delivered the anticipated outcome, at the most crucial time to save the world from total annihilation. This secret is only known to the current and past Directors of the CIA. It had been hidden from all past Presidents including the current sitting President Trent. For the CIA's director's eyes only. If only they knew, he thought as he glanced at the ceiling, and quietly thanked the three scientists that made this possible.

The President was deeply troubled by Barnaby's calmness at this time of crisis, and studied him more closely.

'From the chatter that we have intercepted, I can confirm that their nuclear launch sites have experienced catastrophic electrical meltdowns, so from our observation, they cannot launch any nukes at present, Mr. President,' said Barnaby, conscious that the President was studying him.

'Our satellites have captured images of chaos around all their launch sites, and the chatter we have intercepted confirms this,' continued Barnaby.

General Mitchfield interrupted, 'this is the ideal time to attack Mr. President.' 'We will never get another opportunity to take Ivan out, so I recommend we attack right now.'

President Trent turned to face him directly, looking him squarely in the eye and said, 'that's not the American way General.' 'We have never initiated an attack in our proud history.' 'We have always responded to any attack on the USA or our allies by defending ourselves, and I remind you that the radiation fallout will kill billions of people.'

Continuing he stated emphatically, 'let me remind you, we are not the aggressor here, and I can assure you that this will not happen on my watch.'

Barnaby confirmed that the CIA had intercepted a communication between Pushkin and all his generals. He had demanded to know exactly what had happened, so it appeared that the crisis was over for the time being. The President kept calm, sat staring at the array of monitors on the wall, and focused on the images being beamed from the satellites over the Russian nuclear sites.

A feeling of uncertainty crept into Rafael's thinking as he pondered whether the CIA agent that he had used to interpret the Russian language had done it correctly. All hell would have broken loose if the self-destruct sequence that he had installed in the Russian and Chinese launch code sequences did not work, he considered. It appeared that what I have done has worked as anticipated.

He whispered silently to himself, 'sweet Jesus, please don't let this happen again.' 'I promise that I will come to church twice a year, and reward you if you stop this madman.'

Director Heathcott excused himself from the room and called the Embassy on a secure line. He asked Rafael, whether he thought that the self-destruct codes that he had installed into the Russian launch code sequence had worked, or whether he thought it could have been a malfunction.

'I can't be one hundred percent sure Director, because I can only hope that the CIA agent that I used to interpret the Russian language, actually got it right, however, I am confident that he did and that it did work Director.' 'As mentioned previously, I altered the memory used to hold instruction, and the data within their system, so I am very confident that it was successful.'

'Well young man, the President and all of us are thankful that we have not ended up firing nukes at each other because the consequences of that are way too horrific to even contemplate..' 'Thank you for what you have done Rafael, and the world without their knowledge, also needs to be thankful,' said Barnaby ending the call.

Hours later the President stood and made his way out of the situation room. He asked Barnaby for a minute of his time. They made their way towards the oval office. The President walked to the sideboard and poured two triple scotches.

Clinking glasses, he said, 'well the world has come close to annihilation for a second time, and I mean real close this time.' 'Thanks to your agent, it appears that whatever he did, actually worked, and that it has managed to destroy the nuke in its silo, so the world owes him a great debt of appreciation for what he has done.'

'I want to meet him when he is next in the US.' 'Please bring him to the White House.'

'Tell me how you could stay so calm in this crisis, and what you know?'

'What have you not told me, Barnaby?'

Trying as best he could to divert the question in another direction, Barnaby said, 'well Mr. President, we all experienced the incredible work of our agent, who as you know managed to infiltrate the Central Processing Units of the Russian and Chinese military installation systems and plant an encrypted instruction, that resulted in the nuke exploding in its silo when they activated the launch code sequence,' said Barnaby.

'One can only hope that Ivan never finds out what caused the explosion.'

The President pursed his lips and looked Barnaby squarely in the eye.

'I think you people in the CIA are so secretive.' 'I feel that you know something that we all don't know, and I am convinced that you have many cards up your sleeve, so again, tell me what you know Barnaby?'

'The world is full of surprises Mr. President, and nobody can be exactly sure what has happened in Saratov, however, I believe that our agent has done an exceptional job.' 'I was always sure, and convinced that our agent would prevent a launch resulting in the explosion at the Saratov nuclear site.'

'As I have said, he has successfully manipulated the data, which when they activated a launch code sequence, resulted in the nuke exploding in its silo.' 'However, having said that, I am extremely pleased that we are all still here to tell the story,' replied Barnaby.

He knew that he could not lie to the President nor could he reveal the CIA's involvement in the development of the UFO's, so he tried as best he could to divert the attention away from what he knew and focus on other issues at hand.

'It may be an opportunity to call Pushkin's bluff Mr. President.' 'Call him and offer assistance, which we could announce on national television.' 'That will be positive in the eyes of the Russian people, even if he turns you down, sir'

'Yes that may be something worth considering,' said the President.

Continuing he said, 'I want to meet this agent and thank him personally Barnaby, so make sure that happens the next time he is in the US.'

'I will do that Mr. President, however, he is not a person that wants to be in the spotlight nor does he want his name up in lights either, so if I may suggest, don't offer him a medal or any type of official ceremony.' 'He is a very private person, Sir.'

The President merely nodded.

It was well after midnight when Barnaby jumped into the SUV and instructed his detail to drive him back to Langley. He realized that his detail had not eaten for the past twelve hours, so he instructed them to go to the drive-through at MacaBurgers and order a meal. He ordered a large coffee for himself as he had lost his appetite. Sitting in the rear of the SUV, he reflected on just how close the world had come to total annihilation. Scary, real scary he considered, and he had somehow managed to keep the CIA's secret of the UFO's to himself, a tradition that CIA Directors pass on from one to the next. He wondered why the UFO had not flown over the site at Saratov, and considered that they simply may have run out of time.

Back in his office, Barnaby dialled Colonel Emmanuel Dolivo, the officer in charge of Area fifty one on a secure line.

Speaking in their gibberish code he said, 'sorry to wake you, Manny.' 'Dad wants to thank you and the drivers for delivering the goods, albeit that I see that one of them did not make it to their last delivery point.'

'Thank you, Director, yes they made the deliveries, however, they did not get to their last drop-off point as they ran out of time,' said Manny.

'I see, well I am glad they were able to deliver the rest of the orders,' 'Please thank the drivers for making it all possible,' replied Barnaby.

A short while later he dialled Rafael on a secure line.

'Hope I did not wake you Rafa, but I feel that it is appropriate to thank you most sincerely for saving the world from annihilation, yet again.' 'We were all very lucky that your encrypted instruction worked,' said Barnaby.

'Thank you, Director,' came the sleepy reply from Rafael as he glanced at the clock, noting that it was zero six hundred hours.

'The President wants to meet you and thank you personally when you are next in the States.' 'Thanks again young man,' he said as he ended the call.

Claire turned to face him and asked who had called.

'Just the Director calling to touch base,' said Rafael as he snuggled up.

'At zero six hundred hours?' said Claire looking at the bedside clock.

Now fully awake, Rafael gently kissed Claire on the cheek, fully waking her up from the slumber she was in, then moved the blankets off her, revealing the athletic contours of her naked body as the filtered light streamed into the apartment from the street lamppost. Fully erect, he mounted her in the missionary position. Claire merely offered a slight groan. Five minutes later he rolled off her almost out of breath. Happy that the world has not found itself in a nuclear war with Ivan so we can continue our lives and I can use my joystick, and make love whenever I want to, he thought to himself.

Claire propped herself up on the pillows, turned to face him, and said, 'what's wrong my handsome man.' 'I sense a lot of tension in you.'

'All good Mon Pétale,' he responded as he got out of bed, made his way towards the bathroom, and took a shower. Claire rolled over and went back to sleep. He towelled himself down, got dressed, and made himself a cup of coffee, then activated his mobile phone.

There was a text message from Director Heathcott, it read, call me when you get to the office. Sitting in his office later, Barnaby suddenly realized that he had not slept for over twenty-four hours so he removed his jacket, shoes, and tie, curled up on the couch, covered himself with his jacket, and was sound asleep minutes later. Hours later his assistant Gizelle entered his office, and was astounded to find him curled up in a ball fast asleep on the couch.

She left him to sleep peacefully, picked up his mobile phone, returned to her desk, and went about her daily chores. A short while later the display on Barnaby's phone lit up announcing an incoming call.

'Hello Rafa, I regret that the Director is unavailable right now, however, I will get him to call you as soon as he is free.'

Barnaby finally woke up from his deep sleep, and noticed that the sun had risen well into the morning sky. He glanced at his watch noticing that it was zero nine-thirty hundred hours. Yawing and stretching he got up, made his way to his desk in search of his mobile phone, and called out to his assistant.

'Gizelle, have you seen my phone?' he asked.

'Yes Director, here it is,' she said handing it to him.

Barnaby called Rafael and again thanked him for what he had done, and told him that the President insisted on meeting him when he is next in the USA.

Chapter 6

Tipsy's Bar

McLean USA

A week after the Russian crisis, the screen on Barnaby's iPhone lit up announcing incoming call from an old journalist friend.

'Hello Jesse, how the hell are you my friend?'

'Outstanding old boy.' 'I thought I would call you to meet for a drink later this afternoon my friend,' responded Jesse.

'Sounds great, say around seventeen hundred hours at our usual hangout,' replied Barnaby.

'Cool see you then,' replied Jesse ending the call.

Barnaby still felt somewhat fatigued and drained after last the week's drama, and needed a change of scenery, so a drink with an old friend felt exactly what the doctor ordered. He sat back and reflected on the drama that unfolded a week earlier, and said a silent prayer of thanks to his maker for saving the world from a nuclear holocaust. He considered, just how lucky they had been to have had William Hikenbothem, a retired admiral at the helm of the CIA in the nineteen fifties, and that he had the vision to appoint three scientists to dismantle, then reassemble the alien craft that had crashed near Hart Canyon on the twenty-fifth of March, nineteen forty-eight near Aztec in New Mexico.

The scientists had learned the secrets of ET's craft, reassembled it, and flew it over various USA nuclear sites, resulting in an electrical failure at all the sites without the knowledge of sitting President Ford or the military. A secret that had been buried for decades, and passed down from Director to Director at the CIA. William Hikenbothem was a man of vision, and had instructed the scientists to secretly develop replicas of these craft as he believed that someday, they would save the world from a nuclear Armageddon. They had successfully tested the four craft that they had built, and stored them at Area 51 under heavy guard, just in case a situation like they had all just witnessed, ever eventuated.

Barnaby turned and looked at the photograph of Admiral Hikenbothem hanging proudly on his office wall alongside other past Directors of the CIA. He stood, saluted him then returned to his desk. The world owes you a great debt of gratitude for your foresight Director Hikenbothem, he thought.

Later that afternoon, Barnaby, contacted Hans Vogel, the head of the Swiss Police in Zurich.

'Hallo Her Hans,' hello Mr. Hans.

'I trust that you are well,' offered Barnaby.

'Ja alles gut, danke schön,' Yes all good, thank you very much.

'Well Hans, we have discovered a group that go by the name of the Three Sixty Degrees Group, and they may well have questionable motives in their modus operandi with a defined agenda that is extremely troublesome,' said Barnaby.

'The CIA uncovered a plot by this group of people, who, as we understand it, have members scattered around the globe that intend to cull the world's population in half through an airborne virus.' 'Also, from what we have been able to find out, the elite members of this group include current and past Presidents, Prime Minister's, captains of industry, the wealthy elite including academics, scientists, medical professors etc.'

Continuing he said, 'from what we have been able to establish, the group intends carrying out this sinister plan in the near future, and as I understand it, they have based themselves in Switzerland, hence the reason for my call.'

'I am giving you a heads up and will call you as soon as we have shed some more light on them, so please keep this confidential and wait for my call.'

'Thank you Barnaby, I will wait for your call.'

Later that afternoon, Barnaby met his old friend Jesse Vozenilek, a freelance journalist working for the Washington News, at Tipsy's Bar on Tysons Boulevard in McLean. Over the years Barnaby had fed him snippets of useful information, which led him to be recognised as one of the best investigative journalists in the industry. Jesse had jealously guarded and protected his sources over the years.

'Hello Jesse, long time no see,' offered Barnaby taking his hand in a friendly greeting as he approached him sitting at the end of the bar.

'Howdy Barnaby,' replied Jesse.

Signalling the barman, he ordered two triple scotches on the rocks.

'So how's life in the world of spooks?' asked Jesse.

'Trying to keep us all safe my friend, so that you can enjoy your annual holidays in the Bahama's,' replied Barnaby.

'So my friend, what exactly happened in Russia a short while ago, and where did the UFO's come from?' questioned Jesse.

Looking him squarely in the eye, Barnaby replied, 'Well as you know we came within a whisker of a nuclear war with Ivan, thanks to the madman running the joint.' 'Pushkin has lost control of the masses, and is trying desperately to cling to power, so in my opinion, he was trying to shift the focus away from the problems he has at home, and blame us for instigating an attack on mother Russia.'

Continuing he said, 'a hell of a dangerous way to try and shift the focus away from himself, because the explosion in the silo at Saratov, has saved the world from a nuclear holocaust because a retaliation from us, would have triggered an all-out nuclear exchange.' 'It's real scary how close we came to oblivion and maybe, just maybe, once he has seen the total destruction at Saratov, he will sober up enough to realise the consequences of a nuclear war.'

'So Barnaby, there have been reports of UFO's flying over the Russian nuclear sites.' 'What part has the CIA played in that?' questioned Jesse.

'What makes you think we are involved Jesse?' asked Barnaby with raised eyebrows.

'Well you guys are the most secretive organization in the world, so I will not be surprised at all to learn that the CIA has somehow managed to copy alien technology,' replied Jesse.

'Yeah right, whatever seems to happen that is out of the ordinary, people tend to think that the CIA is involved.' 'So to answer your question, no my friend, we are not involved in any alien technology at all,' said Barnaby looking Jesse directly in the eye, knowing that was unable to be truthful.

'Do you believe that ET had something to do with the explosion at Saratov Barnaby, and what's your take on the explosion Barnaby?'

'I have no idea what happened there at all.'

'From what we have been able to find out, it seems that whatever happened over there was caused by a malfunction.' 'Thank the good Lord for that, because if Ivan had launched a nuke, either on purpose or not, it would have been met with a massive response from us which would have led to the end of life on earth for sure,' said Barnaby emphatically.

'As you know, the USA and Russia were heading towards a possible nuclear exchange when in July 1962 Soviet premier Nikita Khrushchev reached a secret agreement with Cuban premier Fidel Castro to place Soviet nuclear missiles in Cuba to deter any future invasion attempt.' 'This of course happened after our failed attempt to overthrow the Castro regime with the Bay of Pigs invasion.'

'Whilst we came close on that occasion, it pales in comparison to how close we came to a nuclear exchange this time.'

'The scary part is, Ivan have their finger on the trigger and God forbid, if some moron over there accidentlly hit the button, the entire world would have gone Kaboom.'

Continuing, he said, 'best go to church on Sunday and thank the Lord for intervening my friend, because people have no idea just how close we came to the world going up in smoke this time.'

Barnaby had long come to realise that feeding Jesse snippets of information in the past yielded desired outcomes. Disclosing a minuscule amount of information regarding the Three Sixty Degrees Group, could be useful, and possibly result in many members of the group rethinking their position. He was careful to feed Jesse just enough information for him to investigate the group, as he had a reputation for ferreting out the truth where most thought nothing existed.

Jesse sipped his scotch, looked at Barnaby and simply nodded his head. He accepted that his friend could never tell him the truth, however, would feed him snippets of information from time to time.

'Do you think Pushkin will remain in power?' 'It seems that he has lost the support of the majority of the Russian people, and there have been rumours circulating of a possible coup or even an assassination attempt in the wind.' 'I'm sure you have heard this as well.'

'Yes, it's true that he seems to have lost control of the people as well as the support of the oligarchs, however one can never underestimate Pushkin, because as we have seen, he will go to any length to maintain power, so watch this space Jesse.' 'Things could get very interesting indeed.'

'Barnaby, be honest with me, do you have any further information about the Three Sixty Degrees Group that I can use?'

'Yes, in fact I do have some info for you that you can use.' 'The Three Sixty Degrees Group consists of current and past Presidents, Prime Ministers, the ultra-rich, academics, scientists, presidents of industry and many more.'

'They came to light a while ago, and we have been keeping an eye on their activities, so that's all I can share with you at this time.' 'If ever I am able to pass on some information, I will gladly do that,' said Barnaby.

'Their agenda is to cull of the world's population in half which undoubtedly includes you and I, our families and friends, so we will have to take a very close look at this mob.'

'So, the world without their knowledge, has a massive problem at the moment.' 'If in fact these people were able to carry out their mission and get away with it, then the atrocities they will commit, will make Hitler, Stalin, Pol Pot, Idi Amin, Mugabe, Pushkin, and all the other dictators look like saints,' said Barnaby.

'I believe that the Swiss authorities may well be investigating this at the moment, and will at some time in the future, announce their findings to the world detailing exactly what they have discovered.' 'So if you want to beat them to it, you will need to publish your story within weeks.'

'Best start using your fingers, and get your story out so that you can draw the world's attention to what this group really intends doing,' added Barnaby.

'It seems that there is trouble brewing around every corner,' said Jesse signalling to the barman to bring another round.

'Salute, glad we are still here to enjoy a drink,' he said clinking glasses with his old friend.

'What's up with all these terrorists that keep on popping up Barnaby?'

'Well as you know, we track them, find them, and either arrest or eliminate them.' 'The problem is that as you do that, another group or leader rears his or their head, so it's a never ending problem.' 'I can't see it ever changing frankly, similar to the Jewish/Arabic problem, where neither side will give an inch, so peace is unlikely to ever happen there, nor will we ever stamp out the jihadists.'

'It's not only jihadists that we have to deal with, it is also home grown fanatics that we have to worry about my friend.'

'Well, thanks for a heads up about the Three Sixty Degrees Group.' 'I will investigate this, and hopefully will have a story to be told when I have completed it,' 'I will run it passed you prior to publication Barnaby, and would appreciate any further information you would be able to add,' said Jesse.

Chapter 7

Langley

Virginia USA

Rafael stared at the motivational plaque on the wall in his office at the USA Embassy in Paris.

It read-Yea, though I walk through the valley of the shadow of death, I will fear no evil: for thou art with me; thy rod and thy staff, they comfort me. **Psalm 23:4**

Even though he had occupied the office allocated to him after late Stan Noble's passing, he had never really even noticed it on the wall, nor even taken the time to read it.

His friend Stan, the CIA station chief in Paris France, had been killed when a car bomb exploded during a mission at a panel beating warehouse in Le Blanc-Mesnil a couple of months earlier.

Director Heathcott called Rafael at the Embassy on a secure line, and notified him that he had arranged to fly him to Langley the following day to meet with him as they have another issue needing urgent attention.

'Agents d'Avray and Van Der Jong will pick you up at twelve hundred hours at the Embassy, and take you to the airport where the Gulfstream will await your arrival,' said Barnaby.

'On arrival at Bigler's Mill, you will be met by agents Rodrigues and Conte, and driven to Langley.' 'I do not want you to discuss this with anybody other than your partner Lieutenant Commander Johnston Rafa.'

'Yes sir, you have my word,' replied Rafael.

'Hello Mr. Dujon, dinners in the warmer,' offered the Co-Pilot as he boarded the Gulf Stream, and made to his usual window seat on the port side.

'Pleased to see that my plane is in pristine condition,' replied Rafael.

He was awoken from a deep sleep hours later by the dinging sound of the overhead speaker with the Co-Pilot announcing their impending arrival into Bigler's Mill. He nodded his approval of the smooth landing, and watched as they taxied towards the hanger, noticing the usual black G.M. SUV parked close to the hanger door with agents Rodrigues and Conte leaning against the vehicle. Eight out of ten for that smooth landing he thought.

Agents Marcel Rodrigues and Wilfred Conte offered their hands in a friendly greeting as he made his way down the stairs.

'Good to see you again Rafa,' offered both agents.

Wilfred turned to face the driver and said, 'Langley please Marcel, and make it chop, chop, the boss is waiting.'

'Aye Aye captain,' said Marcel as he turned onto the highway and headed towards Langley.

'Hello Rafa, good to see you again,' said Miss Marple, Barnaby Heathcott's assistant as he exited the metal detector at the front entrance to Langley.

She turned towards Barnaby's private elevator, indicating for him to follow, and tapped lightly on Barnaby's door announcing his arrival.

'Thank you Gizelle,' said Barnaby rising from his chair and rounding his desk.

'Good to see you, Rafa.' 'We have an important issue to resolve,' said Barnaby waiving him to a seat opposite him.

'Once again, thank you for what you have done Rafa, and despite the crisis in Russia, we still face ongoing challenges at the CIA.' 'What I am about to tell you almost seems like a waste of time, due to the crisis that Pushkin was responsible for, however, I am of the view that the crisis seems to have passed, so now he has to deal with the disaster at Saratov, and things should settle down somewhat.'

'Again, I reiterate everything I say is highly confidential, and for your knowledge only Rafa.' 'It came to my attention a while back that a group that you are familiar with, namely, the Three Sixty Degrees Group, has been planning to cull the world's population in half using an airborne virus.' 'We believe that this virus has already been tested in Gabon on the west coast of Africa, hence the need to have you attend their cocktail party in Zurich some time ago,' continued Barnaby.

'The outcome of that test resulted in some two hundred thousand people dying mysteriously twelve months after they had released this virus in Gabon, which in the United Nations charter is deemed as genocide.'

Continuing he said, 'The Gabon authorities are completely in the dark regarding the deaths.' 'They have no clue what has caused it, or even how to treat it, and believe that it is another strain of Ebola.'

'The World Health Organization are also in the dark, and they too believe that it may well be another strain of Ebola.'

'My understanding is, that the elite group of members of this organization has developed an anti-virus that will only be available to their exclusive membership and their respective families.' 'So from what I understand, they have tested the anti-virus which has proven to be one hundred percent effective,' he said.

'We need to put a stop to this idiotic idea, as the success of this would result in these people committing mass murder on an unprecedented scale, the likes of which the world has never seen, and will make Hitler look like a saint that committed a minor misdemeanour.'

'We have been monitoring this group for some time now, and whilst, we have a basic understanding of who some of their members are, we need to act quickly as the group intends implementing their plan shortly,' continued Barnaby.

'I believe that you may shortly be approached by the chairman of the group namely, Dr. Goodfellow to conduct a thorough IT overview of the group's anti-virus and security protocols, and I have it on very good authority that your credentials have been thoroughly checked by one of their Bishops, a retired US congress senator namely, Jim Stratton,' continued Barnaby.

'That's why we set you up as an IT entrepreneur in a company that we aptly named Cyber Logic Solution Inc. and have had you continually work from that office from time to time, to ensure that you have a track record stemming from that location Rafa.'

'I have arranged for you to apply for a job as a barman at the Liberty Club situated on Sid Snyder Avenue in Washington, which is frequented every Friday afternoon at around seventeen hundred hours by two of the Bishops as they are known within the Three Sixty Degrees Group, namely retired Senator Jim Stratton, and a current sitting Senator by the name of Zander Cotalico.'

'Slip into the role and gain their confidence, then when the time is right, squirt the liquid that you will be given in the two vials into their glasses before pouring the drinks.' 'One will be marked with a black cross which is the one I want you use in Senator Stratton's drink, and the other unmarked vial is for Senator Cotalico.' 'So Rafa make sure you get it right young man, and make very sure that nobody witnesses you doing it.'

Barnaby handed a photograph of the two Senators seated at the bar, and pointed to the grey haired gentleman.' 'This is Senator Stratton, so to confirm use the vial with the black cross on it in his drink,' continued Barnaby.

'They always tend to sit at the end of the bar, and from what we understand, Senator Stratton is a Bourbon man and Senator Cotalico's drop of choice is Scotch. Both like it with ice and a dash of coke.' 'Of concern is the fact that there are past and present Presidents, Prime Ministers, captains of industry, academics, scientists, doctors, bankers, and many more wealthy privileged people that are associated with this group.'

'Nobody including your partner, is ever to get a sniff of what you are about to do young man, so you need to be extremely careful,' said Barnaby.

'Yes sir, I fully understand,' 'If you don't mind me asking, what will be in those is vials sir?' questioned Rafael.

'They will contain the same liquid that was used to poison the late Kim Jong-un, the North Korean leader and his sisters, and as you know it led to a regime change yielding positive outcomes and dialogue with them,' 'We need to put a stop to the madness before this group actually commits a cardinal sin, and actually succeeds in killing billions of people around the globe which will include both of us, our families, friends and loved ones, so time is not on our side Rafael.' 'Be extremely careful when handling the contents, and do not get any of it on your hands,' said Barnaby.

'The reason that you need to use two different vials, is that one is more potent than the other, and will result in the deaths not happening at the same time.' 'They will pass about two weeks apart, thus it should not raise much suspicion as they both will die of heart attacks.'

'Also be careful to put the vials into a zip lock bag after you have used them, and dispose of them efficiently later on. Ensure that you do not leave any fingerprints on either the vials or the zip lock bag.'

Rafael, leaned back in his chair and considered Barnaby's remarks. Fuck me, I really have become the Judge, Jury and Executioner all in one. Truth is, the justice system is skewed in favour of the bad guys who somehow always seem to get a slap on the wrist, serve a short-term sentence or are merely let off scot-free. Somebody needs to change that, so frankly I'm glad it's me playing a small part.

'I will have a makeup artist change your appearance before you report for your shift each day at the Liberty Club, as we need to disguise who you really are, and don't befriend anybody at work.' 'Be sure to take great care that you are not followed when your shift ends.'

'I want you to assume the name of René Dubois for this mission, and if anybody asks where you come from, tell them that you were born in Papeete in French Polynesia because it will be hard to disguise your French accent.' 'I anticipate that you will stay on the job for a week or until the mission is complete, then notify the manager that you have accepted a far better paying job elsewhere and leave immediately Rafael.'

Handing a mobile phone to Rafael, Barnaby added, 'I want you to use this phone until your mission is complete, then remove the sim card, clean all traces of fingerprints on it, and destroy the device as well as the sim card.'

A week later the mobile phone rang, and Rafael answered it trying as best he could to remain calm.

'Hello René speaking,' he offered with a distinct French accent.

'Good morning René, my name is Roland Franklin.' 'I am the manager of the Liberty Club, and I am ringing regarding the barman's job that we advertised, which you have applied for.' 'So, I am wondering when you could come in for an interview?' questioned Roland.

'Oui Monsieur, I am available tomorrow morning at a time that suits you, and thank you for the opportunity to meet with you Mr. Franklin,' replied René

'Good, see you at ten a.m. tomorrow then,' replied Roland disconnecting the call.

Next morning René announced himself at the reception desk of the Liberty Club for the interview, and was ushered into a conference room. A short while later he was joined by Roland, who swanned into the room, waving his limp writs indicting that he was openly gay. He was immediately attracted to the neatly dressed dark haired handsome athletic young man seated at the conference table opposite him. No need to go through a rigorous interview process he thought to himself, and skimmed through his resume, finally enquiring when he would be able to start.

'Well Monsieur Franklin, I am available to start tomorrow if that's suitable,' replied René.

'Brilliant, please call me Roland, and to confirm the rate is $20 per hour,' 'I hope that is suitable René.' 'The shift starts at three p.m. and ends at nine p.m.' he continued.

'Merci, thank you that will be fine, so see you tomorrow afternoon then,' said René as they parted ways.

Next day, being a Friday, René reported for duty, and was issued a new barman's outfit of black pants, crisp new white shirt, red bowtie and a red waste coat. He donned the new gear, looked the part as he admired himself in the mirror, and was shown how to use the cash register, then taken on a tour to familiarise himself with the layout of the bar, as well as the cocktail menu, and was informed of the manner in which the patrons expected to be treated in the exclusive club.

The cash register was a standard Casio SE-C450 used in numerous bars with a large lockable cash drawer, eight coin and four note compartments, so nothing too complicated. He went about wiping down the bar counter, started polishing the glasses under Roland's watchful eye, filled the water jugs, neatly placed all the coasters in piles, and cut the lemons into slices.

Generally busied himself with menial tasks around the bar which seemed to satisfy Roland, confirming that he was an experienced barman. A short while later Roland departed and made his way back to his office.

René served numerous patrons and glanced at his watch, noting that it was almost seventeen hundred hours which is the time that the two Senator's normally arrive for their Friday afternoon drinks, so he positioned two tumblers on the rear counter top next to the mirror waited for their arrival. He served other patrons as the bar started to fill up, noticing the two Senators entering and making their way towards the far end of the bar.

He turned his back to the patrons extracted the two vials from a plastic bag in his pocket, identified the one with the black cross, twisted the cap off and squirted the contents into the tumbler on the left. He then followed the same procedure, and squirted the contents of the other vial into the remaining glass. All done very discreetly without any patrons noticing what he had done.

He placed the two vials into a plastic zip lock bag, then placed it into another bag which he put into his pocket before walking to the end of the bar, and greeting the two Senators in a friendly manner. He enquired what they would like to drink. Senator Stratton ordered his usual Bourbon and Coke and Senator Cotalico a Scotch and Coke.

'Make them doubles please young man.' 'You are new here, so what's your name young man?' inquired Senator Cotalico.

'Renè sir,' he replied in his French accent, as he turned and made his way towards the two tumblers taking care to remember that the tumbler on the left contained the poison with the black cross on it. He drew the alcohol from the optic tot measures, added ice cubes, before topping them up with a dash of coke, and placing the two drinks on coasters in front of the Senators.

'Open a tab please René,' instructed Senator Cotalico.

'Certainly sir,' replied René as he turned to remove the dirty glasses from people seated further along the bar. He enquired whether other patrons would like a refill, glancing to see Senator Cotalico and Stratton clinking glasses, and taking a sip of their drop of choice.

So far so good, he thought to himself. From memory, if it is the same poison that we used to eliminate Kim Jong-un and his sisters, it should take around two to four weeks before we see any results. He continued to serve the other patrons, and a few hours later the bar emptied as patrons made their way home, so having cleared the senator's glasses he donned a pair of gloves, and carefully washed them before placing them into the dish washer. He ran the hot water tap in the sink for a few minutes before realising that it was almost twenty one hundred hours, so he busied himself in preparation for the end of his shift.

As he made his way out of the club, he afforded himself a rare smile. Easy as, he thought and farewell to you two bastards, I hope you rot in hell.

He rang Roland the following day and notified him that he had accepted a better paying job.

Chapter 8

Area 51

Nevada USA

Three weeks prior to the Russian crisis, Barnaby boarded the streamlined Gulfstream Aerospace G700 jet, and was greeted by the Co-Pilot as he entered.

'Welcome aboard Director, your meal is in the warmer whenever you are ready sir,' offered the Co-Pilot.

'Thank you,' replied Barnaby as he made his way into the belly of the jet, and found a suitable seat.

The Co-Pilot retrieved the staircase, secured the door, and made his way into the cockpit just as they started taxiing towards the runway. A few minutes later they were amongst the clouds climbing to a cruising altitude of fifty-one thousand feet. The cruising speed of five hundred and ninety-five knots would take around four and three-quarters of an hour, so Barnaby made his way to the galley, and extracted a soda from the fridge. He returned to his window seat, put his feet on the ottoman, and stared at the cloudy sky below.

Having enjoyed the soda he made his way to the galley again, extracted a meal of salmon and vegetables from the warmer, before returning to his seat. He opened the dossier and read its contents for the umpteenth time, focusing on the executive summary towards the end of the file. The summary stated that the four crafts were securely housed in hanger B2 at Area 51, and confirmed that the hanger was heavily guarded, however that was a week ago. They had recently been deployed to a remote part of the Okinawa Islands in Japan, and were securely hidden in thick vegetation on the island. The Footnote Read-All craft had been flight tested numerous times in the recent past, and were ready for deployment whenever the CIA needed them.

The sudden thump and screeching of the Gulf Streams tyres hitting the tarmac startled him, confirming their arrival at Area 51, so Barnaby placed the dossier back into his satchel. He watched as the plane taxied towards hanger B2, and was met by Colonel Emmanuel Dolivo, the base commander at the foot of the stairs.

'Hello Director and welcome to Area 51 sir,' said the Colonel offering his hand in a friendly welcome, as Barnaby made his way onto the tarmac.

'Hi Manny, thank you,' offered Barnaby.

'This way Director,' said the Colonel indicating towards a hanger and leading the way.

As they approached the hanger's side door, Barnaby turned to face the three guards and thanked them for their service, then briskly followed Manny into the hanger through a side door.

'So this is the hanger that the craft were housed in, and to confirm, your team had installed the latest version of UAV, the Unmanned Aircraft System, developed by Northrop Grumman and Martin?'

'Yes Director that is affirmative, sir.'

'I can confirm that we have tested each craft multiple times, and the results have been outstanding with zero defect in all the craft.' 'I have arranged for a demonstration video of the most recent test flights conducted a month ago which is scheduled whenever you are ready Director, and this will give you an update on the technology we have installed in all the craft,' stated Manny.

Barnaby merely nodded his approval.

'As per the classified dossier, I can confirm that these crafts have an unlimited range and ceiling height.' 'They have been deployed to "Area Zero" and as per your instruction, and are ready for action as we speak Director.'

'Well Manny, as you are aware we have a massive problem with Ivan, which honestly may well result in the end of all living matter on earth as we know it, so frankly, humanity without its knowledge, is reliant on the E.T. technology working, and completing its mission successfully if ever it is called upon to do so,' said Barnaby in a sombre tone of voice.

'So please pray that all of E.T's secrets have been uncovered and installed in these crafts, and that it actually works.' 'If not, to be honest, we will be in shit that deep that there will never be sunlight or life on our beautiful planet ever again,' said Barnaby, turning and looking Manny directly in the eye.

Looking towards the heavens and placing the palms of his hands together, Barnaby said out aloud, 'please guide us, my Lord.'

'Director, I have invited the four drone pilots and their co-pilots to join us for the video demonstration, so that you can personally meet the men tasked with the responsibility to carry out any mission you may instruct them to do sir,' stated Manny.

Barnaby merely nodded as Manny led the way towards the office block, opening a door leading to a lounge.

'You may need some private time Director, so make yourself comfortable.' 'Coffee is available on the sideboard, and I will meet with you again in thirty minutes, so that we can begin the video demonstration.'

'Thank you Manny, this looks rather comfortable,' said Barnaby as he made his way towards the sideboard and poured himself a cup of coffee.

Thirty minutes later the four pilots and their backup teams were introduced to Barnaby. He sat at the head of the conference table, and viewed the video being streamed onto a monitor on the wall that lasted ninety minutes. All four of the craft had been put through rigorous manoeuvres over the base demonstrating the ability to change direction in an instant, and propel themselves to ultra-hypersonic speeds at the blink of an eye, and vanish into thin air.

'These craft have the ability to travel at speeds beyond human imagination, change course or simply stop at the blink of an eye Director.'

Barnaby thanked the drone pilots and their backup crews, reiterating the need for absolute confidentiality.

'We have measured the crafts flying at speeds over Mach thirty, and we still have some juice in the tank so we believe we can get to somewhere around Mach forty if needed Director,' said the Colonel as a broad smile creased his face.

'Very impressive indeed Manny.' 'Thankfully nobody has developed missiles that can reach anywhere near the speed that these craft are capable of flying, so in fact they can easily outfly or out manoeuvre any threat of being shot down by a missile.'

'Yes sir, that is correct.' 'They are absolutely safe from any threat such as a missile, however we have never tested it against a laser, so not sure if that could be a problem, however at the speed that they are able to fly, I am confident that it would not be a problem either,' added Manny.

'It has been proven that the further that a laser beam travels, the strength of the beam dims, and weakens, so my theory is that, due to the maximum speed that the crafts can fly, which I believe would be close to Mach forty, I think that we can safely assume that they will outfly any threat from a laser beam.'

'Well let's hope that your theory is correct, and if ever we do get to use any of these crafts, we never find out what effect a laser would have on them, because humanity may well have to rely on them carrying out a number of missions successfully Manny.'

As Barnaby stood, he thanked the pilots and their backup teams. He again reminded them of confidentiality, and the need for zero defect, then bid them all farewell.

'You all need to die with this secret, just the way that the three scientists did.' 'They took the secret to the grave, which is what I expect of all of us,' said Barnaby as he looked at all present.

Walking towards the exit he turned to face Manny and thanked him again.

'The demonstration was very impressive, as well as convincing, and I am particularly pleased that these crafts can perform to expectation.' 'We should all say a silent prayer that these crafts can neutralize Ivan's nukes as they fly over their missile sites, if ever called upon to do that.'

'I have to get back to Washington Manny, so thank you for the demonstration and your hospitality.' 'Let's hope like hell that we don't need to use the technology at all, however, before I depart, I would like to see where you have housed our inter-planetary guests.'

'Certainly Director, please follow me,' said Manny as he led the way to a building located adjacent to hanger B2.

Entering Barnaby suddenly became aware of the change in temperature, as they made their way through two doors leading to a glass enclosure that housed the two alien bodies in morgue drawers.

Manny hit the intercom button and instructed the coroner to extract the bodies of the two aliens, and put them onto the stainless steel embalming tables positioned in the centre of the room. I pray that the technology you brought us will help save the world, thought Barnaby as he stared at the bodies. Strange looking, he considered as he stared in silence.

'Thank you Manny, and God speed.' 'Let's pray to the Almighty that whatever knowledge we have gained from these crafts actually work if ever they are called upon.'

'Au Revoir Manny and thank you for keeping these crafts in a safe environment, and in excellent working order.'

The Co-Pilot secured the staircase, and shortly thereafter they taxied towards the runway, increased speed to full throttle, and were amongst the clouds a couple of minutes later. Barnaby looked towards the west and the setting sun. Truly a beautiful evening he thought to himself as he sipped his scotch from a tumbler. I hope like hell the world will see many more of these. The display on his mobile phone lit up with a message from Gizelle, his assistant notifying him that the President would like to see him in the morning.

Chapter 9

Zurich

Switzerland

D r. Goodfellow, the Chairman of the Three Sixty Degrees Group, known as the Cardinal, had long been concerned about the cybersecurity of their network, and had been searching for an experienced, talented, suitable, and trusted candidate within the Three Sixty Degrees Group to install a secure cyber security firewall into their system. He had taken note of Aaron's name, his expertise in IT, as well as his track record, and asked one of his trusted inner circle, known as Bishop X who was based in America, to check Aaron's credentials. Bishop X used all his extensive connections within the banking fraternity to thoroughly check everything about Aaron Armando.

Rafael had used the alias of Aaron Armando when he met Dr. Goodfellow briefly at the Grand Hotel in Zurich months previously, when President Pushkin's head of security passed on a USB stick containing a video of the meeting between the Russian President Pushkin and the Chinese President Mr. Xiu Jaoping.

Having learned of The Three Sixty Degrees Group, and its intention to drastically reduce the world's population years previously, Barnaby had confidentially monitored them realizing that someday the CIA would be tasked with neutralizing this group, so he went about setting up a business in Paris complete with banking details, an Internet account with hundreds of emails on record, and a paper trail that went back several years. To anybody sniffing around in the future, it would seem that it was legitimate.

The CIA had gone to great lengths to create a track record of business achievements for Aaron as well as setting him up as an IT specialist, with extensive knowledge and expertise in cyber security. They set up an office for Aaron in the district of La Défense, which is the biggest business district in Europe located in the north-west of Paris in the lining up of the Louvre, the Champs-Elysées, and the Arc de Triomphe. The CIA had registered the business name of Cyber Logic Solutions Inc. years previously. This ensured a paper trail going back a number of years, and they created a list of impressive clients legitimizing his business credentials, complete with a bank account, business credit card, a track record of banking transactions, post box, as well as, hundreds of emails from a bevy of reputable corporations. All the relevant company documentation had been registered years previously and his company name, and logo were featured on the outer façade of the building.

Bishop X ran extensive checks on Aaron's credentials, and notified the Cardinal that he was legit, and checked out with a clean record. Aaron was invited to lunch with Dr. Goodfellow at the popular Swiss Gallery restaurant at Kronenhalle which was established in nineteen twenty-four in the heart of Zurich on Bellevue Square, within walking distance of the opera house, theatre, and concert hall.

There are three restaurants within Kronenhalle, the Swiss Gallery situated on the first floor, the Brasserie, and Chagall Hall. The walls of each restaurant are decorated with masterpieces of artwork by various world-famous painters. Aaron admired the artwork that donned the wall of the Swiss Gallery restaurant characterized by Giovani Giacometti, Ferdinand Hodler, Sigismund Righini, and Max Gubler as he made his way towards the table.

The Restaurant specialized in high-quality cuisine, and guests dined beneath these masterpieces of art that gave the room an ambiance of sophistication.

Dr. Goodfellow stood as Aaron approached, offering his hand in a greeting.

'Good to see you again Aaron,' offered Dr. Goodfellow, as Aaron joined him at the table.

'Drink?' asked Dr. Goodfellow, as he summoned a waiter.

'A drink for my friend,' he said turning to face the waiter.

'Double Johnny Walker Blue on the rocks please,' said Aaron.

'Good choice, make that two please, and a bottle of Pertaringa McLaren Vale Tipsy Hill Cabernet Sauvignon,' said Dr. Goodfellow passing the wine list to the waiter.

'Sorry I did not get to chat with you at the cocktail party that you attended a while back Aaron, due to other pressing issues that I had to deal with on the night.'

The waiter brought the whiskies, placed them on coasters, and opened the wine allowing it to breathe.

'To life,' toasted Dr. Goodfellow.

'Santé,' replied Aaron clinking glasses, wondering whose life he was referring to.

'Ready to order gentlemen?' inquired the waiter returning a while later.

Looking at Aaron, Dr. Goodfellow said, 'I recommend the Veal-Filet Geschnetzelte Kronenhalle that is served with hash browns.' 'It's the traditional dish at this restaurant.'

'Sounds terrific, thank you, I will try that,' said Aaron closing the menu, and returning it to the waiter as he sat back in his chair.

'To success,' said Dr. Goodfellow, raising his glass in another toast.

Success at culling the world's population or success at me installing a secure impenetrable firewall wondered Aaron, smiling broadly as they clinked glasses yet again. Aaron was invited to join the group after Inge had introduced his name to Dr. Goodfellow.

'So Aaron, we are looking for an IT expert in cyber security, and I have had your credentials verified, and they checked out, so I am offering you the role of IT Specialist with the group,' 'We specifically need to review our cyber security as a matter of urgency, and that's where you come into the picture,' continued Dr. Goodfellow.

He leaned down and extracted an envelope from the satchel leaning against the leg of his chair, and placed it in front of Aaron. Aaron opened the envelope, read the letter of appointment, and was careful not to reveal his surprise at the salary on offer, which was three times what he earned at the CIA. He went to great lengths to act calmly, as if the salary was no surprise to him whatsoever.

He glanced at the employment contract in silence, flicking through the pages without actually reading them, and was aware that he was being studied by the Doctor who seemed to seek a waiver of surprise at the salary on offer. He studied Aaron closely, and was satisfied that he passed the first test of character with flying colours.

'We have been searching for a suitable, honest, and reliable candidate within the group so I am pleased to say that your credentials are outstanding.' 'I have had your credentials thoroughly checked, and I am satisfied that you meet the criteria,' added Dr. Goodfellow.

'Well Dr. Goodfellow, the task for me to review your current cyber security arrangements, and possibly recommend changes to the current format, is dependent on what's in the employment contract.'

'Perfectly sound to me, and exactly what I expected Aaron,' said Dr. Goodfellow.

Dr. Goodfellow took Aaron's hand in anticipation of him joining the group.

'So to cut to the chase, this is a job offer that I would like you to consider.'

'Well thank you for the offer Dr. Goodfellow, however I would need to read through the employment agreement prior to making a decision.' 'I would like to let you know that I am unable to accept a full time role due to my current business commitments, as I have many clients that are constantly needing my attention, so I would only consider a part time role as a consultant.' 'If I was to accept your offer, I would need offsite access as I may not be able to be in your office when I am required to make any changes to your system.'

Dr. Goodfellow ordered another round of drinks, and sat back seeming to consider what Aaron had just said.

Continuing Aaron said, 'if I do decide to accept your offer, and you agree to me being a part time consultant, I would only be available to start in two weeks-time, as I am currently nearing completion of a project that I am working on at the moment.'

'My client is pressuring me to complete and deliver the task at hand within the next ten days.' 'I will review your offer, and consider either, accepting or rejecting it, and give you an answer tomorrow afternoon sir,' stated Aaron.

Dr. Goodfellow considered Aaron's response, which indicated that he was a successful businessman, and had passed the second test of character, allowing himself a faint smile as he nodded his head ever so slightly. Aaron realised that the good doctor loved the finer things in life.

'I look forward to hearing from you sometime tomorrow then Aaron, and hopefully we can shake hands on the appointment,' he said raising his glass of Cabernet Sauvignon.

He swirled the wine in the glass before smelling the aroma, took a sip which he swirled around in his mouth, parting his lips slightly, then breathed in, and finally swallowed.

'One can tell that it has matured well in oak,' offered Dr. Goodfellow.

Certainly a wine connoisseur, and a lover of fine food. The good Doctor seemed to be getting a little tipsy thought Aaron, as the waiter poured the wine. A second waiter arrived moments later with the meals.

'Guten Appetit,' bon appétit, he said clinking glasses with Aaron in yet another toast.

'Where are you staying Aaron?' enquired Dr. Goodfellow.

'At the Winder Hotel.' 'I leave for Paris early tomorrow morning.'

The small talk went on for the rest of the evening until it was time to part ways.

'Thank you for the invitation to dine with you Dr. Goodfellow.' 'It was an excellent choice,' said Aaron, rising as he bid him farewell.

Dr. Goodfellow watched as Aaron jumped into a cab, and tilted his head slightly, confirming that he had made the right choice. The next day Aaron caught the early morning flight to Paris, and made his way to the US Embassy. He immediately contacted Director Heathcott on a secure line.

'So young man, how did your dinner with Dr. Goodfellow go?' asked Barnaby.

'Good, thank you sir.' 'I will shortly send you the employment agreement, and ask that you get your legal eagles to go through it thoroughly, as there is a non-disclosure clause in the agreement that is binding, and of concern.' 'I need them to review it immediately as I have committed to giving Dr. Goodfellow an answer later this afternoon.'

'Send it now, and I will get you an answer within the next three hours.'

'Thank you, Director.' 'I will wait for your call then.'

Inge Marthaler was more than merely an assistant to Dr. Goodfellow, and she put her skill at sourcing outstanding candidates to join the group to good use, introducing their credentials to him for evaluation.

Barnaby contacted Aaron later that day. 'Well our legal eagles have reviewed the employment contract, and have confirmed that it is certainly binding.' 'Sign it young man, and leave the rest to me,' continued Barnaby.

'Are you sure sir, because this could have serious consequences for me?' replied Aaron.

'I understand your concern, however, be assured that you will have both the CIA, and the US government on your side,' said Barnaby.

Aaron called Dr. Goodfellow later that afternoon, and confirmed his acceptance of the employment offer with the one condition as discussed over dinner, which was that he would not be a permanent employee, rather he would act as a consultant, and work periodically for The Three Sixty Degrees Group. He would need offsite access to their system, should he not be in their offices whenever required.

Dr. Goodfellow agreed to Aaron's request, made the necessary changes, and added an addendum to the contract, then emailed it to him to sign.

Prior to leaving Paris, Aaron had called ahead, and a booked a room for a week under the name of Jon Jones at the Station Hotel, a modest three star hotel close to Zurich Station as a backup. The training he had received ensured that he was on a high alert, and may possibly need to escape and hide for a while, thus he booked a second hotel a precautionary measure.

Having landed and cleared customs, he cabbed it to the Station Hotel, registered by paying in cash, then made his way to the room, and unpacked some belongings. He made his way downstairs though the parking exit, and caught a cab to the Winder Hotel in central Zurich, booked in under the name of Aaron Armando, and unpacked his remaining belongings.

Sitting on the bed, he Googled The Three Sixty Degrees Group, and was not surprised to discover that there was no information about the group on the web.

Having won the trust of the chairman, Aaron was engaged as a consultant to assess the security of their system, and to install a firewall ensuring that no person without the necessary authority could ever be able to access their system. He would spend a week at the group's head office based in the Timedia Office Building that was designed by Shigeru Ban Architects, and housed the Swiss Media Company, Timedia.

The Three Sixty Degrees Group occupied the entire first floor with spacious offices, and a clear contribution to sustainability, on the choice of timber as the main structural material, with renewable construction material, ensuring the lowest CO_2 emissions were used in the construction process. The global mechanical system had been designed to meet the highest standards in energy ratings, and the intermediate space other than its "thermal barrier" function, is part of the public spaces that could be heated, and cooled with the extraction air from the office area.

Impressive, thought Aaron as he entered the building the next day, and announced himself to the receptionist. Dr. Goodfellow met Aaron at reception and proudly took him on a guided tour of the premises, finally showing him to an office overlooking a park with a sweeping view of the city before taking the time to introduce him to his personal assistant, Inge Marthaler. Aaron placed his laptop on the desk, unpacked his belongings, then logged into the hard drive accessing the system, and familiarised himself with the basic architectural layout of the system.

His eyes scanned the office surroundings, and noted the hidden surveillance camera in the air-conditioning duct in the ceiling above the desk, as well as the mirror on the wall positioned behind his chair which he believed concealed another hidden camera. The training he had received from his handler at Camp Perry, fondly referred to as the Hulk by the rank and file at the CIA, had honed his sensors to be ever vigilant. He was acutely aware that his every move would most likely be carefully monitored.

Jose Hernandez, had been his instructor for the gruelling six-month basic training course, and had adequately equipped him with the necessary skills to recognize any impending threat. He accessed the mainframe, logged in, then proceeded to view the resiliency, security, and logic of the system. Later he accessed the email addresses listed, and proceeded to evaluate the current anti-virus software installed in the system, known as Defender Anti-Virus, that had been installed some years previously. It had adequately catered for the company's needs at the time.

The Group had installed the latest version of the IBM Z Mainframe which was overkill for a small company, leaving him to question the logical reasoning behind their decision to buy the latest version available. Aaron set up the remote access allowing him to work offsite, which would give him the privacy needed allowing him to work away from prying eyes, thus making it highly unlikely that he would ever be discovered. He would be able to access the embedded operating system whenever he needed to, and he spent the rest of the day viewing, and assessing the architectural protocols of the system. He evaluated every aspect carefully, and as he progressed, he made notes for a report that he would present to Dr. Goodfellow at the appropriate time.

Dr. Goodfellow tapped lightly on the door later that afternoon, and wanted to get Aaron's opinion on the operating system.

'Well Dr. Goodfellow, it's the latest IBM version as you know, and most impressive, however, it appears to be an overkill for what you require to be honest sir,' 'That said, it is merely my opinion, unless of course you are planning to expand the system in the future.' 'I will need to complete a number of tasks, and do a lot more analysis before I present my report to you.'

'Thank you Aaron, I look forward to the report, and just to let you know, we all leave work at five p.m. sharp as I don't like people slaving on for hours on end, because that does not impress me at all.'

'Well it's almost five p.m. now so I will pack up and start afresh in the morning.'

Earlier in the day Aaron set up the remote access in the system, and was acutely aware that he was most likely being monitored, however, his expertise in computer engineering afforded him the intricate knowledge of being able to bypass any monitoring in the system. Confident that he could not be monitored, he could access the system later, and carefully set up an untraceable sleeper within the system which would allow him to discreetly work offsite, undetected with full access to the server away from prying eyes. He was confident that he could not be monitored or detected, and would be able to work offsite whenever needed.

Later that evening, he sat in his hotel room, and stared at the text on the screen in disbelief. He had accessed the good doctor's emails, and noted the confidential memo from the Cardinal as he is known within the group. The memo was addressed to the executive team of three Bishops.

You have got to be kidding, he whispered to himself, as he leaned back in his chair, and pondered the consequences of what he had just read.

The Memorandum Header read-CWPH which he later understood to stand for Cull the World's Population in Half. If the group in fact carried out that action, and culled half the world's population, it would undoubtedly include himself, his family, the love of his life, Claire and her parents, family members, friends as well as all those he befriended within the CIA, and billions of innocent people around the globe.

Three months previously, the CIA had recruited Dr. Goodfellow's assistant, and she ensured that Aaron's name had appeared on the guest list for a cocktail party that they hosted at the Grand Hotel in Zurich, Switzerland months previously.

Inge Marthaler, Dr. Goodfellow's assistant, ensured that Aaron's name featured discreetly in various discussion notes doing the rounds amongst the hierarchy within the organization, in particular, the Cardinal and his Bishops.

Inge, an avid animal lover had agreed to become an informant for the CIA, after she learned what the Three Sixty Degrees Group had planned for the world's population. Her husband Uri, a professor of psychology at the University of Zurich shared her love of animals, and both looked forward to each Friday evening, when they packed their belongings, loaded their two dogs into the car and headed to their weekend rural retreat. The retreat is based in the mountains at Mt. Rigi, a mountain massif of the Alps, which is almost surrounded by three bodies of water namely, Lake Lucerne, Lake Zug, and Lake Lauerz.

Mt. Rigi, situated a mere forty-five miles from their home on the outskirts of Zurich. An ideal place to unwind away from the rigors of their day jobs. The couple had a childless marriage, and were completely dedicated to each other and their animals. She loved their two-wire head terriers, Scamp, and Tramp, which they treated like their own children, as well as a milking cow that the couple had on their rural property, named Buttercup.

Their neighbor Nikolas Droz, an elderly man in his mid-seventies, tended their land which sprawled over thirty acres with breathtaking views of the surrounding lakes, and was allowed to graze his cattle on their property. He milked Buttercup daily, and was allowed to sell the milk as compensation for the daily chores he did on the property. Each Friday, he would save five litres of milk in a stainless steel milk can for the couple to take back to their home near Zurich.

Aaron downloaded all the contact names, and their respective email addresses. He saved it to a USB stick, then took the time to view each person's profile which took several hours. He was astounded to discover the extent of names listed.

Names of numerous current and past world leaders, high profile wealthy people, leading world academics, scientists, senators and various government officials were displayed on the screen staring back him. He was astounded to discover the extent of the network of contacts displayed.

He sat back and pondered about the consequences of what he anticipated the CIA would do. No doubt they will cut off the head of the snake, and eliminate the rest of the poison which would mean, that they would have to take out the entire hierarchy of the group. Aaron used his expertise in computer engineering to access Dr. Goodfellow's personal database using the sleeper cell he had setup, allowing him to piggyback, and tailgate into the good doctor's personal information. He would be able to view all the Doctor's activities without his knowledge. This gave him access to all the highly confidential memos addressed to the members in the database, as well as archived information that he downloaded to a USB stick, ensuring that it was untraceable. A practice known as "Wardriving" which is highly illegal in most westernised countries, and used by hackers worldwide.

He took the time to alter the security protocol that was setup, aimed at monitoring all activity within the system. It was well after midnight when he finally logged off, and as he lay on the bed staring at the ceiling, his mind wondered back to what Barnaby Heathcott might do. Wonder what plan he would adopt to eliminate the Cardinal, as well as the chief scientist that developed the poison.

He was at his desk early the next morning, and was busied himself setting up the new security protocol in the system, running it parallel to the existing antivirus which he intended testing prior to implementing the software, and deleting the older version. Dr. Goodfellow poked his head around the corner, 'good morning Aaron, you are in early.'

'Good morning Dr. Goodfellow, yes sir.' 'I am about to install the new cyber security system, and run it in tandem with the existing system today.' 'Need to be sure that I have captured all the relevant data, then run it parallel which will take most of the day to complete,' said Aaron.

Continuing he said, 'I will document my findings in my report, which I will present after I have completed all the tasks, in the next couple of days.'

'Excellent, you may wish to join me for a light lunch later,' said Dr. Goodfellow, before he turned and made his way to his office.

Around midday Dr. Goodfellow, tapped lightly on the door, and mentioned that it was lunch time, and wondered whether Aaron would join him for lunch.

'Thanks for the invite, however I am in the middle of testing the conversion, so regrettably I will have to take a rain check sir,' said Aaron.

Hours later Dr. Goodfellow again knocked on the door, reminding Aaron that it was almost five p.m. and time to pack up for the afternoon.

'Goodness me, how time flies when you are busy,' replied Aaron.

Back in the hotel room, Aaron retrieved the mini hidden camera he had discreetly installed on the top of the curtain rail, between the split in the sheer curtains that was not visible to the naked eye. He rewound the tape, and fast forwarded the contents looking for any sign of an intruder. The only person to enter the room was the chamber maid, and he watched as she went about servicing the apartment. He then extracted a scanner, and went around the room checking every nook and cranny before checking the air conditioning ducts. Satisfied that there were no hidden cameras or hearing devices, he walked to the bar fridge, and poured himself a beer. He had been well trained by his instructor the "Hulk", as he was known within the CIA at Camp Perry, at the CIA's secret training facility.

Later that evening, he ordered a meal from the in- house menu, retrieved the information he had downloaded to the USB stick, and accessed Dr. Goodfellow's archived information, seeking confirmation of what the group had been up to.

The confidential memo header staring at him read, Outcomes of the Test at Ndindi-Gabon. He Googled it, and discovered that it is a small remote rural bush village lying on the peninsula between the Ndogo Lagoon and the Atlantic Ocean, in Gabon. A typical African village consisting of huts made of sticks, straw and mud with a small population, ideal for The Three Sixty Degrees Group to conduct an experiment that would not attract any attention from authorities or the media. As cover for their intended operation, they convinced the Gabon Government that they would be spraying the area with a repellent to kill mosquitos, and rid the area of malaria, thus did not draw any unwanted attention to what they were really doing.

The document detailed the procedure that the group had followed, headed by their chief scientist, a German born fifty-five year old male by the name of Joachim Stein, now resident in Bern in Switzerland. Joachim's parents fled Germany during the final days of Hitler's rule, just before the Russians captured Berlin, and made their way through the countryside to Prague in Czechoslovakia as it was known during the second world-war. They made their way to Switzerland through the Allied lines, and finally to freedom.

Despite Joachim's father being a qualified tradesman, he was forced to accept a labourer's job in order to survive, and toiled seven days a week saving part of his meagre earnings to educate his son. Joachim excelled at school, and was eventually accepted into the University of Switzerland as a student in the facility of science. He graduated with a master's degree, as a Bachelor of Health Sciences, after studying for five years, and was offered a job in the laboratory of the University in the Institute of Infectious Diseases (UIID) located on their campus in Zurich, which was a large laboratory combining diagnostic research and translation.

He studied viruses that are highly infectious, for which no therapy or vaccination was available, and are examined under the strictest safety measures in a biosafety level 3 (Biosafety Level / BSL-3) laboratory. Human pathogens are examined, and researched in Switzerland's newest biosafety laboratory. Findings from research are transferred into products and therapies in the spirit of translational medicine. The UIID was setup to study diseases that threaten animal as well as human life, and to research and develop vaccines to treat emerging diseases.

He came to the attention of Dr. Goodfellow due to an achievement award he received for developing the precise genome-editing technology with the ability to cut DNA where you want, that has revolutionized the life sciences. The "genetic scissors" had been discovered a few years previously which has benefitted humankind greatly.

This caught Dr. Goodfellow's attention, and he approached Joachim learning, that he too shared the good doctor's opinion, that the world is over populated, and accepted a role within The Three Sixty Degrees Group. He resigned his post at the University of the Zurich Institute of Infectious Diseases and joined the group.

The group acquired a farmhouse, and setup a laboratory in the picturesque village of Gimmelwald, which is off the beaten path in the Bernese Alps. There are no roads to the village so access is by foot or cable car, and there are no shops or local school. The village is typical of a small farming community. An ideal place to setup a secret laboratory for Joachim to develop the airborne virus that the group intended using to cull the world population in half.

People can only commute to Gimmelwald by train, which is a mere sixty-five miles to the centre of Zurich. Joachim had never married so he was an ideal candidate, tasked with developing the airborne virus and lived alone, able to go about his business discreetly. He did not interacted with neighbours, and was viewed as a recluse within the tiny farming village.

Aaron discovered his name by chance as he scanned through various memos in Dr. Goodfellow's archived notes, and discovered that the good doctor referred to him as J.S. in all correspondence to his fellow Bishops. He Googled the village of Gimmelwald, noted its remote location, and wondered how the CIA would one day eliminate this scientist. He considered that they would need to cut off the heads of the group's hierarchy consisting of the Cardinal, namely, Dr. Goodfellow, his three Bishops and the architect of this deadly poison, J.S. which he now understood to be Joachim Stein. They would need to act rather quickly as it appeared from the notes he read, that the group had intended to implement their plan within the next six months.

Glancing at his watch he realised that it was zero three hundred hours, and he needed to get some rest so he closed his laptop, walked to the door, placed a rubber Jack Hammer Door wedge at the bottom of the door, kicked it lightly to ensure that it was securely jammed under the door, then moved the swing bar security door latch, locking it in place before settling down for some shut eye.

He was up three hours later, and went through his usual morning exercise routine, shaved, showered, got dressed, and poured himself a cup of coffee from the in-room coffee maker. Later he jumped into a taxi, and made his way to the office. He was once again seated in his office when Dr. Goodfellow popped his head around the door.

'Hi Aaron, you really are an early starter.' 'So hopefully you can join me for a sandwich at lunchtime,' said Dr. Goodfellow.

'Thanks again Dr. Goodfellow, I should have completed all the tasks prior to implementing the new cyber security, so I hope to be able to join you,' said Aaron.

He busied himself and prepared the conversion for implementation for later that afternoon, when Dr. Goodfellow again knocked on his door, announcing that it was lunchtime, and they should make their way Café Henri, a local coffee shop at Foursquare within walking distance of the office.

As they settled in for lunch Dr. Goodfellow insisted that Aaron refer to him by his first name, which is Uri. Continuing he said, 'I trust that the system you are installing is hack proof, and will be totally secure.' 'I take it that I will have the keys to it after you have competed the tasks at hand.'

'Yes Uri, you will have the keys to the system.' 'The firewall that I am about to install is state of the art, and the very latest cyber security system available.' 'It is used by the US and French military, as well as all the US government installations, so you can be comfortable that it will secure your system for years to come.'

'However, it may need tweaking on a regular basis, as hackers always seem find ways and means of hacking into various systems, so each time I become aware of any issues, I will need to make the necessary adjustment,' said Aaron.

'I recommend the pastrami sandwich, which is the best in Zurich,' said Uri closing the menu.

'You know, I am not really hungry so I will pass,' said Aaron.

'Are you sure, it's the best sandwich you will ever eat Aaron.'

'I'm fine thanks Uri, you go ahead.'

Don't trust this bastard at all thought Aaron, and he would most likely try to poison me as a faint smile creased his lips. Albeit that he does not have the keys to the system yet, this prick is likely to have a mate in the kitchen that will most likely poison me. He could get another IT expert to give him the keys at a later date. Need to keep a close eye on this enemy he thought, as he stood and walked over to the sideboard, and poured himself a glass of water before returning to the table. I don't even trust ordering something to drink, as that too may be poisoned.

Continuing Uri said, 'so Aaron, I am impressed with your focus and commitment to the job.' 'I and look forward to seeing this new cyber security system in action,' said Uri.

'Glass of wine young man?' questioned Uri.

'No thanks Uri, I never drink on the job, but please go ahead, and enjoy a glass of wine of your choice,' added Aaron.

'So how about yourself Aaron, are you married or still single?' Questioned Uri.

'Still single and who knows what the future holds.'

'How about yourself, are you married with children Uri?' responded Aaron, tactfully repositioning the conversation.

'Not married and no children that I know of.' 'I am a committed bachelor, and have never intended marrying because I simply have not found a suitable partner,' said Uri.

'So how do you spend your spare time, and what hobbies do you have to keep yourself busy Uri, because it can be a little lonely being on your own?'

'Well, I keep myself busy, and do a bit of flying in my spare time.' 'I tend to go flying every Sunday leaving at around eleven, and take a flight over the alps for a couple of hours, then stop off at Chur for a special treat, before flying back to home base,' said Uri.

'I have racked up some two hundred flying hours to date, and will be going up this Sunday, so hopefully you can join me for a scenic flight over the Alps Aaron.' 'You will see some of the stunning landscapes that this magnificent country has to offer.'

'A good friend of mine is joining me for this scenic flight, and I can assure you that the views are spectacular, so really worth coming along,' continued Uri as he opened his mobile phone, and scrolled down to a photograph of his pride and joy.

Aaron took a mental note of the serial number K263 on the tail of the twin engine Piper Seneca with impressive two tone red and grey livery as well as the hanger number, D6 in the background.

'Thanks for the invitation Uri, however I hate flying, even in commercial jetliners, and have never flown in a light plane, as I have heard of way too many light plane crashes, so I will give it a miss.'

'Where do you fly out of Uri, and how long do you spend up there?' asked Aaron.

'My plane is housed in a hangar at St. Gallen-Alternrheim airport which luckily for me is a mere 48 miles dive from my home at Niederdorf, so most convenient,' said Uri.

'Well it's a real pity you won't come along Aaron, because the view of the Alps is really spectacular.' 'As mentioned, I normally spend around two hours flying over the alps, then land at a remote airstrip near Chur, and enjoy the best apple strudel in Switzerland,'

Smiling Aaron thought to himself, yeah right, the poisonous head of this snake must think I was born yesterday. I will hand him the keys to the system on Friday, he then wants me to come along for a flight on Sunday with his mate to this remote airfield at Chur, and his mate will most likely shoot me in the back of the head when we land. The doctor is a dangerous man, no doubt about it. I'm way too smart for this prick. How dumb he is to disclose where he lives, and where his plane is housed in a hanger, as well as showing me the photograph of his plane, detailing the serial number on the tail of it with the hanger number in the background. He also told me how often he enjoys taking it for a flight. Nodding as if he regretted not accepting Uri's invitation, Aaron now had all he needed to know about the head of this organisation and exactly how to eliminate him. Dumb prick.

Need to work out how to leave the company premises without being followed or someone trying to end my life he thought, as he took another sip of his water. Later that afternoon, he completed the conversion, and met with Uri presenting him with the keys to the system, then walked him through the login protocol to be used. He leaned forward, picked up the report he had completed for Uri and handed it to him.

'This is the report I said that I would present to you when I had completed the installation Uri.' 'Take time to read it, understand it, and if you have any questions, feel free to call at any time.'

Just then his office phone rang with the receptionist notifying him that a limo driver had arrived to pick him up, and was waiting in reception for him.

'Well Uri, all done, my ride has arrived, so it's time to bid you farewell, and thank you for the opportunity to work with you,' sir.

Uri seemed rather bewildered, and taken aback with the sudden manner in which the day was ending. He considered that Aaron was most certainly an unusual person, as he stood and took his hand in a farewell gesture. Aaron picked up his laptop, and made his way towards the reception stopping to bid farewell to various staff members on his way out.

Fucking brain dead arsehole he thought to himself, as he made his way towards the elevator. Way too smart for this prick. Aaron had a CIA operative pose as a chauffeur, and collect his belongings at both hotels earlier in the day. He needed backup in case things turned nasty, and had used the online in-house payment system to pay the bills in both hotels, eliminating the need to return to the hotel, and stop at reception to finalise payment.

The undercover agent dropped Aaron at Zurich International departures, and he made his way to the check in desk, and booked in for his flight to Paris.

The next morning he called Barnaby.

'All done Director.' 'I have downloaded the entire database, and to be honest, the names on it will shock you sir.' 'There are numerous past and sitting Presidents, Prime Ministers, and a bevy of ultra-rich people, scientist and academics on the who's who list.'

'OK Rafael, thank you for the excellent work.' 'I look forward to seeing the names on the list.'

Chapter 10

Chur

Switzerland

Rafael was sitting in his office at the Embassy when the phone rang startling him somewhat, until he realised that it was Director Heathcott on a secure line from Langley.

'Bonjour Director,' answered Rafael.

'Hello Rafa.' 'I want you to fly back to the States on our Gulf Stream leaving Paris next Tuesday and meet with me.' 'We need to clear up some of the issues that you are aware of,' said Barnaby.

'The usual procedure, so expect agent's d'Avray and Van Der Jong to pick you up at the Embassy on Tuesday morning at ero seven hundred hours.' 'The pilots will be expecting you, Rafa.'

'Yes sir, I will be ready,' replied Rafael.

'Au revoir Rafa,' replied Barnaby as he disconnected the call.

Agent's d'Avray and Van Der Jong arrived to pick him up from the Embassy, and he assumed his usual position in the rear passenger seat.

'Hi fellows, well here we go again,' said Rafael.

'So back to Langley Rafa?' commented agent d'Avray.

'Oui, got to take care of some business gentlemen,' replied Rafa.

Eight and a half hours later the Co Pilot announced their impending arrival at Biglers Mill, the private airfield used exclusively by the CIA.

Having cleared security at the entrance to Langley's offices, Rafael was again greeted by Miss Marple.

'Hello Rafael, good to see you again,' she offered as she turned, and headed towards the Directors private elevator.

A short while later, she tapped lightly on the door announcing Rafael's arrival.

'Thank you Gizelle,' said Barnaby.

'Hello Rafael,' take a seat young man.

Continuing he said, 'as you are aware, we need to move quickly to eliminate the problem we have with the Three Sixty Degrees Group.'

Barnaby extracted a photograph from a folder, and laid it on the table.

'This is a photograph of the scientist that the group has employed to develop the airborne virus, which they intend using to cull the world's population in half.' 'His name is Joachim Stein, and they have set him up in a farm house in the remote village of Gimmelwald which is really off the beaten track, about sixty-five miles from Zurich.' 'There are no roads to the village, so access is by train then on foot or by cable car, and there are no shops, or a local school in the area.'

Rafael studied the photograph of Joachim Stein facing directly towards the camera, and wondered how the CIA had managed to take a photograph of him front on without him even knowing. These guys know really their stuff he thought to himself.

'Yes Director, I am familiar with the name Joachim Stein because I came across his name in the group's database at the Three Sixty Degrees head office, and the confidential emails that Dr. Goodfellow had sent him.'

'So we need to move quickly as I believe that they have already gone into mass production of this virus, and from what we have been able to find out, they are using a warehouse facility in an industrial zone near Chur to manufacture this virus,' continued Barnaby.

Ah, so that's why the good doctor flies to Chur every Sunday, thought Rafael.

'They have chosen well as there is no possible way of tracing it back to the group.' 'Clearly the head of this group, the good doctor is a sly bugger, so we need to eliminate him, and the hierarchy of this outfit sooner rather than later Rafael,' said Barnaby emphatically.

'You have taken care of both Senators Stratton and Cotalico, so we will need to be rid of part of the head of the snake within the next couple of weeks.'

'I need you to fly to Zurich on Thursday, and have booked you on an Air France flight leaving Paris at zero ten hundred hours. Eliminate both Dr. Goodfellow and Mr. Stein then work your way to Chur, and destroy the facility that they are using to manufacture this poison.'

'I will arrange for explosives to be available once you land in Zurich, as well as a hand gun fitted with a silencer, and will notify our agent to meet you at Zurich airport.' 'He will take care of the explosives for you.' 'It is imperative that we eliminate the last part of the hierarchy of this group sooner rather than later, because they are all set up and ready to distribute this deadly virus very soon.'

'As mention previously, they intend dispersing this poison into the air, posing as a scientific experiment to rid the world of parasites.' 'These are scary people, and whilst they believe that are flying under the radar, you need to be extremely cautious, as they would undoubtedly have a high level of security in place,' continued Barnaby.

Agent's d'Avray and Van Der Jong picked Rafa up at the Embassy at zero-eight hundred hours and drove him the short distance to Paris international airport.

Turning to face Rafa, agent d'Avray said, 'so off to Zurich for some sightseeing Monsieur Rafa?'

'Oui,' yes responded Rafa.

A short hour and a half later, Rafa exited customs in Zurich, and made his way towards the taxi rank, when a well-dressed gentlemen fell in beside him.

'This way Monsieur,' he said indicating towards the underground parking area.

Rafael followed the man who introduced himself as Herr Nikolas Schultz, as they made their way towards a parked SUV.

'Here's the keys.' 'Everything you will need is in the cargo compartment Monsieur, and good luck,' he offered as he turned and walked away.

Rafael, opened the rear door of the SUV, released the cargo cover revealing a couple of boxes and a small suitcase. He loaded his carryon bag into the compartment, hopped into the driver's seat, and meandered his way out of the underground parking. A short while later he joined the traffic towards the La Rèserve Zurich Hotel, situated on the shores of Lake Zurich.

Rafael had assumed the name of Cruze Kerzig for this mission, admiring the sweeping view from the balcony of this magnificent five star hotel. Well, the boss does not waste money on flights having booked him in cattle class, however, he seems to have rewarded me with a comfortable room with a view in a very fancy hotel, he thought.

Better remember my undercover name of Cruze Kerzig he reminded himself, as he unpacked his toiletry bag, leaving all his clothes in the carryon bag which he stored in the closet. He opened the box, extracted the Glock, fitted the silencer, then removed two spare clips, and put them on the bedside table. The case contained a remote as well as a detailed map of the small town of Chur with a series of photographs of a warehouse in an industrial area on the outskirts of the town. There was a photograph of a hanger, and a light plane in the case, which he immediately recognised, identifying it as the light aircraft owned by Dr. Uri Goodfellow.

The serial number of K263 detailed on the tail of the twin engine Piper Seneca was imbedded in his memory as well as the two tone red and grey livery, confirming that he was looking at the correct plane. He looked at the access card to the St. Gallen-Alternrheim airport which was most convenient, allowing him easy access to the airfield without having to pass through security. Bugger me, the CIA seems to think of everything he thought, as he picked up a key which he believed would be the key to the hanger's side door. Unbelievable.

He, removed his scanner, and went around the room checking every nook and cranny, as well as the air conditioning unit to ensure that there were no hidden cameras or eavesdropping devices, then positioned a mini camera on top of the curtain rail amongst the sheer curtains. Satisfied that the room was clean, he walked to the door, and placed the Do Not Disturb Sign on the outer door handle, then drew the curtains, and unpacked the explosives, laying them out on the carpet next to the bed. He carefully sorted, and checked the explosives following the procedure he had been taught by his handler at Camp Perry, before placing them back into the case and locking it.

With three days to himself, he punched in the coordinates given to him, and drove towards Chur which was a mere thirty-eight miles from Davos, the highest town in Europe famed for its diversity of sports, leisure and culture, the Kirchner Museum. The town is famous for hosting the World Economic Forum. As he drove slowly past the warehouse on Felsenaustrasse, he noticed that there was no sign writing on the façade, and took note of the electrical box situated at the end of the street.

He returned to the hotel as the sun was setting, and made his way to the lounge. Positioned himself in the corner with his back to the wall, pretending to be reading a tourist brochure, all the while scanning the room for anybody he deemed suspicious. Satisfied that there was no apparent threat, he ordered a cold beer, and watched the patrons engrossed in conversation. Later he returned to his room, and ordered an in-house meal before once again Googling an aerial view of Chur.

The next day he drove to St. Gallen-Alternrheim airport, used the gate access key to gain entry to the airport, and parked the SUV in the designated parking area, then took a leisurely stroll towards hanger D6. Passing the open hanger door, he noted the Piper Seneca positioned towards the rear of the hanger, and made his way around the hanger, towards the side door. He inserted the key, and was pleased to see that it unlocked the door.

The hanger had a couple of aircraft parked in it, and he took the time to look around the hanger, before locking the door, and making his way back to the parking area.

A while later, he pointed the SUV in the direction of the hotel, and made his way back. All seems to be in order he thought to himself, so I best get to the airport on Saturday evening, install the explosives, and be ready for action on Sunday.

It was almost twenty-hundred hours as the SUV made its way out of the hotel basement parking, and headed in the direction of St. Gallen-Alternrheim airport. He stopped a mile short of the airport, donned a blond wig ensuring that his collar was up, and pulled down peaked cap visor, put on a pair of rubber gloves as well as dark rimmed sun glasses. Hope that the peaked cap covering his eyes, the wig, as well as the black rimmed glasses will hide my real identity, he thought. He drove towards the access gate of the airport, scanned the access card, and parked the SUV in the designated parking area. Moments later he opened the cargo door, picked up the box, and made his way towards hanger D6. He donned rubber gloves, the quickly unlocked the side door, activated the light on his tradie's headlamp and made his way towards the Piper Seneca aircraft.

He picked the door lock of the aircraft, installed the bomb under the pilot's seat ensuring that it was secure, positioning it out of sight towards the rear of the seat. Cruze locked the plane door, and made his way out of the hanger, locking the side door as he exited. As he made his way back to the SUV, he noticed the beam of light from a torch light being shone over a hanger in the distance. The security guard on patrol was making his evening rounds. That went smoothly he thought to himself as he jumped into the SUV and departed, hoping that the cameras did not capture a clear image of his face. Maybe even too easy he considered.

Next day he was up early, and having completed his usual morning exercise routine, he showered, got dressed, then made his way to the basement car park, and turned the SUV onto the A3 heading towards Chur, ensuring that he did not stop along the way. The leisurely drive of seventy four miles, took an hour and a half before finally arriving on the outskirts of the town. He found his way towards the airstrip using a rural road, parked on the fringe of the forest, parallel to the runway, and waited. Uri was a creature of habit, so he anticipated that he would approach the airstrip from the north east, and would most likely be on time which would be around thirteen-hundred hours.

Chur is the oldest city in Switzerland, and one of the most authentic with a settlement history of over five thousand years. The car-free mountain city in the heart of the Alps, is very charming, and extremely popular with tourists travelling on the Bernina Express or the Glacier Express.

He waited patiently for the arrival of the Piper Seneca plane, and used his binoculars to scan the horizon for any sign of the aircraft. Glancing at his watch, he noted that it was almost thirteen-hundred hours, so he anticipated that the good doctor would be on time. Leopards do not change their spots he thought. Suddenly he heard the buzzing sound of an air crafts propeller approaching in the distance. Pilots have to negotiate the surrounding Alps, then make a quick descent towards the airstrip at Chur, and have to deal with the swirling wind currents rising from the mountains, testing a pilot's skill.

He trained his binoculars on the approaching aircraft, identified its two tone red and grey livery flying at right angles to where he was hidden on the fringe of the forest, and noted that there was a passenger seated alongside the good doctor. The aircraft was on a final approach towards the runway, so he checked the serial number on the tail as it passed in the distance. Satisfied that he had the correct aircraft in his sights, he extracted the remote from his pocket and activated it.

A huge explosion followed moments later, and the plane tumbled towards the ground engulfed in a massive ball of fire. I hope that the passenger is Joachim Stein, the scientist, and not some innocent civilian, he thought. Satisfied that he had accomplished another mission, having gotten rid of the head of the snake, and hopefully the chief architect of death as well, he nodded gently to himself, and whispered, 'Good riddens, to you two evil men.'

He jumped into the SUV, and made his way towards the outer fringe of the city, found a suitable parking, then walked towards the restaurants noting the frantic activity on the streets, as emergency service vehicles with sirens wailing passed by. No vehicles are allowed in the city, so this allowed him to park on the fringe without anybody noticing, as all eyes were trained towards the plume of smoke billowing in the air from the direction of the airport.

He made his way into the city centre, stopping occasionally to look at the plume of smoke in the distance, then calmly walked into Nonna's Place, a popular Italian Pizzeria, found a corner table facing the window and ordered a pizza. He watched the televised report of the incident at Chur airport, with the reporter suggesting a possible assassination on the two occupants.

Later that afternoon, he stopped at Café Chur a popular meeting place for locals and tourists. He ordered a coffee and a slice of the famous apple strudel that Uri had mentioned, as he needed to kill a few hours, until around twenty-two hundred hours before making his move on the warehouse on Felsenaustrasse. It was almost dark as he made his way to the SUV, drove away from town, and turned onto a rural farm road heading into the bush, before finding a well camouflaged, secluded spot in the forest. He killed the engine, moved to the passenger seat, reclined it, and took an early evening nap.

It was almost twenty two-hundred hours when he started the SUV, and headed back towards town, making his way towards the industrial estate on the outskirts of the city. He turned into Felsenaustrasse, and found a suitable parking area at the end of the road. Quickly out of the vehicle, he released the cargo boot liner that covered the explosives in the cardboard box, picked it up and walked calmly towards the warehouse. He stopped at the electrical box, picked the lock, killed the electrical connection to the entire street, then made his way towards the warehouse, and picked the lock on the door. Moments later he donned his biosecurity suit before entering the warehouse, scanning the premises as he entered looking for an alarm system or any surveillance cameras, and was relieved to discover that there was a total lack of security. The group must have been comfortable that they were flying under the radar, and did not deem it necessary to draw unwanted attention towards themselves.

He activated his forehead tradie light, walked around the ten vats, tapping each one as he made his way further into the warehouse, noting that they seemed to be full of some kind of liquid. He stopped, and stared at the label on one of the vats, identifying the contents as Strychnine, which is white odourless bitter crystalline powder primarily used to kill rats. The label on another vat identified that it contained Sarin, which is a quick acting chemical nerve agent, and one of the deadliest nerve gases, hundreds of times more toxic than cyanide. Just one whiff, and you'll foam at the mouth, fall into a coma, and die. Originally synthesized for use as a pesticide, it was outlawed as a warfare agent in 1997. How the fuck has the architect of death managed to manufacture this amount of deadly poison, and fly under the radar he thought.

Moving between the vats he took note of the label on one that contained Ricin, a poison that works by getting into the cells of a person's body preventing the cells from making the proteins needed. The labels on the other vats indicated that they were filled with Anthrax, Botulinum, Variola, Francisella Tularensis (Tularemia), Aflatoxin.

He stopped in his tracks, as he read the label on another vat identifying that it contained Novichok, which if you inhale it or it is absorbed through the skin will first cause a constriction of the pupil in a person's eyes.

The last vat appeared to be empty and merely had a number on it, EV11. It seemed that the architect of death was planning to merge the contents of all the vats into the empty vat, combining all of them into a deadly poison, which when released into the air would kill billions of people.

Sweet Jesus in Heaven, how on earth have they had managed to manufacturer this amount of deadly material without ever having been noticed, he thought. He stood momentarily, and stared at the vats wondering how the scientist planned to merge all these deadly chemicals, and in what quantities.

How would it be released in densely populated areas, and how on earth would all of these poisons when combined, actually work, he considered.

Fuck me, this is extremely poisonous and dangerous, he considered. Best be very careful, and I simply cannot blow this lot up, because it will kill tens of thousands of innocent people right here in Chur, so he exited the warehouse. Ensuring that he had locked the door, he removed his biosecurity suite, then made his way towards the electrical box, and reactivated the electrical connection restoring the power to the area. He jumped into the SUV, and called Barnaby on a secure line.

'Hello boss, I have taken care of the good doctor, and if I am not mistaken, hopefully the architect of mass destruction as well, however I am not one hundred percent sure that it was the scientist that has also passed on.'

'I cannot simply blow this warehouse up, as it contains highly poisonous chemicals that will kill tens of thousands of people anywhere near an explosion, so I suggest that you get in touch with the Swiss authorities, and get them to seal off this warehouse, and get rid of the deadly poisons stored in here,' said Jon.

Barnaby reminded himself to use Rafael's undercover name whilst he was on this mission, and whilst, he believed that the line was secure, he knew that he had to take measures to conceal his identity at all times.

'OK Cruze, secure the warehouse and leave immediately.' 'I will contact my counterpart in Switzerland and inform him.'

A rare smile creased Cruzes' lips and he nodded to himself, as he considered that he had just saved half the world from certain death. Biological warfare agents have been banned after World War 1, and the international community reinforced the ban in nineteen seventy-two and nineteen ninety-three prohibiting their development, stockpiling or transferring any of these weapons. Biological warfare agents are most likely to be dispersed in the air, and easily spread amongst large populations.

He drove to a secluded area on the other side of city, parked and reclined the passenger's seat, making himself as comfortable as possible for the evening. The chill was evident as the temperature started plummeting, so he snuggled up under his jumper, and waited for the coming dawn. He knew that the evening would be chilly.

The early morning sun shone on his face which woke him, so he got out of the SUV stretched, and relieved himself. There was a feint smell of something that had burned wafting in the air. It was just after zero-eight hundred hours, so he started the vehicle and made his way back towards the edge of town. He parked near the Mountain View Hotel on the outskirts of the city that offered a scenic view of the Eastern Alps and opened the cargo door, engaged the cargo cover, ensuring that it covered the box containing the explosives, then removed his bag, locked the vehicle, and placed the vehicle's keys on the inside of the front rim. As he made his way towards the station, he noticed that the police were conducting identity checks at various points along the way, so he bypassed them, taking a roundabout route towards the station without being noticed, and bought a ticket on the Bernina Express from Chur to Tirano in Italy.

The train journey takes around four hours, crossing the beautiful Graubünden from north to south showcasing an impressive piece of railway engineering. The train reaches an altitude of two thousand two-hundred and fifty-three meters, without the help of a cogwheel track, requiring lots of spiral loops, fifty-five tunnels, as well as one hundred and ninety-six bridges to accomplish this. The landscape varies greatly, from high alpine scenery in the Poschiavo valley to Tirano.

He decided to change his plans, ensuring that he did not fly out of Zurich as a precaution, and found his way to the window seat allocated to him. The seat was comfortable, so he settled in for the scenic journey. The landscape varies greatly, from high alpine scenery on the Bernina Pass to Mediterranean scenery in the Poschiavo valley to Tirano. There is a connecting Bernina Express bus from Tirano to Lugano that adds another 3 hours to the journey, which he considered was worth taking.

He sent an SMS to the number given to him by the agent he met at Zurich airport, and left a message stating that dad had left the car at a certain spot to be picked up. A rare smile again creased his lips, as he considered that he had just saved half the world from certain death.

This would be an ideal place to propose to my partner, so got to make plans to revisit this place with Claire.

Chapter 11

Montana

USA

R afael stared at the photograph of Malcolm McGivern, the Chief Justice of the Supreme Court of Montana, emailed to him by Barnaby Heathcott.

So this is the last part of the head of the snake of The Three Sixty Degrees Group, he thought.

Amazing, how a person in the justice system like this guy is involved in planning to kill billions of innocent people. He sits on the bench, and judges those that have committed a crime, and sentences them, yet he could be guilty of committing a mass killing, the likes of which has never been perpetrated in living memory.

The last remaining part of the hierarchy of the group, that needs to be eliminated.

Fucking hypocrite he considered. These elitists think that they can do as they please, and never be prosecuted. They really think that they are above the law, and their shit does not stink. I need to kill this bastard real soon. No good arresting this prick, because he will never be judged.

Barnaby rang to confirm that Rafael had received the photograph that he had emailed.

'Yes Director, I am looking at it right now, sir.'

'So Rafael, from what we have learnt, "Your Honor", packs up his gear every Friday afternoon, and heads to the rugged countryside of Yellow Stone to do some trout fishing. Traditionally people use a barbless hook when fishing for trout in Yellow Stone Lake, Maddison River and the north fork of Shoshone River. They are the best places to catch native Yellowstone cutthroat brown rainbow, or brook trout. Blue ribbon trout is great at the scenic Big Hole River.

Ideally fishing starts towards the end of May on the Saturday of the Memorial Day weekend, and lasts until the first Sunday in November. Luckily this has fallen within the timeframe that Rafael, was available.

'So Rafa, I suggest that you pack up your camping gear, and head for the hills.' 'We know that the Chief Justice heads to a secluded spot along the Shoshone River every Friday, as he loves fishing.' 'From what we have seen, he tends to camp at the same spot every time he goes fishing, so I will send you the coordinates shortly.'

'I want you to assume the guise of a French Tourist, making your way towards the Yellow Stone National Park, however, decided to stop, and try your hand at trout fishing.' 'Use the alias of Claude Del la Croix, and if he asks tell him that you are from Réunion, a French island off of Africa.

Rafael arrived at the coordinates given to him by Barnaby, and set up camp mid-afternoon. He gathered some fire wood, lit a camp fire, before jumping into a pair of fishing waders, and tried his hand at trout fishing.

Useless at this he thought. Geez this fly fishing takes some perfecting, he thought as he tried to cast repeatedly.

He tried to come to grips with the technique he had read in the Fly Fishing Magazine, on the flight to Wyoming. Looks easy enough he thought, however, in reality it takes a long time to perfect the casting technique.

The spot that Malcolm normally used, was deep in the bush, with a well secluded flattened area alongside the river. An ideal place to camp, and for the privacy one may want, away from the daily hustle and bustle of life.

As the late afternoon sun dipped towards the horizon, suddenly a white Jeep Grand Cherokee made its way towards the camp site that Rafael had set up.

A grey haired man parked the Jeep and exited the vehicle.

'Wow, this is a surprise.' 'I come here every weekend, and have never encountered another person in this secluded spot.' 'How on earth did you find my hiding place?'

'Bonjour Monsieur, my name is Claude Del la Croix.'

'Pleased to meet you Claude, my name is Malcolm McGiven,' he said, offering his hand.

'So how on earth did you manage to find this spot?'

'Well as I was driving along the gravel road, when I noticed some tracks leading towards the river, so I followed them, and came across this spot, which seemed like an ideal place to set up camp.' 'I want to try my hand at some fly fishing.'

'You have come to the right place for sure.'

'I have to admit that I am rather useless at fly fishing, because where I came from, we don't have any rivers with trout in it, so I am a novice for sure.'

'No need to worry, I will give you some tips, as I fish here every weekend.' 'So let me unpack and we can cast before it gets too dark.'

Malcolm unpacked and set up his tent.

'I see that you have collected enough firewood for the evening so let's head to the river, and get started, because it will get dark soon.'

'Let's have a small wager, whoever catches the first fish, has the loser serve his drinks for the evening.' 'I have to admit, it is rather nice to have someone to chat to, as it is somewhat lonely out here, because no one ever seems to find this hidden spot.'

'Great idea, not that I think I have any chance of winning the bet at all,' replied Claude.

An hour later as the sun kissed the horizon, both sat alongside the fire. Neither had caught a fish, so they poured their own drinks.

'So Claude, where are you from, because you have distinct French accent?'

'Well I live in Réunion, which is an island off Africa, and I am travelling through America, heading towards Yellow Stone.' 'It is a beautiful part of the country, rugged and unspoilt.'

'So what do you do in Réunion Claude?'

'I am a police offer sir.' 'I followed my father into the Gendarmerie.'

'Oh, that's interesting.' 'I am in the justice system in Montana.'

'Wow, we police catch the bad guys, and you prosecute them.'

'Well actually, I judge them, as I am the Chief Justice of the Montana Supreme Court.'

'Awesome, I hope that you deal severely with the bad guys, and lock them up for a long time Malcolm.'

'Yes, I don't tolerate those that have committed severe crimes, and I send them away for the maximum allowable sentences.'

You have got to be kidding, thought Claude, as he looked at the old guy seated opposite him. I wonder whether he will actually take control of the group, now that his mate the good Doctor, and his other two Bishop mates have departed.

'Would you like a drop of the Johnny Walker Blue I brought with me, Malcolm?'

'That would be great, thanks.' 'I just need to have a piss,' he said as he headed into the bush.

Claude extracted the vial from the zip lock bag, and inserted the contents into the tumbler that Malcolm was using, then dropped a few cubes of ice into the glass. He placed the vail into the bag. Seems like a decent type of person, however, proves you cannot judge a book by its cover, because you just don't know, he considered.

'Cheers,' he said, lifting his glass.

'So where do you live Malcolm?'

'Well my home is in Broadwater which is around thirty-five miles from my office, so rather convenient.' 'My office is in Helena.'

'Are you married Malcolm?'

'Yes I am, and my wife is lawyer specializing in divorce law.'

'Any children Monsieur?'

'No kids.' 'Our careers saw to that,' he said.

He watched as Malcolm took a sip of scotch. Going to suffer the same fate as those before him, and will most likely not wake up in about a week from today. Glad that there are no kids to mourn the passing of this bastard, he thought.

'Thanks, this is really smooth Claude.'

'So tomorrow, we need to get up early, and try our hand at catching some trout.'

'Oui Monsieur, however, I will be leaving mid-afternoon, as I want to make it to YeLow Stone before dark.'

A few drinks later it was apparent that the old boy was rather intoxicated, so he excused himself, and made his way into his tent. He was sound asleep a short while later. Claude looked at his tent, and smiled broadly to himself. Going to be rid of the last piece of this poisonous snake real soon. Fucking bastard.

Hours later, neither had caught a fish, so Claude packed up his camping gear, and turned to face Malcolm.

'Well Monsieur, it was a pleasure meeting you.' 'I have to be on my way, so thank you for the company last evening.'

Chapter 12

USA Embassy

Paris

The sudden screeching thump of the tires hitting the tarmac, announced the arrival of flight AF1415 at Paris Charles de Gaulle international airport, startling him from his stupor and back to reality. Maybe six out of ten for that bumpy landing he thought to himself, reminding himself to once again use his CIA undercover name of Rafael. Makes me sick to keep track of who the hell I am at any given time he thought. Wish I could get posted permanently to the Embassy here in Paris, and revert to my actual name which reminded him, that he had not called his parents for months. Shit, what excuse am I going to give them this time he pondered.

He made his way into the Embassy, stopped to kiss his partner along the way, and found his way to his office. A short while later, he dialled Barnaby Heathcott on a secure line.

'All done Director,' said Rafael.

Later that afternoon, Rafael met with Capitaine Bastienne Pétit of the French Police who also acts for the DGSE, the French secret service which is the equivalent of the CIA acting under the Ministry of Defence.

'Bon après-midi Monsieur Jon,' good afternoon Mr. Jon, offered Bastienne as he entered the conference room situated on basement level two.

Here we go again, he thought to himself. Bastienne knew him by the name of Jon, as he used that undercover name whenever in France. This is driving me crazy, he thought to himself as they discussed a plot that the

French Police had recently uncovered.

'We have intercepted communications between two middle-eastern brothers namely Tahir and Talib Faizan, and from what we have been able to understand, they are planning to detonate a car bomb outside the Embassy's front gate here in Paris,' said Bastienne.

Jon stared at the photograph of the brothers, and noted the scar on the right-hand side of Tahir's face that stretched from his temple, over his cheek, and down to his jaw line. It was visible through his beard.

'We need to remind ourselves of the devastation that a car bomb explosion can cause, just like those that exploded in front of the US embassies in Nairobi, Kenya, and the one in Dar es Salaam in Tanzania.' 'Two hundred and twenty-four people died in those explosions,' continued Bastienne.

Jon's partner, Lieutenant Commander Claire Johnston put her head around the door, and mentioned that she was leaving for the afternoon. She bid Bastienne farewell.

'See you later Mon Pétale.' 'I'm sure that Bastienne will give me a lift.'

'Au revoir Mon Beaute, drive carefully,' said Aaron giving Claire a peck on the cheek, and watched as she turned to leave.

The two discussed the latest threat indicating a possible attack on the US Embassy in Paris for a few hours.

'We have identified where Tahir lives, however, not where Talib lives, and we are unsure how many people live in the flat that Tahir is renting.' 'Talib may well also live in the same flat, but we have yet to confirm that,' said Bastienne.

He put a photograph of an apartment block in the Chêne Pointu housing estate down on the table, which is in the run-down Parisian suburb of Clichy-sous-Bois, consisting of one thousand five- hundred apartments.

'It's a suburb where slumlords rule the roost, and more than two-thirds of the inhabitants live below the poverty line.' 'The overcrowded flats are rented room by room for as much as one thousand eight hundred euros per month. Local authorities complain that they are largely powerless to combat the blatantly illegal practices,' continued Bastienne.

'So, as you can see, it's not an option to conduct an operation there.' 'We do not have the time to try and find out whether Mr. Talib lives in the same flat, or in fact exactly where he does live, so we need to concentrate on Tahir, and move quickly Jon.'

Continuing he said, 'time is not on our side, as I believe that the threat is real and imminent, so we need to eliminate these two very soon, and we cannot consider using the same method that we used when we took care of Rafiq Zahida and Abdul Sinai.' 'If you recall, we nearly blew the farm house to the moon in the peaceful village town of Villeneuve-d'Ascq and Dunkerque in Nord-Pas-de-Calais.'

'That's not an option because of where Tahir lives, and as I said, we don't know where Mr. Talib lives, so blowing up the flat would result in many innocent people losing their lives.' 'We are not in the business of killing innocent people, only the bad guys, so we need to follow this bastard, take him out well away from the apartment block, away from prying eyes,' continued Bastienne.

Later, the fading sunlight reminded them of the coming darkness.

The next day as Bastienne meandered his way through the underground parking at the Embassy in an unmarked police car, and headed towards the exit. He joined the traffic, heading towards the center of Paris. As they exited Jon noticed a dark-colored sedan parked a short distance from the driveway entrance to the underground parking of the Embassy, and shifted his posture in the seat to get a better view of the sedan in the passenger rear view mirror. He noticed that it was following them two vehicles back, and kept his eyes on the vehicle as they turned into a side street. The vehicle continued following them albeit some distance behind.

He mentioned it to Bastienne, who acknowledged that he was aware that they were being tailed, and suggested that they act normally. Bastienne stated that he would turn at the upcoming intersection to see if the vehicle continued following them. Shortly after they turned, both noted that the sedan was still following albeit some distance behind, so Bastienne once again turned at the next intersection, and Jon mentioned that he should slow down and turn right at the upcoming intersection.

He pulled up a short distance down the road, and used his indicator to confirm that he was waiting for a vehicle to exit a parking spot.As they approached the intersection, Jon pulled up the collar of his windbreaker, donned a pair of dark sunglasses, and jumped out of the vehicle as it slowly rounded the corner. He flicked the passenger door closed behind him, and quickly made his way between two parked vehicles. He rounded the front fender of one of the parked cars, and hid behind the front wheel, estimating that the sedan would come to a halt slightly ahead of where he was hidden. This would give him a chance to jump into the rear seat of the vehicle to ascertain who these people were.

A short while later the dark sedan rounded the corner as anticipated, and came to a halt a short distance ahead of where he was crouched. In an instant, moving like a leopard about to pounce on its prey, he meandered his way through the two parked cars, opened the rear passenger door using a tissue to ensure that there were no fingerprints left on the door handle, and slid into the rear seat before the occupants had fully realized what had happened.

He quickly placed the barrel of his Glock fitted with a silencer onto the top of Talib's left shoulder, and ordered him to put his hands on the dashboard. He told the driver to keep his hands on the steering wheel, and studied him for a moment, noticing the scar on the right-hand side of his face, then leaned slightly forward between the bucket seats, and said, 'hello Tahir, nice to meet you, and you too Talib.'

'So gentlemen why are you following us?' said Jon in a raised voice.

Both brothers tried to explain that they were on their way to the Mosque, and had to stop at the supermarket to pick up some groceries.

'Like hell you are.' 'You were tailing us to see where we live, you two pieces of shit.'

As Talib shifted in his seat, and tried to turn around to face him, Jon fired two quick shots into the deltoid muscle on the top of his shoulder, angled in a downward direction ensuring that the bullets would pass through the various other muscles that are attached to the shoulder, through his left lung, and into the heart bringing instant death. Talib slumped forward slightly just as Tahir made a move to extract a weapon, and Jon quickly positioned the barrel of the Glock onto the top of his right-hand shoulder angling it inwards towards the heart and fired two quick shots. Tahir's body jolted forward and his head come to rest against the door. He picked up the tissue, used it to open the rear door, and exited the vehicle, looking back to see both brothers slumped in their seats appearing to be looking at something in their respective laps with no blood splatter visible.

He quickly made his way towards where Bastienne had parked and jumped in.

'And so Monsieur Jon, I take it that these are the two we were discussing earlier, Oui?' Questioned Bastienne.

'Well Capitane, we have had a very lucky break.' 'These are the two we have been discussing, and I have taken care of both of them, so we need to get out of here,' said Jon.

'To quote your favorite line Capitaine, no need to capture shit like this and jail them, because they will simply have an extended holiday, costing hundreds of thousands of taxpayers Francs, and will continue where they left off after they have been released from our penal system.'

'Oui, très vrai Jon,' yes very true Jon.

'I will drop you off a few blocks from here, and drive around the neighborhood as I am sure that sooner or later somebody will report the incident,' said Bastienne.

'Well it is a worry that we have been followed, so I wonder how these two knew about us,' said Jon.

'Monsieur Jon, it's not you they are after, it's me, because I arrested their cousin two days ago on suspicion of a drug-related matter, so no need for you to be concerned at all.'

'You must come and work for us Monsieur Jon, we make a good team you know.'

'Merci beaucoup Capitaine, maybe someday.' 'Please drop me off at the supermarket around the next corner, and I will walk home, it's only a few miles from my partner's apartment,' said Jon.

An hour later the radio crackled to life with the central command communication center reporting that two men in a car appeared to have been shot. Bastienne responded immediately, and was on the scene a short while later. Reporters were quick on the scene as reports started to filter through the various television networks, notifying the public of the incident. The police cordoned off the area. A reporter from TF1 television stated that it appeared that the men had been assassinated, and that the police were investigating, however, there was no confirmation of a drug-related incident.

Images of a dark-colored sedan with two men slumped in the front seats played out on television screens. A reporter cornered Capitaine Pétit, and asked him for a comment.

'Well, we are unsure of exactly what took place here, and we are not ruling out a drug-related hit, however, once we have completed our investigation, I will make a statement,' he said as he turned and made his way into the cordoned off area around the crime scene.

Reporters continued hurling questions at the Capitaine, who simply ignored them.

Later that evening, Claire mentioned the incident of the two men that had been shot in a car, not too far from her apartment.

'Wonder what that was about,' she said.

'Not sure Mon Pétale, sounds like someone had a beef with the two guys, or possibly a drug-related hit,' said Jon.

Their sexual spark had not waned, however, their lovemaking had changed from an intense sexual lust when they first met, to a deep physical connection and loving devotion of each other. Later, after he rolled off Claire, the pair lay on the bed gathering their breath staring at the ceiling in silence.

Claire turned to face her partner, 'I know that you are called upon to do many dangerous things that involve eliminating bad people, and I fully understand that you have to get rid of the bad guys.' 'I just want to say, I fully understand, and accept what you do.' 'I also accept that you do not want to talk about it,'

'As far as I am concerned, you are eliminating the bad guys which is a good thing, because that is what needs to happen to make the world a safer place, my handsome man,' she said, placing her head on his chest.

'I am very concerned about your safety, and think that you should consider changing jobs and taking the role that Bastienne offered you.'

'Well to be truthful, that role also has a lot of dangers attached to it, so if I was to quit the CIA, I think it best that I change my profession entirely, and maybe go farming or something like that,' he said.

The couple were committed to each other, having cemented their relationship over time, and had assumed healthy sexual activities four times a week, whenever they were together, making them somewhat different from the typical married couple who only had occasional sex.

Chapter 13

Ardennes Hills
Northern France

Jon, Capitaine Bastienne Pétit of the French Police, and Joseph Diamond an agent from Mossad were seated in the conference room of the American Embassy in Paris, discussing the problem of a new terrorist cell that the CIA had uncovered recently. Of concern, was that there were three scenarios. They intend to kill the Chief Rabbi of France, Isiah Guldin, the Presidents of the USA and France, as well as the USA ambassador to France, Ezequiel Arrabito.

'The new terrorist movement is known as, "Qutl Ghayr Almuslimin," calling for the killing of all Non-Muslims,' said Jon.

'You know, most Muslims are peaceful people, who only want to be able to feed their families, avoid confrontation and practice their religion.' 'I have no problem with that at all, however, I have a huge problem with the jihadists that want to kill innocent people.'

'Well gentlemen, we have multiple problems to deal with, all of which have far-reaching implications,' continued Jon using the undercover name that he always used when in France.

'Oui Monsieur Jon,' replied Bastienne.

Joseph knew Jon as Aaron, the undercover name he had used in Zurich Switzerland, and was confused when Bastienne referred to him as Jon.

'Right you two, who the hell is Jon?' Questioned Joseph.

'As the late Stan Noble told you on several occasions, it's my middle name,' replied Jon with a wry smile on his face.

Joseph merely stared at him, now convinced that he was using an alias whenever in France.

The CIA had intercepted chatter on the wire, passed on the information to Mossad, and the French police, which was how Capitaine Pétit and Joseph Diamond became involved. The movement had a cell in the UK, and Joseph had familiarised himself with all the details concerning this new threat that had recently reared its head. Jon had befriended Joseph months previously after the two had successfully eliminated Ali Darwish, a known terrorist in the Jihad Council of Hezbollah in Lebanon.

The CIA had tracked Ali Darwish to an apartment block where he was living months previously, keeping track of him, then shared the information with Mossad. They needed Mossad's guidance, as they were familiar with the area, and far better acquainted with the surroundings than they were.

Joseph and Aaron, the alias Jon used in the past, posed as Jihadi fighters, and had entered an apartment building attached to the building where Ali Darwish lived in the early hours of the morning, while most jihadists guarding him had fallen asleep. They waited until the evening, and killed him while he was having his evening meal, then made a daring escape later that same evening, as jihadists fired wildly at their fleeing car.

'This is what our intelligence is telling us about these multiple threats, and what we have managed to find out so far,' said Jon as he fired up the laptop.

'Our intelligence is solid, and we believe that the planning of all of these threats are in the advanced stages.' 'They intend carrying out the assignation of the Rabbi within the next two weeks, then from what we have learned, they will attempt to kill the Presidents at the VE Day celebrations in Paris a week later, and finally the USA ambassador to France, the following week,' added Jon.

'All in that order gentlemen, so we have a very busy time ahead of us, and we had best ensure that these bastards are not successful in carrying out any of these attacks,' stated Jon emphatically.

'So, gentlemen, there are six terrorists, and we know of two of them, namely, Akeem Hasan and Omar Najjar, however, whilst we have images of two of the other terrorists, we have not yet identified them, nor do we know their names at this time.' 'We have no idea who the last two in the group are, and believe that they may all be residing in an apartment block that is privately-owned, which was built in the 1960s called the "Chêne Pointu" housing estate.'

'This is in the run-down Paris suburb of Clichy-sous-Bois, and there are one thousand five- hundred apartments in the complex,' he said pointing to the images on the laptop.

'Slumlords rule the roost there, where more than two-thirds of inhabitants live below the poverty line in insalubrious, overcrowded flats that are rented room by room, for as much as 1,800 euros per month.' 'Local authorities complain that they are largely powerless to combat the blatantly illegal practices.'

Continuing he said, 'from the intelligence reports we have in our possession, we have uncovered a training ground that Akeem and Omar use regularly in the Ardennes Hills at the northern tip of France near the Belgium border, around two-hundred miles from Paris.' 'It's deep in the bush, and ideal for clandestine activities, as it offers excellent cover from prying eyes.'

'We are seeking confirmation whether the other four that we have not yet identified, also live in the same apartment block, so we have a huge challenge ahead of us.' 'Our team is desperately trying to identify them, however, we have photographs of two of them,' said Jon, placing a photograph of two of the unidentified suspects on the table.

'These two look like typical jihadists with shaven heads and long beards'

Jon inserted the USB stick into the laptop, and satellite images of the mountainous region of the Ardennes Hills, lit up the screen detailing the surrounding bushland.

'As you can see, this is in a rather remote part of the countryside, allowing Akeem and Omar to go about their training undetected.'

Capitaine Pétit interrupted, 'thanks to the tip-off by the CIA, we have monitored Akeem and Omar for the past few weeks, and have learned that they travel to this remote site every Saturday morning.' 'They set up a tent and from the images we have, it appears that they undergo some sort of training in preparation for an attack.'

'From what we have learned, Monsieur Akeem and Omar possibly intend to attack Rabbi Isiah Guldin, after the congregation has dispersed having attended the Sabbat on a Friday evening and kill him.' 'The Grand Synagogue of Paris, generally known as Synagogue de la Victoire or Grande Synagogue de la Victoire, is situated at 44 Rue de la Victoire, in the 9th arrondissement.'

'It is extremely worrying that we have not yet been able to identify the other four, so the pressure is on to find them.' 'Our understanding is that

Akeem and Omar intend to attack the Rabbi within the next two weeks,' emphasized Jon.

'So from the intelligence we have been given, it appears that two of those we are yet to identify have been tasked with killing Presidents Trent & Macon when they are together for the VE Day celebrations in Paris.' 'We had best establish exactly who they are, and how these two intend to do it gentlemen.' 'We understand that the other two are tasked with killing the USA ambassador to France,' reiterated Jon emphatically.

'Ambassador Arrabito is scheduled to open the Eurosatory, an International Weapons Industry Trade Fair that is held every two years in the Paris-Nord Villepinte Exhibition Centre, Paris a week later.' 'So that is what the terrorists are tasked with, and that's where we believe they will try to kill him,' continued Jon.

'In 2018 the trade fair gathered over 1,800 exhibitors, attracted over 57,000 visitors, and is organized by COGES Events in partnership with the French Ministry of Defence.' 'This year's fair is sponsored by the United States, and from the snippets of information we have managed to find out, it appears that the terrorists possibly intend to assassinate the ambassador, as he exits the vehicle at around seventeen-hundred hours on the Saturday evening.'

'Bastienne and I have reviewed the intelligence given to us, and we are sure of the accuracy of the information, so we need to eliminate them, ensuring that they are not successful.' 'We only have a limited time left before they intend to carry out the first attack.'

Continuing, he said, 'we intercepted a phone call that Akeem Hasan made to one of these two terrorists a few days ago, which is rather rare.' 'They don't normally use a mobile phone, and as we understand it, they appear to have dumped the mobile phone after having made the call, making it hard to identify and track.' 'As soon as we have them in the cross hairs, we will have eyes on them twenty-four seven, and track their every move, so I am hoping that we will have more information in the coming days.'

'I think we need to prepare ourselves for a camping trip on Friday afternoon a week from today, get set up, and be in position when Hasan and Najjar arrive on Saturday morning.' 'We are sure of the accuracy of the intel, so we need to be ready to eliminate both of them,' said Bastienne.

'You both know my philosophy regarding the arresting of terrorists, who are then given lenient sentences, and once released, they simply continue on their murderous ways.' 'My preference is to simply eliminate people like this, and not arrest them, which means we no longer have a problem,' he continued.

'Oui, je suis d'accord,' yes I agree, said Jon

Joseph nodded in agreement.

'I don't believe that taking them into custody is the answer, because they will most likely end up getting off free, or with a limited jail sentence, thus I prefer to take them out, so that we don't have to give these terrorists a holiday at tax the payers expense,' emphasized Bastienne.

'I will pick you both up here at the Embassy on Friday at zero-nine hundred hours, so pack your camping gear boys, and be ready for action,' he said rising, and bringing the meeting to an end.

Bastienne arrived at zero-nine hundred hours, and parked the Grenadier, the French version of the British Land Rover with false number plates in the basement. He rode the elevator to reception on the ground floor, and was met by Jon and Joseph waiting patiently. They picked up their gear, made their way towards the elevator, and loaded it into the rear cargo compartment of the Grenadier.

Bastienne meandered his way out of the basement, and pointed the vehicle in the direction of the Ardennes Hills. The travel time was around three and a half hours, so they stopped along the way at Reims, a city ninety miles northeast of Paris situated in a vine-growing country where champagne and wine are produced. It is overlooked from the southwest by the Montagne de Reims, an ideal place for a light lunch.

Two hours later Bastienne turned onto a gravel road, and the Grenadier made its way towards the GPS coordinates he punched in before leaving Paris. He noticed the well-worn track leading away from the gravel road into the undergrowth as they passed, so he purposely continued along the road for a hundred yards before coming to a stop. They exited the Grenadier, walked back to where the track left the road, and followed it, ensuring that they walked on the track leading into the bush, eventually finding what appeared to be a camping ground that appeared to have been used regularly.

Having returned to their vehicle, Jon ran point as Bastienne drove further along the gravel road, then turned, and drove deeper into the bush, eventually turning back in the direction of the tracks they had seen earlier. He stopped well short of the tracks as he did not want to alert the two terrorists to the presence of other human activity in the area, and parked in the dense bush. They made their way through the thicket on foot until they saw an opening ahead which appeared to be a campsite, and were careful not to leave any tell-tale signs of anybody having been in the area recently. Bastienne scanned the area through a pair of binoculars, and was convinced that they had discovered the campsite used by these two terrorists.

They returned to the Grenadier and drove deeper into the undergrowth, eventually pulling up at a small clearing in the dense bush, ideal for a well-camouflaged campsite for the night. Bastienne confirmed the coordinates on the GPS, and was careful to step exactly in Jon's footprints to minimize any disturbance of the undergrowth. He viewed the site, checking the surroundings from a distance, and it was clear that this site had been used on many occasions in the past. Both were careful not to leave any tell-tale signs of human activity in the area.

Jon and Bastienne backtracked, and returned to where he had parked the Grenadier. They noticed that Joseph had camouflaged it with netting, so they set up their tents which were well hidden in the bush and not visible, even from a short distance. The campfire warmed them as the evening temperature started dropping. They enjoyed a late afternoon meal with a few beverages before finally settling in for the night. Bastienne, took the first watch, while both Jon and Joseph got some shut-eye. Jon was awake when Bastienne unzipped the opening to his tent, informing him that it was zero-one hundred hours and his turn to stand watch.

The hours slipped by slowly, giving Jon the time to reflect on what he does for a living. Capture them, judge them, sentence them, and execute them all in one move he considered. Well, at least I am part of a one-stop solution to some of the world's problems he thought. Finally, Jon handed over the watch to Joseph, and crawled back into his sleeping bag.

'Best not light a fire this morning Monsieur's as the smoke tends to leave a feint smell of burnt wood lingering in the air, and thankfully there is a slight breeze that will clear the air of last evening's campfire.' 'We don't want to warn these two of the presence of anybody in the dense bush,' said Bastienne.

Bastienne handed Jon a FR F2-7.62mm (French: Fusil à Répétition modèle F2), Repeating Rifle, which has been the standard sniper rifle of the French military since 1986 that was disassembled, and packed into a carry case. It is designed for shooting point targets at distances up to eight-hundred and seventy-five yards. He assembled the rifle, attached the silencer, then set the scope to its maximum range, took aim at a branch in a tree in the distance, and fired.

It was slightly off target, so he sighted the rifle, making the necessary adjustments, before firing another test shot at the tree. He continued to fire several test shots making minor adjustments, until he was satisfied that he had sighted the rifle accurately, knowing that he would need to make allowance for the wind and distance when the time came to take the shots.

Most shooters do not take the alignment of their reticle into consideration when zeroing in their scope. When the crosshairs of the scope are not perfectly aligned to the directions of the elevation and windage adjustments, it is referred to as a "Reticle Cant."

A canted reticle can cause shots to miss right or left of the target, especially when engaging a target at a distance of 250 yards or more. The greater the distance the sniper is shooting, the lower the accuracy, as natural forces like wind resistance work on the bullet while it travels through the air, so Jon knew he had to compensate for wind speed, direction, and distance. He had been well taught at the CIA's basic training course, and took the time to study the surrounding terrain. The rifle was fitted with a specialized scope, so he needed to make calculations for distance and angle, as well as having Bastienne read the wind direction and speed.

They were up early the next morning, decamped, and packed up their gear before having a cold breakfast of tinned corned beef and a bread roll. Joseph made his way towards the gravel road remaining in the dense bush, and hid near to where the track led into the bush. Albeit Jon was not familiar with the French spotter's rifle, he quickly familiarised himself with the weapon, and practiced loading it repeatedly until he was comfortable that he had perfected the handling of the gun. Bastienne would act as his spotter, using a Vectronix Range Finder to gauge distance, wind speed, and direction.

Both took the time to measure out the distance to where they believed the two terrorists would set up camp in a small opening in the wooded area, taking great care not to walk around in the bush, and leave tell-tale signs of human activity around the site. Joseph positioned himself in the thicket closer to the track in the dense bush, and would warn Jon and Bastienne when the two terrorists drove towards their intended campsite.

Jon and Bastienne found an ideal hiding place in the bush, and waited patiently for the signal from Joseph that Akeem Hasan and Omar Najjar, were on their way. It was a calculated guess that these two would make their way towards the campsite that they seemed to have used previously, as they would be familiar with the surroundings which were well hidden in dense bushland.

Two hours later, Bastienne's earpiece came to life, and Joseph reported that a dilapidated old van had just passed him on the track heading towards the campsite that these two appeared to use regularly. Minutes later the van passed close by to where Jon and Bastienne were hidden in the dense bush. They got a good look at both terrorists as they passed, confirming that they were the two people that they were waiting for. Jon and Bastienne watched patiently as Akeem and Omar set up their camp. A short while later they started their ritual, by positioning themselves on mats facing toward the Kaaba, the sacred building at Mecca, to which Muslims turn at prayer time, called the qibla. What they face, strictly speaking, is not Mecca but the revered Kaaba, the central shrine in Mecca's Great Mosque, which is Islam's holiest place.

They picked up their mats, and stored them in the cargo compartment of the van, then set up numerous cardboard dummies of people scattered around, depicting a scene of multiple people surrounding a person of importance, which in this case would have been assumed to be the Rabbi.

The two then took up a position on the fringe of the dummies amongst what appeared to be a throng of people that they had set up as well as a dummy of a parked vehicle. They were enacting a scene of two people walking towards the throng of people, when both suddenly extracted handguns, and started shooting at the dummy placed in the center, which Jon assumed was to be the Rabbi.

'Bastienne, whispered, so that is their plan, Monsieur Jon.' 'Shoot these two fucking pieces of shit Monsieur, and let's get rid of them, then get out of here.'

'Oui Capitaine.'

He waited for the ideal opportunity when one of the terrorists had turned his back on the other, and did not have his compatriot in his line of sight, thus would not even be aware that his friend had been shot, as the noise of the shot would be subdued by the silencer.

Bastienne, read out the wind speed, direction, and distance. Jon adjusted the setting on his scope, took aim, and waited until one of the terrorists turned, and made his way toward the van. He fired a head shot that split the terrorist's head open like a melon, and he fell silently to the ground in the long grass. Jon quickly reloaded, and repositioned his scope on the other terrorist, his finger gently touching the trigger, then as the other terrorist turned and called out an instruction to his friend. He was horrified to see him lying in the grass with half his head shot off. Jon squeezed the trigger gently, and a moment later the second terrorist fell backward to the ground, suffering the same fate as his fellow companion.

'OK, Monsieur, let's pack up here, sanitize the area, and get the hell out of here.'

'Oui Capitaine, but we need to collect as much information as we can from these two before we leave,' said Jon as he collected the two shell casings, and put them into his pocket.

'We need to be very careful as we make our way towards them, and use the tracks left by their vehicle with you following exactly in my footsteps, so that we minimize any disturbance of the grass, ensuring that we leave no clues,' said Bastienne as he donned a pair of rubber gloves.

They made their way toward the two deceased terrorists, removed their mobile phones, wallets as well as all other useful information they were able to find, Bastienne photographed the van's number plate, opened the bonnet, and took a photograph of the VIN, for comparison later to ensure that these two had not used stolen number plates. Both were extremely careful to ensure that they left no clues, then backtracked covering their tracks as best they could as they made their way towards their hideout. Jon and Bastienne went about clearing up any sign of them having been in the area, before picking up their equipment, and making their way back to the hidden Grenadier.

Bastienne started the vehicle, and drove towards the gravel road where Joseph was hidden, stopping to pick him up, ensuring that he stayed on the same tracks he had made earlier. He parked the Grenadier on the gravel road, and the three of them then broke off some branches from trees, made their way along the tracks in the grass to where they had parked earlier, using the branches to cover the tracks in the grass as best they could. Not ideal, but it appeared to have camouflaged the tracks somewhat.

'Well Capitaine, I understand that you did not want Joseph to witness what we have done, as he is a foreign subject, which therefore exonerates him from any future possible prosecution,' said Jon.

'Oui Monsieur Jon, we need to cover every angle, because the judicial system in this country would not look too kindly at what we did, and would jail us for life if ever we got caught, as they would deem it as murder, so we need to be very careful.'

'Well Monsieur's Jon and Joseph, as I have said on many occasions, if we have irrefutable evidence that we have identified a terrorist cell, I believe that we need to kill them, rather than take them prisoner because the legal system is way too lenient in the western world.' 'They would either get a light sentence or be let off entirely, thanks to some smart arse lawyer.'

'The French government has no idea of the way I operate, or my view on terrorism, and if ever they found out, I would be charged and jailed, not the terrorists, so I hope both of you agree with my opinion. We should never discuss any of this with anybody other than the three of us, and only in person.' 'Never call on a landline or mobile phone.'

He continued glancing at Jon seated alongside him, then looked at Joseph in the rearview mirror.

'I know that we are acting as prosecutor, judge, and jury, however, we need to get rid of all these terrorists my friends,' said Bastienne in a somber tone.

Both fully agreed with Bastienne's methods, as they too shared the same view.

'Two down and four to go Monsieur's, so we need to stay focused in the zone.'

Chapter 14

Avenue des Champs-Élysées

Paris

B arnaby Heathcott was patched directly through to Rafael at the Embassy.

'Hello Rafa,' said Barnaby, using his usual CIA undercover name.

Here we go again, now I'm Rafael. I really must consider taking up Capitaine Pétit's offer to join the French police, because these name changes are making me sick, thought Rafael.

'Hello, Director.'

'As you are aware, President Trent will visit Paris for VE day, and will drive with the French President down Avenue des Champs-Élysées in Cadillac One, or the Beast as we know it, celebrating the end of world war two.' 'As you are aware, we intercepted some recent chatter on the wire, and as discussed a terrorist cell stated that they intend to kill both Presidents, so we need to ensure that this does not happen,' said Barnaby emphatically.

'President Trent will celebrate this historic occasion with French President Emile Macon, and from the chatter we intercepted, it is apparent that they are planning to kill both at the same time.' 'They deem it an ideal opportunity to deliver a massive blow to our westernized way of life, so I need you to fathom out exactly how they intend to achieve their objective, and ensure that they are not successful.'

'We have come across this new terrorist cell known as "As-Sirāt fefore" before, which according to Islam, is the bridge every human must pass on the "Yawm al-Qiyamah", the Day of Resurrection to enter Paradise.'

'So we should assume that they will be true to their word, and attempt to kill both presidents at the same time.' 'Clearly, this would then have to happen when they are together, possibly as they exit the Beast, or stop to address the world at a news conference,'

'There will be numerous occasions when the two Presidents will be together during the VE day celebrations, offering these terrorists an ideal opportunity to try and kill them, which could include some type of a bomb, or possibly an RPG type of attack.'

Champs-Élysées, officially Avenue des Champs-Élysées, as it's known in French or "Avenue of the Elysian Fields," Broad Avenue in Paris, is one of the world's most famous, stretching one-point one-seven miles from the Arc de Triomphe to the Place de la Concorde. The Avenue des Champs-Élysées is an avenue in the 8th arrondissement of Paris in France, and is divided into two parts by the Rond-Point, a roundabout known as des Champs-Élysées. The lower part, toward the Place de la Concorde, and beyond, the Tuileries Gardens, is surrounded by gardens, museums, theatres, and a few restaurants. The upper part, toward the Arc de Triomphe, is traditionally the site of luxury shops, hotels, restaurants, pavement cafés, theatres, banks, and offices. Progressively, however, its character has changed, although its tourist appeal remains strong. Airline offices, fast-food restaurants, car showrooms, and cinemas, as well as American-style shopping arcades, have become increasingly dominant.

Frequently described as "the world's most beautiful avenue," the Avenue des Champs-Élysées is a Paris must-see when in Paris. Tourists and Parisians can be spotted strolling at any time of day or night, at any time of year along this iconic one point one seven-mile stretch, between the Place de la Concorde, the Arc de Triomphe, and the Eiffel Tower. The Avenue is a symbol of Paris.

It is also the setting each year for major events such as the Bastille Day military parade, the end of the Tour de France, and the Christmas lights. The Avenue des Champs-Elysées has some of the top museums in Paris, the Grand Palais, the Petit Palais, the Palais de la Découverte and the Espace Culturel Louis Vuitton. The fountains at the roundabout of the Champs-Elysées have rediscovered their magic thanks to the Bouroullec brothers that collaborated with Swarovski, to design their six bronze fountains that are embellished with over three thousand crystals. Tourists usually round off their visit by climbing to the top of the Arc de Triomphe for a spectacular view of Paris.

Victory Day in Europe is celebrated as V-E Day, commemorated on the eighth of May, and is a national holiday in France, known as "Victoire 1945" or La fête de la Victoire. The day is also celebrated worldwide as a holiday in countries around the world.

'We cannot rule out an attack from the air either, albeit that the Beast has been built to withstand an attack of almost any magnitude, however, these bastards may have something else up their sleeve.' 'I need you to do your best to establish exactly how these killers intend to carry out their mission, and to ensure that they are not successful Rafael,' emphasised Barnaby.

'You don't have much time to try and sort this out Rafa, so I will send you all the relevant information we have at hand right now, and I want you to keep me fully in the loop young man.'

Rafael, placed both elbows on the table, cupped his chin in the palms of his hands, and stared rigidly at the wall, wondering how this terrorist cell would attempt to pull this off.

While Muslims believe that dying as a martyr will guarantee them a passage to their heaven, which is described in the Qur'an as a beautiful garden, "Jannah is Paradise," where those who have been good go. It is described in the Qur'n as "gardens of pleasure" (Qur'an 31:8). Muslims believe they get to Paradise by living religiously, asking Allah for forgiveness, and showing good actions in their life. They believe that according to these traditions, Muslim men that die waging jihad against the enemies of Islam, will be rewarded by Allah in heaven (Jannah) as martyrs (shuhada), and receive seventy-two virgins to enjoy in blissful ecstasy.

I need to think like them, he thought. So if I was going to try to pull this off, it would be extremely difficult to kill both Presidents with high-powered rifles, as all areas along the route will be highly guarded, including all surrounding areas, as well as all areas in, and around press conferences. They could not possibly plant a bomb in a vehicle along the route that the Presidents will travel, as secret service agents from both countries will remove all vehicles along the intended route.

So how the hell would they try to pull this off, he pondered, and whilst, this is their belief, I think that most jihadists don't want to die, until of course they have inflicted maximum death upon non-believing Muslims, then they are happy to enter their heaven, and reap their reward, considered Jon.

Not sure if there are any virgins left in their Muslim heaven after Bin Ladin and his cronies arrived, he thought, with a wry smile on his face.

Jon, using his undercover name, called Capitaine Pétit and arranged a meeting for later that day. Bastienne arrived shortly after fifteen-hundred hours and was ushered into the conference room.

'Bonjour Capitaine,' offered Jon.

Continuing he said, 'I believe that Director Heathcott has copied you with the latest information he has on the possible attempt on the lives of both President Trent and President Macon, so we had best review what we have at hand, as time is fast running out.'

'Oui Monsieur Jon, this is extremely serious, so let's get started.'

Jon inserted the USB stick that he received from Director Heathcott into the hard drive, and the monitor on the wall came to life with images of two males matching typical jihadists. They had long black beards, and wore white Taqiyah skullcaps, which are usually worn by Muslims for religious purposes.

'You know Jon, we eliminate one lot of these fanatical people, and another rears its head a day later.' 'That's why I prefer to kill them, rather than arrest and charge them because, as I have stated numerous times in the past, the judicial system is way too lenient.' 'They let these bastards off with a slap on the wrist or light sentences, and the next day they are planning some other attack.'

'Oui Capitaine, I think just like you, and yes we act as prosecutor, judge, jury, and executioner.' 'I know we both believe that our actions are fully justified, so we need to kill them, and not bother trying to arrest them, therefore we do think alike.'

'You will note that these cells keep on popping up, and as we eliminate one cell, another pops up,' 'Curse the day we let these people into France,' said Bastienne.

'So Capitaine, I can only see one way that these terrorists can pull this off.' 'In my opinion, they cannot attempt a shot at the Beast because it is bulletproof, even taking a shot from an RPG would not destroy it, because it has been built to withstand an attack of that nature.'

'Nor can they plant a bomb in a parked car along the route that the Presidents will travel as all parked vehicles will be removed by secret service agents, so I believe that they will plant a massive bomb in the underground stormwater system, which as you know runs down the middle of the Avenue des Champs-Élysées.'

'A huge bomb exploding in a stormwater drain would cause massive damage, as the heavy metal cover on the road would be catapulted upwards underneath the Beast as it passes over it, and whilst, the Beast has heavy armor plating, a massive explosion directly below the rear seats where both Presidents would be seated, could be fatal,' said Jon.

'Oui Monsieur Jon, that's an excellent assessment of what these people may well be planning,' said Bastienne.

Jon pulled up satellite images of the Avenue des Champs-Élysées. Images of various stormwater manhole covers came into view.

'The heavy cast iron manhole covers usually weigh two-hundred and fifty pounds, and a massive explosion would most likely see the cover penetrate through the underbelly of the Beast, and possibly kill both Presidents.'

'So, that's what I believe these people may be planning.' 'We need eyes on all these manholes along the Avenue des Champs-Élysées twenty-four seven, and we need to get down into the stormwater drain running along the avenue, and check it thoroughly before the motorcade passes over it.'

'From what I understand, the Avenue des Champs-Élysées is the only road that has these manholes in the middle of it, as all other roads that they will travel down, have concrete manholes situated in the gutters on the sidewalks, so in my opinion, this is the most likely area that these terrorists will target,' said Jon.

At around midnight on the evening prior to when the Presidents and their motorcade were scheduled to drive along the Avenue des Champs-Élysées, Jon and Bastienne donned overalls and drove towards Place de la Concorde. They parked their van in a remote spot, out of sight of any tourists and Parisians strolling along this iconic one-and-a-quarter-mile stretch ending at the Arc de Triomphe. The avenue, a symbol of Paris is lined with restaurants, luxury boutiques, and nightclubs. So a massive explosion would not only kill both Presidents and some of their security detail, but also hundreds of onlookers. Bastienne arranged for traffic management to place bollards around a manhole a half a mile further up the road, directing traffic around it hoping that it would not attract any attention.

Traffic management arrived in a big truck with a heavy-duty jack, connected a hook to the cover, and lifted it from its cradle. As soon as they opened it, Jon and Bastienne entered the stormwater drain, activated the lights on the headgear, and made their way down the ladder into the bowel of the stormwater system. A moment later the traffic management team replaced the heavy manhole cover, removed the bollards, and drove the truck towards a secluded area a mile away from the scene. They parked the truck well away from any prying eyes with the whole manoeuvre taking a couple of minutes to complete.

'Geez it's as dark as hell down here,' commented Jon as he carefully stepped onto the concrete floor of the drain ensuring that he did not place his foot into the gutter in the middle of the drain. There is a constant flow of water which is gravity fed, and the stench was unbearable.

'Mind your head Capitaine,' he said crouching as he entered the stormwater drain.

Jon turned his head, and the beam of his headgear light lit up the drain for a distance of thirty feet. He noticed rats scurrying away from the light.

'Fucking disgusting down here,' he said as he turned to face Bastienne.

They made their way along the drain in the direction of the Place de la Concorde, checking each manhole along the way, and finally, Jon stopped as the beam of his light caught a glimpse of what appeared to be explosives hanging from a manhole in the distance.

'Sweet Jesus in heaven Capitaine, look at this.' 'The entire shaft is packed with explosives,' he said as he cautiously approached, trying as best he could to look deeper into the shaft.

'There are enough explosives in here to blow the whole of Paris to the fucking moon.'

Bastienne tried as best he could to see past where Jon was crouched.

'This is the fourth manhole from where we entered, so around midway down the Avenue des Champs-Élysées,' said Jon.

'From what I can see, the detonator appears to be hidden behind this layer of explosives,' he said pointing to a massive bundle fixed to the ladder close to the manhole cover.

'It's zero-one hundred hours now, so we had best check the other manholes, then work our way back, and get the bomb squad to remove the detonator, and defuse this lot well before daylight, so let's get moving Capitaine,' said Jon leading the way.

They made their way towards the other manholes thoroughly checking each one, then doubled back to the manhole where they had entered earlier, and Bastienne radioed the traffic management truck instructing them to open the manhole. A short while later they were out of the stormwater drain and Bastienne called the operations center. He spoke with his commanding officer who was the head of the French Police on a secure line, explaining what they had discovered. Within minutes the French authorities had members of their bomb squad at the scene accompanied by USA Special Task Force members, and two bomb disposal experts.

The traffic management team arrived minutes later, again placed bollards around the manhole detouring traffic, removed the heavy manhole cover, and the two bomb disposal experts, as well as the USA and French Special Task Force Members, entered the manhole. Once inside, the traffic management crew replaced the manhole cover, and removed the bollards opening the road to normal traffic. The two bomb disposal experts made their way towards the manhole where the terrorists had assembled the explosives, and went to work.

Special Task Force Members secured the area in the drain on either side of the manhole, and the two bomb disposal experts went to work removing the detonator. They slowly removed explosives around the detonator until it was visible, then checked to ensure that there were no other detonators hidden behind the mass of explosives, noting that the detonator did not have a timer on it, thus the terrorists would activate it remotely once the Beast passed overhead. Having removed the detonator, they radioed the traffic management team who once again placed bollards around the manhole before opening it, allowing the teams to exit the stormwater drain.

The entire procedure was done with lightning speed, to minimize any suspicion that there was a problem on the eve of the President's traveling down the Avenue des Champs-Élysées.

'How certain are you that your guys have identified, and removed all detonators?' questioned Agent Banasiewicz, the head of President Trent's detail.

'According to both the bomb disposal experts that he removed the detonator, they are one hundred percent sure that there was only one, Monsieur,' replied Yves Toussaint, Directeur général de la police nationale.

'Continuing Yves added, 'I am confident that my guys have removed the only detonator, so they have eliminated any possibility of the explosives being detonated remotely, and I have arranged to have two officers positioned in the stormwater drain on either side of where the explosives have been placed.' 'Nobody can enter the stormwater drain from another manhole along the road.' 'These officers will be relieved after a four-hour stint, and a new crew sent into the drain.'

'Monsieur Banasiewicz, I recommend that we leave the explosives in the drain so that our officers, and your agents can try to identify these terrorists, then apprehend and charge them.' 'And yes, I know that you may see this as taking a huge risk, so feel free to go into the drain, and see for yourself that they have removed the detonator, and that there are no other detonators, and it is safe.'

Thousands of people lined the Avenue des Champs-Élysées in the hope of getting a glimpse of the Presidents as their motorcade passed nearby. Yves and agent Banasiewicz had dozens of plain-clothed agents mingling in the crowd trying to identify the terrorists as well as snipers strategically placed on rooftops along the route.

Jon studied the terrain, and concluded that the two terrorists would not position themselves in harm's way, however, would most likely be close by, possibly directly opposite the manhole where they had placed the explosives. This would allow them to accurately assess when the Beast passed over the manhole that contained the explosives. He moved to the outer fringe of the throng of people casually making his way in a ninety-degree arc, his eyes searching for anybody that seemed suspicious. Bastienne, followed close by, maintaining eye contact with Jon, and noted that Jon had stopped, and had scratched his head, a signal that he had identified the possible terrorists.

The two terrorists were seated on a blanket on the lawn some distance from the road, and diagonally across from the manhole in which they had planted the explosives, enjoying an afternoon meal. The white Taqiyah skullcaps had been replaced with peaked caps, however, their long black beards remained, which were evident in the video that Director Heathcott had sent. It confirmed that he had identified the correct two people that were about to attempt to kill both Presidents and hundreds of innocent bystanders.

Got you, you bastards thought Jon, as he slowly circled these two terrorists, making his way closer to them from their rear. Bastienne leaned against a tree nearby, pretending to be speaking on this mobile phone, conscious to not look in their direction, however, managed to keep Jon in his peripheral vision. His earpiece crackled to life with the Directeur général de la police nationale wanting an update on whether anybody had made eye contact with the suspects.

'We only have a few minutes left before the motorcade will pass by, so gentlemen, we need to find these bastards real soon,' said Yves in a demanding voice.

'Oui Directeur, we are doing our best,' said Bastienne.

Facing the road, with his back towards the terrorists Bastienne shouted 'Vive le France.'

Both terrorists turned to face him, and Jon extracted his Glock fitted with a silencer, covered the distance between himself and them in an instant. He pointed the gun at the head of the terrorist holding the remote. Bastienne turned and faced them, his weapon trained on them as well. The terrorist holding the remote realized what had happened, and pushed the button on the remote repeatedly, finally realizing that it was not going to activate an explosion, he attempted to extract a gun from the picnic basket, only to find the barrel of Jon's Glock resting firmly against his temple.

'Go ahead and try.' 'I will blow your fucking brains all over the lawn here, so lie down on your stomach, and don't even breathe,' said Jon placing his knee in the small of the terrorist's back.

Bastienne frisked them, extracted two pairs of handcuffs, and cuffed both of them. He pulled them to their feet, and marched them away from the throng of people lining the street that were waving French and American flags as the motorcade passed by.

Jon looked in the direction of the manhole cover, held his breath as the motorcade passed over the manhole, then leaned towards Bastienne and whispered, 'what a pity, we should have killed them you know, however, there are way too many cameras about that would capture images of what we would have done, as well as hundreds of people that would witness it, so this is their lucky day.'

Bastienne, radioed the Directeur général de la police nationale Yves Toussaint, and informed him that they had the two terrorists in custody, and that one of them had tried to activate a remote only to discover that it did not work.

'Excellent Capitaine.' 'Congratulations to both you and Jon.' 'Job well done,' he said as he turned to face Agent Banasiewicz and watched the television coverage as the motorcade safely passed over the drain that has the explosives in it.

Jon turned to Bastienne and said, 'I do not doubt that we will meet these two again after they have enjoyed their holiday at the taxpayer's expense.'

Chapter 15

Paris-Nord Villepinte Exhibition Centre

Paris

B arnaby called the Embassy and was patched through.

'Excellent outcome Paris Rafa.' 'Congratulations, and please pass on my thanks to Capitaine Pétit.'

'The President has been fully briefed by our Secret Service, and has asked me to convey his thanks to you for a job well done.' 'I am sure that the French authorities have done the same, and informed President Macon, so thank you again for the excellent work, Rafa.'

'Yes sir, as you know we apprehended the two terrorists, and the French police are in the process of questioning them.' 'We believe that they will shed a lot more light on other activities that this lot have been planning,' said Rafael.

A week later Bastienne and Jon were discussing the possible assassination of the USA ambassador to France, Ezequiel Arrabito which they believed would take place later that evening.

'Well, we eliminated the two terrorists in the Ardennes Hills that were going to kill the Rabbi, as well as arresting those that would have tried to kill the Presidents of the USA and France, so that's taken care of, and now we must focus on the possible attempt on the US ambassador, Arrabito's life,' said Bastienne.

'To date, nobody has reported finding the bodies of the two that we eliminated in the hills, and it may be some time before a bushwalker possibly discovers the bodies.' 'This suits us perfectly as the rain would have washed away any traces of us having been there, as well as the regrowth of the grass covering our tracks,' continued Bastienne.

Jon fired up the computer and images of the Paris-Nord Villepinte Exhibition Centre in Paris were displayed on the monitor.

'From what we understand, the ambassador's motorcade will pull up at the main entrance at around nineteen-hundred hours, and this is where we believe that an attack may take place, because these terrorists need a quick escape route.' 'From what we have seen at their camp site in the Ardennes Hills, it appears that this is their plan.'

'I have alerted the ambassador, and he will wear a bulletproof vest.' 'We will have multiple undercover police officers scattered around the drop-off point, covering every possibility,' continued Bastienne.

Jon looked at his watch and mentioned to Bastienne that they had best relocate to the Exhibition Centre. An hour later he noted that the Ambassador was five minutes late. His eyes scanned the throng of reporters, anticipating that the terrorists may attempt to kill the Ambassador as he exited the limousine. He slowly made his way around the fringe of reporters doing his best not to draw attention to what he was doing, and hoped that he had interpreted the intelligence correctly, so he focused on the hordes of the press gathered at the entrance, waiting for the arrival of the ambassador and his wife.

Maybe we should have had him, and his wife enter through a rear door of the Exhibition Centre he thought just as the ambassador's limousine pulled up at the front door. Bastienne was positioned at the front door, and made his way towards the parked vehicle, his eyes scanning the reporters surrounding the limousine making it impossible to keep an eye on all the people.

Jon focused as best he could, his eyes darting from one face to another. The cameras covered their faces, and he wondered if the terrorists could be hiding behind one of them. He looked at the throng of reporters closest to the parked limousine, albeit it that his view was obstructed. A security agent riding shotgun jumped out of the limousine, and opened the rear door allowing the ambassador to exit. Flashes of light from the reporter's cameras blinded Jon momentarily as he stared at the reporters. Moments later, the ambassador was joined by his wife, and he stopped to offer a comment to the waiting media, before making his way towards the entrance. He had not noticed Jon as he was preoccupied with answering questions from reporters. Jon and Bastienne followed closely behind as he entered the complex, continually scanning the area ahead, and behind them to ensure that the terrorists would not take a shot while the ambassador's back was turned.

OK, nothing happening here, thought Jon as he leaned over and whispered to Bastienne, these bastards must be somewhere inside. Bastienne barked orders into the hidden microphone in the cuff of his jacket, and multiple agents surrounded the ambassador and his wife, as he shook hands with dignitaries on his way to the podium. Jon worked his way towards the front of the podium, his eyes darting from one person to another, as he tried to identify any possible threat. The ambassador stepped up to the microphone and addressed the dignitaries, finally declaring the exhibition open.

Bastienne whispered into the hidden microphone in his sleeve, 'nothing here Jon, I think they will try to take a shot as he walks around the various exhibitor stalls, so we need to follow him closely and kill these bastards.'

A short while later, the ambassador and his wife made their way along the passageway, stopping at various exhibitors to offer compliments and words of encouragement. Jon's eyes worked the surroundings as the ambassador stopped to admire the USA exhibit. Watching the ambassador closely, Jon folded his arms as he considered that there had been no threat thus far, so what do these bastards have planned, he thought. Could be an attack from one of the roving waiters, an exhibitor, or a cleaner sweeping up droppings on the floor. Jon kept close to the ambassador and his wife, his eyes darting from one exhibitor to another, scanning every corner of the exhibition center, wondering where they could possibly be. If I was them, I would attempt to kill him in the most unlikely place which would allow me to escape he thought.

Of course, the men's urinal would be an ideal place, as there are never many guys relieving themselves at any given time, so an accomplice could place a no entry cleaning sign on the door after the ambassador had entered, whilst his mate slit the ambassador's throat as he was relieving himself. Yes, that's it he convinced himself. An ideal place to commit the killing, and get out of there unnoticed. An hour later the ambassador excused himself from the bustling crowd, and headed towards the man's toilet.

Right on cue, so let the games begin, thought Jon as he followed closely behind. The attendant had busied himself refilling the paper towel dispenser as the ambassador entered the man's toilet, and offered a courteous, 'Bonjour Monsieur.'

The ambassador, unaware that this person was about to kill him merely responded with, 'Bonjour,' as he passed the attendant on his way to the urinal.

Moments later, Jon approached the men's toilet door, lifted the tail of his jacket, removed the Glock fitted with a silencer from the rear of his pants, and entered the men's toilet. He noticed the ambassador standing in front of a urinal relieving himself, just as the attendant started walking towards him holding a knife in his hand. The attendant noticed Jon in the mirror, quickened his pace as he moved towards the ambassador, and was about to lunge towards him, when he felt the barrel of the Glock against his temple. Jon had covered the distance between them at record speed like a cheetah chasing its prey, and secured the hand that held the knife twisting his palm backward and forcing him to release the knife.

He placed his leg behind the assailant's legs, dropped him to the ground in an instant, flipped him over, then placed his knee on the perpetrator's neck, and secured both his arms behind his back. The ambassador was astounded to discover that it was one of the ambassadorial staff members standing over the person on the floor.

'Where the hell did you come from?' asked the ambassador recognizing the CIA agent based at the Embassy.

'No need to worry Mr. Ambassador, I have your back,' he replied.

Bastienne entered a moment later, cuffed the assailant, then turned and said, 'we will take it from here Mr. Ambassador, so best we keep this between us and under wraps.'

Bastienne added, 'Monsieur Ambassador, we have another suspect somewhere in the crowd, so I think you should consider making a discreet exit soon.' 'I will have agents escort you and your wife to the front door, and arrange for your limousine to be available as soon as you are ready to depart.'

As the ambassador made his way out of the toilet, Jon whispered to Bastienne, 'pity it has ended this way, because I would have liked to kill this fucking bastard, rather than take him into custody.' 'Unfortunately, or more appropriately, fortunately for this prick, the ambassador has witnessed this, and there are way too many surveillance cameras scattered around the place, so in time after he has served a short sentence at the pleasure of the French Government, he will be released and I have no doubt we will meet him again.'

'We need to find the other bastard Jon,' said Bastienne as he pulled the assailant to his feet, and marched him out of the toilet heading towards the loading dock at the rear of the premises without anybody even noticing.

They made their way to a parked squad car, and loaded the terrorist into the rear passenger seat with Jon assuming a seat alongside him. Bastienne pointed the car towards the exit, and made his way out of the complex.

'Well you bastard, I am going to give you one opportunity to tell me where your friend is.' 'Only one opportunity, then if you refuse to tell me, I will beat it out of you, you fucking piece of shit,' shouted Bastienne as he turned to face the terrorist.

'I don't have a friend,' replied the terrorist with a defiant smile on his face.

'OK tough guy, we will shortly see just how strong you are,' continued Bastienne.

Bastienne turned into an old derelict warehouse on the outskirts of Paris. Jon pulled the terrorist out of the vehicle, and they made their way into the warehouse as rats scurried to get out of their way.

'See these, they are hungry, and they are going to eat you after I have finished with you,' said Jon in a raised voice.

Jon bound the terrorist's mouth with duct tape, clenched his fist, and smashed it into the terrorist's face, breaking his nose and jaw. Muffled noises from the throat of the terrorist were evident as he screamed in pain, blood oozing out of his nose. Jon leaned down and grabbed his testicles, and squeezed as hard as he could. The pain on the terrorist's face was evident, his eyes wide open with tears and blood streaming down his cheeks. Jon extracted an Emerson Specwar Custom Knife from the sheath on the side of his pants, and positioned the tip of the blade against the terrorist's testicles.

'After I have cut them out and made you eat them, you won't be enjoying the seventy-two virgins waiting for you in Muslim heaven.' 'I don't think there are any left after your mate Bin Laden entered the Promised Land,' said Jon forcefully.

Bastienne, leaned against a pillar admiring Jon's technique, and watched as the terrorist screamed in pain, tears again welled up in his eyes, shaking his head from side to side, begging for forgiveness as best he could through the duct tape.

'What's your mate's name?' shouted Jon, as he cut the front of his pants open exposing his penis.

'See this knife.' 'I am going to cut your dick off as well as your balls and make you eat them, you piece of shit.' 'So they will be no good anymore, and you won't be able to use them when you get to the Promised Land.'

The terrorist tried as best he could to offer an inaudible comment through the duct tape, so Jon emptied his pockets, took possession of his mobile phone, flipped him onto his stomach, and removed his wallet.

'Ah Monsieur Muhammad Jaafar,' said Jon as he extracted his identification card.

'So you bastards run from Iraq, Afghanistan, and Syria, come to France seeking asylum bring your jihadist shit with you, then bite the hand that feeds you.' 'Curse the day we ever let you murderous bastards into France,' shouted Jon.

'Every second Muslim is called Muhammad,' said Jon as he flipped him onto his back, staring him directly in the eye.

Jon activated Muhammad's mobile phone, and noted several calls to a person by the name of Kidadl Tazi. He noted that a call had been made shortly before the attempt on Ambassador Arrabito's life.

'So your friend is Monsieur Kidadl Tazi I see,' said Jon as he flicked through calls made on the mobile phone.

He scrolled through the photo album on the phone, pointed to a photograph of Muhammad and another man, then turned to face him and said, 'is this Mr. Tazi?'

Jon moved closer to Muhammad, pushed the blade of the knife against his testicles and said, 'best you tell me where I can find this bastard or you will eat these shortly,' he said.

In fear of his life, Muhammed again murmured something inaudible, so Jon ripped the duct tape off, and he screamed in pain as the duct tape removed part of his beard.

'Yes that's him,' cried Muhammed.

'Not so fucking tough now are you, you piece of shit.' 'So where does he live?' questioned Jon as he pushed the blade of his knife deeper into Muhammed's testicles.

He screamed with pain and said, 'we arranged that he would leave the exhibition center if he saw I had been caught.' 'He lives in the Saint-Denis migrant camp in northern Paris,' shouted Muhammed.

Jon pulled Muhammed to his feet, and guided him towards the side of the warehouse, opened the dumpster lid, picked him up, and threw him in. He extracted his Glock and shot him between the eyes. Rid of another jihadist prick, he thought to himself. I am sure that no one saw us marching this prick out of the exhibition centre, and the ambassador will not question what had happened to this arsehole, so let's hope that nobody in the media even noticed us taking him towards the rear of the exhibition center, Jon thought to himself.

'Right Capitaine, we now need to find this other prick,' said Jon as they made their way out of the warehouse.

The next morning Bastienne arrived in a garbage truck, picked Jon up at the Embassy, and drove to the migrant camp in northern Paris. He parked a short distance from the entrance, waiting patiently. Jon picked up a pair of binoculars, and scanned the multitude of tents, finally focusing on a green tent with a yellow zip. Same as the one he saw in the photograph on Muhammad's mobile phone.

'Yep, got it,' said Jon.

'I can see a group of men gathered around a fire drinking something, which I assume is tea, and if I am not mistaken, Mr. Tazi is the guy in the light blue windbreaker,' said Jon.

'OK, let's wait and see what he does,' said Bastienne.

Two hours later the suspect walked out of the camp heading towards the railway station. Bastienne fired up the engine and followed at a discreet distance. Jon jumped out of the truck and followed on foot, quickly closing the gap. The suspect stopped at a garbage bin outside a restaurant, and scrummaged through the waste bin seeking something to eat from leftover scraps. Jon approached him, and stopped to ask him if he was hungry.

'Oui Monsieur,' I am very hungry stated the suspect.

Jon reached into the rear of his pants pretending to extract his wallet, however, extracted his Glock, and pointed it directly at the suspect's head.

'Ah, Monsieur Tazi, pleased to meet you,' said Jon.

The suspect taken by surprise, looked somewhat bewildered. It appeared that he thought of making a run for it, so Jon moved closer to him and said, 'don't even think of running because I will shoot you before you take one step, so lie down on your stomach and keep quiet.'

Jon glanced around to ensure that nobody saw what he was doing, then bound his hands with Flexi cuffs, lifted him to his feet, frisked him, and pushed him towards the garbage truck.

'Get in Monsieur Tazi,' instructed Jon assisting him into the cab, then jumped in alongside him.

'Oh, I almost forgot, meet Capitaine Pétit of the French Police,' said Jon.

'Now then, we arrested your friend Muhammad last night.' 'That's why he did not answer the eight calls you made to him on your mobile phone,' continued Jon.

'You will shortly join him unless, of course, you tell me everything I want to know, and yes, he is on his way to Muslim heaven right now.' 'He will soon discover that there are not seventy-two virgins waiting for him because your other buddy, Mr. Bin Laden has taken them all for himself,' said Jon sarcastically.

'So best you tell me who else was involved in planning to kill the Ambassador,' continued Jon holding an image of a person on Kidadl's mobile phone to his face.

'I have no idea what you are talking about,' said Kidadl sarcastically.

'Yes, of course not,' replied Jon as he activated Muhammad's mobile phone, and accessed the message that Kidadl left on his phone.

'Well there you have it, loud and clear, you calling your friend wanting to know if he had killed the ambassador,' said Jon.

'So we have a surprise in store for you, unless of course, you tell us who else is involved, and what else they are planning,' said Jon as he leaned towards Kidadl, grabbing him by the throat.

Bastienne drove the truck into the same warehouse where they had dumped Muhammad's body. Jon dragged him out of the cab, marched him towards the dumpster, opened the lid, picked him up, and shoved Kidadl into it He stared at the body of his friend at his feet, and started shaking uncontrollably, pleading for mercy.

'Nobody else is involved in the operation,' shouted Kidadl trying desperately to get out.

Jon jammed the blade of the knife into his nose and said quietly, 'whose idea was it to kill the ambassador Mr. Tazi?'

Petrified, Kidadl said, 'if I tell you, please do not kill me.'

'Depends on what you tell me, so best you tell me the truth,' said Jon.

Jon pushed the blade a little deeper into his nostril and Kidadl cried in pain with blood streaming out of his nostril.

'We were recruited by Faisal Syed, and he promised to pay us each five thousand Francs after we killed the ambassador,' Kadadl cried in pain.

'So where does he live?' Questioned Jon.

'He lives in the Maghrebi Community in Paris and owns a delivery van business that delivers goods to several stores.' 'He is an early riser, and is normally at his desk at four in the morning long before any employees arrive at work,' volunteered Kidadl in a great deal of pain.

'The business is called, Paris Express Delivery Service, and is situated in a warehouse complex at Aubervilliers and Saint-Denis, Les Entrepôts et Magasins Généraux de Paris.'

Jon Googled it, and the warehouse appeared to be situated on a huge 70-hectare warehouse complex used for storing non-perishable goods. He took note of the delivery vans parked neatly in a row at front of an old office block, and noticed that there were other warehouses scattered around the complex, however, the warehouse appeared to be in an isolated corner of the complex, well away from the other warehouses. Very convenient he thought to himself.

Jon turned to Bastienne and said, 'I think we have all we need Capitaine, so time to go.'

Bastienne, extracted his Glock deactivated the safety switch ensuring that the weapon was ready to be fired, positioned the barrel against Kadadl's forehead, and shot him between the eyes. Both understood that having extracted the maximum intelligence, they would eliminate the terrorist, so no need for any commentary. They closed the dumpster's lid and left.

'OK, Monsieur Jon, let's take a drive, and see what we have.'

They parked some distance from the warehouse. Jon scanned the surroundings with his binoculars, noting some activity inside, which appeared to be mechanics servicing some trucks. He noted that the vegetation around the facility was overgrown which would give them excellent cover when they decided to revisit the location, and trained his binoculars on the sign-writing, confirming that they had located the correct warehouse.

'Capitaine, I suggest that we pay Mr. Faisal a visit early tomorrow morning, say around zero-four hundred hours,' said Jon.

'Oui Monsieur Jon, let's do that my friend.'

Early next morning, Bastienne, pulled up outside Claire's apartment block in a van with the EUS Electricity Utility Company logo on it and Jon jumped in. This was the same van that they had used when they eliminated the two terrorists in a barn house in the rural village of Anvin Pas De Calais months previously. They drove to the complex at Aubervilliers and Saint-Denis, Les Entrepôts et Magasins Généraux de Paris in silence, parked a short distance away with a clear view of the warehouse and the office block. They jumped out of the van, and made their way towards a pile of pallets near the warehouse roller door, and waited for around fifteen minutes until a beam of light from an approaching car warned them of the arrival of Mr. Faisal.

'Dead on time, so let's wait until he is about to unlock the office door, then pounce,' said Jon.

Bastienne turned to face Jon and whispered, 'you and Joseph are the only people that I trust and have shared my views with, regarding the elimination of these terrorists.' 'I know that I have said it many times, and that both you and Joseph share the same view.' 'We best never allow ourselves to be suspects of committing a killing, or we could find ourselves in court charged with multiple murders.' 'We can only share our views in private.'

'These idiotic civil libertarians make me sick, they defend human rights with everything they have.' 'When we catch these murderers, judges give them a couple of year's holiday in our prisons then set them free,' added Bastienne.

'I know deep down that many French people share our views, however, they can never say that in public.' 'OK, the bastard is about to unlock the door so let's grab him,' said Jon as he sprung to his feet.

He quickly closed the gap between them, and was behind Mr. Sayed in an instant, positioned the blade of his knife at his throat, and whispered, 'good morning. nice to meet you, Mr. Sayed.'

Bastienne and Jon had donned gloves earlier to ensure that they left no fingerprints that could implicate them in any way.

'This way Monsieur Sayed,' said Jon pushing him towards their parked van.

'So Mr. Sayed, when are your mates arriving from London?' questioned Bastienne as he turned to face him.

'I have no idea what you are talking about,' replied a defiant Faisal.

'Is that so,' said Jon as he punched him in the stomach. Faisal buckled over in pain, and Jon repeated what he had just said, then cuffed, and bundled him into the rear of the van.

'Well a good friend of yours namely, Kadadl Tazi, says otherwise,' said Jon.

He activated Kadadl's mobile phone, and scrolled down to the message from Faisal that was made the previous evening, then leaned forward, grabbed him by the throat and squeezed.

'Here's the evidence you piece of shit,' shouted Jon

Bastienne started the van, and headed out of the complex towards the derelict warehouse where they had killed Muhammad Jaafar and Kadadl Tazi. A short while later they pulled him out of the van and headed toward the dumpster.

Jon lifted the lid of the dumpster and said, 'see, we have a surprise for you, Monsieur Sayed.'

'So unless you tell me everything I want to know, you will join your two friends shortly.'

'I want my lawyer,' shouted Faisal in a demanding voice.

'Yeah right, I will call him after you have told me what I want to know,' said Jon calmly.

'Now then, when are your comrades coming to France?' demanded Jon forcefully.

'I will only speak when you get me, my lawyer,' shouted Faisal.

'OK, you idiot,' said Jon calmly, as he grabbed Faisal by the testicles and squeezed as hard as he could.

Faisal screamed in pain and bent over as the tears welled up in his eyes. He begged Jon to stop.

'Please stop,' pleaded Faisal in a hushed voice.

'They are arriving tomorrow at lunchtime in a container full of goods being trucked by my company.' 'After the driver has made his first stop at the Remise Express Supermarket Warehouse, the large Discount Express Store, and unloaded some of the goods.' 'He will then drive to Rue du Louvre railway station, and drop off the two guys before making his way to Méga Magasins de Rabais, the large Mega Discount Store Group, where he will drop off the remainder of the goods.' 'After that he will head back to the UK,' said Faisal.

'So to confirm what you are saying, after the driver has made his first stop, there will be several cartons left in the container which he then has to deliver to Méga Magasins de Rabais, and these two people will be hiding behind these cartons.' 'He then drops them off at the station, and continues to the last stop to unload?' questioned Jon.

'Is that correct?' insisted Jon forcefully seeking clarification.

'Yes that is correct,' said Faisal, tears streaming down his cheeks.

Doubled over in pain, Faisal fell to his knees. Jon took one step, and kicked him squarely on the side of his face with a "Yoko-Tobi-Geri," a flying sidekick he had learned as a martial arts student. Faisal fell unconscious to the ground, so Jon pulled him up by the collar, slapping him repeatedly.

'Right, you bastard, do you want some more, or are you going to tell me anything else I need to know,' said Jon.

'That's all I have, so stop beating me, and call my lawyer?' demanded Faisal bleeding profusely.

'Yes, I told you that I would do that before, so one last chance, is there anything else you want to tell me, or must I beat it out of you,' said Jon in a forceful tone of voice.

'No, I have told you everything I know,' said Faisal defiantly.

'What color is your truck,' pressed Jon.

'The cab is white with my company's name sign written on it which is, Paris Express Delivery Service,' responded Faisal.

'What else,' he demanded.

'So to be clear, these people will be in the container that is being transported by your company which means that you are an accessory to a crime about to be committed, which makes you guilty.'

'What color is the trailer?' demanded Jon.

'It's white like the cab,' said Faisal.

'So where were you born, and why are you involved in this mess, when you have a successful business?' questioned Bastienne.

'I was born in Syria, and you people have murdered hundreds of thousands of our people including women and children.' 'You think that you own the world, and can do just as you like,' said Faisal defiantly.

'So you come to France as a refugee, and somehow start a business with a grant given to you by the French government in good faith.' 'You are able to start a new life, yet, you harbor this hatred towards the French people,' said Bastienne forcefully.

Smiling, Faisal said, 'yes we need retribution for the atrocities the Americans, French, and British have committed, so I have no regrets, because as a Muslim, I am committed to Jihad.' 'You people must pay for killing Muslims.'

Bastienne, smashed the butt of his Glock against Faisal's head knocking him to the ground.

'You fucking piece of shit,' 'You abuse our hospitality, bring your murderous ways to our beautiful country, and plan atrocities as if it was a school kid's play game,' shouted Bastienne.

Faisal somewhat dazed, simply smiled broadly and said, 'I want my lawyer now.' 'Allahu Akbar,' he shouted defiantly.

'Fuck you, and fuck your lawyer, you have no rights now.' 'I will deal with you, you murderous bastard,' shouted Bastienne.

'I demand that you call my lawyer right now,' screamed Faisal.

'Shut up you fucking prick,' said Bastienne in a demanding voice.

Jon turned to face Bastienne and said, 'Well we have everything we need to know, so help me put this bastard into the dumpster while we wait for his lawyer.'

They picked him up, and bundled him into the dumpster with Faisal begging for mercy understanding that he was about to face the same fate as his accomplices lying in the dumpster. Jon extracted his Glock, and shot him in the back of the head.

Bastienne fired up the engine, headed towards the Embassy, and dropped Jon off at the entrance.

He called Joseph Diamond in London on a secure line, and asked him to position himself at the UK border exit point of Folkstone the following day at around midday. He asked Joseph to wait until he had identified the white truck sign written with the words, Paris Express Delivery Service depicted on the cab. Arrangements were made with the UK and the French authorities to waive the truck through border control without inspecting it. The next morning, Bastienne, picked Jon up at the Embassy at zero-seven hundred hours, and they drove the one-hundred and forty-seven miles to Calais, found a suitable parking spot along the road. They waited patiently for the truck to pass by.

Around midday, the display screen on Bastienne's mobile phone lit up with an incoming call from Joseph.

'Thought I would tell you granddad has just left, so expect him soon,' said Joseph.

'Merci Beaucoup,' replied Bastienne as he disconnected the call.

They waited for around fifty minutes. Jon scanned the road through his binoculars, finally turned to face Bastienne, pointing to a truck in the distance, and said, 'that's our man.'

Bastienne made a U-turn, and joined the traffic some distance behind the truck ensuring that he maintained a suitable speed and distance, following the truck as it made its way towards Paris. He closed the gap between the truck and the van as it approached the outskirts of Paris, then watched as it drove into the Remise Express Supermarket Warehouse.

He parked further down the road and Googled the address for the Méga Magasins de Rabais warehouse, noting a possible route that the truck would most likely take. It would likely pass them en route to the Rue du Louvre railway station, so he took a calculated guess, and drove towards the station, parked at the most likely place where he thought the truck would stop to offload the two terrorists hidden inside in the container. He considered that it was a calculated risk, however acting on the intelligence that they had gleaned from Faisal, he believed that it was worth the risk. Jon and Bastienne scanned the area, and believed that the driver would stop towards the end of the parking lot, as he did not want anybody to witness him allowing people to get out of the container which would raise suspicion.

An hour later, Jon warned Bastienne of the approaching truck, as he had positioned himself amongst the parked vehicles, with Bastienne parked further down the road towards the middle.

The driver stopped a short distance from where Jon was hidden amongst the parked vehicles, and exited the cab. In an instant, Jon was alongside him as he rounded the rear end of the container, and was about to open the doors. He looked up to see the barrel of Jon's Glock pointing directly at his head.

'Bonjour Monsieur,' offered Jon as he positioned the weapon directly against his temple.

Bastienne was alongside an instant later, pushed him towards the cab, and told him to get in. Jon jumped into the passenger side of the cab, and instructed the driver to follow Bastienne. The truck followed the van as it made its way towards a derelict container boneyard depot.

'Well we have a surprise waiting for you,' said Jon as they turned into the depot.

He instructed the driver to exit the cab as Bastienne approached pointing the Glock in his direction.

'So what's your name, and how many people do you have hidden in the container?' asked Bastienne.

'My name is Abdullah Qadir, and I have no idea what you are talking about,' he insisted.

'Is that right Abdullah, well I will give you one opportunity to come clean and tell me the truth?' 'If you lie to me, I can assure you that you will feel a great degree of pain, so speak up,' shouted Bastienne forcefully.

'I have no idea what you are talking about.' 'I am just the delivery driver.' replied Abdullah in a defiant manner.

'Is that so' 'So how do you explain the phone call that Faisal made to you yesterday confirming that you will pick up the two people, hide them in the container, then drop them off at the Rue du Louvre railway station,' said Bastienne forcefully.

'I have no idea who Faisal is,' replied Abdullah.

'OK, I warned you,' said Bastienne as he struck him in the face with the butt of his Glock.

Abdullah tumbled to the ground, and Jon positioned himself on top of him, turned him over, and frisked him. He removed his wallet, emptied his pockets, pulled him up by his collar. Stunned by the blow, he staggered towards Jon, who smashed his fist into his face. Abdullah fell to the ground unconscious. Jon picked him up, looked at Bastienne, and said, 'funny how they all don't know anything until they feel the pain, then somehow it seems to jog their memory.'

'OK, OK, I will tell you he said as he staggered to his feet, blood streaming down his face, but I want a guarantee that you will release me if I tell you,' 'I have the right to an attorney you know,' said Abdullah through his bloodied mouth.

'Oh, is that so.' 'This is not England, and I doubt that you will need one, however, if you give us the information we require, I will consider getting one for you, so start talking,' replied Bastienne calmly.

The container depot boneyard was located near the Paris Terminal, Route de Bassin in Gennevillers, in the north-western suburb of Hauts-de-Seine department of Île-de-France, conveniently located some five and a half miles from the center of Paris. The boneyard was used as a graveyard for these old discarded containers that had most likely traveled millions of miles over many oceans, and had seen better days.

Bastienne noticed that the containers were stacked in rows of three alongside each other, three containers high and ten deep, thus some ninety containers in a section. There appeared to be around twenty batches of these derelict old containers in the yard. Luckily the roadway between each batch of containers was sufficiently wide enough to drive the forklift comfortably between the batches with enough space to be able to pick up a container, back up, and turn around without any problem.

He found an old forklift that appeared to be in reasonable condition, hot-wired it, and surprisingly managed to start it the first time. Bastienne noted that it had an eighth of a tank of fuel in the tank, so he tried all the levers to see if they were functional, and to understand exactly what function each one did. He drove it towards a stack in the middle row, proceeded to remove the top two containers, and parked them a short distance along the driveway.

Then he drove the forklift back to the container truck, and unloaded the container from the trailer, placing it on the ground. The people inside were shouting, and banging on the walls pleading to be let out. Jon pulled the truck driver out of the cab, and forced him to his knees, pointed the Glock at the back of his head, and watched as Bastienne opened the container doors.

Both trained their weapons on the men standing near the door, and instructed them all to move to the rear of the container. One man tried to make a run for it, so Bastienne shot him in the thigh as he tried to escape. The man fell screaming with pain, and the others that had witnessed what had just happened, all backed up towards the rear of the container.

Jon grabbed the driver by the collar, and pulled him to his feet as he pleaded for mercy. He pushed him towards the door. As they got to the door, he kicked him in the small of his back resulting in the driver being catapulted into the container, then dragged the man that Bastienne had shot back into the container.

Bastienne closed the doors, and used the ties to secure the levers in place, then placed the clips in possession which securely locked the doors. He jumped onto the forklift, picked up the container with the terrorists in it, and placed the container above the one positioned on the ground ensuring that the containers were tightly secured against each other, with no way of the terrorists ever being able to escape. He then picked up one of the remaining containers, and positioned it above the container with the people in it. Finally he moved the remaining container to the end of the line, before parking the forklift back in its original parking place. As he jumped out of the forklift cab, he could hear the people inside the container banging madly on the side, pleading for mercy.

Not a nice way to die, he thought to himself, but these bastards were going to kill innocent people, so fuck them. They made their way out of the boneyard and headed toward the Embassy.

'Another successful outcome,' said Bastienne.

'Oui, got rid of them,' replied Jon.

Chapter 16

Tvet

Russia

Barnaby's assistant tapped lightly on the door announcing the arrival of Victor Portnorsky, the Russian President's former head of security.

'Thank you Gizelle,' said Barnaby as he rounded his desk, extending his hand in a greeting.

'Hello Victor, good to see you looking so well,' he said waiving him to a seat alongside Aaron.

'The American way of life seems to suit you.'

'Yes sir, I love the outdoors. I have spent many months hiking, fishing, and hunting in this beautiful country of yours, that is free of dictators like my ex-boss Mr. Pushkin,' said Victor in his broken English accent.

Pointing to Aaron Barnaby said, 'Excellent, you remember meeting Aaron at the Grand Hotel in Zurich of course, when you passed on the USB stick that contained vital information from the meeting between Pushkin and the Chinese President Mr. Xiu Jaoping, so thank you for what you did Victor.'

'Hello Mr. Aaron, good to see you again,' said Victor.

'Privet,' hello in Russian, replied Aaron.

'You speak some Russian I see,' said Victor nodding his head in approval.

'No, not really, I took the time to find out how to say hello, when I discovered that we would meet again,' said Aaron.

Continuing Barnaby added, 'I invited Aaron to join us as you may have something interesting to tell us about your ex-boss.'

Rafael used the undercover name of Aaron on that mission, which is why Barnaby referred to him by that name in Victor's presence. Victor had passed on a USB stick of a video recording detailing the meeting between these two communist Presidents to him in the men's toilet at the Grand Hotel in Zurich.

'So Victor, you called, and said that we should meet rather urgently.' 'What do you have for us?' questioned Barnaby.

'Well, Director, firstly thank you for opening the way for me to come to America, and live a normal peaceful life,' 'Something I have always dreamt of, and I am grateful for everything you have done for me.' 'I do not like what Mr. Pushkin has done to millions of Russians, and he has killed a huge number of people that do not agree with him, jailed thousands in gulags which he refers to as dissidents, in the most appalling conditions as well as having eliminated his opponents at will.'

'Everybody is too sacred to question anything he does,' said Victor.

'He also killed my uncle and his family for demonstrating against his rule.' 'He never discovered that they were my family, so I lost, not only an uncle and his wife, but two female cousins, both of whom were raped repeatedly, then killed,' said Victor with a trait of hatred in his voice.

'I hate this bastard, and have been waiting for an ideal opportunity to eliminate him without being implicated in any way,' 'As you know he is an extremely dangerous person, and I know of a way to get rid of him,'

'I remind you that Pushkin came very close to ending all life on earth when the nuclear explosion happened at Saratov.' 'If that launch was successful, America would have responded, and an all-out nuclear war would have ensued, leading to the elimination of everything on earth, so we need to get rid of this madman.'

'Pushkin and three of his cronies meet in his office at the Kremlin Senate Building every Friday evening for drinks.' 'His drinking buddies are Mikhail Andreev, Alexei Belov, and Sacha Novikov, who form the trio of Leningrad KGB alumni, and act as his close advisors.' 'Mr. Andreev is the secretary of the Security Council, and these four get stoned on Vodka every Friday evening,' said Victor.

'I have had to pick these drunks up, carry them to my car, and drive them home more times than I can remember.' 'Pushkin merely flops onto the couch in his office, and nods off to sleep.'

'As you have seen, he is not afraid to use nuclear weapons, so the world needs to be rid of him, and hopefully, we can all live peacefully.' 'I know how we can do this without drawing attention to America, its allies, the CIA, or any of us,' said Victor.

'Pushkin's grand plan is to reunite the Baltic States into the Russian Federation, and he won't hesitate to use military force to achieve this objective.' 'I have witnessed his plans, as he is planning to invade Ukraine, and once annexed, he intends to expand the invasion to Latvia, Lithuania, Estonia, and the Czech Republic, because he sees an opportunity to unite them into the Russian Federation.' 'He believes that the west and NATO are too weak to intervene.'

'This would coincide with his plan of shutting down the world's electricity grid, effectively crippling the western world militarily, so we have to get rid of this maniac as a matter of urgency.'

'Wow, what you are saying is extremely dangerous Victor, because if ever, any word of this got out, it would most certainly end up in a world war, and we all know the consequences of that, let alone what would happen to all of us,' 'Even if Pushkin has been eliminated, who it to say, that whoever becomes President will not be as bad as or even worse than him?' questioned Barnaby.

'Well, we are all aware of Alexei Navalny, a long-time critic of the Kremlin, who has been jailed by Pushkin, and has been described as "the man Vladimir Pushkin fears the most" by the Wall Street Journal.' 'He is a trained lawyer that received a scholarship to the Yale World Fellows program at Yale University in 2010, and had since entered the world of politics, however as you know he has been jailed by Pushkin,' said Victor.

'Well, he would no doubt be released after Pushkin has been eliminated, and I believe that Russia would move to a general election quickly after that.' 'I have no doubt whatsoever that Alexei Navalny would be elected, and he harbors a friendly attitude towards the West, so things will change dramatically for the better if he was in charge in Russia.'

'So, how do you believe, that this could be achieved successfully without a finger being pointed at America, or God forbid, any of us?' asked Barnaby.

Continuing he said, 'this has to be contained to the three of us only, and regarded by us as highly classified, most secretive and strictly confidential.' 'None of this can ever be discussed.' 'Only amongst the three of us in the privacy of my office.'

'I hope that you both agree, and understand that what you are about to suggest has far-reaching implications, hence the need for this to be a closely guarded secret that has to go to the grave with us, and never become public, even if what you suggest is never carried out.'

Both Aaron and Victor agreed, and gave their word that it will never be discussed outside of Barnaby's office.

'OK Victor, give it to us chapter and verse then,' said Barnaby.

'Years ago, when I was a young Lieutenant in the FSB, which as you know stands for the Federal Security Service, I was tasked with finding the best quality Vodka in Russia for Pushkin.' 'This is his favorite drop of alcohol, and luckily I knew just such a person, an elderly peasant farmer that has a unique way of distilling Vodka, that is legendary in the village where he lives on the outskirts of Moscow,' said Victor.

'I befriended him years previously.' 'A man by the name of Evgeni Varkov, and introduced his unique brand of Vodka to Pushkin.'

'The old man lives in the outskirts of Tver, a rural village that is around one-hundred and ten miles from Moscow, and he exists on a subsistence farming lifestyle, however, he is renowned as the best maker of Vodka in Russia, by those living in the same village.' 'The still is in an old dilapidated barn that is about half a mile from his homestead, and his claim to fame is that the Vodka is distilled to an alcohol content of seventy percent, unlike the way other Vodkas are made which he ages in an oak vat.'

'Vodka is traditionally colorless, flavorless, and odorless, however, each batch he does is distilled several times increasing the alcohol content each time.' 'Enough to blow a person's head off his shoulders,' stressed Victor.

'He named his Vodka, "Bomba Zamedlennogo Dejstviya," which translates to "Time Bomb" in English, and believe me, it is as potent as one can ever get,' said Victor with a wry smile creasing his lips.

'Unlike traditional Vodka, each of his batches has a slight tinge of color, and the ageing process in the vat adds to the unique flavor.' 'He introduced wood in the ageing process which is not the traditional way Vodka is made, and this enhances the complex flavors with a richness that has been purposefully absent in straight vodka, including aromas of the source which are, potato wheat or honey,' continued Victor.

'This aging process not only mellows the vodka much like whiskey, but gives it a much more palatable flavor which Mr. Pushkin has found most desirable.' 'Pushkin has banned him from selling his Vodka to the local population, ensuring that he only makes it for himself and his cronies,' stressed Victor.

'Fascinating,' said Barnaby.

'I have watched this old man make his Vodka, and believe that we can poison it, and get rid of Pushkin as well as his group of cronies all at once, without ever being implicated in this at all,' said Victor.

'I used to collect a batch of the Vodka on the last day of every month, so no doubt Pushkin's new head of security would be continuing this tradition.' 'We can sneak into the barn, add poison into the bottles waiting for collection, recap them, and leave without being noticed.'

'I know exactly where the old man stores the bottles of Vodka waiting for collection, and know how to reseal the bottles once opened.'

'The old man stores the cases of Vodka in an underground compartment hidden under the floor boards, which he covers with a mat, then places a wooden table on top of that until Pushkin's head of security collects it.' 'I also know exactly where the old man places a secret mark on the label as an added security precaution, verifying that the batch has not been tampered with.'

'He also cuts a tiny piece out of the seal in a V-Shape directly above the mark on the label, as a further added precaution ensuring that the contents have not been tampered with,' added Victor.

'The barn is about a half a mile from his house, so any noise we may make will be carried away by the wind, as it always blows in the direction directly away from the homestead, ensuring that he will not hear any sound from the barn.' 'I am sure that this mission would be successful because the old man is drunk every night of his life, and sleeps like a dead person.'

'So I am confident that there is no chance of him ever hearing any noise that is made in the barn, albeit that we will take great care to be as silent as possible.'

Aaron sat back in his chair and pondered what he had just been told. Barnaby got up and walked around his desk contemplating what he too had just heard, then fired up his laptop and Googled Tver in Russia, confirming that it was a remote village a hundred and ten miles from Moscow. He beamed the image onto the wall monitor and returned to his desk. He had long considered ways and means of getting rid of Pushkin, however, getting close to him is almost impossible. Poisoning him is one option, albeit that he has everything that he eats or drinks is tasted before consumption. Assassinating him is another option, but finding the right person to do the job would be most difficult, and no doubt, the CIA would be implicated if ever that person was caught.

'So this is the site you are referring to Victor,' stated Barnaby pointing to the image on the monitor.

Continuing, he said, 'well it certainly is a remote village that seems to be in the middle of nowhere.'

He zoomed in on what appeared to be the old man's barn and homestead, noting its remoteness with no other homesteads visible within a radius of five miles, so ideal for a clandestine operation of this kind. The problem is how to get Victor and Aaron into Russia undetected, and then extract them safely after they have completed their mission, he considered.

'OK, Victor, let me give it some thought and consideration.' 'Let's meet back here in my office in a week from today at noon,' said Barnaby rising to end the meeting.

As they were about to part ways, Barnaby added, 'so what makes you think that whoever takes over from Pushkin, would be any better?'

'Well Director, as mentioned, I believe that Navalny will eventually become President.' 'As the head of Pushkin's security, I often overheard rumblings about somebody overthrowing Pushkin, without anybody knowing that I was listening, which I never reported as I have long held the view that the country needed to change direction for the better.'

'From what I have learned over time, the most likely person to succeed Pushkin in the short term would be an oligarch by the name of Olezka Orlov.' 'I don't believe he has any ambition to be President as his focus is on building his financial empire, and he harbors sympathetic feelings towards Alexei Navalny.' 'So if he took over from Pushkin, he would no doubt release Navalny that was imprisoned by Pushkin, who saw him as the most dangerous person in opposition.'

'I believe that Orlov would endorse Navalny to become President, and have no doubt therefore, that Navalny would become the next President of Russia.' 'He is friendly towards the west, and would seek to reconcile relations with the rest of the world.' 'If I am not mistaken, he would encourage Russia, the USA, and NATO to reduce their nuclear weapons.'

'It's ironic how money changes people's views, and that oligarch's would do almost everything to increase their wealth, as is the case with Orlov,' continued Victor.

Barnaby buzzed Gizelle, and asked her to accompany Victor to reception.

'Dasvidaniya Victor,' good bye Victor, in Russian.

'Until we meet again Victor,' said Barnaby as he bid him farewell.

'So, you also speak a bit of Russian, therefore I will respond in English, goodbye Director, and farewell Aaron,' he said as he turned towards the door.

Barnaby waved Aaron to his seat, and resumed his position at the head of the table.

'Well that's an interesting proposal, and certainly worthy of consideration Rafael,' said Barnaby, reverting to his CIA name.

'I asked you to join us as my most trusted operative, so if I decided to go ahead with this operation to eliminate Pushkin and his drinking mates, would you consider being part of it?' questioned Barnaby.

He then added, 'if you opt-out, I would fully understand, as it would be a very risky undertaking, so please give some thought to your answer, as I don't want you to make a hasty decision.'

'No need to think about it, Director.' 'This is exactly what I have been trained to do, so the answer is yes, let's do it, and rid the world of this maniac,' said Rafael.

'Well, before I even contemplate doing the mission, I will have to give it a great deal of thought as well as a lot of planning, because failure is not an option at all.' 'So I will notify you of my decision just before we meet Victor next week, and I again stress the importance of confidentiality,' stated Barnaby as he stood and bid Rafael farewell.

He watched as Aaron closed his office door, sat back in his chair, and stared at the image of the rural village of Tver displayed on the monitor on the wall. Very, very dangerous indeed, to be truthful. The world would be a far safer place without Pushkin, and the only way this could be successful would be to smuggle these two guys into Russia, and then extract them safely. So, I think that Victor could enter Russia posing as a stevedore on a freighter, and probably have Rafael enter by train from Helsinki posing as a tourist.

This would mean that Victor would enter Russia via the port at Tver which would be most convenient indeed, get these two to a safe house, and then somehow get them safely out of Russia again, pondered Barnaby. Extracting them by train is an option, and the trip from Moscow to Helsinki would take some fifteen hours or to Berlin which would be around thirteen and a half hours. The other option would be to have them make their way towards the Lithuanian border, and cross at some point, similar to the route that Victor took when he escaped with the two Russian scientists. Both offer very risky options, he considered.

Barnaby spent the week exploring various options, and finally settled on a couple of ways to insert and extract the two operatives. A week later Rafael was seated in Barnaby's office contemplating whether the plan that was about to be relayed to him could work. Barnaby shared his thoughts with Rafael, who agreed that his plan was the best way to successfully carry out the mission, and extract them safely. An hour later Victor arrived on schedule as planned.

'Firstly gentlemen, as we all know, this is extremely risky, because if ever you are caught, the consequences would be horrific, to say the least, and if Ivan ever discovered that America or myself were involved, there would be a world outcry for not only my head, but that of the American administration, which is why the President or anybody in his administration can never get any wind of this' stressed Barnaby.

'Having said that, the possible outcome out ways the risk, so before we even contemplate going ahead with this, I reiterate the need for absolute and total secrecy.' 'Do I have your word on this,' questioned Barnaby looking at both men.

Both gave him their solemn word offering their hands in a gesture.

'Director, for the betterment of the world, I am prepared to give my life, because we simply need to stop this madman,' said Victor.

'Right gentlemen, as we know the risk factor is enormous, and before I even continue, I want you both to think long and hard, whether you want to do this, yet again' stated Barnaby once again.

Without hesitation, Jon and Victor both immediately agreed that this needed to be done to stop Pushkin from taking over the world by force.

'So, I think the best way to get you guys into Russia would be for one of you to pose as a stevedore on a freighter, and the other to enter as a tourist, then have two of our operatives transport you to a safe place, and finally to the old man's barn in the village of Tver.' 'I think it best that you are transported separately, in case one of you is intercepted which leaves us with the option of the other being able to continue and complete the mission,' said Barnaby.

Looking at both men, he added, 'gentlemen, I know that I have said this before, however, I have to repeat it, yet again.' 'This is extremely dangerous, and if you are ever caught, Ivan will punish you in ways unimaginable.' 'You will suffer unbearable pain, so are you guys sure that you want to do this?'

Again without hesitation, both agreed at once, as they believed that the risk out ways the consequences, because the world desperately needed to be rid of another dictator, such as Pushkin.

'Right chaps, here's my plan,' said Barnaby calmly.

'Victor will pose as a stevedore which I mentioned previously, on board a TRASCO Holdings freighter namely, Ocean Explorer that freights consumer goods from Singapore to Tver every month.' 'TRASKO is incorporated into TransInvest Holding AG, the headquarter of which is located in Sankt Gallen, Switzerland, and is incorporated into the Freight Forwarders Association of the Russian Federation, so yes, a little risky, but it offers good cover for the mission.'

Continuing he said, 'The TRASKO Company cooperates on a long-term basis with Russian, foreign freight forwarding and logistics companies.' 'As well as transport enterprises, shipping lines, port terminals, temporary storage warehouses, insurance companies, and currently has, over 2000 companies that are TRASKO business partners.' 'I happen to know the CEO of the company, so I can arrange for Victor to be employed as a stevedore without any fuss.'

'This offers an excellent opportunity to get Victor into Russia undetected, as this ship docks in Tver which is most convenient, and I don't believe that the Russians will ever suspect anyone trying to enter their country through a trusted sea freighting company, that has been operating into their country for more than a decade,' added Barnaby.

'Ocean Explorer is the name of the ship that sails to Tver on the twenty-fifth of each month, which is a week from today, and docks four days later, so just before the end of the month.' 'I will arrange for you to be on board Victor.' 'You have a couple of days to spend doing whatever it is that you do, then report back here in two days.'

'Take the time to be with your partner Aaron, then catch a flight to Helsinki in three days.' 'Your flight details, and ticket will be delivered to you at the Embassy.' 'I want both of you to reconsider whether you want to do this very dangerous mission, and if you decide to back out, I will fully understand,' reiterated Barnaby.

Turning to face Victor, Barnaby said, 'when the Ocean Explorer docks in Tver, you will need to discreetly make your way onto the dock at around zero one-hundred hours, and walk towards the boundary fence on the western side, where you will find a hole in the fence.' 'Make your way through a hole in the fence that your handler will have cut.' 'He will be expecting you, and take care of getting you to Tver from there.' 'Simply, disembark, and discreetly leave the ship without anybody noticing.'

'I want you to use the alias of Étienne Moreau for this mission Aaron.' 'You will pose as an architect on a fact-finding mission wanting to design a similar structure as the Imperial Palace in Tver, and you will have all the necessary drawings and equipment carried by architects that will convince them of your credentials,' said Barnaby handing Aaron a passport that had numerous entry and exit stamps in it from various countries.

'You will catch the Russian-owned Lev Tolstoy train from Helsinki heading for Moscow, and get off at Tver where you will be met by a handler posing as a taxi driver at around zero six-hundred hours.' 'You will assume the guise of an architect wanting to explore the architectural beauty of the city, especially the beauty of the Russian Orthodox Church, and the Imperial Palace, two buildings you wish to base designs on for a future project,' continued Barnaby.

'Your handler will drive you to the Calypso Hotel where you will book in, and remain at the hotel until around twenty-two hundred hours, then use the staircase, and make your way through the parking lot exit and up the road.' 'One of our operatives will pick you up, and drive you to a safe house not too far from the barn house.' 'Victor will meet up with you there.'

'Victor, I want you to use the alias of Slavik Novakov, which as you know is Russian,' said Barnaby handing him the identification papers.

'After you have completed the mission Aaron, the operative will take you back to the hotel, and the next day you will then need to make your way to Tver station.' 'Catch the train back to Helsinki.' 'The train departs Moscow at around twenty-three hundred hours, and should be at Tver station approximately two hours later.'

'The camera that I will give you will have photographs of various buildings in Tver as a cover for your architectural mission.'

'Your extraction will be a lot more complicated Victor, so I will arrange for your handler to keep you hidden in the bush for a day before making your way towards the border between Russia and Finland.' 'We know exactly where, and how we want you to cross the border at that point,' continued Barnaby.

'You have been booked alone into a first-class compartment Aaron, which will afford you the privacy needed as an architect, so you will have time to relax after the mission.'

The Lev Tolstoy train is owned by the Russians, and runs from Tikkurila in Finland to Moscow with the last stop before Moscow being at Tver. Tikkurila is located in the eastern half of the Helsinki conurbation, some 10 miles north of the capital's downtown district. It is the administrative and commercial hub of Vantaa. Tikkurila's railway station is the busiest in Vantaa, and the third-busiest in Finland.

Rising, Barnaby took both men's hands, and wished them good luck

Later that evening, Claire propped herself up on the pillow and stared at her lover. She sensed the tension in him, leaned over, and kissed him gently on the cheek, as she had become accustomed to him being tense before an important mission.

Using his family name, she said, 'what's troubling you Yonti my handsome man?'

He merely smiled, hugged, and kissed her.

Unbeknown to her, he had used his expertise in engineering to develop a handheld military laser weapon that could destroy a target up to five miles away. The weapon had recently undergone trials in Syria and Iraq, and had proven to be deadly accurate and effective. Previous military-grade laser weapons had proven not to be an option due to their bulkiness, high costs, and poor anticipated results on the battlefield.

That was until the USA military tested Yonti's invention. The general idea of laser-beam weaponry is to hit a target with a train of brief pulses of light. The weapon could be used to destroy conventional weaponry such as tanks and vehicle's. Realizing the changing way that wars would be fought in the future, Yonti believed that conflicts would be driven by unmanned drones with conventional forces used as a backup. His invention was designed to intercept and destroy any aerial threat or missiles launched from the ground, with the power needed to project a high-powered laser beam of this kind that was beyond the limit of current mobile power technology.

He developed a system that could reach a terawatt for 200 femtoseconds, or one quadrillionth of a second, capable of incinerating a drone as well as interrupting electronic signals by emitting electromagnetic pulses. The USA military had tested his invention extensively including tests on aircraft with great success, and had accepted this new technology into their arsenal, paving the way for a huge financial windfall for Yonti.

He had also developed and patented an anti-missile system that he aptly named the Seek and Destroy Missile System (SADMS) which was currently undergoing trials at Area 51, the highly classified United States

Air Force facility within the Nevada Test and Training Range. Barnaby Heathcote, the CIA director was fully aware of his inventions, and had arranged for the testing to take place at the USA's most secretive facility. He was also aware that the wealth that Yonti would be paid for the development of these two innovative technologies, would one day see his best agent retire.

The SADMS system can detect an incoming air-to-air missile fired from an enemy plane, helicopter, drone, or anti-aircraft ground forces and destroy it. The missiles would be mounted on the wings of aircraft effectively facing towards an aircraft's rear, commonly known by aviators as an aircraft's six o'clock, which is where a hostile enemy aircraft would launch their missiles from. The SADMS would identify the inbound threat by the vapor trail left in the wake of the missile, then lock onto its warhead, and once fired, it would hone in on the target and destroy it.

The system makes use of ultra-high synthetic diamond crystals that allows the laser to tolerate very high power inputs, which are made by focusing energy into a crystal that then amplifies a light beam between two mirrors, resulting in a beam that is very collimated and concentrated, rather than dispersed.

Diamond is a new technology that is potentially a disruptive laser technology, because its thermal properties are much better than any other optical material, by order of magnitude. The USA military was seeking ways and means of defending itself against low-end military threats such as drones which are cheap to manufacture. Adversaries could put threats, such as including explosives on a very cheap drone like a quadcopter, and the USA military needed new technologies to combat that.

Yonti turned to face Claire and said, 'I am about to go on a very risky mission, so if I don't make it back, please open my safe.' 'Inside you will find my bank account that has one billion US dollars in it, which is the complete payment for a military-grade laser-beam weaponry system I have developed.'

'I have also developed an anti-missile system designed to destroy a missile fired at an aircraft which I patented that is currently undergoing trials at Area Fifty One by the CIA, and I have been told that the USA military is stoked with the results.' 'I anticipate that they will integrate this into their military arsenal soon, and we have agreed on the compensation of one billion dollars for this technology as well, which as I understand it, will be paid into my account within the next month.'

'I have made you the beneficiary of my assets in my will which is in my safe, so in total there will be two billion US dollars for you to spend on new shoes and dresses if I don't happen to make it back,' he said smiling broadly.

Claire's eyes widened, and she propped herself up on her elbow, astounded to hear what Yonti had just said, raising her eyebrows, and placing the palm of her hand over her mouth in disbelief.

'Yonti, I don't want the money, all I want is for the two of us to be alive, have children someday, and live a normal peaceful life, so I think it's time for you to quit doing whatever dangerous work you do.' 'Let's move to the country and live in peace,' 'Clearly you have an abundance of money as well the meagre savings I have, and you have served both the USA, France and the world without their knowledge admirably, so time to quit doing this dangerous work,' insisted Claire.

'Oui Mon Pétale,' yes my petal,' said Yonti staring blankly at the ceiling.

Continuing he said, 'it's not that easy though, albeit that I will consider quitting once I have taken care of some pressing issues, so I will shortly be away for a week or two.' 'The world needs to be a safer place, so I hope that I can make a small difference.'

'Please be careful Yonti, I want you back alive, and in one piece my handsome man,' said Claire hugging him tightly.

Victor posing as a stevedore made his down the gangway, and onto the dock at zero-one hundred hours as instructed. He quickly made his way towards the fence on the western side of the dock, identified the hole in the fence, crawled through it, noticing the flicker from a cigarette lighter, and made his way towards the darkened image of a person standing next to what appeared to be a delivery van.

'Going to rain tonight,' said Victor using the code words arranged by Barnaby Heathcott.

'Yes, it's going to storm,' came the reply from the person in the darkened shadows.

'I'm Anatoli Yanovski, jump in,' he whispered.

Anatoli extracted a plastic bag from under his seat, and gave it to Victor that contained a facial latex mask.

'From now on I will only use the name of Slavik Novakov when I refer to you, so put the mask on and we can get going,' instructed Anatoli.

The CIA had developed a realistic lifelike flexible facial latex mask complete with a long grey beard, which when fitted, completely changed his looks to that of a wrinkled old man with a bald head and beard.

Slavik removed his jacket and T-Shirt. He pulled the mask over his head, adjusted it as best he could then put his T-Shirt and jacket back on, before donning the peaked cap. He studied himself in the driver's rear view mirror, and was amazed at the transformation.

Should keep this and use it when I next see my partner he thought. Would give her one hell of a fright.

Anatoli fired up the engine of the delivery van, pointed the van onto the main road just as the intensity of the rain gained momentum, and turned into a downpour. Hopefully a good omen he thought to himself. Maybe the police patrols will be rugged up in their patrol vans or would have returned to their stations. He drove towards the outskirts of Tver, and turned onto a gravel road ten miles out of town, eventually stopping at a remote shed in a bushy outcrop that was five miles from the old man's homestead.

'Right, let's go,' said Anatoli as he jumped out of the van, and made his way towards the derelict old shed. The door creaked as he opened it, and Slavik was surprised to see Jon standing in the corner.

'Wow, I did not expect to see you here so soon,' said Slavik using the alias given to him for this mission as he removed the mask, and handed it back to Anatoli.

'Здравствуй, друг,' Hello friend, added Victor.

'Right, so we are about five miles from the old man's barn.' 'Let's get some rest and prepare for the mission tomorrow evening,' said Jon.

The two agents departed after having dropped both off at the shed, and drove towards a remote site deep in the bush, ten miles away. Aaron reached into his backpack, and pulled out a bottle of Vodka, which is the drop of choice for Russians, and reminded himself to use his CIA alias whilst in the company of Victor.

'ваше здорсвье,' cheers said Aaron as they clinked glasses.

'I see you are becoming a little Russian,' offered Victor.

'Well my friend, let's hope that nobody visits this dilapidate old shed because I would hate to have to kill an innocent person because our cover has been blown,' said Aaron.

'So Victor, you said that you know where the old man keeps a batch of his special brew that he has made for Pushkin, who then has his head of security collect it at the end of each month.' 'I hope you have witnessed how he seals the bottles because we will need to uncork each bottle, recap and seal them again without drawing any suspicion.'

'Yes, I know exactly how to do it.' 'This old peasant farmer uses a very basic method to seal his alcohol, corking the bottles rather than using the traditional screw top cork methods that distillers use these days.' 'Obviously, he does not have the machinery to do that, and after having corked the bottle, he then dips the bottleneck into heated lead that seals the bottle over the corks,' said Victor.

'He gathers the lead from an embankment at a local shooting range, collecting the soft-nosed bullet tips which he then melts and later uses as the seals for his legendary Vodka.'

'From what he has told me, he sneaks into the premises of a winery on the outskirts of town, and collects old reject corks from a recycle bin, that have been discarded because of a blemish or have a small chip in them.' 'He then takes them home, and thoroughly washes them before using them at a later stage.'

'He has made a very basic template out of a cast iron pot and melts the lead in it, then pours it into the template he has made.' 'This is what he uses as his homemade seal.' 'As the lead cools, he briefly inserts the neck of the bottles into a homemade stamp that he has made which gives the seal a look of authenticity.' 'I have to admit it is rather primitive but inventive.' 'The cooled lead acts as a seal over the upper part of the bottle, and I have to say it looks rather original.'

'I know exactly how he does it, and where he hides the lead which he melts, using a primus stove.' 'So we will need to do that after we have uncorked the bottles, and you have poured the poison into them, then I will need to mark each seal as well as cut a small V-Shape in the seal, exactly the way the old man does,' continued Victor.

'We had best make sure that we do all of this without making any noise, and do not draw attention to what we are doing, especially not allowing the primus stove flame to brighten the barn.' 'Best make sure that we do not wake the old boy up either, because I would hate to have to kill him which will result in the mission being unsuccessful Victor.'

'As mentioned, he uses an old primus stove to melt the lead, and I know exactly how to fire it up without any trace of a glowing light coming from the flame that will alert the old boy, so relax my friend.' 'I also know where he stores his stockpile of lead, so I am positive he won't miss some of it that we will use to reseal the bottles, so need to worry at all,' said Victor.

'So, what we will do tomorrow night is to get into the old man's barn, then remove the Vodka he has stored in the underground compartment, and I will let you do your thing and add the poison.' 'Then we will reseal the bottles, get the fuck out of there and Russia,' added Victor.

Later that evening they sat down to a meal of tinned corned beef and bread. They buried the rubbish in the bush, and settled in for the evening, however, Aaron's mind was racing, and he simply could not sleep, so he lay there thinking about his life, his parents, and brother as well as his beloved partner. He felt a little tipsy from the Vodka, albeit that he only had a couple of shots as he hardly ever drank alcohol, and always limited his intake to no more than two or three drinks.

Struggling to sleep, he gazed at the roof of the old shed in the darkness, and wondered what his beautiful partner was doing. Got to finish these few assignments then take a break he thought to himself. A moment later Aaron's sensors alerted him to the rustling sound in the undergrowth outside. Fuck me, someone or something is moving out there he thought. He quietly got up and made his way towards the door, peeped into the darkness through a crack in the side panel of the tin shed. Unable to see anything moving he positioned himself to the side of the door, extracted his Emerson Specwar Custom Knife, and waited for the intruder to enter. Moments later the door creaked open as a person pushed gently on the door and entered. The shadow of what appeared to be a male became vaguely visible as he entered the shed. Aaron placed the blade of his knife at his throat, put his leg behind the intruder's legs, twisted his body, and dropped him to the floor.

He positioned one knee on the person's neck and whispered, 'move and I will slit your fucking throat,' then realized that a Russian would not likely understand what he said.

He removed a cigarette lighter from his cargo pants, and as it flickered to life, Victor woke from his snoring slumber. He jumped to his feet realizing that somebody had managed to get into the shed.

'Sweet Jesus in heaven Jon, it's me Joseph Diamond you fucking prick.' 'You could have killed me you arsehole,' said Joseph using the name he always used whenever he was in France.

'What in God's name are you doing here Joseph he demanded?' holding his hand out to stop Victor from attacking his good friend.

'I'm here to watch your back,' said Joseph.

'Relax Victor, he's one of us.'

'So who is Jon?' demanded Victor.

'That's my middle name,' replied Aaron.

Victor eyed Joseph with a great deal of suspicion, and kept his eyes firmly fixed on this stranger.

'We in Mossad know exactly what's happening in the world you know, and I am here to have your back as well as yours Victor,' said Joseph turning to face him.

'How the hell do you know my name Mister Joseph?' questioned Victor.

'As I said, we in Mossad have our fingers on every pulse, so pleased to meet you Mr. Portnorsky.'

A stunned Victor, now fully awake, stared at Joseph without offering a word.

Joseph noticed the bottle of Vodka on the floor and said, 'I can use a swig of that my friend.'

Both turned to face Joseph, 'how the hell did you know where to find us?'

'Well your boss insisted that I came along for the ride, and act as a backup for you guys, just in case the shit hits the fan, so here I am My Lord,' offered Joseph, taking a mouthful of Vodka.

'Fuck me that was a silly thing to do, because I could have slit your throat you arsehole.'

Eventually, all three settled down to get some rest, and remained indoors the next day until twenty-one hundred hours that evening, when they started the five-mile hike towards the old man's barn. They made their way through the thicket on foot, and were careful not to encounter any person out hunting. As they neared the old man's house Victor paused, and stared at the dilapidated farmhouse for some time, ensuring that no lights were visible, then led the way towards the barn, and gently opened the creaking door, taking the time to double-check the surroundings to ensure that nobody had spotted or followed them.

A moment later they were all inside the barn, so he activated his low beam torch, and led the way to the table, lifted and repositioned it, then moved the floor mat exposing a hatch which he opened revealing the hidden underground chamber.

Joseph positioned himself outside the barn door, and kept watch, moving silently around the barn several times to ensure that no person had followed them, or was lurking in the undergrowth or passing nearby.

Victor turned to face Aaron, 'just like I said, here is the batch ready for collection, so let's get to work.'

Both donned a pair of rubber gloves, and removed the case of Vodka. Victor removed the seals and corks from all the bottles, and placed them into a plastic bag. Aaron extracted the plastic vials containing the poison from his backpack, and Victor watched with interest as he poured a measured amount of the deadly poison into each bottle. He only needed a minuscule amount of the deadly poison to be poured into each bottle, as that was all that was needed to kill a human within a month of it having consumed it.

Victor found the pile of lead that the old timer stored in a box ready to be used on the next batch of Vodka that he was due to make, and lit the primus stove. He placed the lead into a pot used to melt the lead, and watched as it slowly melted. The old timer was due to make another batch of Vodka for collection a month later, so he walked over to a shelf, and picked up the box containing the corks. He started inserting the corks into each bottle using a handmade compressor that the old man had made from scrap metal, before dipping the neck of each bottle into the melted lead momentarily, waited until the lead had cooled and hardened, before using the handmade stamp on the top of the bottles which left an indentation mark on the lead.

Victor inspected each bottle and verified that they were sealed properly. He checked that the lead had completely cooled, and hardened before he attached the label that the old timer normally used. He then took the black marker, and made a dot on the label in the exact position where the old man normally puts it, before cutting a small V-Shape into the lead seal, in precisely the same position he had witnessed before.

All done exactly the way Evgeni Varkov normally does it, he thought to himself.

Pushkin's chief of security will carefully inspect each bottle to ensure that it had not been tampered with, then having given it his approval, the old man would close the carton and sign his name on the cardboard box, before sealing the case with clear tape over his signature. This was another security measure.

They placed the case of Vodka back into the underground chamber, replaced the covering board, and mat ensuring that the legs of the table rested exactly in the indentation marks on the carpet. Aaron glanced at his watch, and noted that they had been in the barn for almost two hours, so time to get out of there. They ensured that everything was in place, exactly as they had found it, before making their way out of the barn, and headed back towards the shed in the bush. Along the way, Aaron undid the side strapping on his backpack, removed a small hand tool and dug a hole in the undergrowth. He placed the bag containing the seals and corks that they had removed from the bottles of Vodka into the hole, then carefully replaced the soil ensuring that the undergrowth covered any sign of a hole having been dug. He scattered the remaining soil in the bush. They would dispose of the rubber gloves later.

An hour and a half later they were back in their hideout as the glimmer of light indicated the coming dawn. The three of them holed up in the shed until just after sunset, as the darkness signaled the coming evening. Their handlers drove up to the shed to pick them up with each vehicle departing at fifteen-minute intervals, heading in different directions. Joseph was the first to depart, so he bid Aaron and Victor farewell. His handler turned the vehicle in the direction of the city and dropped him off at the modest three-star Vostok hotel. Aaron was next to depart heading towards the Calypso hotel in Tver. Both would stay indoors and keep a low profile, avoiding any suspicion until later the following evening when they were due to board the train. Finally, Victor turned towards the Lithuanian border, and walked twenty miles into the forest making his way to a rendezvous point deep in the bush and waited. A while later he heard the buzzing sound of a microlight making its way towards an open field so he made his way towards it as it landed. He quickly jumped into the passenger's seat. The pilot engaged full throttle, and they were away moments later heading towards the border between Russia and Lithuania.

The following evening, Aaron stood on the platform and glanced at his watch, noting that it was just after zero one-hundred hours. He looked down the railway line, anticipating that the train would arrive at any moment, and noticed Joseph positioned a short distance along the platform, taking great care not to hold his gaze in that direction, he noticed the headlights of the approaching train as it came into view. A while later they bordered the train headed for Helsinki, and Aaron found his way to the compartment reserved for him, unpacked some drawings, placed them on the bed alongside him, pretending to busy himself viewing the hand-drawn images of the palace.

Fifteen minutes later, two Russian immigration officials knocked on the compartment door, asked to see his passport and papers, as well as his train ticket. Aaron presented them to the curt and rude officials who only spoke in Russian, and courteously notified them that he did not speak Russian, so one official tried as best he could in broken English to question why he had visited Tver. Aaron pointed to his drawing scattered on the seat, and notified them that he was an architect on a fact-finding mission. This seemed to satisfy the officials who then continued to make their way along the corridor in the direction where Joseph had bordered the train.

Aaron followed a short while later pretending to be making his way along the corridor towards the dining car which luckily was in the same direction, as he needed to be sure that the officials did not apprehend Joseph. The corridor was deserted, as all passengers had long retired for the evening, and as he approached the two officials standing in the corridor appeared to be man handling Joseph, so he coughed which was an indication that he was going to confront one of the officials. One official somewhat surprised to hear a person cough behind him turned to face Aaron, who punched him in the face knocking him unconscious.

Joseph quickly took advantage of the distraction, and placed a triangular arm sleeper choke hold on the other official. He placed the palm of one hand over the official's mouth, and a minute later his body went limp as he too fell into an unconscious state. They quickly dragged the two officials towards the carriage door nearby, opened it, and threw them out of the train, just as they traveled over a bridge. The loud thumps were evident as the bodies of the officials hit the bridge structure bringing sudden death to both Aaron and Joseph quickly returned to their respective compartments and got into bed. Hope like hell nobody witnessed that, thought Aaron as he stared into the darkness.

Chapter 17

Moscow

Russia

A month later Rafael was back at the CIA's headquarters in Langley Virginia.

'Hello Rafa, nice to see you again,' said Barnaby using his usual CIA undercover name.

'Good afternoon Director.'

'Good result in Tver a month ago Rafa.' 'Thank goodness all three of you got out without any trouble, concluding a highly successful mission.' 'So now we wait and see if the world will be rid of this madman Pushkin.'

'Important to keep this highly confidential, and take it to the grave.'

They chatted for several minutes about the mission, when suddenly Gizelle tapped loudly on the door.

'Sorry to interrupt Director, but I think you need to watch the news on the television,' she said as she activated the control.

The breaking news story on all the major television networks was that the Russian President Pushkin, had been found dead in his office in Moscow, and the Fox News reporter stated that it appeared that he may have been poisoned. Suspicion naturally fell on the CIA's involvement, and the Russian Foreign Minister Lacrov, stated that a full investigation was underway to determine the cause of his death. Lacrov said, if President Pushkin's death was found to be foul play, then whoever was responsible would feel the full wrath of the Russian military. Barnaby and Rafael exchanged glances, knowing that it would result in the Russians casting suspicion in their direction. Lacrov made scathing accusations that the imperialists had somehow been involved, and openly accused the West of being involved in what he termed, the murder of their beloved leader. Yeah, right thought Barnaby as they sat quietly watching various reports coming out of Moscow.

Barnaby switched from one television station to another, as his mobile phone lit up with an incoming call from Beau Buschini, the bureau chief in Moscow, updating him on developments. He stated that his sources were unable to confirm Pushkin's cause of death, and that they were waiting for the outcome of the autopsy later in the day.

Gizelle buzzed his internal phone announcing that President Trent wanted to speak with Barnaby immediately, so he ended the call with Beau and took the call. Rafael excused himself, and made his way towards the toilet to relieve himself, understanding that any conversation with the President was confidential.

'Hello, Mr. President.'

'I take it that you have seen the report that Pushkin has been found dead in his office Barnaby?' said the President.

'Yes sir, I am up to date on that.'

'Please confirm that the CIA has not been involved in any way whatsoever, Barnaby?'

Trying as best he could not to lie to the President he said, 'from what I have been told by our bureau chief in Moscow, the Reds are unsure how he died, and they hope that an autopsy will put more light on the cause.' 'Someone in Russia may have killed him, however, we have no evidence of that at all right now.' 'Our bureau chief will get back to me as soon as he has managed to find out more.'

'I think it would be advisable to issue a statement of condolence to his family, as well as the Russian people,' continued Barnaby trying as best he could to not answer the question.

'Yes, I intend to call Lacrov shortly, and will issue a statement to the Russian people expressing our sympathy.' 'So Barnaby, I want an assurance that the CIA is not involved in any way whatsoever, because if your guys are involved, the consequences will be dire indeed.'

'As soon as I have any information regarding his death, I will call you Mr. President.' he said sidestepping the question again.

As the President ended the call, he thought to himself that Barnaby had cleverly avoided answering his question, and pondered whether the CIA could have been involved at all. These guys are good at what they do, and this clandestine organization moves in the shadows, so if they were involved in some way or another, he hoped like hell it never sees daylight.

The CIA has succeeded in disposing or killing a string of world leaders in the past. The organization had targeted the Congo's first Prime Minister Patrice Lumumba, and sent a scientist to kill him with a lethal virus in nineteen-sixty, however, he was removed from office by other means. They also targeted the Dominican dictator Rafael Trujillo, President Sukarno of Indonesia, and President Ngo Dinh Diem of South Vietnam. Various other influential people were also involved in the overthrow of Chile's President Salvador Allende in nineteen seventy-three, however, he died on the day of the coup that they had organized. President Gerald Ford signed an executive order in nineteen seventy-six, ordering that no employee of the United States Government shall engage in, or conspire in, any political assignation. Seems that the CIA had ignored this order on several occasions.

The Russian media were speculating whether the CIA had any involvement in Pushkin's death, however, stopped short of accusing America of any involvement. Barnaby switched to the Foxtel channel just as reports of the sudden death of Mikhail Andreev, Alexei Belov, and Sacha Novikov were being aired. All three were part of Pushkin's inner circle of advisors, and it now became evident that all four had been poisoned, so the hunt was in full swing for those responsible. The Russian media immediately switched to a news conference being held by Dimir Lacrov the Russian Foreign Minister, who had just announced the death of these three people, and claimed all had been poisoned. Lacrov claimed that it was an attack on mother Russia, and whoever was responsible would face the full brunt of the Russian military might.

There was a media frenzy in Russia as people spilled out onto the streets in support of the government, and clashed with protesters that were rejoicing at the news of Pushkin's death. Lacrov declared a state of emergency in Moscow, as images of police brutally beating those rejoicing at the news of Pushkin's death, was being aired on Russian television.

All the major television networks reported the sudden deaths of Pushkin's three advisors, stating that it was clear that all had been poisoned.

'Clearly, there has been foul play,' stated Lacrov, as he addressed another news conference. All four appear to have died of apparent heart attacks in their sleep, and all on the same day, so there is no doubt that they have been poisoned.

Victor had just returned from a hiking trip to the Big Horn Mountains of Buffalo Wyoming, and stopped at the local bar for a beer. Having taken the first mouth full of beer, his attention was drawn to the breaking news on television. The breaking news story of the day, was the sudden death of the Russian President, and his three advisors being aired on Fox News. He listened intently to the news conference by the Russian Foreign Minister Lacrov, who had just stated that it was clear that all four had been poisoned, and that they would not leave any stone unturned in the hunt for those guilty of killing their beloved President.

He sat quietly watching the reporter speculate on what had happened, and how it was possible for someone or some organization to have been able to poison the President. The reporter stated that the three advisors had regularly attended meetings in President Pushkin's office every Friday evening, so naturally, the suspicion fell on anybody that had access to his office, including catering and cleaning staff. Lacrov said, that an investigation was underway to identify the person or persons responsible, and that they would apprehend those guilty of perpetrating this terrible crime, be it a person, an organization, a government or a group of people.

Victor's thoughts turned to Evgeni Varkov, the old man that made the special brew of Vodka that Pushkin loved, and wondered what would happen to him. No doubt, they would eventually interrogate him, and most likely conclude that he was guilty of placing poison in the Vodka. Sadly he will die a horrible death. He considered that his death would not be in vain, albeit that he was innocent, and concluded that it would be collateral damage.

He downed his bear in one gulp and ordered a quadruple Vodka on the rocks. 'Na zdarovye,' cheers, he whispered to himself downing the Vodka, and ordering another as he wanted to celebrate the drink with his murdered uncle, his uncle's wife, and his two nieces.

Fucking bastard, may you rot in hell, he thought, smiling broadly.

Gizelle notified Barnaby that the President wanted to see him immediately, so he made his way downstairs, and into the waiting Black SUV with his detail accompanying him to the White House.

'Hello Barnaby,' said the President waiving him to a seat on the couch.

'No doubt you have also heard of the news, that three of Pushkin's inner circle have also died, so we can assume that Lacrov may be correct when he said that they may have been poisoned.' 'I am sure that autopsies will determine the cause of death, however, Ivan may never release that Barnaby.'

'So I want absolute honesty.' 'Is the CIA involved in any way whatsoever?'

Barnaby had to once again dodge the question, as he could not lie to the President.

'Mr. President, we both know that it is impossible to get anywhere near Pushkin, so from where I sit, clearly the Reds have found a way to get rid of him themselves, and no doubt they will blame the CIA and America as usual.'

'I think it would be advisable to keep our troops, as well as NATO's troops on high alter because it is impossible to predict what Lacrov may do.'

'We at the CIA have long considered a possible successor to Pushkin if ever he lost power, and whilst Lacrov is calling the shots for the moment, I am of the view that he will be forced to release Alexei Navalny from prison.'

'I think the dynamics in Russia could change dramatically shortly, and hopefully for the better if they go to a general election and Navalny wins.'

'Mr. President, our Intel indicates that this is a possibility, and to be honest, if Navalny is elected, we believe that he would seek a better relationship with all westernized countries.' 'We know that there have been rumblings about getting rid of Pushkin for years, so I believe that somebody in Russia has managed to get close to Pushkin and his inner circle, and possibly poison them, that's if that is what they have died of.'

'Seems like the most feasible answer for now, however, let's wait and see what the outcome of the autopsy's will be,' 'Well Sir, no matter what happened, I think that the world will be relieved that it is rid of this madman,' stated Barnaby candidly.

'Should they release Navalny, then I think we should throw our full support behind him, and ensure that he gets elected.'

The President merely stared at Barnaby. This bugger has not answered my question, and keeps on skirting around it. I have to admit, he and the CIA are efficient at what they do, so maybe I should just let things just play out, thought the President. The President ordered Barnaby to follow him to the situation room, and as they entered the room all the security advisors stood as a sign of respect.

'Please be seated,' responded the President.

General Mitchfield was the first to offer a comment.

'Mr. President, we have noticed that the Russians have placed their forces on high alert, so I think it advisable that we do the same.'

President Trent thought long and hard before responding.

'No, I think we will just wait and see, albeit that our forces should be put on standby just in case.' 'Placing them on high alert would indicate that the USA is involved in the killing of Pushkin and his three mates.' 'I have been assured by Director Heathcott that the CIA is not involved, therefore we can assume that someone, or some group in Russia has managed to kill Pushkin and his inner circle.'

Continuing he said, 'I intend calling Lacrov shortly, to express my, and the nation's condolences to their families as well as the Russian nation.'

They watched various television stations broadcasting the events unfolding in Russia, and several commentators seemed to be rejoicing at the news of Pushkin, and his three advisors having been eliminated.

'Clearly, the Russians have had enough of him,' stated a commentator from CNN.

'The world is hoping that whoever takes over from Pushkin will seek a more engaging position with the west, and hopefully will end the hostilities that exist,' continued the commentator.

Images of wild celebrations around the globe were being aired on various channels as people spilled out onto the streets, expressing their joy, and happiness at the news of Pushkin's death.

Lacrov placed the military on high alert, and ordered the Russian police, the Politsiya to stamp out any unrest and violent demonstrations in the country. Images of the Politsiya brutally beating up members of the public that were celebrating the death of Pushkin and his three henchmen played out across international television channels.

President Trent convened a video conference with NATO, and world leaders, urging them all to order their military to be on standby, however, suggested that the west remain calm, and not up the ante. He did not wish to inflame an already volatile situation, and assured world leaders that the USA was not involved in the elimination of Pushkin and his three advisors. It is widely believed that some person or organization within Russia had somehow managed to infiltrate Pushkin's the inner circle and terminate them.

Lacrov declared a state of emergency across the whole of Russia, and convened another conference. He announced that the autopsies performed on the President as well as those performed on comrades Mikhail Andreev, Alexei Belov, and Sacha Novikov all revealed that they had been poisoned by something that they had consumed. They could only have died because someone had managed to lace their drinks with a type of poison, or possibly had somehow managed to insert a poison into something they had eaten. He stressed that they would identify the type of poison shortly and bring the person, persons, group, or government responsible to justice, stressing once again, and issuing a warning of the dire consequences for anyone found guilty of this crime.

'We are currently investigating how this was able to be administered without having been picked up, and when we catch whoever is responsible, the person or persons will face the full might of mother Russia.' 'We will not rest until we bring the guilty person or persons to justice, and we cannot discount the involvement of the American Imperialist CIA.'

'If it is found to be the CIA, then that is tantamount to an act of war.' 'I will assume the role of President for the immediate future until we have concluded the investigation, then the country will go to a general election.'

'I again wish to stress to our enemies, not to try to take advantage of the situation, because our army has been mobilized, and we are ready to counter any aggression by NATO and the west.'

Chapter 18

le Creusot

France

Claire, laid her head on Yonti's chest listening to his beating heart. It was pounding in his chest after having made love to her for the second time that evening. He ran his hand gently over her blond hair as both slowly regained their breath. Their lovemaking still had the passion, and lust it had when they first made love, however, had settled into a more consistent routine, similar to people that have been married for many years.

'I think it's time we took a break and went on a vacation, Claire.' 'Maybe somewhere idyllic and romantic, possibly an island.'

'That's a great idea Yonti,' she said lifting he head, and using his family name.

She was the only one that used his real name in private, as he had assumed various under-cover names on many missions, and was known as Rafael within the CIA and to Embassy staff in Paris.

'I have a great place in mind that is picturesque, romantic, and want to keep it as a surprise.'

'Brilliant, I will leave it up to you to organize handsome.'

The screen on Yonti's mobile phone lit us with an incoming call from Barnaby Heathcott at CIA headquarters in Virginia USA.

'Hello, Director.'

'Hi Rafael, have you seen the news,' questioned Barnaby.

'No sir, I have not,' he replied reminding himself of the need to use his CIA name yet again.

'Well young man, switch on your television, and you will see that the French have a major problem.' 'There has been a major derailment on the TGV train line, and from what I have seen, a high-speed train has derailed possibly killing a couple of hundred people,' continued Barnaby.

'The French authorities have requested our assistance, so I suggest you get in contact with Capitaine Pétit, and try to establish whether this is possibly a terrorist-related incident,' 'I will monitor things from our end, and let you know what I have found Rafa.'

'Yes sir, I will report back as soon as I know anything Director.'

He switched on the television, and stared at the wreckage of the TGV high-speed train, known widely as "Train à Grande Vitesse", meaning high-speed train in France. The TGV train is among the most popular transportation modes in France. Carriages were strewn over a wide section of the track, and some carriages appear to have collided with an overhead bridge. Mangled wreckage was strewn all over the tracks. Images of emergency workers were being displayed on the screen with helicopter ambulances landing near the scene, and multiple first responders attempting to find and rescue any survivors.

'Sweet Jesus in heaven, how did this happen,' he whispered, as he realized that there were most likely a couple of hundred people on board at the time.

'I hope that this is not a terrorist incident,' he said as he turned to look at Claire.

A moment later the display on his mobile phone lit up again with an incoming call from Capitaine Pétit of the French Police.

'Bonjour Monsieur Jon, have you seen what has happened to the TGV train en Route from Paris to Marseille,' asked Bastienne.

'Oui Capitaine, I have just received a call from Director Heathcott notifying me of the incident, and I am watching it on television right now.'

'We have requested any assistance that the CIA can offer, and Director Heathcott has offered you to assist, so I hope that you will agree to accompany us to the site immediately Jon,' said Bastienne.

Continuing he said, 'I need to be sure that this is not terrorist related.'

'Oui Captiane, you can count on me.'

'There will be a car waiting for you outside Claire's apartment in ten minutes Jon, and thank you.'

He realized that he had to use the alias of Jon that he always used when dealing with anybody in France, quickly got dressed, kissed Claire goodbye, then made his way downstairs and into the waiting patrol car.

'So, this is what we have so far,' said Bastienne pointing to the monitor on the wall.

Satellite images depicted the carnage, and mangled wreckage of the train.

'As we understand it from the information provided by SNCF, which is the acronym for Société Nationale des Chemins de fer Français, the French National Railways, there were one- hundred, and eighty-five passengers on board when the accident happened.' 'We do not know a final count of fatalities yet,' continued Bastienne.

The train route from Paris to Marseille passes through the industrial town and commune of Le Creusot in the Saône-et-Loire department, region of Bourgogne-Franche-Comté, eastern France. Inhabitants are known as Creusotins which was formerly a mining town. Its economy is now dominated by metallurgical companies such as ArcelorMittal, Schneider Electric, and Alstom.

The derailment occurred twenty miles from the town on a curved section of the rail close to an overhead bridge.

'One can assume it will be horrific because the train would have been traveling at around one hundred and seventy miles per hour at the time.' 'Of concern, is that the satellite images seem to have detected two people doing something on the tracks sometime before the train was due to pass, taking a turn to the left, then derailed crashing into the overhead bridge.' 'Thankfully the CIA has provided us with images of the scene, so let's take the time to study it,' said Bastienne.

The monitors on the wall in the control room displayed images of the crash site being beamed by various television stations with reporters stating that possibly one or two hundred people could have perished in the accident. Bastienne and Jon turned their attention to the satellite images provided by the CIA. The images of two people that appeared to be working on the track came into view. Jon asked the IT technician to zoom in for a closer look, and it appeared that these two were regular track workers carrying out scheduled maintenance, so Jon asked the technician to replay the image, and asked him to freeze the image.

It seemed that the two workers were tampering with the rail approximately two hundred yards from the overhead bridge.

'Freeze it please, and zoom in further,' instructed Jon.

'There, what are those two workers doing?' he said pointing to them on the monitor.

The frozen image depicted two workers seemingly doing regular maintenance on the track, however as the video rolled on, it appeared that they were removing the railway ties along the line, just as the track curved to the left, some two hundred yards from the overhead bridge.

The support technician rolled the video several times, and it became evident that these workers were not inspecting the track, rather they were tampering with it. Removing the ties along a stretch of line, especially where the track curves would result in the line buckling outwards as a train sped over it, causing a derailment with catastrophic consequences.

Bastienne called the SNFC head office, and requested to be transferred to the maintenance supervisor. A short while later he was patched through.

'Bonjour, Monsieur Toussaint parlant,' hello, Mr. Toussaint speaking.

'Bonjour Monsieur Toussaint, this is Capitaine Bastienne Pétit of the French Police.' 'I would like any information you can give me regarding the two maintenance workers that were working on the line before the derailment.'

Continuing, he said, 'I want to review their employment contracts, their maintenance schedules over the past twelve months, their home addresses, and any other contact information you can gather on them.' 'One of my associates will pick up the information from you in thirty minutes.'

'Merci Monsieur Toussaint, Au revoir,' said Bastienne as he ended the call.

He looked at the pictures of the rescue effort being beamed by various television stations, and felt a tinge of hatred for whoever perpetrated this terrible deed. This is not an accident that is a result of a lack of maintenance or negligence, it is due to two people deliberately sabotaging the rail lines he concluded. Going to find these two bastards, and kill them he thought.

Bastienne and Jon were airlifted to the scene by helicopter, and immediately went about examining the track for clues to establish exactly what had happened.

Pointing to the track, Jon turned to Bastienne and said, 'see, the ties have been removed in this curved section of the track for about two to three hundred yards.'

Pointing to a section of track, he said, 'it starts right here, which is about three hundred yards from the bridge so a train passing over the line at the speed such as the TGV train, it would push the track outwards as there are no ties in place to secure the line, resulting in the derailment.'

Continuing, he stated, 'I am convinced that this is sabotage, and the two guys we identified on the video images sent to us by Director Heathcott, has identified those two as the guilty ones.' 'We need to find these bastards and kill them,' said Jon as he scanned the debris field.

Back at police headquarters two hours later, Bastienne accessed the folder containing the names, addresses, and maintenance schedules of the two people he had requested.

'So these are the two people we are interested in, Monsieur's Tareq Ebeid and Qdai Ismat,' said Bastienne.

Both have been maintenance workers employed by SNFC for eight years, and their annual reviews indicated that they were reliable, outstanding employees. They had never been late for work nor missed a day's work in their ten years of service. Tareq Edeid had been promoted to Line Foreman a year previously due to his exceptional work ethic, and the two formed a maintenance crew tasked with track maintenance. Both had performed admirably over several years.

Bastienne closed the folder, and turned to face Jon. 'These two are not at the scene of the derailment right now which is suspicious, and they appear to have simply disappeared right after the disaster.'

He asked the technician to fire up the footage of the two suspects supposedly carrying out the track maintenance, and watched as they left the track. They headed towards a service road that runs alongside the track, and jumped into a parked car which appeared to have a driver sitting in it, apparently waiting for them, then they sped off in the opposite direction to which the train was traveling.

'Can you zoom in on the number plate of the vehicle so that we can try to get a fix on it,' instructed Bastienne?

'Well it is unclear, but I can ask our forensic team to try to enhance the image for you,' replied the technician.

'Thanks, I need it ASAP,' stressed Bastienne.

Thirty minutes later the technician laid a photograph of the number plate of the vehicle on the table and Bastienne was able to identify the numbers on the plate. Got you, you fucking bastards he thought.

'Right Jon, we have the details of the owner of the car, so let's get his address and go pay this prick a visit,' said Bastienne.

The address registered to the license plate of the vehicle was at Seine-Saint-Denis, which is located northeast of Paris and deemed as a "No-Go Area" Muslim enclave housing around three hundred thousand illegal alien immigrants. Seine-Saint-Denis is six miles from the Eiffel Tower, and the area is known as the "jihadi capital of France." Saint Denis is home to the Basilica which holds the resting place of many French kings and queens. The sounds of mosque loudspeakers, and smells of halal food are everywhere. The rule of French law, equality, and religious freedom are nowhere to be found.

There are an estimated one-hundred and thirty-five different nationalities in Saint-Denis. Most are extremely poor, including around six-hundred thousand Muslims from North Africa or Sub-Saharan African backgrounds. Muslim girls aged three to four years of age are dressed in headscarves, veils, and long clothing. Most people rely on the "black economy" to earn money. It is estimated that as many as four-hundred and twenty- thousand legal residents live below the official poverty line in the area with an official population in Saint-Denis of one million, five-hundred thousand.

Rue the day we let these murderous bastards into our country thought Bastienne.

'So this is the place that breeds jihadism,' said Bastienne pointing to the image of an apartment block.

Batienne and Jon donned overalls with the EUC Electricity Utility company logo on them, and drove towards the address shown on the license plate using the same van they used when they eliminated the two terrorists in a remote barn house at Anvin Pas De Calais months previously. They placed a long ladder against a power pole, sat down to enjoy a cup of coffee, and waited for some time until they saw the old beaten-up Citroen pull up outside an apartment complex.

Basteinne checked the number plate, and confirmed that they had located the correct vehicle.

'OK, that must be the driver,' said Jon pointing towards a middle-aged man as he exited the Citroen, and watched as he made his way up the stairs of the apartment block.

Jon activated the remote on the camera hidden in the van so that he could record images of the driver and double-checked the number plate to verify that they had the correct vehicle. He hoped that the two railway workers would show up, so they stowed the ladder, and waited for a couple of hours until later in the afternoon when the driver reappeared. He got into the Citroen, and drove towards "bois de Boulogne," a slum area on the outskirts of Paris. People living in Paris slums are immigrants that come from different countries like Tunisia, Romania, Bulgaria, Yugoslavia, and many others. They don't speak the same language, and don't have the same beliefs, however, even though they come from various countries, there is a majority of Roms in the area.

They followed the Citroen, and watched as the driver turned into a parking lot at the local Lendit market, one of the largest markets in the region of Paris lle-de-France consisting of three-hundred stalls. Bastienne parked further down the road, and watched proceedings through his rearview mirror. Jon jumped out of the van, and followed the driver as he meandered his way through various stalls, stopping to buy fresh vegetables before finally making his way back to his car.

As he unlocked the car, Jon positioned his Glock against the small of his back.

'Bonjour Monsieur, what is your name,' asked Jon?

'Mahmoud Khan,' he replied.

Bastienne was alongside a moment later, instructed the driver to get into the car as Jon made his way around the vehicle, and jumped into the passenger's side.

'Right Mahmoud, drive towards the exit, and wait for my instructions,' said Jon.

Continuing he said, 'follow that van.'

A short while later they turned into the same warehouse where they had dumped the bodies of the other terrorists, and the driver parked behind the van. Bastienne pulled the driver out of the car, and pushed him towards the side of the warehouse. There was an unmistakable odor of decomposing bodies coming from the bin in the corner, due to over eight-hundred chemicals that make up the smell of death according to a forensic anthropologist at the University of Huddersfield in England. About four-hundred and eighty have been identified for human death alone.

'So, Mahmoud, you can smell the decomposing bodies no doubt, therefore you had best tell me everything I want to know, or you will soon join them,' said Jon.

'You picked up the two railway workers thirty minutes before the TGV derailed at a section of the line where they were working, then drove them away from the scene in a hurry, and dropped them off somewhere,' said Bastienne.

'How am I doing so far?'

'Oh, I forgot, the two you picked up are Monsieur Tareq Ebeid and Qdai Ismat, so I will only give you one opportunity to tell me the truth, and if you don't, well, you will feel a great deal of pain,' continued Bastienne.

Jon fired up the laptop, and replayed the video of images of Mahmoud picking up Tareq and Qdai on the service road alongside the track.

'See we have a video of you at the scene.' 'It seems you forgot to smile for the camera, and if you look closely, you can even see your Citroens number plate displayed, so as the police Capitaine said, where did you take these two bastards that have killed a couple of hundred innocent people?' said Jon forcefully as he smashed his fist into Mahmoud's face.

Mahmoud fell backward, hitting his head on the concrete.

Dazed with blood streaming out of his broken nose he said, 'I dropped them at Charles de Gaulle international airport.'

'Oh, you did and why did you do that?' questioned Jon.

'Because they caught a flight,' said Mahmoud.

'Where are they flying to?' questioned Jon.

'They caught a flight to Islamabad,' answered Mahmoud reluctantly.

'And when they get there, where will they go,' questioned Jon.

'I don't know, my instructions were to pick them up and drive them to the airport,' said Mahmoud.

'Who instructed you to do that Mahmoud?' asked Jon, as he grabbed him by the throat.

Choking, he said, 'Muzaffar Ghanem.'

'So where does Monsieur Ghanem live and work?' pressed Jon.

'He owns a stall selling fruit, vegetables, and spices at Rue de Grenelle Market in the fifteenth arrondissement near the seventh, across from Champ de Mars.' 'His stall is called Oriental Fruit and Vegetables,' volunteered Mahmoud.

'So how will I recognize Monsieur Ghanem and where does he live?' questioned Jon.

'He is an old man, and always wears a black long-sleeve Jubba Thobe Kaftan with a black skull cap, and has a long grey beard.' 'He usually sits on a stool at the entrance to his store near the spice section, and he lives at the back of his stall,' volunteered Mahmoud.

'Can I go now?' asked Mahmoud.

'No, you can't.' 'How come you are involved in this mess?' questioned Jon.

'Monsieur Ghanem offered me two thousand francs to pick them up, and drive them to the airport,' said Mahmoud.

'I see, so I want to show you something before we send you on your way to meet your buddies in the Promised Land,' said Bastienne grabbing him by the collar, and marching him towards the dumpster.

The stench of decomposing bodies was unbearable as they got closer to the dumpster, and Mahmoud started trembling as he realized his fate. He begged for mercy, offering to forfeit his payment.

'Please, I am only the driver, and did not commit a crime,' begged Mahmoud.

Bastienne, picked him up and threw him into the dumpster, pulled the Glock from the rear of his pants, and shot Mahmoud in the temple. He shut the dumpster, and they made a hasty exit as the stench was unbearable.

Jon called Director Heathcott on a secure line at CIA headquarters.

'Hello Director, I have Capitaine Pétit alongside me,' he said.

Realizing that, Barnaby reverted to the undercover name that Rafael was using whilst in France.

'Hello, Jon, and hello Capitaine, what have you managed to find out,' questioned Barnaby.

'We captured the driver of the getaway car, interrogated him, and he confirmed that he dropped the two people we saw working on the track at the airport.' 'They apparently caught a flight to Islamabad, so can you have some of your people follow them when they land in about four hours from now.' 'The flight time is around eleven hours, and they caught the PIA, Pakistan International Airways flight PK750 a few hours ago,' said Jon.

It was almost midnight when Jon and Bastienne made their way into the Rue de Grenelle Market. They parked a few blocks away, making their way to the Oriental Fruit and Vegetable stall owned by Muzaffar. The place was deserted, and they noticed a dim light coming from the stall, and heard the old man conversing with someone on this mobile phone.

Bastienne scouted the area, ensuring that they had not been followed or were being monitored, and watched as Jon quietly approached the stall. Jon placed his Glock against the old man's head and shot him.

Have to admire his work, thought Bastienne, as Jon emerged.

'Right lets the fuck out of here,' said Jon.

Back at police headquarters, they accessed the international airport security footage and from what we had seen these two gentlemen, namely Tareq Ebeid and Qdai Ismat were still dressed in their orange high-vis jackets.

Both were carrying, dark green carry-on sling bags, and immigration has confirmed that neither checked in any luggage,' continued Jon.

'Director, they may have changed clothing, however, I doubt that, so I will send you the photographs of them that we got from SNFC, the French National Railways, and hope that your people in Islamabad can identify and follow them when they land,' said Jon.

'Thanks, Jon, I will get onto it right away, and you and Capitaine Pétit should prepare for a trip to Pakistan,' said Barnaby as he ended the call.

Flight PK750 landed in Islamabad on time, and forty-five minutes later Tareq and Qdai emerged from the international arrivals hall having cleared customs. A CIA operative by the name of Souma Haq was seated, pretending to be reading messages on his mobile phone, however, he was studying the photographs of the two males sent to him from CIA headquarters in Virginia. Neither suspects bothered to change clothing, nor had they discarded their orange Hi-Viz workwear vests making them easily identifiable.

He watched as the two suspects were greeted by a middle-aged man, then made their way towards a parked car and jumped in. Souma called a fellow operative who had parked his motorbike on the side of the road exiting the airport, and notified him of the type of car and color that the two suspects were traveling in. He jumped onto his bike, and made his way onto the motorway maintaining a reasonable distance behind the car in which the two terrorists were traveling for around twenty miles. His fellow agent positioned himself slightly ahead of the vehicle, keeping a watchful eye on the car in his rearview mirror as they made their way towards Faisalabad which was formerly known as Lyallpur. The city was named after the founder of the city is the third-most-populous city in Pakistan after Karachi and Lahore respectively. It is the second-largest in the eastern province of Punjab.

The car turned onto a gravel road, and headed towards a remote village on the outskirts of Jaranwala which is one of the historic, and beautiful Punjab provincial cities in Pakistan. The eastern boundary of the city borders Nankana sahib while Sangla hills are located in the south and the northeast, where the village of Sir Ganga Ram, Gangapur, is situated. Canals surround the city, and it is one of the famous and largest Tehsils (districts) of Faisalabad but Pakistan.

Moreover, the city is almost 400 years old, and its history is recorded on the famous 100-year-old historical monument, Pakistan gate. The village was considered to be the most modern of its time, and the car with the two suspects in it, eventually pulled up at a rural contemporary dwelling and stopped. The house was made of straw and clay. Both operatives continued down the road on the motorbikes, before stopping a mile further down the road at a roadside food stall. They ordered a helping of Haleem which is considered to be the "king of curry" in Pakistan, wrapped in Mitho lolo, the traditional local Sindhi flatbread accompanied with a cup of tea, and settled down to enjoy the meal.

Souma dialed Director Heathcott, and notified him that had followed the suspects, and gave him the GPS coordinates. Barnaby ordered Souma to dismiss his assistant and leave. He arranged for Souma to meet the inbound Emirates flight EK72 from Paris the next day.

The flight departed from Charles De Gaulle international on time. Jon and Bastienne made themselves as comfortable as possible in the crowded cattle class for the thirteen-hour flight to Faisalabad. They ordered a couple of beers, and having enjoyed the evening meal, both settled in for the long flight, trying as best they could to get some shut-eye.

As they cleared customs and made their way into the arrivals hall, agent Souma greeted them by name indicating for them to follow him as he led the way to a Honda Bolan van, one of the most commonly seen vehicles on the roads of Pakistan. They loaded their gear in the rear cargo compartment, hopped in, and were introduced to the driver, a fellow operative by the name of Joud Yousef.

He dropped them off at the Deluxe Comfort Inn a four-star hotel situated in the center of the city, and Souma informed them that he would pick them up at zero nine-hundred hours the next morning.

Later that evening, Jon and Bastienne were sitting in the bar enjoying a cold beer, when Jon turned to face Bastienne and said, 'did you notice Capitaine?'

'Oui Monsieur Jon, I noticed that the driver seemed a little nervous, and kept looking at us in the rearview mirror which I thought was a little strange.'

'Glad you noticed it as well, so I think we best keep an eye on him, my friend.'

'Good morning gentlemen,' offered Souma as they jumped into the van the next morning.

He handed them a picture of the clay hut, and said that they would need to be careful as the locals would deem them suspicious because of their European looks. They are weary of strangers so they would need to be on high alert. Jon took note of the direction they were headed, and studied the driver more closely, watching the image of his face in the rearview mirror. The driver constantly glanced at Jon and Bastienne in the rearview mirror which troubled him.

Thirty minutes later, the driver turned onto a gravel road, and headed towards the hut that the two suspects had entered the previous day, slowing as they passed. Souma pointed it out to Jon and Bastienne. The driver continued towards the food stall about a mile further down the road, then pulled up and stopped to order a cup of tea.

The driver went to relieve himself and Souma opened the cargo door. He handed Jon and Bastienne a Glock each, fitted with a silencer, and five clips of ammunition. Jon removed the magazine and cocked the weapon removing the round in the chamber. He checked the weapon before cocking it again and pulling the trigger to ensure that it worked, then removed all the rounds from the magazine and counted them to ensure that it was full, before replacing them, and inserting it into the gun. He cocked the weapon ensuring that it was ready to be fired, and placed the spare clips in his pocket, before putting the Glock into the back of his pants.

He watched as Souma ordered tea, and leaned over to Basteinne and whispered, 'I don't trust this driver so we had both better keep a close eye on him.'

Joud seemed to have been away for a prolonged period, so Jon took a walk in the same direction that he had taken, and stood behind a tree. He watched the driver who was speaking with someone on his mobile phone. This bastard is warning someone that we are here, he thought, so he made his way back to where Bastienne was leaning casually against the Honda.

'I think we can expect a welcoming party soon because I think this driver is a rat.' 'I saw him speaking with someone on his phone, so check that your weapon is loaded and ready, because I think the fireworks are about to begin.'

Joud, the driver returned and appeared to be on edge, so Jon turned to face him, and put his right hand behind his back, firmly gripping the Glock hidden in the back of his pants.   He kept his eye on the driver, and a short time later, two people arrived on a motorcycle. Jon noticed that the passenger held a gun, so he shouted to Bastienne and Souma to take cover, just as the passenger opened fire. Jon dove for cover, extracted the Glock and shot the gunman twice in succession in the head, and as the motorcycle driver tried to turn the bike around and flee, Bastienne shot him three times. Joud extracted a handgun, and fired wildly in their direction. Souma, quickly returned fire killing him instantly.

The motorcycle catapulted sideways, and Jon instantly ordered Souma and Bastienne to get into the Honda, and high tail it out of there.

He turned to Bastienne, 'I am not sure, but I managed to get a look at the driver of the motorcycle, and I am almost sure that he is one of the two that caused the train to derail.'

'Yes Monsieur Jon, I am also sure that the one I shot was his accomplice.'

Chapter 19

London

England

Rafael stared at the photographs of the former Directors of the CIA hanging on the wall in Barnaby's office, and wondered what secrets these people had held close to their chests for many decades.

'Well, thanks to your successful mission to Tver, let's hope that whoever will be in charge of Russia changes direction for the better.' 'Thankfully the world is rid of Pushkin, and as I have said a number of times, let's pray that the Russians never find out that the CIA was involved, and that we are never implicated, because you and I, will spend the rest of our lives incarcerated.' 'This secret must be taken to the grave by you, Victor, Joseph and myself.' 'We now need to wait to see what the future holds, and we can only hope that whoever takes over from Pushkin, will foster a new beginning for Russia and the world,' said Barnaby.

'There is always another challenge, and we need to concentrate on this new threat.' 'A new group has raised its head, called "Almawt Lilkufaar," meaning "Death to Infidels" in Arabic, and it appears that there are six members in this group.' 'They intend to carry out mass murder in each country, namely the UK, the USA, and France.'

'All in that order.' 'I understand that they have split into groups of two, hoping that this will not draw attention to what they intend to do.' 'Seems that each time we identify one of the fanatical groups, and eliminate the threat, another rears its head.'

'Our intelligence, in conjunction with our Israeli friends in Mossad, have uncovered the names of the two people currently living in England that are tasked with the responsibly of carrying out an unimaginable atrocity on English soil.' 'The two that we have identified in England are Anwar Abadi and his cousin Jabir Osman.'

'So, from what our intelligence sources have managed to uncover thus far, it appears that the group is planning several terrorist attacks in the UK, France, and the USA.' 'It appears that they are planning attacks on civilians because they know that this will give them maximum exposure, and result in a mass panic amongst the public in these three countries,' said Barnaby.

Continuing he said, 'the first attack is planned to coincide with the Trooping of the Colour that starts at Buckingham Palace marking the celebration of the Queen's birthday which takes place on a Saturday in June each year in London.' 'This has been a British tradition for over two-hundred and sixty years, when over one thousand four-hundred soldiers parade, accompanied by two-hundred horses including some four-hundred musicians in a great display of military precision, horsemanship, and fanfare, marking the Queen's official birthday.'

'The Streets are lined with tens of thousands of people waving flags as the parade moves from Buckingham Palace, and down the Mall to Horse Guard's Parade alongside members of the Royal Family on horseback and carriages.' 'The display closes with an RAF fly-past that is watched by the Royal Family from the Buckingham Palace balcony.'

'The second attack is planned for Independence Day in the USA which as we all know is the fourth of July, and as we understand it, they will target civilians at the Washington Monument where traditionally hundreds of thousands of people gather to enjoy the festivities, culminating in a massive fireworks display in the evening,' said Barnaby.

'And lastly, the third attack is planned to take place at the end of the Tour de France as the riders make their way towards the finish line, which takes place on the eighteenth of July on the Champs-Élysées, in Paris,' 'Traditionally there are hundreds of thousands of spectators gathered along this part of the route, with massive celebrations planned on the day.'

'Clearly, they aim to maximize the impact, and make people believe that they can strike anywhere and at any time, causing mass panic,' stated Barnaby candidly.

'So if one considers the significance of the targets that they have chosen, there is no doubt they have chosen well, and one would have to admit, that should they be successful in carrying out any of these attacks, they will have achieved their objective.' 'I remind you that these fanatics adhere to calls from Allah, and believe that he has Islamic leaders, seeking to motivate would-be suicide bombers, inciting them to murder in the name of Allah.' 'The Qur'an, quoting Islamic sources, promises 72 Virgins in Paradise to those who kill, and are killed in Jihad for Allah.'

Many Muslims, especially those exposed to Western culture, are aware of the jokes, and the ridicule that the 72 Virgins legend has brought upon them, and upon their brother believers. Consequently, they blame the Jews for spreading the myth in an attempt to downgrade the image of the Islamic "freedom fighters".

Despite the disclaimer by some Muslims, the truth is very clear. The *72 Virgins* notion has its origins in the Qur'an. Although the holy book does not specify the number as 72, it does say, that those who fight in the way of Allah, and are killed, will be given a great reward. It goes on to stipulate that Muslims will be awarded women in Islamic heaven. It even describes their physical attributes—large eyes (Q 56:22) and big, firm, round "swelling breasts" that are not inclined to sag (Q 78:33). The Qur'an refers to these virgins as houri, companions of equal age, but the highly-flavored emphasis of their bodily characteristics, including their virginity, gave rise to many hadiths and other Islamic writings.

Hadith 2687, is where the number 72 is mentioned. "The smallest reward for the people of Heaven is an abode where there are eighty-thousand servants and 72 houri, over which stands a dome decorated with pearls".

'So, I have informed the British, French, and FBI authorities as well as keeping Mossad in the loop, and I am sure that all agencies will do everything in their power to stop this madness.' 'The British and French have been offered our assistance which they have gladly accepted, hence our meeting today Rafa.'

'I believe that Mossad has been tracking this group for some time, since they are affiliated with al Qaeda, and the Israeli authorities believe that they may well be planning a terrorist attack in Jerusalem shortly, so we need to neutralize them as soon as possible Rafa.'

'I have planned for you to fly to London in our Gulf Stream leaving later this evening, and meet with the heads of Scotland Yard, Metropolitan Police, National Crime Agency, Specialist Operations, as well as MI5 security Service scheduled for tomorrow evening, at twenty-hundred hours at the head office of MI5 at Thames House, 12 Millbank, London.'

Barnaby fired up his computer, and beamed the names of the security officials in the UK onto a monitor on the wall. He reminded himself that he only had three days to intercept these two suspects, and nullify whatever plot they intended to carry out.

Rafael stared at the names on the wall headed by the Ministry for Home Security-Sir John Anderson

The heads of the agencies are: -

MI5-Director General Ken McCullum

Scotland Yard-Ms. Cresida Dick

Metropolitan Police- Sir Stephen House

National Crime Agency-Graeme Biggar

Specialist Operations-Assistant Matt Jukes

'These are the people responsible for security in the United Kingdom, and are the people you will be meeting,' said Barnaby.

Continuing he said, 'we need to apprehend or eliminate these radical people Rafael, however, I wish to inform you that the British are not in favor of eliminating people.' 'On the contrary, they believe in apprehending anyone that has, or is about to commit a crime in their country, and charge them.' 'Stiff upper lip way of doing things in the UK old boy, as the saying goes over there.'

Later that evening Rafael made his way up the staircase of the CIA's Gulf Stream, and was met at the door by the Co-Pilot.

'Bonjour Monsieur, long time no see,' offered the Co-Pilot as he closed the door.

'Oui, it's been a long time, and I'm glad to see my plane in a pristine condition,' said Rafael as he stowed his carry-on bag in the luggage cupboard near the door.

'Dinners in the warmer whenever you feel like eating, and I have stocked the bar for you as well,' said the Co-Pilot.

Rafael made his way into the belly of the jet, and assumed his usual seat on the port side. They were amongst the clouds minutes later, so he put his feet up on the ottoman, stretched out, and settled in for the eight-hour flight. He wondered what awaited him in London, and was awoken by the announcement from the Co-Pilot to buckle up for landing. He reminded himself that he had not eaten. Right let the games begin, he thought as he watched the houses disappearing below, as the plane was on its final approach into Heathrow.

A security agent was waiting for him at the base of the staircase as he exited.

'Good morning Monsieur Dujon, and welcome to London sir.' 'My name is Jett Dalton, please follow me,' he said as he led the way towards the black Land Rover.

'I will pick you up at nineteen-hundred hours,' said Jett as he dropped him off at the front entrance to Shoreditch Hotel on Bedford Street in London, where he was met at the door by the hotel manager who guided him to his studio suite on the top floor. He reminded himself that he had not booked in at reception. Typical of the way that the English organized important matters, he thought.

'Thank you.' offered Rafael as the manager opened the door to the suite.

'Please do not hesitate to call, should you need anything at all Monsieur Dujon.'

He unpacked his belongings, then made himself a cup of coffee from the in-room coffee machine, sat down, and wondered how these terrorists would attempt to carry out this mass murder operation.

Could be aerial, maybe by smuggling a bomb through security, maybe create a diversion, and try to get through security with automatic rifles, then open fire on the unsuspecting crowd.

A dozen ways he thought to himself. So, if I was one of them, what would I do, he considered. Need to think like them he concluded. He ordered a meal from the in-house menu as he was starving, having not eaten on the plane.

Later that evening Jett picked Jon up at the hotel, and drove him to the office of MI5 at Thames House, 12 Millbank in London.'

Rafael was escorted into the conference room, and introduced to the heads of the various departments. He assumed a seat at the conference table, and a moment later the satellite feed beamed a live feed from CIA headquarters in Virginia, and Barnaby's face came into view.

'Good evening gentlemen and madam.' 'I wish that we could be meeting under far more pleasant circumstances.' 'I take it that you have all met one of our leading agents, namely Rafael, so let's get down to business,' said Barnaby.

'Our latest intelligence indicates that this threat is imminent, and from what we have managed to glean so far, this group, known as "Almawt Lilkufaar," meaning "Death to Infidels" in Arabic has based themselves in Newham in South London.' 'They have split themselves into three groups of two, and intend to attack civilians which as we all know are easy targets, and hope to kill multiple innocent people that will result in mass panic.'

'The first group of two are intending to kill as many people as possible in London to achieve their objective, which is to send us all a message that they can attack us wherever, and whenever they chose.' 'They are planning to attack civilians at the Trooping of the Colour which will be held in a couple of days from now, which is why this is an emergency, and why we are meeting.' 'If they were to be successful, they would have achieved their objective, by sending a clear message to the authorities, and the population of Britain that there is very little that we can do to stop them.'

'The second group of two, intends to kill as many civilians as possible on Independence Day in the USA which as we all know is the fourth of July, and from what we have learned, they intend to carry out this attack at the Washington Monument, while people are enjoying the festivities, and the fireworks display.' 'The third group is planning to carry out their attack to coincide with the end of the Tour de France on the Champs-Élysées, in Paris where hundreds of thousands gather to witness the end of the race.'

'So clearly we cannot allow this to happen in any country,' stated Barnaby emphatically.

'Rafael has thwarted several attacks in France and the United States.' 'His experience is invaluable, so I suggest you allow him to be involved in the coordination, and execution of the exercise to eliminate this treat,' said Barnaby.

'With your permission, I ask that you consider what he has to say,' said Barnaby.

All agreed and turned to face Rafael.

'Thank you, Director.' 'Need I say, that we must all act in concert to identify, and bring these fanatics to court?' 'There are several ways that these people could carry out their mission to inflict maximum death, and destruction upon innocent people.' 'It could be aerial, or planting a bomb in dustbins where people would gather to view the parade, strap suicide vests to their bodies, drive a truck laden with explosives into the crowd, or they may just charge into the crowd with guns blazing.'

'One needs to think like these people to identify what they intend to do.'

Sir John Anderson, the Minister for Home Security was the first to offer a comment.

'I want to put it on record, that we in the United Kingdom, believe strongly in justice, so it is our preference to catch, and arrest the perpetrators of any violence committed in the United Kingdom, then prosecute them.' 'Then let the justice system do its work and sentence them.' 'We abhor violence, and wherever possible we prefer to apprehend a criminal rather than take his or her life, then we will charge that person for the crime committed, and leave it up to our judges to decide their fate.' 'Our system will then hand down an appropriate sentence.'

Rafael clasped his hands with his fingers interlaced, and placed them beneath his chin. He considered what the Minister had just said, and came to the conclusion that the British, like so many other countries, were happy to have taxpayers pay for an extended holiday for the perpetrators of crime, and finally release them to continue with their tirades. Yet another civil libertarian, who does not understand that catching and jailing perpetrators of violence, then setting them free after they have done their time, will result in them continuing along their murderous ways after they have been released. Dumb and dumber, he thought to himself. The world needs to be rid of people like that, not give them a holiday at the taxpayer's expense.

'So, I want to make it very clear, catch these people, and let the law take its course,' added Sir John.

The heads of all the security services started planning a coordinated response to the threat, and Rafael merely watched as they excluded him from the discussion, and did not seek for his input. Typical English arrogance he thought to himself, as his eyes darted from one face to another. We, the French, have experienced this for many decades.

Later that evening, he tapped on the table, stood up, and emphatically stated, 'I believe that these people will put explosives into the heavy-duty traffic plastic barricades that you use as safety barriers to control traffic during roadworks.' 'These are also used to control large crowds as well.'

Every person in the room stopped and stared at Rafael.

'I noticed that some have already been placed around the perimeter of Buckingham Palace.' 'These barricades are normally filled with water making it impossible to be moved by hand, so that is where I believe the terrorists will have hidden explosives, which they will detonate remotely when the time is right,' continued Rafael.

Continuing, he said, 'I suggest that you get sniffer dogs to check the barriers already in place, and if you have handheld X-ray machines, I suggest you use them as well.' 'Best to carry out these checks well after midnight, as you don't want the people responsible to become suspicious that you have discovered their plot.'

The chiefs all straightened up from the bent-over posture, and were rather surprised that nobody had thought of this previously. Sir John immediately ordered the Metropolitan Police to conduct a thorough search of all the safety barriers later that evening as suggested by Rafael. It was well after midnight when Rafael made his way into the entrance of the Shoreditch hotel, and noticed his old friend Joseph Diamond sitting in the lounge.

'What on earth are you doing here my friend?' he said as he took his hand in a greeting.

'Best come up to my room where we can talk in private,' he added.

'So Joseph, why are you here?'

'Well I heard that you are in town my friend, so I want to share some information that we in Mossad have.' 'These bastards have been planning this attack in England for some time, as well as the intended attacks in France and the USA, so we have been tracking them for several months because we believe that they will also attack Israel sooner or later,' said Joseph.

'I know where the two bastards that are planning to attack innocent people at the Trooping of the Colour live.'

'Yes, so do I. 'They live in the affluent Borough of Knightsbridge, located south of Hyde Park' replied Jon.

'OK, let's eliminate them then,' said Joseph.

'Not so fast my friend.' 'Sir John Anderson, the head of the Ministry for Home Security, has clearly stated that the United Kingdom believes strongly in justice, and that it is their preference to catch and arrest the perpetrators of any violence committed in the United Kingdom, then bring them to justice.' 'If we did happen to kill these bastards, I can assure you that they will charge us with murder, so slow down my friend.'

'You and I share the same views, which is to eliminate terrorists rather than arrest terrorists, and put them on trial, so, if we are to do what we always do, then we would need to move in the shadows and not be seen,' 'We have very little time to find these bastards, so let's Google their address, and see what we come up with Joseph.'

'No need, I have already done that,' said Joseph as he fired up his laptop.

Images of Knightsbridge in South London lit up the monitor. He clicked the mouse on Google Earth, and selected the area detailing an apartment block called Brompton Apartments in Terrance Square. It is in an upmarket part of Knightsbridge, and is not the typical type of accommodation frequented by terrorists.

'These two have wealthy parents in Saudi Arabia, and we believe that they have been radicalized, so mom and dad pay for their playboy lifestyle, and whilst Muslims in public, they do not drink alcohol or frequent bars, however away from prying eyes in private, they make use of prostitutes, liquor, as well as all of the pleasures that we westernized people seem to enjoy.' 'All of which is against their religion,' added Joseph.

'Funny when mom and dad are not within eyesight or anywhere near, these radicals turn rogue.'

'I have images of the two suspects,' he said as he flicked to the photo album on the laptop.

'There you go old boy, as the English would say.' 'Look like typical playboys, not mommy and daddy's good Muslim young men are they'

The next morning Jon met Joseph in reception, and they walked to Knightsbridge which took them around twenty-seven minutes. They made their way into the One Hundred Steps coffee shop on Brompton Road that had a view, of the appropriately named Brompton Apartments complex. Jon studied the photographs of the two suspects, and the intelligence report handed to him by Joseph. He noted that the two were employed by the local road maintenance company, Highway Authority situated in Birmingham, a distance of one-hundred miles from Knightsbridge.

'They commute by train each day which normally takes around an hour and a half.' 'So once again, the suspects have rich parents, live a lavish lifestyle, and are prepared to kill innocent people,' said Joseph.

As they sipped their coffee, Jon noticed both suspects making their way out of the apartment complex, so he dropped a ten-pound note on the counter, and they made a hasty exit from the shop. They followed them on foot as they headed towards the railway station, bought a train ticket to the end of the line, and boarded the train in the same carriage as the two suspects. The ticket enabled them to get off at the last stop as a safety measure, because they were unsure how far these two would travel. An hour later both disembarked at Birmingham station. Joseph and Jon followed some distance behind, as the suspects entered the premises of the Highway Authority through the main gates, and made their way towards one of the warehouses.

Jon and Joseph stood at the local bus stop nearby posing as commuters waiting to catch a bus, and noted the lack of security at the premises. A few minutes later both made their way through the front gate, walked towards the rear of the warehouse, and looked through the open roller door noting the two suspects changing into overalls.

Jon gazed deeper into the warehouse, and noticed a row of traffic safety barriers. He watched as the two went about filling them with water. So as anticipated they were preparing the barriers for transportation, and he wondered whether the ones that they had already installed around the palace could already have explosives hidden in them. They may just be filling the extras with water as a cover or to be placed elsewhere.

'Bet they have placed the explosives in the barriers that are already in place around the palace, he whispered.'

'So let's grab these two as they leave work later this afternoon, interrogate them, and once we have confirmed that this is what they have done, we will need to take them back to the office of Home Security,' said Jon.

'Why?' 'Let's just kill them, Jon,' 'You know we don't take prisoners,' said Joseph forcefully.

'No can do my friend, because Sir John Anderson the head of Home Security made it crystal clear, that he wants these people captured and not eliminated.' 'So when in England, you do what the English want.'

'We can say that they tried to attack us, so we had no option, but to eliminate them.' 'Nobody would know Jon.'

Jon left Joseph at the bus stop close to the entrance to the warehouse Highway Authority warehouse, and walked towards the outskirts of the town, eventually finding his way towards a car hire business and hired a car. Two hours later he picked Joseph up at the bus stop, and parked close to the warehouse entrance. They stayed on point for a further five-hours until late afternoon when the two suspects made their way out of the warehouse, and headed towards the railway station. As they passed them, Jon was quick out of the car, approached both suspects pretending to be a lost tourist asking for directions to Knightsbridge in his best French accent. He convinced Anwar Abadi that he was merely a lost tourist, and they happily offered their assistance in guiding them to their location.

'Actually, we both live in Knightsbridge, so if you are headed that way, we can guide you in the right direction if you give us a lift,' offered Anwar.

'Thank you, that would be wonderful,' said Jon.

'So where are you guys from' he enquired in a friendly manner as he glanced at them in his rearview mirror.

'We were born in Saudi Arabia,' offered Anwar.

'I see, so how are you enjoying life in England?'

'Life is great over here, and very different to our Arabic way of life back home,' said Anwar.

'Well guys, I just need to pick something up on our way, then we will drop you guys off wherever you want to go,' said Jon.

As he drove towards Knightsbridge he noticed a warehouse with a real estate agents for lease sign, so he turned into the premises, and stopped at the rear of the building. A moment later both Jon and Joseph were out of the car, and opened the two rear doors with their Glock's pointing directly at the two suspect's heads. Both suspects were totally surprised.

'Right you two, get out, turn around, face the car, and spread your legs,' instructed Jon.

They frisked the two, cuffed them with Flexi cuffs, and Jon removed a detonator from Anwar's pocket.

'Well, well, what do we have here?' he demanded.

'That's a remote for my television,' said Anwar.

'Like hell it is.' 'This is the remote that you two are going to use to trigger an explosion at Buckingham Palace tomorrow.' 'You see, we know that you have put explosives in some of the traffic safety barriers that you have already placed near the gates to the palace, and wired them together so that when you trigger the remote it will detonate, causing a massive explosion that will kill hundreds of innocent people.'

'No, no, no, that is not true,' pleaded Anwar as he tried to turn around and face his captors.

'Well, I will only give you one chance to come clean, and tell me the truth, because if you don't, I am going to shoot both of you right here.' 'In case you have not noticed, there is nobody around, and nobody can see into the complex over the high-security fence, so again, only one chance to come clean.' 'Who instructed you to do this and why,' demanded Jon forcefully.

Anwar pleaded their innocence, so Jon cocked the Glock and pointed it at his testicles.

'So before I kill you, I am going to shoot you in the balls, then I am going to cut your magic wand off and make you eat it as well as your balls.' 'When you get to Allah's Promised Land you won't be able to use your joystick on the seventy-two virgins he promised you.' 'Oh, I forgot, there won't be any virgins left in Muslim heaven because Bin Ladin has taken them all for himself, so one last time to come clean, and you may live to see the sunrise tomorrow morning.'

'You have no right to detain us.' 'I want my lawyer.' 'This is England, not France,' demanded Anwar.

'OK, don't say that I did not warn you,' said Jon as he instructed Joseph to undo Anwar's belt and remove his pants.

Jon moved the Glock to his left hand, then smashed his fist into Anwar's stomach, and as he slouched forward, he cupped his right hand, and ear slapped him creating an air vacuum that shattered his eardrum. Anwar fell unconscious to the ground.

This was a technique he had learned in martial arts.

As Jabir turned and tried to run, Joseph tripped him, and without his hands able to cushion the fall, he tumbled head first onto the concrete driveway. His head crashed against the concrete. Joseph pulled him to his feet, as the blood streamed from a gash on the side of his forehead.

Joseph leaned towards Jon, and whispered, 'let's kill these two bastards, and get the fuck out of here.' 'Nobody would ever know.'

'I told you, we can't do that, my friend, because they would suspect us of the killing, so let's bundle them into the car and take them to MI5.'

Jabir stared at his unconscious cousin in horror and offered to reveal the truth.

'Right, Mr. Jabir, give it to me chapter and verse then,' he said holding the knife to Anwar's private parts.

'If you don't tell me the truth you are going to suffer the same fate as your friend over here.'

'Yes, we filled five of the barriers with explosives, and were going to detonate it as the trooping of the color commenced.' 'You American, French and English bastards kill innocent people in Syria, Iraq, and Afghanistan, and think that you can get away with it.' 'We Arabic people want to revenge our brothers that have died at your hands, so it would have been payback time,' shouted Jabir defiantly.

As Anwar groggily regained consciousness Jon pulled him to his feet, and slapped him several times, telling him that Jabir had confessed, and had revealed everything. He had told them how they had wired explosives into five of the traffic safety barriers, and that they intended to remotely detonate it just as the trooping of the color was about to begin. Joseph checked that their hands were securely cuffed behind their backs, and bundled them into the trunk of the car. It was almost eighteen hundred hours when Jon parked outside the office of MI5, pulled the two suspects out of the trunk, and marched them into the complex.

As they exited the elevator, and made their way towards the office, Jon's mobile phone lit up with an incoming call from Sir John Anderson notifying him that they discovered explosives in five of the barriers near the palace gates. Not wanting to rudely interrupt, Jon glanced at the people seated around the table as they entered the room, and watched as Sir John looked up in surprise, astounded to see him enter the room holding a person that appeared to have been handcuffed. He noticed that the cuffed person was bleeding from his forehead, and watched as another person entered the room, holding the arm of a second person that also appeared to be handcuffed.

'Oh, I suppose there is no need to continue our call,' said Sir John staring in disbelief as he noticed Jon and the others enter the room.

All the other people looked up in amazement at Jon, rather bewildered by the presence of these other strangers.

'No Sir John, I did not want to be rude and interrupt your call, and to be honest, I thought it would be a nice surprise to present the two people that were planning to commit mass murder at Buckingham Palace to you and your team.' 'Please meet Anwar Abadi and his cousin Jabir Osman.'

Not wanting to reveal that Joseph was a Mossad agent, he merely stated, 'I would also like to introduce you to a good friend of mine, namely Joseph Diamond from the Israeli Embassy here in London.'

The people seated at the table were taken completely by surprise, sat back, and stared in disbelief.

'Well, Sir John, Joseph and I have apprehended the two people that were about to possibly kill a couple of hundred people and wound numerous others.' 'You have stated that you want to bring them to justice, so we will hand these two over to you for processing.' 'Oh yes, this is the remote that they intended to use to detonate the explosives,' said Jon as he placed it on the table.

Chapter 20

Voie Triomphale

France

Jon, Bastienne, and Joseph studied the Google Map of Avenue Champs-Élysées, which is part of the Voie Triomphale (Triumphal Way) in Paris.

The Avenue Champs-Élysées plays a major role in opening the outlook from the Louvre towards the West and the setting sun. Its current name was adopted in 1709, and derived from the Elysian Fields, a place of final resting for the souls of the heroic and the virtuous in Greek mythology. But the thoroughfare on the axis is nowadays known as *"la plus belle avenue du monde"* (the most beautiful avenue in the world). The long avenue of one point two four miles is 70m wide, therefore not the widest in Paris (Avenue Foch is 120m wide with its central gardens).

The magnificent vista runs through some of Paris' most celebrated monuments and squares, towards the Louvre, and the gardens of the Tuileries to La Défense, passing through the Champs-Elysées, which are dominated by the famous Arc de Triomphe. The Grand-Palais and the Petit-Palais are grand additions to the area from the La Belle Epoque period.

The wide processional avenue had been in Le Nôtre's mind when the urban architect designed the Tuileries Gardens back in the 17th century. But it was the Duke of Antin who pursued the Grand Cours or *"Perspective"* up to the mound of Chaillot (Butte de Chaillot) where the Arc de Triomphe now stands majestically. In the 18th century, the promenade was bordered by trees formally planted in a straight line, and English gardens were laid out on each side, from the Place de la

Concorde up to the Rond Point des Champs-Élysées.

'This is such a beautiful part of Paris.' 'No wonder these bastards want to use this part of Paris to commit a heinous crime, which would be horrific, to say the least, and if they were successful, it would yet again, send a message to us, that they can strike wherever and whenever they like.' 'They believe that we cannot do anything to stop them,' said Jon using the undercover name that he always used in France.

'As I have said on several occasions, I have no problem with peaceful Muslims whatsoever.' 'They don't harbor hatred as the jihadists do, and all they want is to have a roof over their heads, a job, enough food to feed their families, and be able to practice their religion.' 'No problem with that all, however, the radicals are the people I cannot stand, as they bring hatred to our country, and despite what France has done for them, they seek an opportunity to cause chaos and kill innocent people.'

'So gentlemen, we simply cannot allow that to happen.' 'I think these jihadist fanatics have several options available to them to attack this time.' 'Wasn't so long ago when you and I, prevented an attack on Presidents Trent and Macon as they traveled down the Avenue des Champs-Élysées, so planting a bomb in the underground sewer could be a possibility because it would kill several riders, and many by-standers.' 'I think we cannot discount that threat, so we would need to check the underground sewer thoroughly once again,' said Jon.

'If I was planning an attack like this, I would pose as a council worker, and busy myself picking up papers, bottles and general rubbish on the sidewalk, that has been strewn all over the place by spectators.' 'Then when I have the opportunity, I would pretend to be placing a new garbage bag into one of the bins, however, it would contain a bomb.' 'I would insert another bag over it, covering the bag containing a bomb.'

'Effectively that would hide the bomb that I placed in the bin, and no one would ever discover it until of course it goes "Boom," and all hell breaks loose,' said Jon.

'You would only need to do that in say, four or six garbage bins, and when they go 'kaboom", the number of people that would die would be in the dozens, if not hundreds.' 'There are numerous bins scattered along the sidewalk which is where hundreds of onlookers would be gathered to watch the riders as they pass on their way to the finish line.'

'Several blasts along the Avenue Champs-Élysées would cause massive casualties, and devastation that will kill many bystanders and riders as well,' reiterated Jon.

Pointing to the Google Map image of the Avenue Champs-Élysées, he pointed to the numerous garbage bins positioned along the sidewalk. They seemed to be positioned twenty yards apart, which would result in maximum casualties, if they coordinated multiple explosions at once, it would have catastrophic consequences.

A moment later, the display on Jon's mobile phone lit up with an incoming call from Barnaby Heathcott at the CIA's headquarters in Langley.

Using his undercover name, Barnaby said, 'hello Jon, I take it that you have Capitaine Pétit with you?'

'Yes Director, as well as Joseph Diamond from Mossad,' replied Jon.

'Bonjour Capitaine and hello Joe,' offered Barnaby.

'I can confirm that we have picked up some chatter on the wire, and we have identified the two terrorists that have planned this attack, to coincide with the end of the Tour de France, which as you know will take place in two days, so we need to act quickly,' added Barnaby.

'The two suspects are of African descent, known as Faruq Rahmani, who from what we have managed to find out, is from Algeria, and Omar Naji who hails from Morocco.' 'It appears that both come from the Maghreb a region in North Africa, bordering on the Mediterranean Sea, and integrated themselves into the predominantly Muslim area that offers them an ideal place to hide amongst other like-minded people.' 'Both are domicile in the community district of Clichy, Hauts-de-Seine a northwest suburb of Paris, located four miles from the center of Paris that has a population of around sixty-four thousand people.'

Clichy, Hauts-de-Seine, sometimes referred to as Clichy La-Garenne is the headquarters of global corporate giants such as the L'Oréal Cosmetic Group, Bic the largest pen producer in the world, and Sony France, a large electronics and media company. The Beaujon Hospital, one of the largest, and most modern in the Paris region, which is located in the town, and the church of Saint-Vincent-de-Paul, that was built when the saint was the village priest at Clichy (1612–25). It is on the boulevard Jean-Jaurès. The suburb's manufacturers include mechanical, electrical, and chemical products. Hardly the place you would expect to find terrorists.

'So, over to you Capitaine to ferret out more about these two, and make sure that they are not successful in carrying out their plan of mass murder.' 'As you are aware, we are almost out of time, and as mentioned, we only have two days to the end of the race, so this is certainly a matter of urgency.'

'I have notified the French President of the threat, and he has welcomed the CIA's support, so gentlemen, it's time to find these two, and bring them to justice,' continued Barnaby.

'Thank you, Director, I will take it from here,' said Bastienne as they ended the call.

Bastienne used all the resources at his disposal, and finally managed to uncover an address registered to the wife of Omar Naji, They Googled the Joli Perspective apartment complex which was situated on Rue Villeneuve, that seemed to be a middle-income complex.

'It appears that these two have steady jobs at the Parisian Garbage Disposal Company, so why on earth are they involved in terrorism?' questioned Jon.

'As we have seen numerous times, it seems that they have been radicalized,' responded Bastienne.

'OK, guys, we have an address, which is a start, so I suggest we take a look at this apartment complex,' said Bastienne.

The chief of police placed his force on high alert, and contacted the head of the intelligence services updating him on the threat. Later that afternoon, Bastienne parked the garbage truck close to the apartment complex they had identified and waited.

Joseph and Jon jumped out of the truck, and made their way toward the apartment block. They split up at the entrance with Jon waiting patiently at the front entrance, and Joseph making his way towards the rear of the building. Jon busied himself, tying his shoelaces, and a couple of minutes later he noticed a resident leaving the building, so was quick to keep the entrance door to the complex ajar. He entered the complex without drawing any suspicion to what he was doing, and Joseph walked around the rear of the building inspecting any escape route that the two suspects could use. Jon climbed the staircase to the second floor, and made his way down the passage towards apartment number twenty-three. He paused at the front door, and listened intently for any sign of activity in the apartment, then continued down the passage towards the elevator. A short while later he and Joseph both jumped back into the garbage truck.

'Seems like no one is home, so I suggest we sit, wait and see,' said Jon turning to face Basteinne and Joseph.

'That's the part of the job that is boring,' he added.

Jon, called the company that both these people worked for, and asked to speak with Faruq Rahmani, pretending that it was an urgent family matter. A few minutes later the receptionist notified him that Faruq was away on three days of annual leave. How convenient he thought to himself. Bastienne then called the company, and asked to speak with Omar Naji. A couple of minutes later the receptionist notified him that he had taken three RDOs (Rostered Days Off), and that he would be back after the weekend. Well, well, I wonder where these two could be, he pondered.

'Where would you go if you were them Jon?' questioned Bastienne.

'As I have said, I think these two will pose as council workers so I believe that we should look in that direction.'

Four hours later Bastienne arranged to have a surveillance vehicle position itself near the front entrance to the apartment block later in the day, and take over the duty of keeping a watchful eye on the complex.

They waited patiently for several hours until the surveillance car arrived to take over.

Early the next morning they were back at the apartment block, and parked in the same spot. Around zero eight-hundred hours, they noticed the two suspects making their way out of the complex and heading towards the bus stop further down the road. Joseph quickly jumped out of the garbage truck, and made his way towards the bus stop, pretended to be reading the timetable attached to the pole in front of the bus shelter.

He boarded the bus, seated himself behind the two suspects towards the back, and watched intently as the two suspects chatted idly in Arabic, then activated his mobile phone, and took numerous pictures of them side on.

Fifty minutes later, they rang the bell, made their way towards the exit at the front of the bus, and exited with Joseph following at a leisurely pace some distance behind. He watched as they donned their orange safety vests before entering the Enterprise d'élimination des ordures ménagères, the Parisian Garbage Disposal Company's site office.

OK, let the games begin he thought as he jumped back into the garbage truck driven by Bastienne, which did not look out of place parked on the side of the road.

'Right guys, here are a few photographs of the suspects that I took on the bus.' 'Not ideal but we have clear images of the sides of their faces.' 'Both are wearing baseball caps, and as you will notice, one is orange and the other is blue, so easily identifiable.'

An hour later a council utility vehicle driven by one of the suspects, made its way out of the Garbage Disposal site and headed toward Paris. The driver was easily identifiable by the orange baseball cap he was wearing, so Bastienne fired up the engine, and followed at a discreet distance. The utility vehicle had the Parisian Garbage Disposable Company's name and logo printed on the doors, making it easy to identify.

They followed the vehicle as it drove down Avenue Champs-Élysées, eventually turning into a site reserved for council vehicles, so Bastienne continued past the turnoff, and turned at the next intersection. Jon and Joseph jumped out of the truck, and made their way back to the council site, before parting ways. Both lingered in the park opposite the council site and Jon scanned the park, reminding himself of the time that he and Bastienne arrested the two bombers that had placed explosives in the underground sewer. Both were sitting exactly where he stood. Bastards, I hope they rot in hell he thought.

Joseph pretended to be inspecting the barrier erected along the road that would keep pedestrians at bay as the Tour de France approached the end of the famous avenue. A day to go he reminded himself, so he watched as the two suspects went about cleaning the avenue of any debris, and he took note that both looked into various bins close to where the race was due to end. I think these pricks will place explosives in the bins at the endpoint he considered.

Bastienne, Jon, and Joseph were up early the next morning, and made their way back to the Avenue Champs-Élysées. The crowd was already massing, so they lingered around the end point of the race, and watched as the organizers put the final touches to the finish line. Joseph positioned himself close to the entrance of the council site, and noted the arrival of the utility vehicle as it entered.

He radioed Bastienne and notified him that the two suspects had entered the site, then watched at a discreet distance as the two suspect's donned backpacks, noticing that the backpacks appeared to be rather bulky, and he took note of the rolls of black garbage bags that they had in hand, as well as a water bottle attached to the side of each backpack.

Jon positioned himself closer to the front of the throng of people, and kept his eye on the two suspects as they made their way out of the council site towards the finish line. They meandered their way through the masses, stopping at several bins close to the finish line, removing the filled bags before extracting a bundle of what appeared to be a replacement black bag from their backpack, and placing it at the bottom of the bin. They placed another garbage bag over the top of the bundle. He watched as they did this to six bins positioned near the finish line. Jon glanced at his watch noting that it was approximately half an hour before the group of riders would slowly peddle past the throng of people that had lined the famous avenue heading towards the finish line, so he made his way towards one of the suspects. He radioed Bastienne and Joseph to close the gap, and to position themselves directly behind the other suspect.

A short while later, Bastienne gave the order to move in, and arrest the suspects, reiterating that they needed to secure the arms and hands of both of them, to ensure that they were not able to activate any remotes they may have in their pockets.

Jon approached one of the suspects, secured both arms, placing his leg behind him, then dropped him to the ground. He looked up to see Basitenne and Joseph follow a similar procedure securing the other suspect.

They cuffed the suspects using Flexi cuffs, frisked both of them, and then carefully removed a remote from each person's pocket. The crowd was amazed at what had just happened, so Bastienne notified them that they were police officers, and ordered them to move back.

'Ah Monsieurs Rahmani and Naji.' 'I am so pleased to meet you both.'

He looked at the remotes, and noted that did not have a timer attached, so he presumed that the suspects would remotely trigger an explosion at the appropriate time. He radioed for backup, and moments later, several plain-clothed police officers ordered the crowd to move away from the bins. They cleared a fifty-yard radius around the six bins. Members of the bomb squad arrived shortly after, and went about making the area safe, checking all the bins along the route, just as the riders passed by, totally unaware of the possibility that they, and many people could have died.

Bastienne watched as the riders passed him, heading for towards the finish line.

'Fuck me that was a close call.' 'It could have been catastrophic if those bombs went off,' said Jon.

'Oui Monsieur Jon, you are correct, so thank you for everything you have done, and to you too Monsieur Joseph.'

'Let's take these pricks, and get rid of them guys,' whispered Joseph.

'No we cannot do that, there are way too many witnesses, so this is their lucky day,' replied Bastienne.

Several police officers arrived, and took the two suspects into custody, then led them towards a police van. They were taken to the central police station for processing.

Bastienne notified the Chief of Police that had taken the two suspects into custody, and that the bomb squad had disarmed the bombs and removed them.

An hour later, Bastienne's mobile phone range with an incoming call from an unlisted number.

'Bonjour Capitaine Pétit speaking.'

'Bonjour Capitaine, this is President Macon speaking.' 'I have just been informed by the Chief of Police that you have successfully apprehended the two people that intended to explode bombs that they had placed in refuse bins at the finish to the Tour de France.'

'Congratulations and thank you most sincerely for making the arrests, and avoiding what most certainly would have resulted in many deaths with multiple people being injured.' 'Thank you and please thank any other people that were involved in the operation because you guys have saved many lives,' said the President as he ended the call.

Chapter 21

Washington Monument

Washington-USA

Rafael stared at the Lincoln Memorial Reflecting Pool, which is the largest of the many reflecting pools in Washington, D.C., United States. It is a long and large rectangular pool located on the National Mall, directly east of the Lincoln Memorial, with the Washington Monument to the east of the reflecting pool. Part of the iconic image of Washington. The reflecting pool hosts many of the twenty-four million visitors a year who visit the National Mall, and is lined by walking paths with shade trees on both sides. Depending on the viewer's vantage point, it dramatically reflects the Washington Monument, the Lincoln Memorial, the Mall's trees, and the expansive sky.

The Lincoln Memorial Reflecting Pool was designed by Henry Bacon, and was constructed in 1922 and 1923, following the dedication of the Lincoln Memorial. It is approximately two thousand and thirty feet long, and one-hundred and sixty-seven feet wide. The perimeter of the pool is four thousand, three-hundred and ninety-two feet around, and has a depth of approximately, eighteen inches on the sides, and thirty inches in the center, holding approximately six-million, seven-hundred and fifty-thousand U.S. gallons of water.

Why the fuck is there so much hatred in the world. Millions of ordinary Muslims only want to live in peace, have enough food to feed their families, and shelter for their families, then of course, as is the case with many other religions, you have the radical elements that just want to kill people out of hatred, he thought to himself.

Such a peaceful place, no wonder these radical jihadists want to come here to one of the most iconic features of the capital of the United States, and commit mass murder, which would send a very clear message to the US administration, and the world at large, that they can strike wherever or whenever they choose. Best make very sure that this does not happen, thought Rafael.

Barnaby fired up his laptop and images of the Lincoln Memorial were beamed onto the monitor on the wall.

'From the snippets of information we have gathered, this is where we believe that these bastards will try to kill as many people as they possibly can,' he said looking at Rafael.

'Rafael, as you know there will be tens of thousands of people attending the Independence Day celebrations, as well as viewing the fireworks display later in the evening, so we need to try and figure out what they intend to do.' 'Chatter on the wire has gone silent, so that complicates our task.'

'We think these two bastards entered the US via Canada on false passports, and we have the immigration border officials of both countries reviewing their CCTV security footage to try to identify these two people.' 'I am expecting a call from the heads of immigration at the border crossings to call me later this evening, so I am hoping that will be able to identify these suspects.'

'I was down at the Lincoln Memorial earlier today Director, and in my humble opinion, there are many ways that they could try to kill a multitude of people.'

'We need to consider that they could attempt to smuggle explosives into the area, either with suicide vests attached to their torsos, or to drive a truck into the crowd which is unlikely, because of the bollards in place, or even possibly an aerial attack of some sort,' said Rafael.

'The authorities will have searched the area repeatedly, so planting bombs in garbage bins can be discounted as security will check them constantly.' 'I think that we can discount the threat of them driving a truck into the crowd, which therefore leaves the last two options, namely, they strap suicide vests to their bodies, then activate them amongst the crowd or an aerial attack.'

'And yes, security will conduct body searches, making suicide vests a risky option for them, because they could be apprehended before they can carry out their intended mass murder plan, and detonate their bombs,' continued Rafael.

'In my opinion Director, I believe that they will attempt to hijack a light plane, fill it with explosives and crash it into the crowd, which in some way, would remind Americans of 9/11.' 'This would give them maximum impact resulting in the deaths and injury to hundreds of people,' he said.

Barnaby sat back in his chair and considered what Rafael had just said. That is a real possibility he thought. The CIA alerted all law enforcement agencies of the threat, and they coordinated the correlation of all intelligence, analyzed it, and shared their findings through the US Department of Homeland Security, the National Security Council (NSC), and the FBI. Barnaby would represent the CIA at all the meetings, as he needed to ensure that another attack on US soil did not happen on his watch.

Days before Independence Day, the FBI cordoned off the area, erected crowd control barriers, and fencing around the perimeter that would corral people towards numerous turntable checkpoints staffed by armed officers as well as sniffer dogs. People would be guided through metal detectors, and all baggage would be X-rayed. It was a massive security operation, and people were warned that they should expect some delays.

Rafael studied the list of all the airfields within a two-hundred-mile radius of Washington, and was surprised to learn that there were a few hundred of them. How the hell we are going to check all of these, he wondered. An impossible task, let alone the manpower it would take to thoroughly check every airport.

So what the fuck am I going to do he thought?

The FBI had fifty agents visit all the airfields close to Washington, to ascertain the names of all pilots that were registered at each airfield, how often they flew, and whether they owned or hired aircraft. They established that there were around a hundred and thirty people that flew regularly that did not own a light plane, so they searched through their databases for any criminal history on all those people. Twenty were female, which they did not believe would possibly commit mass murder, and focused on two names in their database, both of which were males namely, Ilyas Abu and Abdourahman Abdulaziz, and cross-referenced it with the companies that had employed them.

Comfortable that they had identified the possible suspects, they focused their efforts on an airfield, aptly named Leesburg Executive Airport at Godfrey Field, which is a general aviation airfield. Leesburg Executive Airport is around forty miles from Washington, however, Rafael believed that these people would merely hire a plane for a couple of days, fly it to a remote landing strip, load the plane with explosives, then fly it to the

Memorial. He thought that they would then crash the plane into the crowds, committing mass murder, which would guarantee them a passage into the Promised Land, and the seventy-two virgins in Islamic Paradise. Jihadists are convinced that they will be rewarded in Muslim Heaven.

From the information that the CIA received from the Federal Aviation Administration, they discovered that Ilyas Abu had obtained his pilot's license twelve months previously, and was licensed to fly a light two-seater sports aircraft. He had completed his twenty hours of training, and was viewed as a model student.

Rafael, accessed Google Maps and searched for a remote town near Washington, focusing his attention on the small town of Port Tobacco. It dates back to the seventeen-hundreds with a population of sixteen people, and around twenty-seven miles to Washington making it an ideal place to land a light plane on a remote strip of grassland, fill it with explosives, then fly it to Washington, and crash it into the hordes of people.

Barnaby Googled the town of Port Tobacco, and agreed that it was in a remote location. He searched for a possible landing strip, and focused on a long grassy strip on the fringe of the town in what appeared to be the edge of bushland, making it an ideal place for clandestine activities away from prying eyes.

'I think that Mr. Abu will hire a light two-seater plane, and fly it to that remote strip of grassland where he will be met by his jihadist mate Mr. Abdulaziz, who will most likely have driven a truck laden with explosives to the area, then both would load it into the plane, and take off for the Washington Memorial the next day.' 'I do believe that they plan to crash it into the huge crowd of people,' said Rafael.

Barnaby called William Knowles, the COO of Leesburg Executive Airport on his mobile phone.

'Hello William, Barnaby Heathcott speaking.' 'Can we speak privately, so are you able to excuse yourself from any other colleagues you may have around you, because, what I am about to reveal to you, is classified.'

A couple of minutes later William confirmed that he was able to speak with Barnaby in private.

'Thanks, William, we have uncovered a plot that could result in hundreds of people dying from an attack which we believe may come from a light plane being flown deliberately in the crowd at the Washington Memorial on Independence day.' 'If these people are able to carry this out successfully, it would remind Americans of 9/11, so we need to ensure that this does not happen.'

'As you know that is in two days, so I am asking you to access your database, and extract any information you have on two suspects we have our eyes on namely, Ilyas Abu and Abdourahman Abdulaziz.' 'We think one, or both of them have completed a pilot's license course, enabling them to fly a light aircraft, so we need everything you can give us on these two ASAP,' continued Barnaby.

'Certainly Director, I will get onto it immediately and get back to soon,' replied William.

An hour later Barnaby's mobile rang with an incoming call from William Knowles.

'Hello William, I hope you have some useful information for me,' said Barnaby.

'I can confirm that Mister Ilyas Abu completed his light aircraft pilot's license some twelve months ago, and from the information I have on my desk, it appears that he was an outstanding student.' 'Very diligent, however, there is no record of Abdourahman Abdulaziz having either applied for, or having completed a pilot's license'

'I have all the information available for you, so if you would like to send a couple of agents to pick it up, I will wait for them to arrive, and if there is anything else you require, simply call me,' said William ending the call.

An hour later Gizelle, Barnaby's assistant tapped on his door, and handed him the dossier containing all the information sent by William Knowles.

'Thanks, Gizelle.' 'I don't want to be disturbed.'

Barnaby read through the notes in the file and turned to Rafael, 'well this is where these two appear to live,' he said as he handed the file to him.

'OK Boss, I will take a drive and see what I can find out said Rafael.'

Rafael noted that the two were of Palestinian descent, and lived in the affluent Arabic neighborhood of Columbia which is a distance of around three and a half miles from DC. So why on earth are these two people living in a wealthy Arabic community wanting to commit mass murder? Beggar's belief. Both are employed by multinational corporate giants, and have steady jobs, so how the hell has it gotten to this, he thought?

He parked outside the Pinnacle Apartment complex situated on Park Circuit, and waited patiently. Later he made his way into the complex, found the building Super and asked to view a couple of one and two-bedroom apartments for rent. He specified that his preference was to be on the second floor, which was the same floor that the two suspects resided on. Having viewed a couple of apartments, he made his way back to his car and waited. Four hours later with no sign of either of them, he returned to Langley.

'Well Director, I visited the apartment complex that they live in, however, there is no sign of them, so I believe that they have already made their way to another location, possibly the grassy strip of land we identified at Port Tobacco,' said Rafael.

He called several car/truck hire companies, and discovered that a four-ton delivery truck had been hired for four days, and that it had been rented to Abdourrahman Abdulaziz. Ah, got you, you bastard he thought.

He called Barnaby on a secure line, 'hello Director, I discovered that Mr. Abdulaziz rented a four-ton truck from Affordable Truck Hire in Gateway, so we can almost be sure that they plan to transport explosives from a location, possibly a storage warehouse to where they intend landing the light plane, which I believe may be Port Tobacco, fill the plane with explosives, then fly it to the Washington Memorial, and crash it into the crowd.'

Barnaby repositioned the satellite images and focused on Port Tobacco and zoomed in on the grassy strip on the edge of town, He noticed a light aircraft parked on the fringe of thick bushland. Got you, he thought.

'We only have a day to investigate this so, I will be on my way boss, and will report back to you once I am there,' said Rafael.

'The FBI has a couple of people keeping an eye on the apartment complex, so we will know exactly when these two return home.' 'Let's hope that they show up, and that we can intercept them before they commit mass murder, however, I think they have already left,' said Barnaby.

'What do you want me to do with these two if I catch them.' 'Do you want me to arrest them, and bring them back alive, so that you can interrogate them or do you want me to eliminate them,' asked Rafael.

Barnaby sat back, and considered what Rafael had just said for a few moments.

'Just kill them.'

Rafael had a broad smile on his face as he looked at Barnaby. He is thinking just me. Don't arrest terrorists, terminate them.

He called the Leesburg Executive Airport, and established that Ilyas Abu had rented a light two-seater plane a day ago, and that it was due to be returned three days later. The plane is a single prop two-seater Explorer light aircraft with the registration number of S-GAN, and that the aircraft had a blue livery, so easily identifiable.

Next day, Rafael, drove to Port Tobacco in an old Chevy pickup, and parked in the town. He jumped on a bicycle, and rode around the town eventually identifying the open grassland area that he had seen on Google Maps, then placed the bike in the bushes and worked his way on foot towards a truck he saw hidden in the bushes some distance away. These pricks have not done a good job of hiding the truck he thought. As he got closer, the blue tail of a light plane became visible, and the registration number confirmed that he had the correct aircraft.

The terrorists had tried to park the plane deeper into the bush, so he moved closer using the shrub as cover, ensuring that he was not visible. He carefully made his way towards to the two people that were loading cartons into the aircraft, and crept to within thirty yards of the aircraft, double-checked that the registration marking coincided with the information that Barnaby had gained from the airport manager at Leesburg Executive Airport. He watched for an hour as the two people continued to load the cartons into the plane. A lot of cartons he thought so I wonder whether this plane will ever get airborne because of the weight.

A short while later, one of the terrorists removed two mats from the rear of the truck, then closed the tailgate doors and made his way towards the front of the light plane, He laid the mats down facing Mecca. Both men made their way into the thicket to relieve themselves, and Rafael quickly covered the ground between himself and the plane, slit the packaging tape on the top of one of the cartons, carefully opening it. Yep, just as I thought, it's laden with explosives. He hid behind the rear wheel of the plane where the tail of the aircraft almost touches the ground, and waited for the two to return. A few minutes later both returned, washed their hands, then stood on the mats facing towards the west which he believed was Mecca. Luckily for him was in the opposite direction to where he was hidden.

He extracted his Glock fitted with a silencer, checked to ensure that the weapons safety switch was activated and ready to be fired, and reminded himself that his gun was always ready to be fired. The two stood and raised their hands in the air shouting, "Allahu Akbar (God is Most Great) aloud. They folded their hands across their chests, and recited the first chapter of the Quran.

Moments later after they had completed bowing three times, Rafael was standing behind them, and placed the barrel of his gun at the back of one of the terrorist's heads. He ordered both of them to move off the mats, ensuring that he was out of reach of the other terrorist in case he lunged toward him.

'Hello, Mister Abu, and greetings to you too Mister Abdulaziz, what a pleasure to see you both' 'Now I want you both to lie down on your stomachs with your hands spread out beside you,' he instructed.

Dismayed, Abu glanced at Abdulaziz in disbelief that they had been discovered.

'Right, so where did to you get the components to make homemade bombs,' questioned Rafael.

'If I tell you, will you let us go?' asked Abu.

'Well that depends on whether you tell me the truth,' replied Rafael.

'Making bombs is easy.' 'We got the raw material from the local hardware store, like fertilizer, nails, chemicals, etc which we then assembled,' said Abu.

'So where did you assemble this lot Mister Abu?' questioned Rafael forcefully.

'We hired a storage unit at Red Branch Road, and assembled it there.'

'I see and who else is involved,' questioned Rafael.

'Nobody else.'

'So why are you doing this?' questioned Rafael.

Continuing he said, 'you both have good jobs, so please explain to me exactly why you want to commit mass murder amongst innocent civilians.'

'Israelis and Americans killed my parents, my younger brother, and sister in Palestine, so do you think I would forget that,' replied Abu defiantly.

Rafael placed his boot on Abu's neck, and looked down at him for a short while, almost pitying him before removing his boot, then shot him in the back of the head. His accomplice Abdulaziz, tried desperately to get to his feet, so Rafael trained the Glock at his temple and fired.

A while later he called Barnaby on a secure line, and notified him that he had eliminated both terrorists. Barnaby sent the coordinates to the FBI, and instructed Rafael to wait for their arrival, as they need to secure the explosives.

Chapter 22

United Nations

New York USA

Jon stared blankly at his cup of coffee, deep in thought about his life, and focused on the people seated at the tables on the sidewalk. He wondered what it would be like to be one of them, leading a normal lifestyle, have a job, and lead a peaceful life with a home, wife and kids, without putting his life in danger every day.

Using the undercover name that he always used when in France, he met Bastienne at Café Floret, his favorite coffee shop, situated at one-hundred and seventy Boulevard at Saint Germaine in Paris. His friend, the late Stan Noble loved stopping there for a coffee.

'Capitaine, do you know that there are twelve groups that control the world and everything that happens in it,' said Jon as he turned to look at Bastienne.

'Oui Monsieur Jon, I know, so why are you telling me this?'

'Well, the CIA supposedly has a reputation of using, then disowning operatives if they are ever caught, and may well turn their back on them,' said Jon.

'So all the more reason for you to come and work for us Monsieur Jon,' replied Bastienne sensing a change in Jon's attitude.

'A while back the Swiss authorities uncovered yet another group, called The Three Sixty Degrees Group which is of great concern.' 'These groups control the world, and The Three Sixty Degrees Group has a wide range of influential people amongst its membership, including past Presidents, Prime Ministers, Academics, Captains of Industry, Scientists and the wealthy elite,' continued Jon.

Jon knew that he could not confirm that the CIA had eliminated the hierarchy of this group, and were still concerned that other influential people may step up and take control of the group, so they continued to monitor them.

Bastienne knew that the Swiss authorities were investigating The Three Sixty Degrees Group, and had not released their findings to date, so Jon felt comfortable to openly discuss the group amongst themselves.

'Oui, I am aware of the group from CIA briefings passed onto us, so what's your point?' asked Bastienne.

Continuing Jon said, 'the twelve groups that control the world, and everything that happens in it, are extremely influential, and can be very dangerous.' 'All of these groups were formed many years ago, except for the Three Sixty Degrees Group, which appears to have been formed in recent times.'

'From what I understand, The Three Sixty Degrees Group intends culling the world's population in half using a deadly airborne virus, and they have already tested it in Africa, which is detailed in the CIA briefings.' 'What is of concern to me, is that I have discovered that the CIA has its tentacles in some of these organizations, which means that Director Heathcott could possibly be involved.'

'This may well be a strategy by the CIA so that they can keep tabs on what these groups are doing, however, I cannot be sure of that, and if I ever uncovered the CIA's involvement, more particularly Director Heathcott's direct involvement, the comment you made earlier may well eventuate for me.'

'The Three Sixty Degrees Group is the twelfth group, and they appear to be the most dangerous.'

Jon laid a sheet of paper on the table detailing the names of the various groups.

Bastienne picked it up and read it.

The Knights of Malta-is a Catholic Religious Order traditionally of Military, Chivalric, and Noble Nature. They have members all over the world, with ties to banking and politics, as well as in the CIA, and provide humanitarian aid to countries in need.

Club De Berne-an intelligence agency that has twenty-seven states of the European Union, Norway, and Switzerland in it, as well as the USA, including Australia, and the Canadian CSIS.

Skull and Bones-are one of the most secretive societies based in the USA, known as the brotherhood of death, formed at Yale University in 1832, and some forty-six US Presidents have been members of this group.

The Bohemian Grove-is another secretive group, located in California and Sonoma County. They were founded in 1872 by journalists, artists, and musicians.

Le Cercle-is yet another very secretive group, which is a less known British and American Group frequented by spies and politicians, with an agenda that encompasses political arms deals. The Group meets annually in Washington DC. It is believed that their funding comes from the CIA.

The Illuminati-is a Secret Society of Freedom, supposedly operates in defense of all humans, and of all generations. Their motto is "Freedom is an Idol of the Human Species." Their charter states "For happiness, the human desires freedom; for prosperity, the human requires leadership." Outsiders cannot infiltrate this group. Members are supposedly better informed, and knowledgeable than those not in the society. The society was set up as a secular non-religious sect, with extremely influential members within the group. It operates in defense of all humans, in all places, and of all generations.

The Bullingdon Club-was formed as an all-male club by students of the University of Oxford, consisting of wealthy members including current and past Prime Ministers in the UK.

The Bilderberg Group-was established in 1954 consisting of politicians, financiers, military leaders, and heads of corporations.

Chatham House-known as the Royal Institute of International Affairs has its headquarters in London, and claims to provide authoritative comments on world events and global challenges. The Group is funded by the Bill and Melinda Gates Foundation, as well as the Rockefeller Foundation.

Cfr-also known as the Council of Foreign Relations, is a United States Non-Profit Think Tank, specializing in US Foreign Policy and International Affairs that gives direct orders to politicians.

The Trilateral Commission-is a non-government, nonpartisan discussion group, founded by David Rockefeller in 1973. They make political and business decisions. Members are chosen by the Chairman and Executive Committee consisting of past USA Presidents.

Director Heathcott may have discovered a link between these groups, and the new group that was formed recently, namely The Three Sixty Degrees Group. He was extremely troubled by this group's agenda, as it appears that this group is planning to cull the world's population in half.

'So why are you showing me this Jon?' questioned a rather confused Bastienne.

'Well, the truth is that these groups are made up of the ultra-wealthy elite who do not care about people, they only care about increasing their wealth.' 'So it seems odd that the Three Sixty Degrees Group wants to cull half the world's population, which seems ridiculous, because it is the masses that help the elite increase their wealth,' said Jon.

Continuing he said, 'I imagine that their agenda may include controlling the entire world's population in a new world order, because they are scared of possible diseases that could kill them.' 'Rather stupid, because we all have an expiry date.'

'What if a person could access all their banking details, then suddenly one day, they all realized that their accounts had been cleaned out, and they had no money,' 'I wonder how they would feel about that,' said Jon with a wry smile on his face.

'And you think that's possible?' questioned Bastienne.

'Who knows, however, anything is possible if one thinks about it Capitaine,' replied Jon leaning confidently back in his chair.

'The CIA has recently uncovered a group of people that are currently hacking into various infrastructure facilities globally, such as electrical grids, banking, strategic military installations, big corporations, and governments.' 'This group of hackers appears to be located in the most unlikely place, and over the past few weeks, I have used my expertise in IT technology to infiltrate this group,' said Jon candidly.

'Believe it or not, they have based themselves within the headquarters of the United Nations, situated in the Turtle Bay neighborhood of Manhattan in New York, and from what I have learned so far, it appears that the group is Chechen.' 'It seems that they have been trained by the Russians, and they have been offered huge sums of money if they successfully shut down the western world economies.'

'What I have discovered, is that the group consists of three Chechen's that the Russians have managed to position within the UN's IT department many years ago, and these people have been sleepers until the late Pushkin recently activated this cell, prior to his death,' continued Jon.

'Another dangerous, and desperate plot by this late despot.'

'The Russians have been planning this for well over a decade, and have systematically infiltrated various departments of the U.N., positioning their operatives in strategic roles,' stated Jon.

'Before Mr. Pushkin passed on, he planned to shut down everything that drives the economies of the western world, then attack us, which means that we would have been rudderless as all our infrastructure, military, banking, and communications would be unable to function.' 'This would cause mass panic in the western world, and we could have found ourselves in a very dangerous position.'

'So if this was ever to happen, despite Pushkin's passing, and they were successful, Ivan would be able to start a war without much resistance from the West,' said Jon candidly.

'Nobody really knows who will take over from Pushkin, so we need to be on our guard, and eliminate this problem, once and for all.'

'From what I have managed to find out, it appears that somebody in Russia instructed this lot to ready themselves to shut down the word's infrastructure, on his command.' 'Maybe whoever is calling the shots in Russia right now, has issued that instruction.' 'Not sure, however, we think Mr. Lacrov may well have issued the instruction, however, we are not certain.'

'We know that Lacrov believes that NATO and the West may be planning to attack his beloved mother Russia, and he may think that it's a good idea to keep the group active, just in case.'

Bastienne sat back in his chair, and contemplated what he had just heard.

'So how can I help Jon?

'Well, Director Heathcott asked me to approach you for assistance, and has suggested that one of us apply for a cleaner/janitors job, and the other applies for the role of a security officer at the U.N., thus I would have a backup in case it is needed.' 'These Chechens are extremely dangerous people, and would most likely have found a way to smuggle weapons into the United Nations headquarters, so we would need to be extremely careful,' said Jon.

Continuing he said, 'no doubt Director Heathcott will use his CIA connections to ensure that we are employed, and I am sure that he will clear the way for your participation with your superiors shortly, so sit tight for the time being,' continued Jon.

A few days later Barnaby called the Directeur Général de la police Nationale Yves Toussaint on a secure line in Paris.

'Bonjour Yves, J'espère que tu vas bien Mon ami?' I hope you are well my friend, said Barnaby.

'Oui merci, et comment vas-tu mon vieil ami,' yes thank you, and how are you old friend, replied Yves.

'Que se passe-t-il au pays des étoiles et des rayures?' What's happening in the land of Stars and Stripes, continued Yves.

'All's well on our end my friend, except for what the late President of Russia did while he was still alive, which I believe still poses a massive problem for the West.'

'We recently uncovered a plot that Pushkin had organised in his living years, which was that he had some Chechens hack anonymously into the infrastructure of various NATO countries, and from what we have discovered, it appeared that they intend shutting down the entire world's electrical grid,' said Barnaby.

'Believe it or not, they have positioned operatives in the I.T. department at the U.N.'

'We know the implications of a total electrical shutdown, which will affect not only NATO's military capabilities, but also banking worldwide, water and electricity supplies, as well as all communications.' 'So we have a nation with one finger on the nuclear button, and another on the world's infrastructure button.' 'Clearly, we need to negate this threat as a matter of urgency,' continued Barnaby.

'You are familiar with our agent that assisted Capitaine Pétit in finding the two terrorists that were planning to kill President Macon and Trent, as they traveled down Avenue des Champs-Élysées during the VE celebrations,' said Barnaby.

'Oui, from memory your agent's name is Jon, and these two guys did an outstanding job,' said Yves.

'Well the Chechens were employed at the UN a decade ago, and from what we have managed to find out so far, I can confirm that they are employed in the IT department.' 'So a huge problem for the West.' 'The team leader is a man by the name of Daud Dudiyn, and his two accomplices are both female namely, Malaika Sishani and Dagmara Mutsuray,' said Barnaby.

'I understand that the three of them live in a one-bedroom apartment at Midtown East, and it appears that Daud is servicing both females.' 'So I am asking that you to allow Capitaine Pétit to be involved in this operation, and with your permission, I will arrange for our agent and Capitaine Pétit to be employed at the U.N., and they can get to work to neutralize this threat,' continued Barnaby.

'This is extremely serious Barnaby, and I can confirm that I will make Capitaine Pétit available to assist.' 'That will be fine from our end,' confirmed Yves.

Two weeks later Jon and Bastienne found themselves waiting in the reception area of the Human Resources department at the United Nations headquarters, pretending not to know each other.

'So Monsieur, what job are you applying for?' enquired Bastienne.

'I am applying for the cleaner/janitor's job, and how about you?' questioned Jon.

'Well, my hope is to be employed as a security officer,' replied Bastienne.

The next day Jon and Bastienne reported for duty.

'Good to see you again Monsieur,' said Jon.

'Oui, you too, and good luck in your new job,' replied Bastienne.

Both reported to the heads of their respective departments, were given the relevant uniforms, and introduced to their colleagues. They started their training, and having been appointed as a cleaner/janitor, Jon had access to all areas in the building including the IT Department. He went about diligently cleaning the various areas, and gained the trust of the personnel with his friendly manner.

Females drooled over the handsome janitor, and ensured that they were at their respective work stations when he arrived to clean their office. Rather embarrassed by the attention he was getting, he concentrated on the task at hand.

He noted that the three IT Technologists seemed to be a very close-knit bunch, so he continued to with his duties, and noted their daily routine, focusing on their habits. Albeit that he heard everything they were saying, he was unable to understand, as they were conversing in their own native Chechen language. He activated a hidden tape recorder which was later sent to the CIA's technical department to decipher what these people were discussing.

A week later it was clear that the two female IT Technologists took their orders from the team leader, Daud Dudiyn. Jon took note that all three took their lunch break at the same time, so he purposely arrived to clean their workstations, and surrounding areas just before thirteen-hundred hours. They seemed to follow the same routine each day, which was that they would visit the toilet to relieve themselves, then make their way to the kitchenette, and warm their lunch in the microwave oven, before settling down in a recess area in the kitchenette to enjoy their meal.

Jon noticed that they did not have a clear view of their office from the recess, and quickly identified a place where he could hide a hidden mini camera that had a view of Daud's computer screen. Excellent he thought to himself as he climbed the ladder and attached the mini camera to the rail head that holds the vertical blinds. An hour later whilst on his break, he activated his mobile phone, and checked the footage to ensure that he had placed the camera in the correct position. Images of Daud's monitor came into view Excellent he thought to himself.

Later that evening Jon fired up the recorded video, and whilst he was unable to understand the Chechen language some of the recordings were in English as Daud conversed with various people within the U.N. organization. He forwarded the video to the technical department at the CIA's headquarters for analysis.

The following day, Barnaby called Jon on his mobile phone.

'Nothing to report, however, we did hear Daud answer his mobile phone, and from what we were able to hear, it appeared that he had a heated discussion with someone in Russian.' 'It sounded like he was demanding payment before he took action, so it seems as if they are getting closer to them enacting their plan.'

'We heard him say that he did not give a shit who was in command after Pushhin's death, but demanded payment before he proceeded.'

'We tapped his mobile phone, however, we were too late to intercept the entire call but we discovered that the call was made from Grozny in Chechnya, so our team is tracing the address as we speak.'

'Clearly someone in Russia must be calling the shots after the departure of Mr. Pushkin, so we need to identify who that person is, and eliminate him or her as well.'

'Best take action as soon as you can Jon, as I think we are almost out of time,' said Barnaby.

'Leave it to me, Director.' 'As soon as I have completed the mission, I will call you.'

Jon arrived a little early to clean the office, and went about his chores in the usual way. He donned plastic gloves, and emptied the waste bins, then made his way into the kitchenette cleaning all the bench tops. As usual the three made their way to the toilet to relieve themselves, so Jon made sure that he could not be seen, in case they returned unexpectedly. He opened the fridge, removed a small vial from his pocket, and poured the clear contents into the milk bottle before capping, and replacing the bottle in the fridge. He put the plastic vial into a zip lock bag, and placed it into his pocket

The clear liquid was the same poison that the CIA used in the clandestine operation to eliminate the two United States Senators, namely, Stratton and Cotalico who were members of the Three Sixty Degrees Group, as well as the leader of North Korea Kim Jong-un, his sisters, Pushkin and his three cronies.

The batch was far more potent than the batches that they had used to eliminate the other people in the past, and would result in the death of anybody that had consumed it, within an eight-hour period. Jon made his way out of the kitchen, and started dusting the office just as Daud, Miliika, and Dagmara returned from their toilet break.

He noted that all three followed their usual routine daily, and poured themselves a cup of milk, prior to warming the lunch, exactly as he had anticipated. They assumed their usual position in the recess, poured themselves a cup of milk, followed by their lunch, that they had warmed in the microwave and sat down to enjoy their lunch, followed by a cup of coffee. Creatures of habit he thought, and was confident that they would not see the morning sun the following day.

The poison would take around eight-hours to take effect, meaning that all three were likely to die in their apartment later that evening negating any suspicion of his involvement.

The next day Jon arrived early to clean their office, and noted their absence, so he emptied the contents of the milk bottle into the drain, then ran the hot tap in the sink for a full fifteen minutes, before rinsing the milk bottle with boiling water. He then poured drain cleaner into the sink, waited a further ten minutes before flushing boiling water into the sink a second time.

Satisfied that they were not reporting for duty, he checked their desks for any evidence of their involvement in the scheme to shut down the world's power grid, however, was unable to find anything that implicated any of them. Comfortable that he had gotten rid of any evidence that could incriminate him, he made his way down the passage, continuing with his daily chores in adjoining offices.

Later that afternoon, he called Barnaby on a secure line, and notified him that he believed that he had successfully eliminated all three. He suggested that Barnaby arrange for FBI agents to send a team to their apartment to recover whatever they may have hidden there.

The agents sent to the apartment discovered the three bodies, and the local police were called to the scene to investigate the cause of their death. Later a police report declared that the three had died of unknown causes, and that investigations were ongoing. Before reporting the deaths to the police, the agents cleared the apartment of all intelligence they could find including laptops and mobile phones which contained a treasure trough of information.

The CIA traced the person that regularly communicated with Daud, and discovered that the three were acting on instructions from someone in Russia, and that they were days away from enacting the plan to shut down the electrical grid of the world's leading economies, which would have led to chaos.

Clearly Pushkin had planned this with a trusted ally whilst still alive, so Barnaby knew that he would need to identify this person or organization, and eliminate him, her or them very soon.

This would be an ideal way for Russia to launch an attack on the west, and become the dominant world power able to dictate terms to the world at large, he considered.

Chapter 23

Zermatt

Switzerland

The cab driver dropped them off at international departures at Charles de Gaulle airport, and Claire could hardly contain her excitement as she exited the cab.

'Where are we going Yonti?'

'Well as you know, it's been two years since either of us has had a holiday, and I promised to take you on a mystery trip Mon Pétale, so don't ask, just enjoy the ride,' he replied smiling broadly.

Having checked their luggage in at the counter, and taken possession of their boarding passes, they made their way towards customs, joining the queue of Christmas and New Year holidaymakers. A customs official fell in beside them, and instructed them to accompany him to an office situated to the side of the customs processing cubicles found at international airports.

Claire, using his family name whispered, 'what's going on Yonti?'

Yonti shrugged his shoulders as they entered the office.

'Bonjour, my name is Pierre de la Coupetat.' 'Passports please.'

He scanned the passports, stamped both, turned to face them, and bid them a pleasant flight. He pointing towards a side door, indicating the way into the main passageway leading towards the departure gates.

'What on earth just happened Yonti?' asked Claire, somewhat bewildered.

He merely tilted his head as they made their way into the duty-free shop. Claire found her way to the display of Louis Viton handbags, so Yonti took advantage of the distraction, made his way to the perfume counter, and bought Claire a bottle of Tom Ford Limited Edition Eau De Parfum, priced at one thousand two-hundred and twenty-six Euros. He asked the assistant to gift wrap it, then ordered a bottle of Johnny Walker Blue, and a bottle of Chateau Lafleur Pomerol Cabernet Franc Merlot from the Bordeaux wine region of Haut Médoc.

A while later they headed towards the departure gate. Claire leaned over asked Yonti, what on earth had just happened, and how they were granted special treatment. She reminded him that they did not even have to make their way through the metal detector. He knew that he had security clearance because of his involvement with the CIA, and always had his Glock hidden in the rear of his pants, ready to face any threat, which would have caused the detector to bleep, resulting in it being discovered. The CIA always ensured special treatment for their operatives in total secrecy, so he merely shook his head.

'Well it's not only Presidents that don't have to clear customs you know,' he said with a broad smile on his face.

Claire stared at him in amazement, and concluded that it was likely due to his involvement with the CIA. He had become accustomed to receiving special treatment at various customs departure and arrival points, because Barnaby Heathcott had always cleared the way for him to enter or exit countries, without having to go through rigorous security procedures because he was always armed.

They made themselves comfortable at the departure gate, and waited for the announcement to board Air France flight A51614 to Zurich.

'So, we are going to Zurich,' she said, looking at the destination lit up on the overhead signboard above the gate at the departure lounge.

Yonti merely nodded. Can't keep it a secret any longer, however, she still does not know exactly where we are going he thought to himself. They settled into their first class seats for the one hour and fifteen-minute flight, sat back, and enjoyed the silver service that accompanies this exclusive method of travel.

'Wow Yonti, this is a big surprise to be flying first class.' 'I have never had the pleasure, so thank you,' she said as she leaned over and gave him a peck on the cheek.

The Co-Pilot announced their impending arrival in Zurich an hour into the flight, instructing all passengers to buckle up for landing. Ten minutes later, Yonti and Claire disembarked through the forward door of the Boeing 777X, and were headed towards customs, when a smartly dressed young gentleman in a customs uniform fell in beside them.

'Follow me,' he instructed.

Claire shot an inquiring look at Yonti, who merely shrugged his shoulders, as they were ushered into a side room where they were met by an immigration official.

'Hello Mister Dujon and Lieutenant Commander Johnston.' 'Welcome to Switzerland.' 'My name is Herr Meier, and I am the senior Immigration Official here at Zurich airport.'

'Passports please.'

He scanned them into the computer, stamped them, then handed them back.

'Your luggage will be waiting for you as you exit the office, so I wish you a very pleasant stay while you are in Switzerland.' 'Good day,' and with that, he turned and left the room.

'What on earth just happened Yonti?' 'Twice in a matter of hours, maybe I should call you sir,' said Claire smiling as she continued to use his family name.

Yonti merely smiled, and did not offer a response as he was sure that Barnaby Heathcott or Capitaine Pétit had arranged for him to bypass immigration, and the usual detector procedure, as they knew that he would be carrying his Glock which he had appropriately named, "The Equaliser". They picked up their luggage, loaded it onto a trolley, and made their way out of the customs hall, and into the arrivals hall where another person approached them.

'Hello, Rafael,' he said using his CIA undercover name.

Turning to face Claire he said, 'and I take it that you are Lieutenant Commander Johnston,' he said offering his hand in a greeting.

'My name is Frédéric Muller, and I have been instructed by Langley to drop you off at the Grand Hotel.' 'Welcome to Switzerland.' 'I hope you have a pleasant stay, and enjoy the scenery as well as the hospitality we have to offer in this picturesque land,' he said.

Claire was dumbfounded by the royal treatment, and turned to face her handsome partner.

'Is this the treatment you always get when you travel?'

'Just for you Mon Pétale.'

These name changes are making me sick he considered. I don't know who the fuck I am half the time. Rafael, Jon, or Yonti, who knows he thought to himself. As they approached the entrance to the Grand Hotel, he was reminded of the meeting he had with the Russian President's chief of security, when he took possession of a USB stick containing footage of the meeting between Russian President, Pushkin and Xiu Jaoping the Chinese leader. He smiled broadly, and gently nodded his head at the memory of a successful mission.

Claire unpacked a few belongings, as they were only due to stay at the hotel for two nights, and Yonti opened the bottle of wine he bought at the duty-free shop, poured a glass for Claire, then splashed a three-finger tot of Johnny Walker Blue over ice cubes.

'Merry Christmas Mon Pétale.'

He handed Claire the perfume he bought at the duty free shop, and kissed her passionately.

'Oh wow, how thoughtful of you Yonti.' 'Thank you ever so much handsome.' 'What a terrific gift.'

'Here's to our first holiday in two years,' he said clinking glasses.

'Santé, Mon Pétale,' said Yonti as he admired her beauty.

Two days later they boarded a train from Zurich to Zermatt.

'Where are we going Yonti?' 'You are driving me mad you know.'

The train to Zermatt normally covers the distance of one-hundred miles in around three hours, so they settled in for the journey. The town of Zermatt is one of the best places to visit in Switzerland. Near the famous mountain, known as the Matterhorn, and is a car-free village. The train arrived on time, typical of Swiss precision, and they caught a cab to the luxurious five-star Zermatt Lodge Hotel, featuring breathtaking views of the Matterhorn. He planned to spend five nights in Zermatt, then catch the Glazier Express to St. Moritz where they would spend a further five days before flying to Spain.

Claire unpacked while Yonti made his way to reception to confirm their booking for the New Year's Eve dinner in the crow's nest, which was situated in the loft area overlooking the restaurant. An ideal place that offered complete privacy, away from the throng of patrons. Later that evening, both dressed in their evening attire, and were escorted to a table in the nest. Claire looking radiant in her red evening gown, was overwhelmed by the dining choice that he had made.

'You are full of surprises Yonti Barr, and such a romantic.' 'This is most unusual and beautiful,' she said.

The service was outstanding, and having enjoyed a scrumptious meal, Yonti went down on one knee, opened a box containing a four-carat round-cut diamond engagement ring.

He looked at Claire and said, 'will you marry me?'

Claire burst into tears nodding her approval before standing and hugging her lover tightly.

'Yes, yes, yes and yes again,' she said as he slid the ring onto her finger.

Their lovemaking changed from the routine it had assumed, like that of long married couples, to the lust they had when they first made love. He moved his middle finger and slid it over her feeling her wetness and continued to massage her, as her cries of pleasure intensified. Claire reached multiple orgasms until he thrust his member deep into her vagina. Claire grabbed his hair as his rhythm intensified. He finally rolled off her spent. Both lay panting, staring at the ceiling. Claire ran her fingers through the crop of hair on his chest, leaned over, and kissed him passionately.

'I know how committed you are to the CIA and Barnaby Heathcott, but you need to quit before something awful happens.' 'From what I gather, you have used up all of your nine lives, and more Yonti Barr, and to be honest, I want to grow old with you, and hopefully raise a couple of children, and be a happy family leading a normal life.'

'Well to be truthful, I do intend resigning when we get back.' 'We will then get married, and I think we should move into the country possibly even here in Switzerland away from the hustle and bustle of city life.' 'Maybe buy a small farm, grow vegetables, have a cow so that we can have our own milk, make cheese, have a few chickens, and maybe have a farm stall at the edge of the property.'

'Part of this trip was to showcase the beauty of Switzerland to you, hoping that you would fall in love with the countryside, and maybe someday we could consider settling here.'

The next morning Yonti was up early, got dressed in his tracksuit, put his Glock into the back of his pants, and made his way downstairs. He went for a five-mile run, and had gone to great lengths to hide his gun from Claire which he hid amongst his dirty washing in his suitcase, ensuring that she was not aware that he carried a firearm. Feels good to be out in the fresh air he thought to himself, as he completed the run, and made his way up the stairs at the entrance to the hotel. An elderly gentleman stopped him and introduced himself as Hans Vogel, the head of the Swiss police.

'Hello Rafael,' he offered, using the usual CIA undercover name given to him by Barnaby Heathcott.

'I received a call from your boss yesterday warning me of a threat in our beautiful country by two Neo Nazis.' 'He mentioned that you are holidaying here in Switzerland, and that I should contact you to assist in taking care of our problem.' 'We in Switzerland are unaccustomed to threats, and to be honest, we don't know how to deal with something of this nature.'

Oh, sweet Jesus in heaven, here we go yet again. Rafael, Jon, Yonti. I can't keep up, and I am sick and tired of these name changes every ten minutes he thought to himself. Can't even have a holiday without there being some sort of a problem.

'We never have any trouble here, so this is a first for many years, to be honest.' 'I would prefer to take care of this problem quietly, and get rid of it without anybody even knowing.' 'So from what Barnaby Heathcott told me, you are just the person to do that.' 'I am hoping that you will agree to assist us to eliminate this problem quietly.'

An instant later his mobile phone lit up with an incoming call from Barnaby.

'Hello Rafa, I'm calling to let you know that you can expect an approach from a person by the name of Hans Vogel, the head of the Swiss police regarding a problem they have, and he will most likely ask you to assist them in getting rid of that problem.'

'Well boss, I am having a conversation with him as we speak.'

'OK, I will leave it up to Hans to fill in the blanks, and for the record, I insisted that they give you immunity from prosecution should you be implicated in anything to do with this issue,' added Barnaby.

'Au revoir Rafa,' he said ending the call.

Hans turned to face Rafael, 'the two people I need taken care of are having breakfast right here in the hotel, so if you care to join me, we can have a coffee, and I can point them out to you.'

As they sipped their coffee, Hans added, 'if you look behind me, you will see two people seated near the window.' 'Both are dressed in kaki jackets, so they are easily identifiable.'

'Look closely, and you may catch a glimpse of a swastika hanging around the big fella's neck.' 'You can barely see it, but it's there,' he added.

'Yes I can see a small part of it protruding out of the side of his shirt,' replied Rafael.

'I am asking that you take care of this discreetly, without being spotted or caught, so please be careful.' 'I know that you guys don't like taking prisoners, so I am guaranteeing you immunity from prosecution should you be caught,' he continued.

'I also know that you guys move in the shadows, and are extremely efficient at what you do.'

Rafael was used to taking orders, and carrying them out without questioning the reason, so he merely nodded.

'I see, OK leave it up to me,' he said, as Hans stood and bid him farewell, paying for the coffees as he departed.

Rafael made his way to reception and waited for the two to leave the hotel. Half an hour later both exited the hotel, and Rafael pulled his baseball cap down covering his eyes, and as much of his face as possible, then followed them at a discreet distance as they made their way across the road towards a parking garage opposite the hotel. Rafael quickened his pace, ensuring that he closed the gap, as they made their way towards the staircase leading to the first level.

He was behind both of them as they turned to climb the last flight of stairs leading to the first-level parking, extracted his Glock fitted with a silencer from the rear of his tracksuit pants. A moment later he shot both in the back of the head, then quickly made his way to the first level parking, walked calmly down the ramp, and out of the parking complex.

He walked around several blocks, removed his cap, and placed it into his pocket, as made his way into the hotel through the car park. He chose to use the stairs making his way up to the room.

Claire was seated on the couch, and questioned why he had taken so long.

'Gee you must have been for a long run.' 'What took you so long?' she questioned.

He knew that he could never tell her exactly what he does, and always tried as best he could to divert questions in another direction. Wonder how she would react if ever she knew or what my parents and brother would think if they knew. Have to keep it hidden forever.

'Yes, I think it was about ten miles, then I popped into the gym to round off with some martial arts training.'

As he finished towelling himself, the wailing sounds of sirens intensified, so he wrapped the towel around his midriff, and made his way towards the window. He watched as the ambulance and police cars stopped at the entrance to the parking garage.

'Wonder what the hell is going on,' he said.

A while later he sent Barnaby an SMS on a secure line notifying him that daddy and son had departed.

The five days passed quickly, and they made their way back to the Zermatt Railway station. They boarded the Glazier Express heading to St. Moritz, a distance of one-hundred and eighty-one miles that takes around eight hours.

The Glacier Express is the slowest express train in the world, offering travellers full panoramic views of the countryside passing over the Rhine-Canyon and Oberalp-pass. Special panoramic windows offer the best views, and is the best way to discover the most beautiful parts of the Swiss Alps. The staff serve snacks, drinks, and a special three-course meal at passenger's seats.

The journey from Zermatt starts at the dead end of an Alpine Valley, known as the Mattertal which is just below the world-renowned Matterhorn, at an elevation of five thousand two-hundred and sixty-nine feet, before it descends towards the Valley of Valais in Brig. The train travels through the center of the Swiss Alps, over two-hundred and ninety-one bridges, through ninety-one tunnels including the nine and a half mile Furka Tunnel, at an elevation of four thousand nine-hundred feet as it circumvents the Furka Pass.

The train stops at Andermatt on a secluded high Aline Valley, then traverses to its highest point on the Oberalp Pass at an elevation of six thousand six-hundred and seventy feet, before descending to Chur at one thousand nine-hundred and nineteen feet. The train then backtracks to a higher altitude to reach St. Moritz situated in a valley to the south.

The entire line is a meter gauge commonly known as a narrow gauge railway, with fifteen miles of track using the rack-and-pinion system, both for ascending steep grades, and to control the descent. It is operated by Glazier Express AG, and is jointly owned by Rhaetian Railway, passing through the World Heritage Site known as Rhaet, showcasing the Albula/Bernina Landscapes

'This is truly stunning,' 'Thank you Yonti, it's really beautiful,' said Claire as she took in the panoramic views.

Claire had absolutely no idea of what he had done, and he did everything in his power to ensure that she remained in the dark regarding what he does daily. He gazed at the panoramic view reminding himself that he had become a ruthless killer in the line of duty, and questioned whether what he does on a daily basis was justified.

Chapter 24

Barcelona

Spain

The travel time from St. Moritz to Barcelona on board the Eurail train took around thirteen-hours and fifty minutes to complete the five-hundred and nineteen-mile journey.

The train arrived on time, and they disembarked following the throng of passengers heading into the arrivals hall. As they entered the hall, Yonti's eyes darted around the hall glancing at the hordes of people making their way towards the concourse exit, with many headed in the direction of various departure platforms. He noticed two young men walking ahead of them, and focused on the one that had a backpack slung loosely over one shoulder.

Something alerted him to manner in which these two seemed to constantly be looking around to ensure that they were not being followed. He took note of the star tattooed on the right hand of the man carrying the bag. His long dark hair was neatly tied into a ponytail. The backpack and black hoodie jumper had the same star printed on the back of them. Strange that a person would have the same star on his hand, backpack and hoodie, he thought.

The training he received at the CIA's training facility at Camp Perry had honed his sensors to be aware of his surroundings at all times, and his instructor, aptly named The Hulk, due to his physical size and physique, had drummed it into him. He needed to be on guard at all times. Something about the way these two moved troubled him. They seemed rather nervous, which is a sign that they may be up to something, so he focused on the one carrying the backpack.

He kept his eyes on both, and watched as they were headed in the same direction, towards the exit. A short time later, he noticed that the man carrying the backpack had placed it into a refuse bin, and both seemed to have quickened their pace towards the exit.

Yonti held his hand out to stop Claire, moved in front of her, and shouted for everyone to take cover. He instructed people to move away from the refuse bin because there may be a bomb in it, pointing towards the bin positioned in the middle of the concourse.

'There is a bomb in the bin,' he shouted.

Chaos broke out as people scurried to move away from the bin dashing in every direction. He placed his leg behind Claire, and gently dropped her onto her back cushioning her fall with his arm, landing with his body on top of hers. A moment later there was a loud explosion, and the carnage became evident as he lifted his head.

'Stay put,' he instructed.

He was on his feet in an instant, and ran towards the exit in pursuit of the bombers, stopping at the edge of the road, and searching for any sign of the two suspects. It soon became clear that both had disappeared. Bastards he thought, hopefully, their images have been captured on CCTV. As he turned to make his way back into the concourse he looked directly into the barrel of a police officer's gun.

'No te muevas.' Do not move.

'No hablo español,' I don't speak Spanish.

The police officer ordered him to lie face down on the concrete, and frisked him.

'Ah, what do we have here?' he said, as he removed the Glock from the back of his pants.

A moment later another police officer was alongside, cuffed him, and pulled him to his feet.

'So you are trying to run away?'

'No, I am trying to find where the two people that planted the bomb have gone,' 'I saw one guy place a backpack into a refuse bin, before he an accomplice made a hasty exit, and shortly after that, a bomb exploded,' said Yonti.

'My partner is inside, so if you don't believe me, go and ask her.'

'Why are you carrying a weapon?' questioned the officer.

'Because I work for the CIA.'

'Yes right, you work for the CIA.' 'That's just an excuse to try and wriggle out of this.'

'No officer, my mobile phone is in my pocket.' 'Look up the number for my boss listed under Big Daddy and call him.' 'He is the Director of the CIA and his name is, Barnaby Heathcott.' 'He is based at the CIA's headquarters in Langley, Virginia USA.'

The officers bundled him into the back of a police van that had just arrived, and instructed the driver to take him to Guàrdia Urbana de Barcelona's head office, and place him in a holding cell until they arrived.

A short while later they located Claire who was assisting the injured, as the wailing sound of more police vehicles and ambulances grew louder. Claire had no idea that Yoni had been arrested, and did her best to aid the injured, eventually glancing around, and letting out a sigh of relief that nobody appeared to have been killed. Various people pointed in her direction, as police tried to establish what had happened. Onlookers notified the police that her partner had most likely saved dozens of lives by alerting them to the danger.

'I am Capitán Santiago Domingo of the policéa Española señora, and I am hoping that you can shed some more light on what just happened here, so please follow me,' he instructed.

As paramedics took over the duties of tending to the injured, Claire looked around trying to find Yonti, however to no avail as he had simply vanished. So she picked up their belongings, and dragged their suitcases towards a side door that led to a control room.

'I take it that you are tourists, so firstly I wish to apologize for the terrible experience you have witnessed, and thank you most sincerely for assisting the injured.' 'People have mentioned that you shouted a warning which has helped save dozens of lives señora, so thank you once again.'

'I need to find my partner officer.' 'He is the one that shouted a warning for people to scatter away from the bin,' said Claire.

'Let's start with your name please?'

'My name is Claire Johnston and my partner is Yonti Barr.'

The moment she mentioned his name, she realized that he was using his CIA under cover name of Rafael Dujon.

'Can I see your passports please,' instructed Santiago?

He perused through the passports noting that the name of Yonti Barr mentioned by her, did not match the name on his passport.

'Señora, you said his name is Yonti Barr, so how come the name on the passport is Rafael Dujon?'

'My partner works for the CIA, and sometimes uses an alias when traveling.' 'Fell free to call the USA Embassy in Paris, and talk to the ambassador.' 'Or call the CIA's head office in Virginia USA, and ask to speak with Director Heathcott.' 'I suggest that you do that because this could become a diplomatic issue, so best you call, and find out for yourself.'

'I will send some officers to locate your partner, so what is he wearing?'

'He has a dark blue windbreaker on, with white sneakers and a red baseball cap, so you should easily be able to identify him.'

'Well Capitán, I know it sounds a little confusing, however, I urge you to call and speak with the Director of the CIA.'

'I am afraid that I cannot do that because you, and your partner seem to have false passports so I have to place you under arrest.' 'Please stand so that we can cuff you.' 'I will get one of our officers to drive you to the police station for further questioning.'

'As I said, find my partner, and we can clear this all up,' demanded Claire.

The officer cuffed Claire, and a fellow officer dragged the luggage towards a parked police van. He instructed her to get in. Half an hour later, she was led to an adjacent cell that housed Yonti, and she turned to face him as she passed. They locked the cell door.

'There you are Yonti.' 'What the hell is happening?'

'I have no idea at all.' 'This is ridiculous.'

'What are we going to do Yonti?'

'No idea, let's just wait and see.'

Two hours later, Capitán Domingo arrived, and ordered that they both be taken to an interrogation room. He walked slowly around the table staring at them, then sat down, studied both passports, and noted that Claire's passport only had an exit stamp from France, an entry and exit stamp into and out of Switzerland as well as an entry stamp into Spain.

'I find it very suspicious that according to your companion, your name is supposed to be Yonti Barr, yet the name on the passport is Rafael Dujon,' said the Capitán.

'Capitán, please call Director Heathcott at the CIA, and he will verify exactly who I am,' 'The number is in my mobile phone,' said Yonti emphatically.

Thirty minutes later, Capitán Domingo returned to the interrogation room, and his attitude had completely changed. It was clear that not only had he spoken to Barnaby, but he must have received a call from a higher authority in Spain.

'So, I spoke with your Director, and he confirmed exactly who you are.' 'He said that I should embrace any assistance you can offer to find the persons that planted the bomb.' 'He has also contacted the DSN, which is the department of homeland security here in Spain, and they have ordered your immediate release, so please accept my apologies for the inconvenience.'

'I would like to take this opportunity to thank you most sincerely for warning people of the possibility that there was a bomb placed in the refuse bin.' 'This helped save many lives, so once again, I apologize and thank you.'

Capitán Domingo handed Yonti's gun back to him.

'You are free to go, and I will have an officer to drive you to your hotel.'

'I would be most grateful if you can offer any assistance in identifying those responsible, as they seemed to have vanished into thin air.'

'All that I can offer you, is that the person that placed the backpack into the refuse bin had a tattoo of a star on his right hand.' 'His hoodie and the backpack that he was carrying, also had a star printed on it.' 'Not sure if the star means anything at all, but it seems that it could be some sort of emblem that a group may well have adopted as their motto,' said Yonti.

'Surely you have CCTV surveillance cameras around the station entrance.'

'Yes, we are reviewing the footage right now.'

The Cápitan handed his Glock back to him, as well as a business card, then offered another apology as he led the way towards the exit, and bid them farewell.

Claire turned to face Yonti as they made their way into the Grand Barcelona hotel and said, 'how on earth did you manage to hide your gun from me, mister Barr?'

'I always have it with me Claire, so don't ask.'

'Well, that's a first.' 'Neither of us have ever been handcuffed before, or arrested, and placed in a holding cell.' 'Then to crown it all, I am accused of having a fraudulent passport.' 'A real warm welcome to Spain.' 'What an experience.'

They settled into their room and unpacked.

'I have been thinking about the people that placed the bomb in the bin, and believe that they may be members of the Catalan Independence Movement, which is a political movement that supports an independent Catalonia from the rest of Spain.'

'Spain's government rejected any ultimatum from Catalonia on moving towards self-determination, and remained focussed on having a wide-ranging dialogue with the Restive Catalonia Region to resolve a secession crisis.' 'They allowed self-government, but no independence.'

'So, there is no doubt that those that have not accepted this outcome are determined to carry on fighting for independence.'

They casually meandered their way out of the hotel, then made their way into the center of the city enjoying its beauty, eventually hiring two bicycles, and pedalling their way up the hill to Gaudi's Landscape Gardens. They stopped at the iconic viewing terrace, and visited the Hypostyle room. The Dragon Stairway offered a spectacular view. Park Guell was one of the highlights. They also visited La Sagrada Familia, the UNESCO-listed Casa Batllo as well as Casa Mila.

Eventually, they found their way to Montjuic Castle, on a coastal hill that is home to a veritable treasure chest of attractions that include, the Olympic Stadium, the Botanical Gardens, and the Joan Miro Foundation, on one side of the hill, Poble Espanyol, with the MNAC museum, and Magic Fountain on the other side.

They made their way to the top of the hill by cable car enjoying the sensational views over the city as cable car ascended. The day ended with them attending a Paella cooking class in the late afternoon, enjoying a couple of glasses Cava which is the Spanish version of Champagne, before taking a stroll through the narrow labyrinthine of the Gothic Quarter, one of the medieval districts that make up the Old Town.

Later that evening they watched the flamenco dancers strut their stuff at a rooftop concert before making their way back to their hotel.

'I'm exhausted,' said Claire as she headed for the shower.

'Well, Mon Pétale, tomorrow we will go to Camp Nou, which is the home ground of the Barcelona Football Club, and watch the soccer match between Barcelona and Real Madrid, two giants of Spanish and world football.' 'I have always supported Barcelona, so I think we will experience a very competitive game, and I hope that you will enjoy it.'

The next day they found their way to their reserved seats amongst the Barcelona supporters. The game was electric with the score tied at zero all, and both teams trying desperately to find a winner. Barcelona scored the winner five minutes from full time, and their supporters went crazy celebrating. All the Barcelona supporters were standing and cheering, and Yonti noticed a person five rows in front of them with his hands in the air in celebration. He noticed the star on his right hand as well as the star printed on the back of his hoodie.

Sweet Jesus, that's the person that placed the bomb into the refuse bin he thought, as he looked at his long dark hair tied into a ponytail. He settled back into his seat, keeping his eye on the suspect. Looks like the same guy he thought to himself. The game ended in a one-goal victory to the home side. Yonti and Claire made their way down the stairs heading towards the exit, and he ensured that he kept the suspect in his eyesight.

They followed a short distance behind. Claire had no idea that he was focused on the suspect that may have placed the bomb in the refuse bin. The crowd thinned out, and the suspect accompanied by a friend made their way towards the Olé Bar a short distance from the stadium. The bar was crowded with Barcelona fans celebrating the team's victory, and Yonti guided Claire towards the bar, ordered a beer and a glass of wine.

He kept sight of the suspect, reached into his wallet, extracted the police captain's business card, and sent him an SMS notifying him that he had a visual of the suspect that placed the bomb in the refuse bin. He suggested that the Cápitan send a dozen plain-clothed police to the bar. They could identify him by the dark blue windbreaker, the Barcelona peaked cap, and scarf he was wearing. He suggested that the captain instruct one of his officer's approach him, and utter the word Asombroso, meaning amazing in Spanish.

Twenty minutes later the group of police officers arrived at the pub, and made their way separately into the bar. Yonti noticed the Cápitan pausing at the door, his eyes working the bar, as he tried to find Yonti in the crowded bar, eventually making eye contact, he made his way through the throng towards him standing at the far end of the bar.

'Asombroso señor,' offered the Cápitan.

'You know my partner Cápitan,' he whispered over the boisterous throng.

'Sí señor, hello señora,' he said turning to face Claire.

Claire was totally surprised to see the Cápitan standing next to her.

'What on earth are you doing here?' she said with raised eyebrows.

Yonti leaned over, and whispered that he had identified the bomber, who was enjoying a beer right near them, and instructed her not to look around or act surprised. Stay calm, and leave it up to the police to arrest him. A while later, the suspect and his friend made their way toward the exit. Suddenly twelve police officers surrounded the suspects and cuffed both of them, then led them towards an unmarked police car nearby.

The Cápitan turned towards Yonti, 'thank you ever so much for identifying this bomber, and once again, I apologize most sincerely to both of you, for the way I treated you.'

As they walked back to the hotel, Claire turned to face Yonti. 'Wow, how secretive you are handsome.'

Yonti merely nodded and offered a slight smile.

Chapter 25

Wood Village

Oregon USA

'So Rafa, in our line of business, the problems keep coming thick and fast.' 'We have uncovered yet another extremely serious problem that needs urgent attention.' 'This time it involves a group of home grown fanatics here in the USA, who intend to assassinate the President, as well as several people in the current administration, to sow panic amongst the population here.' 'They seek to change the government's stance on racism, and possibly install their own President, which from what I have learned, is a person by the name of Arlo Dallarosa.'

'He is a current sitting member of the senate, and harbors a radical right-wing agenda, so we need to treat him as hostile, because he is also a member of the secret White Patriotic Front.' 'This is a group of radical fanatical racist's, intent on taking the USA back to the days of slavery.' 'Clearly, we cannot allow this to happen.'

'So here's a short history of our country Rafa.' 'Abraham Lincoln's legacy, is that of the Great Emancipator, liberating over four million slaves, which is well documented in the annals of US history.' 'He was killed on the fifteenth of April eighteen sixty-five and on the eighteenth of December of the same year, the thirteenth Amendment was adopted as part of the United States Constitution.' 'The amendment officially abolished slavery, and immediately freed more than one- hundred thousand enslaved people, from Kentucky to Delaware.'

'Slavery in America began early in the sixteenth century and ended in eighteen sixty-five.' 'Slaves, mostly from Africa, worked in the production of tobacco crops and later, cotton.' 'The invention of cotton gin in seventeen-hundred and ninety-three along with the growing demand for the product in Europe resulted in the use of slaves in the South that became a foundation of their economy.'

'In the late eighteenth century, the abolitionist movement began in the north, and the country began to divide over the issue between North and South.' 'In eighteen twenty, the Missouri Compromise banned slavery in all new western territories, which Southern states saw as a threat to the institution of slavery itself.' 'In eighteen fifty-seven, the Supreme Court decision known as the Dred Scott Decision, said that Negroes (the term then used to describe the African race at the time) were not citizens, and had no rights of citizenship, therefore, slaves that escaped to free states were not free but remained the property of their owners, and had to be returned to them.' 'The decision antagonized many Northerners, and breathed new life into the floundering Abolition Movement.'

'The election of Abraham Lincoln, a member of the anti-slavery Republican Party, to the presidency in eighteen-hundred and sixty convinced many Southerners that slavery would never be permitted to expand into new territories acquired by the US, and might ultimately be abolished.' 'Eleven Southern states attempted to secede from the Union, precipitating the Civil War.'

'That's a shortened version of some of the history in the USA Rafa.'

'So to compound the problem, this group intends further attacks on various sitting members of the senate.' 'They hope to achieve a clean sweep, and form a new government as soon as they have removed people from positions of power.' 'From what we have learned, they intend to carry out their attacks within a few weeks from today.' 'As I understand it, they intend to take America back to the dark years of white domination and deport African Americans, which we know is simply not feasible or achievable as no African nation is ever going to take millions of people back into their countries.'

'So they hope that by assassinating the President, and killing members of his administration, as well as various senators, they will achieve their objective, leaving Americans to wonder who will lead the nation, which will create mass panic,' continued Barnaby.

Barnaby knew the legalities of killing fellow Americans in America.

'From what I understand this group was formed in Wood Village in Oregon, which is around three-hundred and twenty-four miles from Washington where fathers work in wood mills or drive log trucks.' 'You can always tell by their stained teeth, and the circle worn into the back pockets of their jeans from their Copenhagen tins that hold their snuff or tobacco. Most families invest a large portion of their disposable income on weapons and giant 4x4 trucks.'

'These people tend to be racist with narrow-minded opinions.' 'The population of Wood Village is around seventy-five percent white, of which some fifty-two percent are males, with a mere one percent African American.'

'The history of racism in Oregon began before the territory even became a State in the USA' 'The topic of race was heavily discussed during the convention where the Oregon Constitution was written in eighteen fifty-seven and eighteen fifty-nine.' 'It became the only state to enter the Union with a black exclusion law, although there were many other states that had tried that before, especially in the Midwest.' 'The Willamette Valley was notorious for hosting white supremacist hate groups with an agenda of discrimination and segregation.'

'Portland is the largest city in the state, and continues to have one of the largest proportions of white residents of all major U.S. cities.'

'Some more American history for you Rafa.'

'So Rafa, I want you to drive to Wood Village, and pose as a tourist. Sniff out where these people meet, and try as best you can to identify those involved in this conspiracy.'

'They have been very secretive with everything they do, and it's almost impossible to infiltrate their network, albeit that we have been monitoring their leader, the honorable senator Dallarosa for some time.' 'He has been extremely cautious in everything he does, and he travels to Wood Village every weekend.'

'Our intelligence is solid, but limited regarding this senator, however, we need to gather far more evidence before the FBI can charge him for treason, so I need you to be extremely careful as this group is most likely well-armed and very dangerous.'

A couple of days later, Rafael, drove into Wood Village late on a Saturday afternoon and parked his old beat-up two-door nineteen forty-six Chevy truck outside the local saloon bar. Barnaby had arranged for a middle-aged African American agent to loiter near the pub's entrance, so he positioned himself against a lamppost near the entrance to the bar, and pretended to be reading the local newspaper.

Dressed in a pair of American Bib farmer overall jeans complete with over-the-shoulder straps, making him appear like a typical farm worker, he approached the entrance to the bar, and stopped to warn the African American not to touch his beloved truck.

'Why the fuck don't you go back to Africa where you belong, and where your ancestors came from?' said Rafael loudly in an agitated voice.

'You add no value to this beautiful land, so just fuck off and make sure that you are not here when I come out, because if you are, I will personally pack you up into a cardboard box, and mail you back to Africa nigger.'

The term nigger is an ethnic slur widely used during the sixteen to eighteen-hundreds when Americans referred to African slaves. Many local red necks witnessed his aggressive attitude towards the man before he entered the crowded bar. He made his way to the end of the bar and ordered a beer. The locals entered a short while later, eyeing him suspiciously, and made their way towards a group standing at the far end of the bar. They seemed to whisper something amongst each other, and he noticed that they all seemed to have tattoos, many appeared to be missing teeth, and the remaining teeth appeared to be stained by tobacco.

One of the rednecks made his way toward Rafael.

'You are a stranger, and not from around here?'

'No sir, I am French, and passing through, so I thought that I would stop and have a beer.'

'So where is a Beauf like you headed, he asked arrogantly?'

Beauf is French slang for an undereducated and annoying white dude that is vulgar, unsophisticated, unintelligent, arrogant, uncaring, and chauvinistic, without any taste for etiquette or good manners.

'I am looking for a log trucking job so that I can earn enough money to continue on my journey across the USA,' said Rafael without taking offense.

'Well, maybe you have come to the right place, because the company I work for is looking for a couple of drivers, so come and meet my workmates, and have a beer with us.'

'Merci Monsieur that would be great.'

The group of rednecks crowded around him, and were interested to hear why he confronted the African American in the manner that he did.

'Well in my country, France, we have the same problem, because of the number of black refugees both legal and illegal that our government has allowed into the country.' 'They have no skills, live off government handouts, and are constantly causing problems, so curse the day that France ever allowed them entry into our country.'

'I cannot stand these black people, who continue to be a problem in my country, so fuck them.'

'Well, you have come to the right place, because we too cannot stand them, and we would like to see them all sent back to Africa.' 'My name is Buck Zade and I am the foreman at the Forest Trucking Company.' 'So do you have a heavy-duty license Beauf?'

'Oui, here it is,' he said as he extracted it from his wallet and handed it to him.

'OK, come and see me on Monday morning at six o'clock at this address,' he said scribbling it on a piece of paper.'

'You will be paid twenty-four dollars an hour, so make sure you are not late.'

Hours later, feeling a little under the weather, Rafael watched as the bunch of rednecks, now well and truly intoxicated, got louder and louder, so he excused himself and bid them all farewell. He jumped into his truck and headed towards the outskirts of the village, full well knowing that he was well over the legal alcohol limit, hoping that he would not be stopped and breathalyzed along the way.

He booked into the Wood Village Truckers Motel, a modest three-star motel, and unpacked his belongings, then walked to the local bakery and bought a pie for dinner.

The next morning he was up early, and went for his usual ten-mile run, returned, and took a shower, before taking a leisurely drive around the village making a mental note of its outlay. He then drove into the forest along a well-worn dirt track, eventually finding his way to the logging truck company's site office, and familiarised himself with the surrounding area. As he drove deeper into the forest, he took note of a clearing that appeared to have been used on regular basis with some tree stumps positioned in a circle that appeared to be seating.

Later that day, he sent Barnaby an SMS on a secure line informing him that he had made contact with a group of rednecks that had openly stated their hatred of African Americans, so he was relatively confident that he may have identified them as part of the group that they were seeking to infiltrate. He confirmed the GPS coordinates and told Barnaby that he had been offered a log trucking job, and was expected to start the next morning.

Unbeknown to law enforcement agencies, Barnaby was tracking the trucking company's activities by satellite.

He knocked on the door at exactly zero six-hundred hours before entering.

'Right Beauf, take a seat instructed Buck.' 'Fill in these forms, and we can get you into one of the logging trucks.' 'Here's your clock card, so make sure you clock in and out every day, or you won't get paid.'

'By the way, the company deducts ten percent of your wages, which goes towards a fund that will guarantee that our state remains independent of Washington.'

Thirty minutes later, he jumped into the cab of a filthy logging truck, and followed another logging truck deep into the forest. He parked, waited, and watched as the deforestation hydraulic forklift loader, loaded logs onto the trailer. Ten minutes later he eased his truck and trailer into the loading area, and waited until it was stacked to the correct height, then followed the lead truck heading towards the mill.

Having dropped his load off at the mill, his two-way radio crackled to life.

'Right Frenchie, you know the drill so you are on your own from now on.' 'See you at the end of the shift.' 'Oh, by the way, there is no break for lunch, so you will need to eat on the run, and if you need to have a piss or shit, head into the bushes.'

At the end of his shift, he clocked out, and was about to jump into his truck when one of the other drivers shouted for him to join them for a beer at the local pub.

'Oui, see you there,' he responded as he busied himself cleaning the cab of the rubbish strewn on the floor.

Right, let the games continue he thought. This may be the opportunity to fish out some more useful information about this group.

'Cheers,' shouted Virgil. A huge fellow with massive biceps covered in tattoos and missing numerous teeth. The remaining teeth were badly stained from chewing tobacco. Fucking hillbilly he thought.

'Salute,' said Rafael raising his glass, as he looked around at the group of rednecks in the bar.

'So how was your first day Frenchie?' questioned Virgil.

'All good thanks, however, I want to know why the company deducts ten percent of a person's wages, which I find most unusual.'

'Well, that goes to good use.' 'In fact, it is a war chest to fight government's authority, because here in the bush, we run our territory by our own set of rules, and we will not tolerate any interference.'

'I see, so what does the company do with the money, because I too share the view that governments waste taxpayer's money'? Questioned Rafael.

A few beers later and seeming to be well on his way to being intoxicated, Virgil opened up about the activities of the group.

'Well, we have our own army up here, and meet every Saturday.' 'He could not resist bragging about the group's intention to one day get rid of the bureaucrats in Washington, and replace them with their own President.'

'In fact, you seem a decent kind of guy Frenchie, so why don't you come along and join us on Saturday, and I will introduce you to our President.'

'Merci, I will do that, so where do I meet you, and what time'?

'We meet here at the pub at noon, and finish at five o'clock, then come back here for a few beers, so I will meet you here and introduce you to our army.'

Yes, thought Rafael. This may be extremely dangerous, so I hope that this will go well. Best let Director Heathcott know. Later, he excused himself, and made his way into town seeking a place to have a meal. Back in the motel room, he again sent Barnaby an SMS notifying him that he had been invited to join the group at their training site on Saturday.

The week went by rather quickly, and Rafael found himself seated at the crowded bar counter when Virgil tapped him heavily on the shoulder.

'Meet the future President of the USA.' 'This is President Dallarosa.'

Rafael stood and offered his hand. 'Bonjour Monsieur President.'

Arlo Dallarosa studied him for some time, before accepting his hand.

'So from what I have been told, you are French, and according to what I have been led to believe, you dislike blacks as much as we do.'

'Oui Monsieur President that is true, we in France have a massive problem with black refugees flooding into our country, and living off government grants.' 'They are the cause of much of the crime, yet the idiot that runs our country merely turns a blind eye' 'Curse the day we let them in.'

Arlo viewed him with suspicion, and seemed unsure of this new stranger that had been invited to join them later in the day. He was rather annoyed that Virgil had invited a stranger into his group, and made a mental note to discipline him later.

'Right, hop in Beauf,' instructed Virgil.

They made their way towards the clearing that Rafael had seen a week earlier in Virgil's pride and joy, an old nineteen fifty-four Chevrolet thirty-one hundred two-door pick-up truck. His truck was in immaculate condition featuring a two-tone blue and back livery.

'Nice truck,' said Rafael.

'Yes, I love it more than my wife.'

Rafael was astounded to see the number of men standing in the opening as they approached. There must be a few hundred here he thought to himself, as he jumped out of the truck. Virgil introduced him to numerous people, as they made their way toward the center of the circle.

All of them either carried side arms, rifles, or shotguns and most seemed to have the usual redneck tattoos all over their arms, legs and necks. Many appeared to be chewing tobacco and were constantly spitting the brown saliva on the ground.

Looks like a very dangerous lot for sure, thought Rafael as his eyes traversed around the throng.

A while later, the attention turned to the arrival of Arlo Dallarosa, and Virgil shouted out the order, attention. All snapped to attention, and saluted as he exited the new GMC Sierra twenty-five hundred Denali Crew Cab four-by-four vehicle. It seemed that Virgil was some sort of sergeant at arms for the group.

Dallarosa addressed the crowd before they all made their way towards what appeared to be a shooting range, and in a well-coordinated drill, they formed two lines, one in front of the other. Those in the front knelt, whilst those behind remained standing. Moments later the front row fired at targets a hundred yards ahead, and shortly after they had emptied their magazines of all the rounds of ammunition, the row standing opened fire. Rafael watched with interest from the side.

Silence fell over the forest, as all the rednecks reloaded. Virgil walked over to Rafael, and handed him a Custom twenty-eight Nosler Tuebor bolt action precision rifle.

'Let's see what you can do Frenchie.' 'Aim at the tin can resting on the tree stump.'

Rafael knew that he could not display his marksmanship, and possibly expose who he was, so he clumsily pulled the side bolt back, pretending to load the gun, and an unused round flew out of the chamber.

'No you dumb fool, the rifle is loaded, so just aim and shoot,' instructed Virgil as he bent down and picked up the round.

He took the rifle from Rafael, pulled the side bolt back, and inserted a round into the chamber, before handing it back to him.

'This is a single-shot rifle so you need to pull the side bolt back after each shot, then reload it, so let's see what you Frogs are made of.'

Dallarosa watched with interest as he fired numerous shots deliberately missing the target until he had used all the rounds handed to him by Virgil.

'Clearly, you need a lot more practice Frenchie, because you are pretty useless.'

The group performed various drills and formations for a couple of hours before being addressed by Dallarosa. It was nearing seventeen-hundred hours, the time that the group normally packs up and heads towards their usual drinking hole, when Rafael noticed Dallarosa deep in conversation with Virgil. He did his best not to stare in their direction, and watched intently in his peripheral vision as it appeared that Dallarosa was giving Virgil a real dressing down. This does not look good at all, he thought.

A while later Virgil instructed the group to dismiss, and signalled for Frenchie to get into the truck. They headed back into town, and made their way to the pub that the group usually frequented. The place was packed, and dozens of people had spilled out onto the pavement, all with a beer in hand. The President wants a word with you Frenchie, so follow me. They made their way towards the end of the block, and Rafael became aware that a group of four rednecks were following closely behind.

As they rounded the corner, the four men tackled him from behind. One put a stranglehold around his neck, so he used an Ushiro-Geri, a back kick, breaking the thug's leg at the knee, before using a Mawashi-Geri, a round-house kick to the head of the other thug alongside him, both actions that he had learned as a student of martial arts. The thug with the broken leg lay screaming on the ground, while the other had been knocked out.

Virgil swung a heavy-handed blow to his head which Rafael did not see coming, as he was trying to free himself from the grip of those behind him, and was knocked unconscious to the ground. The group started kicking him, and as he slowly regained consciousness, he tried as best he could to cover his head from the continuous kicking. They pulled him to his feet, bound his arms behind his back, and dragged him towards an old derelict warehouse fifty yards further down the road, then continued to punch him repeatedly. Eventually taping his mouth with duct tape. They threw a rope over a roof beam, and pulled him up ensuring that his feet was off the ground. A short while later the thug that he had knocked out with the round-house kick, appeared in front of him, and took his revenge out on him by beating him repeatedly.

They hoisted him further up until he hung with his feet some three feet above the ground. One of the group picked up a plank, and continued to beat him until he seemed to have lost consciousness. He hung there bleeding profusely from a broken nose, his eyes almost shut from the swelling, and he could feel the excruciating pain coming from his ribs. Dallarosa turned to face Virgil.

'Why the fuck did you invite this stranger into our group.' 'I instructed you to never bring a stranger to any of our meetings, yet you thought you could disobey my instruction you fucking backward idiot.'

He nodded and two thugs grabbed Virgil, dropping him to the floor. Dallarosa extracted his sidearm and fired three shots into Virgil's head.

Rafael hung listlessly from the rope, watching through swollen slit eyes at Virgil's lifeless body lying on the floor.

'Now then, who the fuck are you?' shouted Dallarosa turning to face Rafael.

'You are an FBI agent aren't you' 'Pretending to be a French tourist, which you hoped will get you into our group unnoticed.' 'I am not that fucking stupid you moron.' 'I am the President of the United States you idiot, and can do anything I want,' he said as he hit him repeatedly on his legs with the plank.

Dallarosa stared at the limp figure hanging from the rafter, and seemed to be considering what to do with him, when his attention was suddenly distracted by the sound of running boots headed in their direction.

Moments later dozens of FBI agents entered the warehouse, guns pointed directly at the group. They ordered Dallarosa to drop his weapon, and for all of them to lie face down on the floor. The thugs lay their weapons down as instructed, however, Dallarosa stood defiantly, and stared at the agents, with his gun hanging loosely from one arm.

'Do you fucking well know who I am?'

'I am a sitting senator in the US congress and you are trespassing,' he shouted.

'Drop the weapon or I will shoot to kill,' instructed the FBI team leader.

Dallarosa stood motionless, staring at the team leader. An instant later one of the FBI agents lunged forward, securing the hand that held the gun, and dropped him to the floor. The other agents cuffed the rednecks and the team leader accessed his two-way radio ordering an ambulance and paramedics to the warehouse as a matter of urgency.

The FBI team cut the rope and lowered Rafael gently to the floor, removed the duct tape, and untied him, careful to do it as gently as they could, because they could see that he had been badly beaten. One of the agents removed his jacket and covered him. A short while later the whirling sound of a chopper's blades could be heard as it landed near the warehouse. The ambulance arrived a moment later, and the paramedics immediately put Rafael onto a stretcher, and raced off in the direction of the helicopter.

The FBI team placed Dallarosa, and the four thugs under arrest, then escorted them to a waiting paddy wagon, the term used by the FBI to describe a police van. They separated the four thugs from Dallarosa and questioned them.

'My name is Jonas Celoria, and I am the senior agent in charge of this operation, so I am offering you one chance to confirm that your boss, mister Dallarosa shot and killed the man lying on the floor.' 'If you cooperate, you may well get a reduced sentence.'

Having interviewed all four separately, and gotten confessions from all of them, confirming that they had witnessed Dallarosa shoot their brother in arms, Virgil. That was enough to charge senator Dallarosa with first-degree murder.

Dozens of FBI agents surrounded the pub, and were in the process of arresting all the people. Unbeknown to anybody, Barnaby Heathcott had been monitoring the group's every move by satellite all day long, and had arranged for the FBI to have a hundred agents hidden on the fringe of town as he had anticipated that this day would end badly.

Rafael was flown to the St. Michael's hospital in Salem, the capital of Oregon, and rushed into the operating theatre where surgeons immediately went to work on him.

Barnaby called Claire at the American Embassy in Paris, informing her that Rafael had been taken to St. Michael's hospital in Salem in Oregon, and was in a very serious condition. He arranged for her to catch the evening flight from Paris to Salem. She settled into the business class seat reserved for her, and stared at the darkness outside the window.

The plane landed on time, and she jumped into a cab and headed directly to the hospital.

She made her way to reception, and a while later was startled when a doctor wearing a white coat approached her and said, 'hello Lieutenant Commander, please follow me,' as he turned and led the way to a private waiting room.

'Please be seated.' 'I am Doctor Hamish Coleman, and I am afraid that I have some disturbing news.'

Claire braced herself for what was to come, and placed the palm of her hand over her mouth.

'Your partner had a heart attack, and died on the operating table, however, we managed to get his heart pumping again which is the good news.' 'We had to place him in an induced coma, and he is heavily sedated on life support.'

'We were extremely lucky to have brought him back to life using a defibrillator, which administers shock, and then we pumped the heart full of oxygen, blood, and electrolytes which is a ground breaking procedure, that has proven to have saved thousands of lives.'

'He has sustained three broken ribs, a broken arm, broken leg, broken nose, fractured jaw, and has severe facial swelling from the beating.' 'He is truly lucky to be alive.'

Claire sat silently listening intently to what the doctor was saying.

'He is in intensive care, and will be carefully monitored twenty-four seven for several days.' 'We should be able to bring him out of the coma in a day or two.' 'The only reason I believe that he is alive, is due to his physical condition.' 'He has been severely beaten, and from what I have been told, this was by a bunch of rednecks in Wood Village.' 'Luckily the FBI intervened and saved his life.'

'Oh, I almost forgot, he has also lost a few front teeth as well, however, that will be an easy fix once he is strong enough.' 'He is a truly a very lucky man.'

'Am I able to see him doctor?' asked Claire.

'Normally no, however, I have been briefed by Director Heathcott of the CIA, and have been instructed to allow you to see him for a short while, so please follow me,' he said leading the way to the intensive care ward.

Before entering, he turned to face Claire and said, 'please brace yourself, and only stay for a short while.'

Claire stood motionless at the door, and stared at the man she knew as Yonti Barr, not able to recognize him. His head was bandaged, and his eyes were badly swollen. She glanced at the beeping sound of the heart monitor, urging it to keep him alive, then noticed the plaster cast on his arm and leg. She looked at the ventilator that was hooked up via an endotracheal tube inserted into the trachea.

'Dear Lord, please keep him alive, she whispered.'

She made her way to a chair, and pulled it closer to his bedside, reached out, and held his hand as the tears streamed down her cheeks smudging her mascara.

'Please don't die Yonti Barr.' 'I am going to type out your resignation.' 'I want you to be able to sign it, and personally hand it to Barnaby Heathcott when you have recovered.'

'This is the second time I have been put through nearly losing you, and I don't want to go through this ever again.' 'So when you have fully recovered, and after you have resigned, we will then go and live in the Swiss Alps and start a family.'

A short while later she made her way back to the private waiting room. Realizing that she had not slept for over thirty-six hours, she folded her coat, used it as a pillow, and was sound asleep minutes later. She was awoken by the sun rays on her face the next morning, and realized that it was almost zero nine-hundred hours, so she stood, stretched, made her way to reception, and asked the nurse whether she was able to see Yonti again.

'Please take a seat in the waiting room, and I will check with Doctor Coleman if you can see him.'

A while later the nurse confirmed that she could see him, however only for a very short while.

She made her way back to the ward, sat quietly, and watched, as the nurse checked his vital signs. The nurse turned to face Claire and said, 'all his vital signs are normal, so hopefully he will slowly regain his strength.' 'From what I have heard, Doctor Coleman said, that he may bring him out of the induced coma in the next day or two.'

'He is heavily sedated, and the Doctor will bring him out of the medically induced coma by gradually reducing the amount of anaesthetic, and other drugs in his system.' 'Very lucky to be alive.'

Claire sat next to his bed and whispered, 'please recover Yonti, I want you back.'

A couple of minutes later the nurse notified Claire that she should leave, and could visit again in the early evening, however only for a short time.

Claire jumped into a cab, and made her way to the Majestic hotel in the center of the city.

She dialled Barnaby Heathcott, and updated him on Yonti's condition, then called his parents and broke the news.

'No, not again,' responded his mother.

'My husband and I will fly to the US to be with our son, so I hope to see you there in a couple of days.'

The next day when Claire visited the hospital, she bumped into Barnaby in the passage.

'Hello Director, thank you for coming.' 'He is still in an induced coma, however, the doctor seems optimistic that he will bring him out of it tomorrow which is good news.'

'I have just met with Doctor Coleman, and he has fully briefed me, so let's hold thumbs that he will recover fully.' 'I have just spent an hour sitting at his bedside, and read him a couple of short stories of the amazing survival of people that found themselves faced with impossible odds, and in dire circumstances.' 'I hope that he could hear the stories, as it offers hope that people can overcome the worst possible situations.'

'I will pop in later this afternoon before I have to return to Virginia, so let's keep the faith, Claire' 'See you later,' he said as he turned, and made his way towards the exit.

Two days later the doctor successfully brought him out of the induced coma, and Claire was sitting beside his bed watching him breathe slowly when his parents suddenly appeared. His mother burst into tears at the sight of her son lying in the bed.

As devout Catholics, both parents made the sign of the cross, then both hugged Claire, and asked what had happened. Claire knew that she could not disclose what he did for a living, so she tried as best she could to divert the inevitable questions that were to follow in another direction. He had never told his parents what he does in his day job, and Claire fully understood his commitment to Barnaby Heathcott to never disclose any information regarding his job to anyone, including herself and his family.

'I have no idea what happened, only that he was attacked by a gang of thugs, and as you can see, they have beaten him to within an inch of his life.' 'The doctor that treated him, put him into an induced coma, and said that he is extremely lucky to be alive.' 'He said that he has only lived because of the physical condition that he is in.'

Having been brought out of the induced coma the day previously, and unable to communicate, Claire noticed some tears rolling down his cheeks, as he seemed to recognize his parents. He moved his head slightly, looked at Claire, parted his lips, as he seemed to try and smile.

His parents complained that he had not contacted them for over a year, and made Claire promise that she would see to it that he called regularly.

He recovered over the following few months, slowly regaining his strength, and was able to get around unaided, albeit with a slight limp. The daily physio exercises were taxing, and the swelling eventually abated. He proudly displayed his new set of front teeth.

Claire printed the letter of resignation for him, and watched as he signed it. Tomorrow we are both going to resign, and then look for a place to settle, and yes Yonti Barr, I too love the idea of settling in the Swiss Alps.

Chapter 26

CIA Head Office

Langley Virginia USA

Rafael, reached into his jacket pocket, and extracted an envelope, handing it to Barnaby.

'Well, if this is what I think it is, to be truthful, I have been expecting it for some time.'

He opened the letter and read it, then offered his hand across the table.

'You have been the best agent I have ever had under my command, so I would like to take this opportunity to thank you most sincerely for your service to the CIA, America, France, and the world at large.' 'Nobody knows the part you have played in saving the world we all live in from total destruction.'

'I cannot thank you enough for what you have done, so once again, thank you Yonti Barr.'

He used his family name as he was now able to get rid of the various aliases he had used on many missions, and revert to his family name. Barnaby opened his safe and returned all his belongings.

As Yonti stood, he said, 'it has been a pleasure serving you, and the CIA Director.'

'All I want to do, is to live a peaceful normal life with my bride-to-be, hopefully have a couple of kids.'

Barnaby walked him to the door, and bid him farewell.

As Yonti was about to leave, he turned and said, 'I have used up all of my nine lives, and many more a long time ago.' 'Time to spend a peaceful normal life living in the rural countryside, and to enjoy life to its fullest.'

'Au revoir Director.'

'Been, "Right On the Edge," way too many times.'

About the Author

Sid De Beer was born in Johannesburg South Africa in 1950 and is the only son of the late Sam and Joan De Beer.

He immigrated to Australia in 1993 at the age of 43, and has been married to his wife Nadine for 45 years. He is the father of 3 daughters Odette, Shi-Anne, and Kim, and has seven grandchildren.

Sid and his wife are retired and live in Melbourne, Australia where his entire family resides.

'Live Life to Its Fullest-For You Are Not Here For a Long Time.'

-Sid De Beer